I0641947

APOCALYPTIC

VII

SALVATIONS CRY

ARNITA R. LEONARD

This book or any portion thereof may not be reproduced or used in any manner whatsoever without the express written permission of the author/publisher except for the use of brief quotations in a book review or scholarly journal.

Unless otherwise noted, all Bible Scriptures are taken from the King James Version of the Holy Bible.

Scriptures taken from the Holy Bible, New International Version®, NIV®. Copyright © 1973, 1978, 1984, 2011 by Biblica, Inc. ™ Used by permission of Zondervan. All rights reserved worldwide. www.zondervan.com The "NIV" and "New International Version" are trademarks registered in the United States Patent and Trademark Office by Biblica, Inc.™

Scriptures are taken from the New King James Version®. Copyright © 1982 by Thomas Nelson, Inc. Used by permission. All rights reserved.

Scriptures are taken from the New American Standard Bible®, Copyright © 1960, 1962, 1963, 1968, 1971, 1972, 1973, 1975, 1977, 1995 by The Lockman Foundation. Used by permission. All rights reserved.

Author's note: Discussions and scenarios in this book depict real life situations. Characters, names, and incidents mentioned are products of the author's imagination or are used fictitiously. Any resemblance to actual events or locales or persons, living or dead, is entirely coincidental.

DEDICATIONS

To God be the glory for all He has done in my life. I thank God for trusting me with this gift and allowing me to pay it forward for others to walk this path and journey as I learn to navigate these waters called writing and publishing. I never thought I would end in this place of… Truthful Imagination.

In Loving Memory of our Mother, Margo E. Leonard
Born, March 28th, 1941, and to her rest in the Lord,
February 6th, 2020

To my dad who is still with us, Otis W. Leonard

And to their Great-Granddaughter's,
Nevaeh Smith, Amari & Jazzlynn Smith, and Ezryah Lewis
My great nieces, from different parents
with the same last name and my first grandchild.

To their parents Shedrick & Susie, Imari & Jasmine, Joshua & Anayah, and their Uncle David. You have to continue the legacy.

Know that you are the future until Christ returns.
Until then, keep God first and know that you are loved, and you can do anything through Christ who strengthens you!

ACKNOWLEDGEMENTS

This book was fun to write, it allowed me to delve into God's word a lot more by doing research and studying. I am thankful and grateful to God for giving me this dream to create a futuristic fictional world that included His truth, and word through the pages.

The Apocalyptic Series will continue with God's grace and given imagination supplied. Lookout for Apocalyptic 8— Angels of Heavens Army. Only God knows when it will be finished.

- Great thanks to Ret. P.O. III, Stuart B. Guidry for his military expertise and pointers.

- Passionate thanks to all the Beta Readers who gave it rave reviews, even though I made some changes since you've read it. Especially Jonathan Macias, who has waited since 2015, for this book to come out!

- To all who support my dream of writing.

INTRODUCTION

When you know there is a God…

To the Reader: This is a Christian **Fiction** Novel. Apocalyptic 7 (A7) is not a replacement for the Word of God, and not intended for new believers to be confused. The Holy Scriptures used within the pages are for reference, study, and revelation of what is coming truthfully, as described in Matthew 24: 4-8, "Take heed that no one deceives you. For many will come in My name, saying, 'I am the Christ, and will deceive many. And you will hear of wars and rumors of wars. See, you are not troubled, for all these things must happen, but the end is not yet. For nation will rise against nation, and kingdom against kingdom. And there will be famines, pestilences, and earthquakes in various places. All these are the beginnings of sorrow."

My intention is to convey a message with the scriptures used within the book, that God is really going to do those things He's says in His word, but not what's in my book. My imagination with the characters created, is for entertainment purposes only and maybe, a movie in the future. A7 is Truthful Imagination from the writer, created from a dream God gave me, but it is not a vision or prophecy that is to manifest, unless God says Yay and Amen. My goal was to create a work that was adventurous, fun spirited and pleasing to God. So, enjoy, and take the ride with each character you meet as the Apocalyptic team goes on their missions.

The Dream, I had was about me being in the military, and I was to print out five names. When the dream came, I was in the midst or two-thirds finished with writing my first novel, Unconditional Counsel. This dream gave me the idea for this two-book series and I had so much fun researching scripture and reading the apocryphal writings, like Enoch. It was fun creating these characters I had never known before. Each character provides a glimpse of reality and imagination on what we see every day, whether in real life or on the news. The everyday feelings and experience we have as human beings. Our faith, our doubt, our triumphs, our relationships with others and how we maintain that relationship with our Heavenly Father.

Have you ever thought about how our modernistic society became so morally bankrupt? Apocalyptic 7 embarks on and reveals some reasons that have led our United States and even the world to be lost.

CONTENTS

PROLOGUE

Apocalyptic 7-Salvations Cry is a story of battles between God's earthly warriors and malevolent forces. The Divine Scriptures guide A7's missions, as they must learn how to count on each other and put their hope and trust in God.

In a government system that is morally bankrupt in 2043, Tracy, a former government assassin, learns who she is in Christ and leads a team (Michael Being-Euphrates, Kelton Johns-Shadow, Kendrick Roberts-Xerxes, Carsen Philips-Leopard, Joshua Wells-X-Ray, and Kim Acai-Minah Bird) to unearth a key organization who presumes they're descendants of fallen angels.

A7 accepts orders from their mysterious leader, Mr. Zinkes. While chaos breaks out between the team, only their faith will carry them from mission to mission to stop the Apollyon. The Apocalyptic 7 comes together to block the Apollyon from creating a world built of chaos. During their missions, they learn Black Rain, a vigilante group, craves to dispose of the Apollyon for good. But is this part of God's plan? A7 must stop them both, before God consumes the cities in the Middle East, as He destroyed Sodom and Gomorrah in generations past. Through evidence and acceptance, they prepare for battle, which is their only hope for survival in this life and into eternity.

"Hi, I'm Mr. Zinkes, the director of the Compound. Yes, I'm speaking to you, the reader. I want you to know the part I play in all of this. I watch their every move. You'll understand who I am later. I'm not any of their handlers, nor do I work for any government. I have not interfered with any of their lives unless instructed. I am aware of everything they have done or will do. Like Saul, who persecuted the church, Tracy was an executioner for the U.S. Government, who wanted certain people eliminated in 2033. I've tested each one of them, because they will be a part of what's coming. I can only imagine what it will be like in the next few years when I gather them for God's purpose. All of them right now are in trouble. Searching for who they are inside. What will they find out about themselves? What shall they become?"

Chapter 1

Blow Back

In Rome, Italy, 2039. Executioner for the government, Sublimes' McMillan TAC-338 scopes toward the hunter green convent entrance door. Nuns in crisp Habits walk the pathway singing. Her mind was not on the job, and it wasn't like her to be unfocused. Her eyes close for a moment, listening to their voices carry songs of hope in beautiful, haunted Italian. She thought about being somewhere else. Far from there, but she had to complete this job first. 'How did I get here, anyway?' Sublime understood her assignment. Her life took this path because she was searching. Searching for that one thing that would make her life fulfilled. A life of purpose and realized dreams.

Finally, in the moment, as the birds coo and scurry away as patrons walk by. They stand and listen as Sublime listens at the window. Her mind was not on what she needed to do.

Hidden in Hotel Rastelli across from the convent. Sublime moves from the nuns to the door, waiting on her target. The Mother Superior was a mother of the church and the head of the Sicilian Mafia (The 'Ndrangheta). In order for this organization to break up, there had to be someone else in charge.

The buzzing of the imagery device on the nightstand also disturbed Sublime's focus. There was no reason for the call.

She dares not answer.

"What's the urgency? I'm in position." Sublime said.

"Get back as soon as it's done. There's another job of higher importance." The mysterious man said.

'They said this about every job,' she thought. "My plane leaves in a few hours," losing the connection, saying nothing else.

Staring out the window as the curtains fold, tingling pricks roll up her arms. She's in position again. It was unlike them to call during a mission—why this time?

Raising her rifle, she feels a brief rumble, then glass shatters from the windowpane where she's standing. Her rifle tumbles, sliding underneath the dresser. Sublimes head slams against the wood paneled floor as her body is inches from crashing into the dresser leg where her rifle slid. A few seconds she lies dazed. Hearing the muffled car alarms blaring, the shaking finally stops, and her eyes focus on the still swinging ceiling fan and the mustard-colored ceiling. She wasn't so sure she was okay. Her life didn't matter in the scheme of things. If she didn't finish the job, they would send someone else to finish the job and her.

Undeterred, she searches the ground in front of the convent. Pages of the hymnals flutter as the nuns scramble on the ground, covered in debris and ash. They rise to their feet, covering their faces from the smoke. A pungent odor of flesh fills the air through what remains of the windowpane. Burning her nose, it wasn't unfamiliar. The dirty cloud moves past, and her gaze is now focused again. The Mother Superior appears, and Sublime's Barber .308 ammo spins through her heart, and another, more significantly, through her frontal lobe. She grabs a hold of her chest. She falls holding a secret from the Catholic church.

They wanted to remain hidden from the world and the other cartels. Information that was hazardous to one's health, she kept. This was a favor for a favor from the U.S. Government.

Relieved to complete this mission. The discomfort of what she was feeling was almost unbearable. In times past, the jubilance of the kill would have given her a spark of purpose. This time, there was nothing. There were too many questions running through her mind. Is this all I am?

The screams from down the street and the nuns across the way from the hotel fill the air. They hasten to the Mother Superior, as bystanders run away from the bombing. Those around her work to save her life. Her blood flows down the steps. There was no saving her. Sublime never missed.

Siren's blaze, as management evacuates everyone to ensure those in the hotel remained a safe distance from the bombed building down the way. Sublime exits the hotel and sees one nun advance toward the screams for help at the bombed site. As Sublime glances in that direction, she sees electrical sparks fall from the destroyed building. There were those who ran towards the site. She heads in the same direction as the cries grow louder, but stops. Remembering the call from earlier, 'I know they're watching me now. It wouldn't be wise for my handlers to see me head toward the bombing,' she thought. Her only solace in the moment, the bombing, was a perfect cover for her disappearance out of the country. She arrives at the airport unnoticed, and hours later, she lands in Egypt.

Tracy Pimbridge, Sublime, was born in Washington. It was the only home she knew and did not want to leave. Folding her arms, her brother Myron was indifferent to the whole moving situation. He was used to it—she wasn't. She was six years old, and he was sixteen. Myron sat with Tracy inside the Hungry Harbor Grille, while their father, Major Pimbridge, concluded a round of golf for the last time in the state. They ate cheeseburgers and cheddar fries in silence. Tracy's somber demeanor didn't go unrecognized. Her father said nothing to explain why this move was so important to him. If he had, maybe she would have understood then as she does now—you go where they tell you to go. Mr. Pimbridge had their dreaded station-wagon since Myron was born. They both could agree on that one thing. The station wagon was an eyesore. "You would think with his rank in the Army, he could buy something new by now," Myron said.

After eating, they drive two miles to the Pacific Beach End, standing and observing the sunset. Tracy's mood shifts, amplified by the dramatic symphony of waves clashing against the powerful rock arrangement to the left of them. The mist from the sea was calming. They always admired the wood formed benches from early twentieth century fallen trees that sat on the beachfront to the right of them.

Their father guides them down the sand filled steps to sit for the last time to spectate the sand sculpting competition. He hugs them, one in each arm. They watched in amazement as the artists along the beach shore rushed to complete their multi-level, three-dimensional sand figures before the downpour, which was expected within the hour and typical of Washington.

Leaving the beach, she knew it to be the last time seeing this place as a child. Colorado was their next home destination.

Sixteen years later in Tracy Pimbridge's life.

"Ugh. I hate not knowing what career track to choose now. I just want to start all over."

After finishing West Point, Tracy was in her first year of active duty in the Army at Fort McClellan in Alabama. At nine a.m., sitting on her bed in the barracks alone, she calls her father after travelling to Fort Leonard Wood, in Missouri, for 20 weeks. Her career path as a Military Police (MP) was not progressing the way she had hoped. She resolved to be the best. Making daddy proud was the ambition. Boot Camp had been a breeze, studying to be all she could be. Lamenting about the career path she signed up for and now Tracy wanted to shift gears. Her training was not challenging enough, so she called to get advice.

Her dad, now Colonel Pimbridge, didn't want her to be anything like him, but it was too late. He challenged her thinking and direction, "You are my daughter and as much as I would have preferred you had elected another path, I can only respect that this is who you are. I cherish you and wouldn't change a thing about you. We are along for the ride until the established time of your purpose reveals itself. Having an epiphany, that discovery of what you're supposed to be doing for the rest of your life."

"The military has served you well, Dad. I'm preparing for the rest of my life. Is the military all there is for me? I just feel like my path should go down another road."

"Tracy, you have many more choices than I did at your age. You can't do life for anybody else. The decision is yours alone to make. If you choose something specific, then maybe I can help, but right now you're blowing in the wind."

As a twenty-seven-year Army man at Fort Lee in Virginia, Colonel Pimbridge was full of wisdom, integrity, and focus. Both Myron and Tracy followed in his footsteps—somewhat, as Myron joined the Marines. He was dad's favorite until Tracy came along. It didn't bother Myron, though. He was her protector and best friend. He never tried to deter Tracy from joining the military, either.

In 1952, Fort Bragg became the home of the Army's Psychological Warfare Center. Now, the U.S. Army Special Operations Command, and the headquarters for Special Forces Soldiers. Tracy transferred to Fort Bragg in North Carolina to do Special Forces training in the Ranger Regiment. While there, North Korea attacks Tracy's parents' base, and both succumbed to their injuries. At their dad's funeral, Tracy recalls her dad saying, 'Organizations fail for lack of knowledge, vision, and goals. Organizations fail because they lack the communication skills of planning and implementing change from top to bottom. Change is imminent, and we must welcome it, or we won't endure to see another day.'

Tracy realized then her father was right. Not just about the Army, but about my life.

After completing her initial tour with the Ranger Regiment, she left and trekked through the region of Asia. Struggling to make sense of her life and searching in all the wrong places. Her journey to discover who she was on her own terms, she had to find her way to that one thing she was missing. In solitude, she studied with monks for two years, seeking to find herself and any meaning to it all. They pitied Tracy at first and that's why they allowed her to stay. Settling in Hengshan, or Mount Heng, which is in Shanxi Province. It is one of China's Five Majestic Mountains, high in altitude, and has a scenic view all around with inset dwellings. Monuments on the cliff side allowed for liberation from the outside world. She was away from the maddening thoughts of a world lost. After learning the disciplines of the monks, it was time by the monks' standards for her to return to civilization. Unfortunately, she found it worse than before. Tracy couldn't elude her calling and had to go back to what she craved and knew best—military life.

A Test in 2033

Biological Weapons became the norm, and Tracy was now a Naval Intelligence Officer (NIO). Tracy marveled at the fact that she was back in the place where she was born—Pacific Beach, Washington. A place she never thought she'd see again.

On a normal afternoon, sitting at her desk, she received an unmarked package with only her name and no return postage. Nothing about the packaging seemed out of the ordinary.

"Was this examined?" she asked.

"Yes. A brief look in the box. It appears to be a pair of slippers," Petty Officer Justin said. Placing the box down, the brown paper wrapping was loose, with the folded edges pointing to the sky.

"Thank you for delivering this parcel. I will explore it further."

"You're welcome, ma'am."

"You're dismissed," she said. Without looking up at him, she put on gloves to pick up the package and take it to the containment area. The shoebox remained closed as it rested on the examining table—under the biohazard ventilation hutch. Putting her hands through the opaque green barrier gloves, she opened the lid slowly. Taking out the thong sandals from the box, she scanned the soles and the seams, not realizing she was taking shallow breaths in moderate apprehension until she got a little light-headed.

Glancing toward Dr. Omar Spin, a chemical scientist and the lab's director, recognized her concern. "Dr. Spin, we need a thorough x-ray of these flip-flops. I suspect there is something in between the soles. These types of sandals shouldn't have two separate uneven parts. If something is in the interior, all I had to do was wear them and whatever it is, could've been airborne."

Although concerned, her demeanor remained unshaken. 'Who would send this to me?' she thought.

Dr. Spin, a man in his early fifties with strands of gray hair and a little hunch in his back, directs Tracy to take her hands out of the gloves and don a lab contamination suit. He follows his own instructions and places his hazmat suit on. Once they are both protected, Dr. Spin places the sandals back into the box. Unlocking the hutch, he walks them to the radiation area for an x-ray scan. He places the box in the x-ray machine. They both could see two vials, one in each sandal. After the exam, Dr. Spin removes the sandals and takes them to the contamination hutch, and he splits the thong soles open and extracts the vials. It was VX-Nerve Gas, a clear and odorless liquid. Dr. Spin notifies their superiors, and the entire base went on immediate high alert. They launched an investigation to find the individual or individuals responsible.

A year later, the person responsible stayed anonymous. Tracy viewed the situation as blind luck and decided her gut didn't let her down this time.

Tracy's changes careers in 2035

A couple of years after that incident, she changed career path again and transferred to the Navy Seal Team 6. This was what she needed. This level of training required her to give everything she had inside. An environment that provided combat and intelligence. Tracy thrived and broke the records of her predecessor and a few of the men, too. She was not the first, but only the second woman to make it through BUD/S (Basic Underwater Demolition/Seal Training). If you know anything about BUD/S, you know it's grueling and almost impossible for women to complete.

Her father's memory was a constant reminder of what he told her when she began down her many career paths. There was no turning back. The military was in her blood. Running from it did her no good. She craved the action, adventure, and found where she belonged.

Alone in a bunker in 2037

On the USS Momsen, an Arleigh Burke-class destroyer, Tracy's team, returned from a mission. Walking off the ship, heading toward headquarters, fifty feet from the ship, missiles rain down on the base. The administration building took a direct hit, resulting in the loss of hundreds of lives. Shrapnel struck Tracy between my clavicle bone and shoulder. She screamed bloody murder. Jason, her other team member, grabbed her and drug her behind the closest trash barrel. As he went to grab another fallen teammate, a shot to the chest instantly killed him.

Explosions, deafening with every stride to save her own life, making a run for it, if she could get into the shelter barracks. This was the time where she admittedly regretted her choice to switch career paths, but she had to keep running. Images of the past flash through her mind as she dodges flying dirt and other dangerous metal debris. Tracy's chest burned from the fast-paced breathing and it didn't make her injury any better. Tracy had to stay levelheaded and focused. She had to fight through the pain while searching for safety with every move she made. Vulnerable in the open, she ran toward a barracks opposite of where they were targeting to take cover. She ran past the water's edge, seeing bodies floating. She scanned to see for any survivors. Most of them were unrecognizable. Blood oozed from every orifice. No one could save them. The heat threatens to suffocate her. The feeling as if a dragon had flown through and scorched everything in its path. Her stomach churned from the acrid smell of burning flesh. Her survival was unsure. She didn't want to bleed to death, and no one knew where she was.

Becoming A Master Chief in 2039

At the Navy Seal Training Camp, which was no longer a six-month training camp. In the past, it was about teamwork, physical and psychological qualifications. Now, it was a year of training, adding in biological and chemical warfare. Fresh recruits sit in class, listening to Tracy speak of her ordeal during the 2037 attack from parts of Asia. She glances around at their faces as they cling to her words.

"Most of the time, we could identify when our enemy was about to attack us. On this occasion, to say they surprised us is an understatement. Ballistic missiles hit our base. Those who ran to get away from the explosions, like I did, ran toward closer barracks. A lot of them didn't make it into the buildings in time. No one was around me now. Alone in my pursuit to survive, the invader attacks us from behind. No one else had the specific intelligence that I had. Being captured was not an option.

"Thirty seconds from the last missile, I ran into the dark, empty barracks, hoping a Hsiung Feng IIIG Missile wouldn't hit it. I knew this simple building with tan-white walls and charcoal-gray floors wouldn't save me from the bombs dropping. I could feel my heart pound against the wall of my chest. My wound was bleeding consistently, but slowly. This was the only time I felt fear. Not the fear of dying, but of being alone. At least if I bled to death, I would go quietly. 'I have to get in here now,' I said to myself. Gritting my jaws to cover my pain as I pulled up the loud squealing steel door from the floor. I jumped onto the ladder and sealed the hatch top, sliding twenty feet below. I punch in the code to the bunker and another hatch door opens. A mechanical sled takes me the rest of the way. I punch in my military access code and the final hatch sucks the air from the door opening. I pull on the vertical bar to get in. The smoke and pain caused me to have labored breathing. I knew I could not stop to rest. The fluorescent lights come on and I focus. The sound from topside was faint to the ear. I turn to look up at the ceiling.

"The tunnel bunker was at least fifty feet long and wide, stocked with everything needed to survive a nuclear attack for 100 years. Searching the desk to find the manual codes to the black ops radio, once I find it, I send out the signal for contact. Not hungry, but thirsty. I took in as much water as needed. I could only rest once I pulled out the shrapnel and cleaned and stitch my wound. It had not gone through to the other side, so I had to stop the bleeding. I then rested on the cot closest to the radio panel. Not knowing the answers to what was going on up there and what I needed to do next, I close my eyes, fatigued but not willing or able to stop trying to figure out my next move. My mind raced with the visions of those in the water. My pulse stays rapid, as I couldn't stop seeing the images of those already dead in my head. I open them for temporary relief from death. I close them again to see the next move, and my heart slows to a normal pace.

"After five hours, I heard nothing. Then the radio sounds, "This is Captain Lorenzo of the USS Makin Island. We received a distress signal. Anybody out there?'"

"Jumping up to push the com button, 'Captain Lorenzo, it's Tracy Pimbridge of the DEVGRU (Naval Special Warfare Development Group) ST6 Blue Squadron. They hit our Murat base, and I am not sure of any other survivors. I'm in a bomb shelter, 98658. No other command staff is with me. Can you tell me if the friendly's have taken back the base? I've heard no bombings for the last hour.'"

"Pimbridge, please hold," he said.

"For ten long minutes, I pace. Captain Lorenzo comes back to give information. "Pimbridge, confirmation, friendlies have taken back the base. The enemy has deserted the area. It was missiles from a submarine. It's being pursued but not identified."

"Thanks Captain, I will get back with you as soon as I get topside."

"Although the time frame to get into the barracks and shelter seemed quick, it took much longer to get out. The sled took me back to the opening. I climb up the ladder slower because of the pain. Opening the hatch door to see the white-tan walls again. It relieved me to be topside. The stench of the dead hit me again. I took a moment to reflect and adjust to what I was about to walk into. My eyes took in the remains of smoke clouds, and bodies floating out to sea like driftwood on an ocean wave. Trying not to look at those lost, I had to stay focused on the living, some pleading for instant death. My ears block the noise of wailing, and I look for the triage, which was helping those wounded and still alive.

"Inside the medical tent, I found my Commanding Officer holding on to life. The explosion blew off his leg and arm on the right side at the elbow and knee. There was no other way to save his life but to close the wounds as best they could under the circumstances. At the sight of the wounded, I could only help and there was not much I could do. My team had just come back from our first mission, victorious. Was this retaliation? Why didn't we see this coming? Did I blame myself for abandoning my post, surviving in one piece, while others had not? Could I handle the pressure of this much loss? Was I strong enough for the people I was helping?"

Tracy asks the class without expecting an answer from the recruits. "As I conclude my summation, these are the questions you need to answer in your written assessment of this debrief. The details given will be the basis for your assessment. Ultimately, you need to decide, did I abandon my post? Did I do the right thing? Was I selfish? Should they have court-marshaled me? Could I have helped the others sooner?"

Tracy paces the floor. Her glance is staunch and unmoving. Her gaze locks onto their body language, the slight shifting in their seats to get comfortable. She knew what they were thinking. She allows them to take forty-five minutes to answer a few of those questions. After reading a few of the recruits' answers, she addresses them.

"Well, your answers are typical, and I suspected you would answer the way you have. Chief Petty Officer (CPO) Bradford over there owes me a hundred bucks, and this is the reason I'm Master Chief Petty Officer (MCPO) and you're not — yet. Just to be clear, none of those questions could be yes, because there is a paper in my file that states, "Under no circumstances should the enemy capture me. There was information that I did not provide to you."

"Why and what, you ask in those new questioning brains of yours? Well, here's the answer. I was the only officer left on that base with access codes to Nuclear Weapons from here to NORAD. They could have taken Commander Rodgers, but he was dying from the wounds he sustained and they didn't know he would survive. It just so happens. The first hit to the base was to the administration building. The Generals, and other higher ups, were sitting in their offices unaware. I don't know if that was the enemy's intention to kill those who could give them information, but they did. Unfortunately, the enemy hijacked one of our U.S. subs and used it against us. This is the reason no one knew. There were no survivors in the administration building. Can you imagine what a catch I would have been, had the enemy hacked into our files and received intelligence about me or any other DEVGRU member like me? So, I had a choice to make. Die as my superiors had or run like hell to get into one of those bunkers. Also, when we came back from our mission, I was carrying a very important briefcase with intelligence that I was to hand over once we arrived."

Tracy finished her part of the lecture for the day. As she walks out of the class, she turns to them, "Never judge a writer by the fatness of a Silverfish's molted skin." It was a tradition to keep them guessing about a metaphor.

~

During missions and after becoming Master Chief, Tracy lived in Egypt and continued to do their bidding, even though she questioned her part in the scheme of things. She continued to receive high praise, which allowed her to rise in the ranks so quickly.

The property of the U.S. until the realization came. She had no life outside of them. No love, no family, no friends — no Sublime, without them. Her heart ached with longing for someone she would never meet until one day she did. While lying low in Memphis, Egypt, she planned the doom and execution of those who took her life and love away. They threatened to decimate an entire island the day before their wedding. They knew the secrets she held. This island where she was to spend the rest of her life with the love she so wanted. It was their mistake. They wanted complete control over Sublime.

Standing at the window looking out at the sand dunes, not regretting wanting to be free, "I have to kill them all."

'There was no other way to be free,' she thought.

~

It was a world filled with sparks of light to guide the course of man. A wake-up call that failed to sound the alarm in the sense of urgency. It was a volatile time, and they desensitized us to the truth of what was going on. Gloom shrouded the earth, even though the sky was blue. The sun continued to rise to the occasion — arraying the seasons as before. Some people couldn't see that things were changing and not for the better. Life itself was temporal. Even with the convenience and access to unlimited self-preservation, lives were mundane in existence. Every human was out for themselves—there was no more village to teach the next generation. Life remained unchanged for those who ruled the nations, their lust for power untamed and unbridled, on the threshold of pure chaos.

They limited faith to greed. The positivity that the universe would return to you is what you spoke to it. New Age nonsense. The truth of God was being eradicated from everything we held dear on earth.

The military scaled back, not because there was no need to secure the country, but enlisting diminished once the true and brave whistleblowers exposed the government for operating the military for less than truthful purposes.

Tracy had become a less than truthful purpose.

She completed her missions to stay alive and got rid of those who knew the military had control over her within three years. Thereafter, she continued to train, as her life would soon take on a different meaning and purpose. Tracy's soul was at stake. One way or the other, her life was no longer hers to own. She understood, she had to turn her control over to the God who created the universe.

Their story together begins in 2043

Amid the chaos, those with a calling could not hide. Someone sent a message to Mr. Zinkes informing him the Apollyon's timetable to bring more chaos to the world was upon us.

Those God chose must interrupt their plans. If they failed, it would be Sodom and Gomorrah over again in the middle east and this time, He would save no one.

Tree leaves rustle with a trivial gust of wind. Mr. Zinkes returns to the Compound from Egypt. Sliding on the loose gravel, he wipes the beads of moisture forming on his brow after balancing himself. He rushes in, as Ms. Giles greets him at the door entrance. Strolling down the lobby, she was almost at a jog. She struggles to keep up.

"Do you consider them ready for what's coming?" They halt in the corridor before entering Mr. Zinkes' office.

"Ms. Giles, it matters not whether they are ready. We will get them ready. God has found them worthy of His service."

"So, who will we start with?"

"Tracy Pimbridge, Sublime. She will be first," he said.

"Why Tracy?" asked Ms. Giles, now sitting in front of him.

"She is first, as she is the first to be called by God."

"Do they suspect what this involves?"

"No. They've never met me, even though my involvement in their lives was significant. Ms. Giles, please notify Mr. Lyemel and Mr. Laemel recruitment occurs in one month."

"Yes, sir," she said. She walks out of his office.

Chapter 2

Why Are We Here?

God had not yet graced us with His Son's Second Coming. The chaotic laws being passed to cut religious freedom were affirming the truthfulness to the *Believer* who followed the ways of Christ. They could see that time was winding up. Only those who depended on and carried steadfast faith could observe and understand what was happening to the world we knew and had grown accustomed to. Why was it so hard to get people to see? Was it selfishness, the gratification of possessions at their fingertips? Humanity was only out for themselves. Yet God was fulfilling His Word and His Promises.

TV Evangelists were failing in their attempt to reach people for Christ. Men and women saved for over fifty years didn't wait on Jesus any longer, taking their own lives or turning a hundred and eighty degrees toward the dark side. The deception took hold. The word of God said that there would be a great falling away. Life in the twenty-first century had changed drastically. It seemed like overnight. *"The love of man had waxed cold."*

Children murdered in their classrooms, snipers killing because they couldn't cope with the matters of life. Domestic and foreign terrorism, parishioners killed, and churches bombed by the spiritual enemy using the flesh and bones of sin.

We once believed that the Forefathers founded the Constitution of the United States of America upon faith. The laws being put in place were contradictory to the Constitution and

God. We lived when that generation moved further and further away from God and faith in the redemptive work of Christ. Where were people running to when disasters struck? They weren't rushing to the churches. They were sinking into narcotics, alcohol, and sexual sin to hide the agonies of their existence.

Suffering from the silencing of the Gospel of Jesus Christ on media broadcasting systems for over twelve years. One World Government and Religion dangled on a string before us. Those keeping the faith didn't know how much longer it would be before they would outlaw all religious freedom. The darkness crept in, oblivious and uncaring.

Winter collapsed into spring—summer folded into the crispness of autumn. God set the four seasons in place for us to see the signs of the times. As a nation, our ideology got lost in translation. None-the-less, those who were standing believed everything was in God's hand.

Those that went before us, we questioned. Did they do nothing because they believed it was pointless? If God purposed everything to be this way in the first place, was it complacency to stand and do our part? God was preparing His people. How many spoke God's truth, and stood, having done all to stand, standing therefore on His Word, and not what they could see? Was there one incident that catapulted humankind into despair?

Those who depended, surrendered, and were obedient to God until the end would continue their spiritual relationship with the Ancient of Days.

What the world didn't consider was that sin existed from Adam and Eve. Sin was the root cause, and only Jesus was the answer.

Recruitment Starts

During this time of sinful discontent, Tracy received a goldenrod envelope from Mr. Zinkes at her home in Egypt. A mild sandstorm covers the mail delivery person from head to toe. Walking away, she opens the door to get the mail. Checking her peripheral before walking back to the door. Inside, she opens the envelope and a book, *'Unconditional Counsel,'* slides out. The faded cover showed a curious image: a rich brown vision of a woman standing before a cross. The subtitle, *'God's counsel, is the wisest counsel.'* Mr. Zinkes marked the worn cream pages with bunny ears. Flipping the pages, she smells the age from the gust of air, to find an invitation and a message. A prophetic word from the author, Erica Manning, in a dream.

> Her journal entry:
> "The world was looking like the last days, as described in the Bible. Everything was chaotic, and I oversaw some type of rebel offense or military operation, which I could not distinguish in the dream. I had to print out seven names significant to the operation."

In a passage, he placed a note as a marker, "Tracy, this unfamiliar voice said seven names needed printing out in her novel, and you are one of them," Mr. Zinkes wrote.

~

That evening, Tracy was on an airplane, headed to the location on the invitation card. She was apprehensive, but she was also sure this is what God had in mind for her life.

Those invited arrive at a secret compound in Northfield, Vermont. Five representatives, including Tracy, were meeting in a vast conference room, seated around a mahogany table with frosted wall glass to the east and west of their armchairs. They gawk at each other but remain silent.

'Why are we here?' Tracy thought, which drew Mr. Zinke's attention. Standing tall, at six feet seven inches, observing them in his charcoal-drab tunic. Mr. Zinkes addresses them over the public-intercom system. "You are here to work for God. Tracy, be glad I am on the Lord's side," he said.

Tracy's memory kicks in as she reflects on when she was operating within government parameters. She kept quiet, contemplating what was next for all those who sat in that room and their fates together.

Tracy Pimbridge, Sublime, was born in Pacific Beach, Washington, to the parents of Colonel Jeffrey and Elizabeth Pimbridge. She is thirty-four. Her specialty is intelligence and hand-to-hand combat. Tracy, the deadliest, five-foot-ten-woman, accepted Christ after working as a government assassin for six years. She speaks many languages besides English: Arabic, Hungarian, Russian, Chinese, Spanish, and French.

Mr. Zinkes continues, "My name is Mr. Zinkes... Giaigo Zinkes. I am the administrator of this facility and its operations. You will meet me in person soon, but first, I must accomplish a task. Please hold your questions for now." Behind the glass, Ms. Giles stood next to him. Mr. Zinkes explains why they have gathered. "You are children of faith in the Most-High God and have no allegiance to the outside world. All of you were at the top of your professions and are no longer connected with any government bureau. Some of you still have access to certain privileges, which will come in handy later. As followers of Christ, you know what is ahead of us and some of you are more acquainted with the Divine Scriptures than others. If what we request of you fails, then God will send others. The faded cover showed a curious image: a rich brown vision of a woman standing before a cross. We must complete whatever God would have us to do. The underlying goal is to learn who you are as individuals and in Christ. Soon, you will become targets of the invisible enemy in the spirit and physical realms of this world. Our intelligence has latched onto new and potential members, but we have started with you. In a few minutes, Ms. Zerah Giles, our Management Director, will meet you to better inform you on your purpose here," he said. His attention now turning to Michael. "Mr. Being, I am not behind this mirror to disguise who I am. I'm behind this glass so that you know I'm aware of everything you say and think."

Michael sat up straighter and puffed out his chest in annoyance. "I didn't even say anything," he said.

"That's the point," Tracy said.

"What's the point?"

"Mr. Zinkes can read your mind."

Michael peers at Tracy as though she had lost hers. "Read my mind!"

"Yes, read your thoughts. Isn't it clear to everyone?" No one offers affirmation. "In my head, I asked, why were we gathered in this place? You didn't hear me say anything aloud. That's why he called out my name and told me to be glad he was on the Lord's side. He just did the same to you, didn't he?"

"I wonder if he was one of those experiments gone wrong?" Kendrick asked.

"I don't know if he's part of any experiment, but they've been running these types of experiments for decades. I can imagine what he's heard over the years. His ability is unmistakable. We should introduce ourselves. I am Tracy Pimbridge, aka Sublime,

and you are?" She asked, looking to her left.

"Kendrick Roberts, aka Xerxes. Nice to meet you all."

Kendrick Roberts, Xerxes, was born in Omaha, Nebraska. His roots are from India, but he was born in the United States. He entered the Air Force after finishing college. At 44, he was the only one born before the year 2000 A.D. His specialty is flying all aircraft. Kendrick became a follower of Christ at age 21. Nicknamed Xerxes, because he rules the sky as king of the airways, and he liked that name from the Bible.

Kelton chuckles at Kendrick. "You know, if he can read minds, he can certainly hear us talking about him," Kelton said.

"Kelton Johns, aka Shadow."

Kelton Johns, Shadow, was born in Paris, France and is now thirty-four. His specialty is computer technology, creating codes and programs. Kelton had no living parents, and grew up in an orphanage, until one day a doctor adopted him at nine. Previously professed himself to be an atheist. He became a follower of Christ at twenty-five. He is fluent in French, Greek, and Pakistani. Nicknamed Shadow because you can't see him coming or going on your computer. He can place a virus in 6.5 seconds.

"Carsen Phillips, aka Leopard."

Carsen was born in Los Angeles, California. Her age, 35. She had established herself as an FBI Archeological Profiler, trained in ancient artifacts and writing. Carsen did eight years of military training with the Army and the Army Reserve. Carsen became a follower of Christ at thirty. Her quickness won her championship medals in college for the 400-meter race, hence the moniker.

"Last but certainly not least, Michael Being, aka Euphrates. Your reputation precedes you," Tracy said. Smiling.

Michael raises his hands again, not understanding why she knows about him at all. Michael was born in Northern Iraq in Anah. At 36, he had a lengthy military history since the age of eighteen. His specialty is explosives and guns. Michael grew up Muslim but converted to a follower of Christ at 24. After training with the Iraqi Armed Forces for four years, he became an athletic phenomenon.

He found himself in the United States, going to college, played football for the Navy, and turned Navy SEAL Gold Squad a year after obtaining his bachelor's degree. The nickname Euphrates was for the river near his home. At six-three, athletic and smart, he grew up with both of his parents, and at eighteen, went into the military. His parents disapproved of his choice, but they had to let him go. They were most proud that he made something of himself, but rejected him once he turned to Christ. Michael excelled in the military, always at the top of his class. He would have been a MCPO or Commander Master Chief Petty Officer (CMCPO) by now had he not turned it down to remain in field deployment.

Tracy had previous knowledge about Michael, as she was a couple of years behind him in Navy Seal Training. She was the only one who broke eighty percent of his training records. Tracy was unassuming. She requested to remain nameless and identified by her initials, so no one could identify her as the record breaker.

"Why, thank you, Tracy. I've heard of none of you here. You seem to know me, but why don't I know you?"

"My clearance level was one step above the President's knowledge—I was top secret. She winks her eye at Euphrates. Pertinent knowledge of my existence and some aspects of what I did within the confines of our lovely government as we know it today remains a secret. My name should be Shadow. And no, I'm not a machine or an AI or an experiment gone wrong. This is not the Terminator films," she said.

Everyone expresses clarity. "Anyway..." Tracy was about to continue when Ms. Giles walked through the door. A statuesque persona, like the woman from Star Wars, part-six, providing the Resistance Pilots the plans to the Death Star that was fully operational. She studies each one sitting around the table before she speaks. "Ladies and gentlemen, what is the aim? To identify the anti-Christ. Not to destroy him, but to expose him to those necessary before he's revealed to the world. The mission, as of now, is to educate and train you. Once we identify who he is, then we must look to the Holy Scriptures to guide us," she said.

"Wait a minute! If we are working for God, why doesn't He tell us who it is? Why go through all the cloak and dagger when God knows all and sees all?" Michael asked.

Everyone laughs.

Ms. Giles smiles, "Michael, we realize what the conclusion will be. What takes place in between time is what we are speaking of. God is revealing those mysteries to us through His Word and *His* Divine Spirit. When Jesus revealed to Peter about who he was and knowing that following Christ would cause him to lose his life, did Jesus tell Peter how he would die? When Paul traveled by boat to Rome to stand before his accusers to proclaim the Gospel of Jesus Christ, God allows the boat to get smashed. Thus, Paul got stranded on the Island of Patmos, and couldn't get to Rome for three months. Yes, God knows who the Son of Perdition is, but we have a role to play before he's announced to the world. Why? Because those who should know will not accept it unless we tell them. We will be their confirmation on the details you are about to learn. Once they are aware, they can prepare."

"May I interject here?" Tracy asks.

"Tracy, you are more than welcome to."

"I thought we knew who the anti-Christ is?" Referring to a message she received over five years ago from an anonymous source.

Ms. Giles, with regret in her stance, "It is in high appreciation and humbleness before God we must admit to our hasty determination. You see, looking for this man has been our mission for quite some time. Unfortunately, the man we call Beniah Zephorah is not the man he alleges to be. We have unearthed his true identity, and a man from the Ukraine cannot be the anti-Christ. Remember, he will come out of the Ten Horns. Tracy, you should be aware, now that you are with us, the information you receive will not be to deceive humanity but to enlighten them. Being told only what you needed to know by your superiors is not the way we do things here. I, too, was under the same impression five years ago. Here, we are honest and will provide the best training, information, and tools you all will need for what is ahead of you. You were above the President's knowledge, but those in charge would not for a second provide you with the truth."

In those awkward seconds, Michael's frustration boils over, "Ten Horns! What about the Ten Horns?"

"Michael, when Mr. Zinkes said some of you need to learn more about the Word of God, he was referring to you," Ms. Giles said.

If nothing else, they determined Ms. Giles did not mince words. As the explanation ends, she passes out portfolios for each member. Ms. Giles waits for them to go over their bios. Clarifying that those in charge of their training understood their strengths, and each member of this team would need to acknowledge and understand their own weaknesses. Their portfolios included intelligence collected on their capabilities and a small, concise biography of the other members.

"In the interim, here are some directives. You will have two weeks to decide your part within this organization. You were all invited with God's purpose in mind. If you choose, know that everyone here is your team and that will not change unless your behavior decides for you or you decide to remove yourselves. We have separate quarters for each of you. You have access to vehicles to leave the compound. All we request is that you keep your identity a secret and stay out of trouble. If you will agree to those terms, then you can have unrestricted access to the outside world for now."

Everyone nods in approval.

~

Leaving the meeting room, chatter increased as they filled the hallway, heading toward their separate quarters. Taking half an hour to settle in, Michael's curiosity to learn how far he could go outside the compound was growing. He was now a rebel with a cause and a goofball with a heart. Michael knocks on Carsen's door. "Get a Spirit of Discernment Michael, I was praying," she said.

He grins and proceeds as if her comment had no effect on his mission. "I'm going out. Do you want to go with me?"

Carsen looked around the doorway to see that no one else was with him. "Is anyone else coming?" Carsen asked.

"I don't know. You're the first person I asked."

"Yes, I will go. Let me know when you're ready," she said.

"Give me five to ask everybody else."

"Okay." Closing the door behind her.

Everyone agreed to go out. Each one with their own motive but one common notion. To hear what everyone else thought about their impending mission and be out of the mind range of Mr. Zinkes, if possible.

~

Riding the hydro-bikes, they needed speed. They were fond of remaining close to the ground since taking a ten-or more-hour flight to the Compound.

The warmest night of the year so far, the hydro-bikes were a welcomed experience. Wearing all black, to be inconspicuous. They rode into the beautiful, green-valley town like a silent biker club. They were out of place, and everyone noticed. The team discusses where to stop, via their helmets' communication system.

"Let's identify a nice, quiet, out of the way place. I'm ready to eat and be joyful," Michael said.

Tracy turns her black helmet toward him. "Nothing about us is inconspicuous at this point. It's a little too late for that, don't you think?" she said.

Glancing around, "Yeah, maybe you're right," Michael said. "Let's go in here."

Although having no reason to be, Michael annoyed Tracy already. They dismount from the hydro-bikes and remove their helmets, leaving them on the bike seat. A gust of air bends the trees to the left of them across the roadway. In the same breeze, the aroma of garlic bends Tracy's taste buds to Gianni's. Tracy's locks flow as they stroll up the mini stairs. Reaching the Italian eatery door, the waiting area was dark. The blue, fluorescent light guided their way as they walked in and headed toward a table, ignoring the staring eyes that followed them. They spotted a red and teal motif booth with a long-checkered tablecloth that seated them all comfortably.

A man and his wife with blonde hair and blue eyes glare at them, stiff, like mannequins. Another couple with brunette hair were sipping on red wine and waiting for their food to arrive, Sublime could only assume. A single man, in his early fifties, with brown eyes and a head full of silvery hair, looked sorrowful and lonely. He sat in the booth alone. Not once did he glance up to acknowledge them with the crimson roses lying at his side.

They sit to eat and talk. Shortly after sitting, the lonesome man roams over to their table and splits the two dozen roses between Carsen and Tracy. He smiles and races away, saying nothing. Carsen pricks her finger on one thorn. As she lifts it to swab the blood, one by one, their heads fall to the table. There would be no dinner or discussion for them this night.

~

At dawn, they wake in their quarters groggy, minds in a haze, and hungry. An unfamiliar voice came over the loudspeaker asking them to report to the conference room—now! They had no clue what was going on, but they had messed up. They emerge from their rooms to meet in the hallway. Michael was scratching his head to cover the strangeness he felt. Reaching the conference room, sitting around the table, they look up in unison as an unknown gentleman enters the room smiling. He stood there for a few moments. "Hello team, my name is Dr. James Eliza. At six-thirty last evening, a group of five women and men walk into a restaurant to eat and converse about what everybody else's views would be on the mission you are about to embark on. Only one of you bothered to pay attention to the other customers in the bistro but they removed all of you from the Bistro on stretchers, none-the-same. You trusted individuals in the eatery to be civilians and not your potential enemy! Lucky for all of you, we own that compact valley town."

The door opens, and the early fifties, lonely man strolls in. In fact, two of them walk in—twins. Dr. Eliza continues, "Do any of you recognize these men?" They immediately acknowledge defeat. "This is Mr. Laemel and Mr. Lyemel, who will instruct you for the duration of time you serve on this team. They are your Support Specialists. Mr. Lyemel was the fellow who set the roses on the table, full of sleeping gas." Dr. Eliza pauses and directs his attention to Tracy. "You felt sorry for him. You assumed he was a lonesome man. And if it had not been a staging operation for us, all of you could be dead right now. Ladies and gentlemen, most of you have been out of the service for at least a year or two. You've been out of harm's way, but there is an enemy out there who's cunning. He craves to sift you as chaff, to crush you, so you cannot fulfill the purpose and plan God sees for your course. Stop your predictability right here and now, or you will die before you can achieve this mission's end. This will be your first and only warning. You've become lenient in your attitude to the world around you. Those you can count on are the individuals sitting next to you, to your right and left, and the person sitting across from you. You cannot trust anyone outside of this compound and you must always be on guard when you are out there. You will grow to discover you can only depend on God, and each other.

"Our purpose is not to tear you down but to bring you up to speed about a system you do not understand exists. There is an enemy we must deal with, living in plain sight and covered in spiritual darkness. The spirit world exists, and so does the adversary, who lurks in that darkness. They use this existence to bring about what they acknowledge as right in their own eyes. You will lose this battle and your lives if you do not recognize the truth and understand the enemy, as they remain ignorant of the truth. They are false portrayers of light. Discern who they are and learn how to avoid them or fight them to win."

Not intended to humiliate any of them, it was to establish their need for further training. Life for them was no longer tiptoeing through the tulips. Their attitude had to shift. Using military tactics would grant them some useful aspects, but they would enhance it with the existence of life's challenges in 2043. Everything they knew was about to change.

Dr. Eliza, Mr. Laemel, and Mr. Lyemel walk out of the conference room, leaving them to contemplate what took place the prior evening. A voice comes over the loudspeaker, "At zero-five-thirty tomorrow, your training will begin. I suggest you get into the Word and read the Book of Daniel."

Everyone files out of the conference room to the cafeteria to eat breakfast. After eating, they enter their quarters and read Daniel.

'The _little horn_ we must find,' they all thought.

Chapter 3

Whose Purpose

Questions remain as Tracy studies the scriptures in her room. In a place that was calming, sitting comfortably on the chestnut chair. She wasn't looking over her shoulder, nor was she on the hunt. Her place in the world was becoming clear. A place where she belonged and didn't have to wonder if her life was in danger at this very moment.

~

At five a.m., the team wakes up. By five-thirty, the training day began with running. Mr. Laemel and Mr. Lyemel are in the thicket, directing their training by sound through the fog. Breathing rapidly, training themselves to calm their pressure, plunging headfirst to slither through mud under barbed wire. They experience a moment of familiarity in their surroundings. Blanks fired in their direction, whizzing by as the smoke fills the air. One ricochets off Michael's arm. Flinching from the burn—he kept moving. There was a ten-foot rust colored wood wall to scale over and a 160-pound dummy to carry on their backs.

By eight a.m., their bodies are in exhaustion mode. Michael and Tracy compete against each other, battling back and forth to determine who could finish first. Surrounded by the timbers that mask them from the outside world. The fog of the night-before follows their bodies as they race through. Their minds had to stay alert, a five-mile hike, a one-mile obstacle course, and an ammunitions test.

A review of the next day's tasks was part of the daily activities to perform, as well as Scriptures to study each day. This was Seal Training, minus the aquatics, which was a constant reminder of the operations they lead during their military service.

It wasn't hard for them to turn up the adrenaline or drive to endure. They now had a mission to look forward to.

~

Standing near her bedroom door, Tracy thought, 'Was God testing me? No, it couldn't have been God. He knew of the outcome I would perform.' She remembered the Nerve Agent that had been in the slippers.

"You are correct, Tracy," Mr. Zinkes said. "Study to hone in your thoughts. React to the spiritual and the natural. I've been standing here for a few minutes, and you never acknowledged my presence. This is your weakness, being in so much thought that you shut out the outside world. Time with the monks proved they can only teach you so much, even though they have impeccable principles. Be in thought, but shutting everything else out leaves you vulnerable to attack. Use the gifts God has given you while praying for discernment and wisdom. And the biological weapons test was from me." The shock of his confession was like almost slipping off a cliff. Tracy was on the edge, and she had to choose not to fall over. Her blood pressure rises. Mr. Zinkes places his palm on the back of her neck and calms her. "I am not your enemy. I am always here to help and be of help to all of you." Standing opposite her. "I know you would like to fight me right now. Know that I only obey God's commands. I don't deviate from it and He knew you wouldn't make the mistake of breaking those vials without investigating the slippers first."

"Why would you risk the chance of me making a mistake of that magnitude? That was a dangerous chemical agent. The exposure to others!"

"God told me to trust because I knew nothing of you. Every one of you had to go through tests and trials, but God chose you all for His purpose. Your test was the most dangerous. I had to know that you had the instinct to think before reacting, as the military enhanced that in you later."

Tracy's body relaxes. "Mr. Zinkes, it's our purpose to find the anti-Christ and Jesus returns to reclaim the earth. If we determine his identity, what do we do then and why do we have a team such as this?"

They walk together to the front of the facility.

"This team will be our eyes and ears for now. There are those who know nothing of the tactics the enemy will use to thwart the saints of God. What we know is, Revelations 13: 12 talks about Satan, a secular power, and a religious compromise (Satan, the anti-Christ, and the false prophet). They join against the cause of God: The Father, the Word(Jesus), and the Holy Spirit. We know a great falling away has been and continues to happen, but the three and a half years of peace have not taken place. In verse sixteen, it talks about the Mark of the Beast. In the last days of the anti-Christ will be the ultimate test of loyalty, devotion, and faith. t is those left behind who must gain the tools and intelligence to recognize the enemy when he's revealed to the world. It is our job to equip those who remain and those who will come to Christ after the Rapture. The tribulation period will be a time when those who remain will suffer, and some will stand. We must realize, even though we are believers, God's plans for us may differ from what we think it should be. This prepares us for the coming battle and those who are sealed."

"So, are you saying there is a possibility that any of us may remain because of what we know and may find out?"

"I'm not saying any of us will remain. God knows what our end will be. What I am saying is there is a possibility we could, and with this knowledge, train others. Remember, no man knows the hour when the Son of Man comes. It may be tonight, tomorrow, or it could be another 100 years from now. The essential point is the five of you, and others are to prepare for what's coming and deal with the present. The future belongs to God. I must warn you, though. Keep this knowledge to yourself. Others are not where you are just yet."

Mr. Zinkes walks away from Tracy. Though he knew she had a heavy heart, he understood the burden she bore by knowing this knowledge for herself and the team.

~

Training day two, surrounded by the forest trees, the group stood in a clearing for target practice. The sun's warmth embraced them as they basked under the clear sky. Weapons training at the gun range in the morning is both enjoyable and cathartic for most of them. Kelton alone wanted to be anywhere but there.

Carsen was more brains than brawn. She could hold her own. With a pistol in hand, goggles, and earphones, Carsen aims at the target and takes one bullseye shot. She exhales and puts the gun down. Smart and intelligent, she graduated at the top of her class. Believing only in science for most of her life. Though her parents were of the Christian faith, she had to discover the truth for herself.

As a Forensic Archeologist for the FBI, Carsen used her weapon in the line of duty from time to time, to draw down on thieves. Traveling the world to discover ruins and examining strange artifacts the FBI would find during their domestic and international cases across the globe. Her investigations involved stolen artifacts, in and out of the United States, such as historical letters, famous paintings, ancient relics looted from historical sites, and wealthy families.

Carsen reminisces to a day while in an ancient ruin five years prior. She was alone, and a man appeared to her. "One day you will believe and work for Yahweh." He walked past her and disappeared in an instant. She could not explain it nor tell anyone. It was that day she believed there was a God.

Carsen too received a letter from Mr. Zinkes stating her invitation to a secret meeting in Vermont and she'd be doing a work for God. Accepting the invitation was no simple decision for her. Her parents were alive and well and didn't understand the level of secrecy she held in her job as an FBI Agent. They knew she was as an archeologist and looked for ancient artifacts in Africa, which was true.

She would visit them twice a year. This time, she'd have to explain to them she wouldn't be home for a while. She could not lie to them but she couldn't give them the complete truth, either. Before making the trip to Vermont, she paid them a visit, as their reaction would determine if she accepted to leave or not.

Her parents were always glad to see her when she came home. Carsen waited until after dinner to tell them the news. Glaring over childhood pictures.

"Mom and Dad, there's an opportunity for me to work for God. I know nothing about what I'll be doing or when I will be back."

"What are you saying?" her mother asked.

"Mom, it's true I'm an archeologist but I've been working for the Government for the past ten years and now, I will work for God."

Her parents gave each other a knowing look. Deep down, they had suspected all along there was more to her career than she had shared. Her mother hugs and kisses her as to say, "You have our blessing." The idea of never seeing them was surreal.

Carsen, holding her pistol in the ready again, broke down as a single tear rolls down to the top of her lip. She brushes it away.

Mr. Zinkes sought Carsen's attention. "Why so cold, Carsen?"

"Pardon me." She breaks down her defense mode when she realized it was Mr. Zinkes. There was no need to hide from him what she was dealing with. "Mr. Zinkes. Not one day goes by where I don't think of my parents and what they are going through. To know they may never see me again, and vice versa. I told them not to worry. How can I expect them not to be nervous that every knock on the door could be the one where they learn their daughter is dead? How do I reconcile the possibility of my parents dying and not attending their funerals?"

"That is your greatest weakness. You must surrender to God. If you believe you will see them in heaven, then you cannot worry about flesh and bones in a box. We don't know what to expect out of this mission. All we know is God has chosen all of you to be a part of it. And let's be clear, no one will go to your parents' home to tell them you are dead and no one ever said that you won't see your parent again in this life. As far as your previous employment goes, if you so choose, you will no longer exist to them. We will expunge you from their files. Carsen, regardless of your thoughts, God makes no mistakes. Deal with loss, even the loss of your parents. Remember, our warfare is not carnal but spiritual, and we are not doing this just for ourselves. This is for those who will come after us, to provide them with the information and tools to fight the good fight of faith. Our enemy uses our minds to defeat us. All of us will face the death of these earthly bodies one day. Will you meet that day with joy or sadness? Both of your parents are full of faith. Pray they continue to stand until their time comes. We all have an individual walk through this life, and we can only make it if we keep our minds stayed on God. I commend you for thinking of your parents, but do not fall short of understanding their knowledge of the scriptures. Ask yourself, why didn't they put up a fight when you told them you were doing a work for God?"

Her cringed forehead realized Mr. Zinkes knew about her visit to her parents. It did not stop her from answering. "Maybe God prepared them. Hey, how did you know they..."

"Haven't you realized already?" He said. Mr. Zinkes turned away from her. "There is no 'maybe' to it. If we abide in Him, He will abide in us and He will always prepare His children." Mr. Zinkes walks away.

~

Assembling in the conference room after breakfast for training day three, Ms. Giles walks in. "Mr. Johns, will you follow me, please?" He followed without question. The rest sat waiting for Mr. Zinkes to arrive. Mr. Lyemel leads Kelton to a white van. Mr. Laemel was sitting behind him and before taking off he puts a blindfold over Kelton's head. He fought at first, but Mr. Laemel spoke to him calmly, to not worry.

They led a blindfolded Kelton into an empty room a mile away. No windows, just cold, gray-painted walls. Mr. Laemel removed the hood and walks out the room.

For the remaining hour, someone led each member to separate quarters, each room containing a lone chair and silence to fill the void of time. Mr. Zinkes stood alongside Ms. Giles on the observation deck. "This is test six, five, nine, four." Mr. Zinkes was recording on the microphone. "This test includes solitude and will test their physical and mental endurance for five days. They will receive no information or supplies. They can't contact anyone, not even each other." Mr. Zinkes observed, as wrinkles fold vertical on his forehead.

"Mr. Zinkes," she whispered. "How do you think they will handle this one?"

Standing up straight, he relaxed the creases in his forehead and uncrossed his arms. "I hope the lesson learned is that this is possible and could be longer out in the actual world. I hope and pray they channel their energy and mind to sustain them for the next five days. Each one, determining their strengths and weaknesses in their bodies. I will only give them water three times a day—no food. Five sounds, one for each day but for today, silence. Each one observed, and no matter the outcome, I will not let them out until it's time. It's one of individual survival instincts to decide their psychological state. They have been out of military service for a year or more. We must make sure of their mental readiness before we send them out. They will learn to how to cope alone and as a team."

Four hours later, "hello", echoes off the walls. Michael, determined to get answers, as he continued to yell out, "Is anyone there?" Kendrick was doing pushups and then prayed. Tracy sat and quoted scripture aloud, to hear them echo off the walls.

Eight hours in, Mr. Zinkes walked onto the observation deck. He studied them for thirty minutes. Michael wondered how long he would be in there. Not too long, he hoped. Carsen asked God to help her survive this. Tracy thought, 'Discernment. He said I should work on my discernment. How long, Lord? How do you prepare for solitary?' She got up and paced the floor, crossing her arms. 'You answered your own question. You go through it. Be positive, you have been in solitary for longer than five days. Remember your training with the monks. Prepare.'

"Ms. Pimbridge is coming along. The Lord is speaking to her." Mr. Zinkes said.

Kendrick, now bored, screamed at the ceiling, "I have nothing to do, and I have to use the bathroom. Can anyone hear me?"

For a normal person, the reality of this experience would be no less than a torturous tactic. No restroom, no noise. Solitude is their only friend.

Kelton resigned himself to the fact that no one was going to let them out yet. "Okay, a test of sorts. Okay, I will go to sleep now." Lying on the floor, he prepared to go to sleep.

Mr. Zinkes, watching them all, sees that they have the same idea and are attempting to get as comfortable as possible with no bedding. He turned and walked to the door. "I will see you in the morning—good night, Ms. Giles."

"Good night, Mr. Zinkes."

The music blasts as they rise for the second morning of the fast. Not overbearing, but loud enough to be annoying. "Oh, God help me." Carsen says under her breath. Knowing their release wouldn't be today, everyone treated this as a serious exercise. Within minutes of waking, each of them picked a corner to release the pressure in their bladders. Their thoughts rambled, and the consensus was that it would soon be smelly.

Tracy conserved energy and moved just enough not to get muscle atrophy. Michael practiced martial arts for an hour, sweat dripping, and then meditation. Conserve mind and body, focus on God, stay prayerful and meditate on the Scripture living inside of them. It was up to them to learn the necessity of communing with God on an intimate level.

As Carsen reserved energy, Kendrick yelled out, "Can we get rid of the noise please?" As though they would grant his request. Kelton exercised for about thirty minutes to get his mind flowing for the day.

The doors automatically open to each room on the morning of the sixth day. A gush of chilly air passes their bodies. Hydrant hoses are let loose on each one. Wet, stinking, and cold, they stood outside in forty-degree weather. Birds chirped in the quietness of the trees. "You have twenty minutes to finish the obstacle course in front of you. If you fail, you will continue until you complete it in less than twenty minutes. You may start now." Mr. Laemel said.

To complete the course, they would run a mile, crawl through a mud pit with barbed wire over it, while ammunition is flying over their heads, sidestep through tires on the ground, climb a wall, while carrying a dummy 300 yards to the finish line.

Carsen took off running and finished in thirteen minutes flat. Tracy finished in thirteen minutes, fifteen seconds. Kelton finished in fourteen minutes, fifteen seconds. Kendrick completed the course in fifteen minutes, twenty seconds, and Michael in sixteen minutes flat.

Mr. Lyemel directs them to the van with the seats covered in plastic. At ten hundred hours, they arrive at the compound. They walk into the hall, exhausted and unafraid. Their adrenaline was high, and they were anticipating what the next test would be?

Within thirty minutes, they take a shower and fall asleep. Sustenance was the last thing on their minds.

Chapter 4

Truth Session

Sunday morning, the Spirit of God fills the church service they were attending. The prayer, worship, and praise allowed the release of tears, fear, and burdens. Raising their hands as a sign of surrender to God, the team was grateful for this moment in time. Even though most churches had been closed, those that remained were in a constant battle to keep their doors open. God would not forsake nor abandon those who had faith. Believers willingly flocked to the churches on Sunday mornings and any other day they could attend. The people of the world saw what was happening, even though they didn't understand what it meant. Some never stepped foot inside because of unbelief or their circumstances got the better of them. The poor, the hungry—the hopeless.

They return from church service to meditate on the Word of God and pray in their secret places. After two hours, they met for lunch and a discussion.

"Michael, do you ever look back and wonder how we got here? I mean, what catapulted us to where we are now?"

"None of us were born then, Tracy. I believe it started when they first took prayer out of the schools."

Kendrick follows that statement, "Yep, in 1963, Madalyn Murray O'Hair won a lawsuit against the Baltimore School System. They voted eight to one in her favor to ban school prayer and labeled it 'unconstitutional.' According to our history, they founded this country on the belief in God, I thought? How could they just discount prayer?"

"The Scriptures and history books I've read don't add up. There is so much out there. We need to question what this country has done and continues to do. Secret Societies, Free Masons, and some conspiracy theorists' information is verifiable. There are speculations this country's leaders followed a god people shouldn't be worshipping," Tracy said.

"Don't tell me you believe in conspiracy theories?"

"Carsen, it's not that I believe in conspiracy theories. I know for a fact that this world is corrupt and the government I used to work for isn't always truthful. There's a lot of information being kept from us…is still being kept from us."

Kendrick chimes in again to give his two cents. "More significant, something happened, and technology just went boom. Microwaved meals, talking and seeing each other on these phones, hydrogen cars, in fact, electric cars and computers. Don't get me started."

"And look at us now, seeming at the end of the world as we know it, fighting the very thing the scriptures are talking about," Carsen said.

Kelton stays quiet and continues to eat. Tracy looks his way. "Kelton, what are you thinking?"

"What am I thinking?… I'm thinking, what are we going to find? Is this an open door for the Rapture to take place and am I living righteous enough to make it in? This way is narrow. Am I reading and studying enough to understand what God is saying to the church or even to me? I believe the Lord orders our footsteps, but the unknown of who we are is what I consider. We have our specialties and are at the top of our professions. Everyone has diverse backgrounds, and we became believers in Christ. That is our common denominator. What if our own self-doubt impedes what God has for us? What if we fail this mission?"

"All of us have self-doubts about this mission. Who amongst us wants to fail God or the people who need our help? The essential point is, as Mr. Zinkes said in our first meeting, if we fail, it is for our learning and God's plan doesn't change," Tracy said.

"But why would failure be in God's plan for us?"

"Michael, no one who has a genuine relationship with our Heavenly Father looks to fail. It happens for our learning and if we are still alive, then we learn from our mistakes and keep it moving. Is our faith in our own ability, or is our faith in Him? How often did we hear the Lord is nigh? Are we going to see this in our lifetime? Maybe, maybe not. Doubt must go out the window. Look around you and see scripture playing out right before our eyes, as Carsen said. The revelation of the 'Abomination of Desolation' will make God's omnipotence clear to every believer and non-believer. Every knee shall bow and every tongue shall confess Jesus Christ is Lord. Why don't people see it's in His Word? God will not change, and His Word will not return void," Kendrick said.

"Think about all the false, world-ending events. We put our own anxiety out in the universe. This Government has controlled people with fear for years. Before we accepted Christ, we could only believe in what we saw. Continue to have faith that God's Word is true, and His promises will happen," Carsen said.

"Amen," Tracy said. "Okay, on to another subject. We have weaknesses. Before they send us into the world, they will test us on them. I need to work on my discernment for spiritual matters. What about the rest of you?"

"He told me I need to let go of people, especially my parents. It is the primary reason I don't get involved with others. I shy away from personal relationships," Carsen said.

Kelton nodded in agreement, then explained his own situation. "At nine-years-old, I was living in the Child's Heart

Orphanage, because my parents left me there. Captain Protector is what the kids called me. It didn't matter who or how big the bully was, I'd fight. I fought for the little guys and dared anyone to defy my protective nature. Because of my willingness to fight, prospective adoptive parents passed me over time and time again. It was noble to defend others but self-defeating in finding a home.

"My parents left me on the doorstep of an orphanage at birth. No record, date, or information about who I am. It's as if my parents never existed. Trust me, I've looked, and nothing of me ties back to anyone. After all the fighting to hide my pain, one man, Dr. Steno, taught me to fight with my mind. He took me in and trained me in every area of my life. He was never abusive or cold, but loving and compassionate, firm, and fair. The spiritual part I didn't recognize until later.

"At eleven, I was writing programs for NASA. My mind was a sponge, and I could never get enough. By eighteen, Dr. Steno was dying. He never told me, and financially, I lacked nothing. I learned the hard way, 'money can't buy you love, nor can it define who you are.' From the age of twenty to twenty-five, I turned into a hermit. Anything that had to do with a computer, they tested through me. Consumed by loneliness, I searched for my identity and still today, my actual identity is unknown. My DNA has matched no one. I know they existed. Someone changed everything about them to conceal their identities.

"Five years after Dr. Steno died, he paid me a visit. Now, I cannot say whether it was him or an angel. He was standing there as real as you or I. He said, "You can search the world over and still never know who you are, because you are no one without God." I thought I had gone crazy for sure. I was adamant in my belief that there was no God. I mean, how can God allow this to happen to a child, a child who didn't know himself in the most basic way? During that experience, my doorbell rang. It scared me back to reality. I looked at the door and turned back toward Dr. Steno, and he disappeared. I opened the door and a boy from the orphanage was standing there, the same age as me. For a moment, I stood, staring, because he looked the same but older.

"You know why I am here," he said.

"There was no question—God sent him. He wasn't there simply to thank me for taking up for him at the orphanage, even though he did. He was there to tell me about his experience with Jesus Christ. We sat for hours just talking about how God directed him to find me. That day, I became a *Believer*. I think for the first time in my life, I gave up the anxiety of never finding my parents. A part of me always knew God was there, but I had to be angry with someone. Why not direct my anger at someone I couldn't see? How crazy is that! To be mad at God, who I didn't believe existed.

"For me, my weakness is the unknown. I've come to grips with the fact I belong to God. I just wonder how I will react if I ever find out the truth of who I am. Biology is only part of the picture that's missing. What if my parents turn out to be horrible people? I've asked God to show me the truth. I used to get anxious about the *what ifs*. Knowing the truth causes you to see yourself. I'm not sure how to handle it." Kelton finished his story with a shrug and a sigh.

Michael and Kendrick said nothing. If you didn't know any better, you'd think they were invincible. Michael wasn't up for discussing his shortcomings. "Do you mind if we pick up this truth session another time? We need to get back to focusing on the training tomorrow?" He postured straight after his statement.

Looking him in the eye. "Sure, I hope you're not ashamed of your feelings," Tracy said.

Michael kept quiet, but smirked to show his frustration with the discussion even more.

Six hours later, the barracks alarm pierced their resting ears. Yes, they were in boot camp. Rising from her bed. "Why?!" Tracy yells in frustration. "Okay, pull it together."

Over the intercom, Mr. Zinkes requests Tracy's presence. She strolls to his office while they escort everyone else to the conference room. Tracy shrugs off the bewilderment as she approaches Mr. Zinkes.

"You have many questions, and I believe your frustration with most of this is, you do not understand, 'why.' Is that correct?"

"Our previous military training was comprehensive. Drills are a part of who we are. Why this focus and what will it serve?" She understood training was crucial, but why these basic tactics?

"It is without dispute this mission is of enormous importance and we must train you all for what is developing. Scripture says for three and a half years. A false understanding of peace will inhabit the land. This unit's mission is to locate the whereabouts of the anti-Christ. God would not have us ignorant, so during this mission, we must prepare. This team's mission and the entire operation will affect people around the world. We, God's soldiers, must train for the end of this worldly system as we know it. His plan to redeem us to Him began at the onset of sin. We must train for those who will turn to Christ after the Rapture takes place. There is a purpose and reason for all we do in God's plan." He stood at his window. "It's your lack of patience with the process and the inconsequential matters that irritate you, which shouldn't. Tracy, lead them and prepare to be a target as the leader of this group."

Tracy walks toward him. "Why can't all of us be leaders? Michael will have major issues with me being the team leader. I don't need any problems from him."

"Again, Tracy, work on your discernment. Michael is not concerned about being a follower or receiving orders from you. The military taught him to do his duty, and it makes no difference who's handing out the plans. I will not reveal what Michael needs. Please discern that for yourself. Prepare to lead because that is where God has called you to serve," Mr. Zinkes stated with finality. Tracy sighs. "This doesn't mean the others can't lead. God placed you in this position because you prefer to work alone, and you can't manage that way with a team. A leader must communicate with their teammates as to the actions to take. This is not about who is better. God is equipping us, and He doesn't always give the in-between details upfront. At this compound, we plan for all possibilities. We opened with fasting for mind and body to receive from the Lord. Fasting in our quiet places is on our own terms or we are doing it because of a need. When the mind thinks it has a choice to eat or not, you will find fasting difficult. What about in the field? Captured and starved? How does your mind, body, and spirit prepare for the unexpected and when you are not in control? When it learns there's no choice, it adapts. Understand, this is not just about you Tracy." Mr. Zinkes sits with his arms crossed. He gazes at her momentarily, then dismisses her. "That is all. Please send in Mr. Being. One last thing, Pimbridge, being in a spiritual place to hear from God is imperative. This is not just physical."

Each member walks in and out of his office in silence. Each told of their own personal mission. Everyone deciding to stay and be with the team on this journey.

~

Within the Darkness Lurks the Fallen

I Timothy 4:1 (NKJV), "*Now the Spirit expressly says in the latter times, some will abandon the faith, giving heed to deceiving spirits and doctrines of demons.*"

On Hallows Eve in Egypt, a torch-lit corridor of the 1800s stonework of spiraled pillars surrounds the hollow chamber of hidden faces. Those who've abandoned faith in the true and living God walk in formed lines, wearing silk, Black-robed shadows, uttering in unison, "It is our mission to deceive man by creating disorder, hatred, uncertainty, and doubt—to control."

Flickering light from a candle bounces off a hooded figure who walks forward to the middle of the gathering and declares, "The son of man they hail as the Christ appeared to save them but billions still do not believe. Those are not our purpose. The three and a half years of peacetime are of the essence. The time is now to launch an accursed accusation against the church to force believers to forsake their hopes. We will appear to adopt their views, and burden those accepting Christ with fear. They will turn to us to preserve them, and we'll provide them with an altered understanding of freedom. Our god's strategy is working."

Chapter 5

Pale Horizon

Tracy sat alone in the courtyard for a while. Spotting the Broad-Winged Hawk in the tree above her. Stepping to the post where the glove was laying, she places the glove on slowly. Tracy doesn't raise her hand right away. He hops past the green leaves on the branch toward the tip in waiting. She raises her hand, and he flies to her. Tracy says nothing to him at first. She then feels his pulse slow. "Thank you for coming. I'm glad you're here today." He squawks in a controlled tone replying to Tracy, as she provides him a live prey to go after. She lets it loose and sees his eyes sharpen and fixed. She knew their visit in time was for only a moment. His pulse raises, the air flutters in her locks as he takes off with grace and precision. Removing the glove, she realizes the cold and gloomy weather was present, as the sweat provides a wake-up jolt from the majestic experience. The air was fresh, allowing her to focus on and contemplate her existence and what it meant. Droplets fall on her face as she looks up to the sky for clarity of mind, feeling closer to God.

She wasted an enormous part of her life looking for the wrong things to fulfill those empty places she was trying to hide. She now knew what was missing. 'I'm not yet fulfilled, but I am close.' Tracy acknowledges. After contemplation, she turns to go inside.

Michael was there staring her way, for how long she didn't know. "Beautiful Bird. I didn't know there were any trained ones here," he said.

"He was once a rescue. He's wilder now, but he has an affinity for humans in their lost existence."

"Yeah, okay."

"You know it's time for this morning's session. The team is expecting us." Her words were relaxed. Tracy giggles as she walks past him. He didn't know why—it intrigued him. They walk toward the building. At that moment, she let him into her life a little.

"You know, you were two years ahead of me in Seal Training. That's why I know of you," Tracy said.

Michael stops in his tracks. "I guess I was in the field with my team by then. Why didn't we cross paths before now?"

"I'm not sure. I kept my identity anonymous regarding the records for the classes. Plus, after the final training, they transferred me."

"Oh, my God! You are T.P., aren't you? I can't believe it! Why wouldn't you want people to know your ability to best the best in certain areas?" Pumping his chest.

"I didn't want the attention. My father taught me to keep a low profile. Colonel Pimbridge was not keen on showboating. Even after he died, it stayed ingrained in me. Respecting his position on the subject allowed me to stay low key. Because of it, the higher ups took notice of my abilities. I didn't ask for it but keeping a low profile was right up the Navy's and the government's alley. I became their personal assassin."

Sensing a less than jovial moment. "Let's get going. We have to get to the meeting," Michael said.

As Tracy turns to lead the way, Michael becomes quiet. He opens the door and allows her to enter first, being the gentleman he was.

~

Entering the conference room, they part ways, sitting on opposite sides of the table. Ms. Giles began the meeting by reading Matthew 24:4 (KJV), *"Jesus answered, watch out that no one deceives you. For many will come in my name claiming, I am the Christ, and will deceive many. You will hear of wars and rumors of wars but see that they do not alarm you. Such events must take place but the end is yet to take place. Nation will rise against nation, and kingdom against kingdom. There will be famines and earthquakes in diverse places. All these are the beginnings of birth pains. Then you will be given over to be persecuted and put to death, and all nations will despise you because of me. Many will turn away from the faith and will betray and hate each other, and many false prophets will appear and deceive many people. Because of the increase of wickedness, the love of man will grow cold, he who stands firm to the end will be saved. And this gospel of the kingdom will be preached in the whole earth as a witness to all people, and thus the end will come.*

"Know that nothing is new under the sun. It happened in Jesus' time and it will happen again. Do we readily see this happening now? The strange things happening across the globe that man can't explain. When you consider the things that you have seen in your lives, do you believe this scripture is being fulfilled right now?"

Carsen speaks. "I believe we are. I can't say for sure when it started, but it's so clear now because I am a follower of Christ and reading the word of God that I can see it in a spiritual aspect too."

~

March 24, 17:00 hours, Michael, Tracy, Carsen, Mr. Laemel and Mr. Lyemel receive orders for their first mission, with Mr. Nordic piloting. No longer using their actual names once in the field. They had been waiting for the day they'd put their training to effective use, needing to feel useful again. Hearing a tap on her door, Tracy hops towards the door while she pulls up the last leg of her pajamas. "Be ready to take off at zero six hundred hours." Mr. Laemel and Lyemel inform each member. One by one, the team opened their 'Pale Horizon' mission modules to identify the target of their summons—Intel on Zephaniah Banks. Without hesitation, they hit the web button. Each one received the same material. Summarizing, there was more unknown than known about this man. There was not enough information to go on, but they identified what he looked like. Tracy got out of her pajamas and headed toward the technology room. She wasn't alone. Each one having the same idea to get more info on Mr. Banks before leaving tomorrow.

~

The next dawn, the sky was overcast but no trace of mist. It would not rain. In the chopper, Mr. Zinkes briefs them as they head to the airstrip to board a jet for Egypt. "Although we ruled Mr. Beniah Zephorah out as the anti-Christ. Our intel says he has contact with an organization called the Apollyon. This is not about the anti-Christ himself. It's about a group of narcissists who are seeking to set Armageddon in motion. Your mission is to collect intelligence. Your assignment is to engage those meaningful to our mission." Mr. Zinkes takes a moment of silence before he proceeds. He rests back in his seat and closes his eyes. They sit in silence for five minutes. There was no relaxation to be had. His mind was racing. When he opens his eyes again, Tracy spoke to Mr. Zinkes, "Why don't men believe anymore? Why is it more attractive to believe in lies than the truth?" she asked.

"Because some of us endure this life in contented ignorance and when we consider other than ourselves being in control, mortal beings can't deal with it. It's simpler to do whatever you crave and have no consequence of how you live this life. Tracy, it has all to do with being swayed by the sins of this world and the condition we find ourselves in. Seems to be the reason God destroyed man before during Noah's time," Michael said.

Mr. Zinkes was just as shocked with Michael's answer as was Tracy. Mr. Zinkes continues his directives.

"The Apollyon claim to know the identity of the anti-Christ. It is undetermined whether this is true. Tracy, use your contacts once in Egypt."

"So, how did we come by this intelligence?" she asked.

"We have eyes and ears everywhere. Some time ago, one of our contacts furnished us some intel on an organization he was not close to but knew of them having information about the anti-Christ. Confirmation of this came in last night before they handed you all the modules. I do not know his name. He's linked with a family who has allegiance to the Apollyon. He's never seen them but has heard the family speak of them." Before Michael could ask his question, Mr. Zinkes responds, "No, Michael, you will not be the lapdog. You both are on an even playing field. I have established Tracy as Team Leader for this mission for a logical purpose. It has nothing to do with your skills or lack thereof. It has all to do with using her contacts. God's selection of Tracy doesn't mean you are not qualified to lead. So, let's get back to what's at hand, shall we?" Mr. Zinkes' pleasant demeanor matched his verbiage. Carsen stays quiet and faces ahead. "Sure, Mr. Zinkes." Michael said.

In a single glance at Mr. Zinkes, Tracy conveyed, 'I told you so.'

"For this mission, Michael, you purchase and sell precious artifacts. Carsen is the restorer. Use Carsen's background as an archeologist to find any ancient writings useful in any form. Your contact in Egypt is Mr. Zephaniah Banks. You will meet him at the Pharaoh Hotel at fifteen-thirty hours on Wednesday, room 304. You will arrive tomorrow evening, settle in, meet Mr. Banks, and Thursday, inspect the archeological site. It's such a buzz right now. Are there questions for me now?"

All echoing, "No."

"Excellent. I expect you to return in three weeks with a detailed report on the Apollyon. Do not, I repeat, do not engage them militarily. All you require will be accessible to you once you reach the hotel. Money is no object. Spend as often as you need to attract attention." Mr. Zinkes finishes.

"But what if we run out?" Michael asks.

"Mr. Being, I'm confident it's impossible, but if it comes down to One World Currency, God will provide what we need. Plus, Tracy has connections to wealth all over the world. Stick with her and you will never run out." Mr. Zinkes smiles. Tracy drops her head into her hands.

There was complete silence for the rest of the trip to the private jet waiting for them. Once the chopper touched down, they grab their gear and head toward the plane, waiting for them. Mr. Zinkes calls out to them, salutes them, and says, "Try to have fun, if that's possible." They glance at each other with smirks.

~

At the Compound, in the conference room, Ms. Giles briefs Kelton and Kendrick on their teammates' mission. "For the next three weeks, you will handle intelligence collection and training. Kelton, you will be with our Information Technology Department. Kendrick will go to our airbase to establish that our airplanes are acceptable. You are to explore any aircraft available, on or off the black market. Money is no object and God is allowing us to prepare. Gentlemen, Mr. Zinkes instructed me to advise you to take this time to have fun. You may not have the chance again. Mr. Roberts, you leave at zero six hundred."

"Yes, ma'am." Kendrick said.

They all file out at the same time. "Hey Kendrick, have fun with the planes."

"Yeah, you do the same Kelton with the computer stuff. See ya when I see ya."

Both head to their rooms.

In the private jet of the Lord, they study about the ancient artifacts found at site 1378. During this briefing, Carsen's expertise is most helpful. Mr. Laemel and Mr. Lyemel are along for the ride to ensure the team has what it needs.

Sitting around the white stone table, they start the briefing process of the hotel and travel arrangements to the site.

Mr. Laemel begins the discussion and brings the floor plans up on the Automated Imaging Map (AIM). He stands, "We have the top two floors of the Pharaoh Hotel. The top floor has a one-way entrance and exit to the elevator. It has five bedrooms, a library, a party room, and a lounge area. The surveillance and communications team are already on the floor below. They have swept the rooms for any devices. We bought both floors, severing access from the lower floors. Each of us will have our own room. No one suspects why or for what reason we are coming, but we will raise eyebrows. All of you must put on an air of power and wealth for acceptance because we are foreigners. For the rest of this plane ride and tomorrow, you need to transform into your identities before meeting with our contact. Are there questions?"

Michael raised his hand like a school kid. "When are we going to have fun?"

"That's totally going to depend on how long it takes for you all to complete this part of the mission and whether your type of fun means going to a museum and the local sites or having fun, the other way you're used to having fun. If things don't go as planned, you may have unwanted fun. Make no mistake, I suspect this group to be armed, well connected, and dangerous."

Michael whistled through his teeth. "I knew it was too good to be true."

With six hours into the plane ride, one by one, they fell asleep, only to be awakened an hour later by a sudden flurry of turbulence. Mr. Laemel comes from the cockpit, flailing his arms. "Do not fret, thirty seconds and we'll be out of it. Mr. Nordic said it's smooth sailing from there." Mr. Laemel comes from the cockpit flailing his arms. "Do not fret, thirty seconds and we'll be out of it. Mr. Nordic said it's smooth sailing from there."

With everyone awake, they ate a light salad with protein and continued with the briefing. Everyone views the AIM of the archeological site and the tentative location of the Apollyon. Mr. Laemel began.

"We know they have several compounds. None of our intelligence has landed us a specific location as to their primary base of operations."

"So, why is this archeological site so important now?" Sublime asked.

Carsen was eager to answer. "Tracy, if you remember, in Luke 24, verses 36 through 53, this is where Jesus appears to the Disciples in Bethany and then ascends to Abba Father. Looks like they found the village house where the Disciples stayed. They are looking for distinctive artifacts to authenticate if this is. in fact, the house."

Viewing the archeological site showed 120 miles away, a possible unverified Apollyon compound site. "The Apollyon organization are Godless men and women (dreamers), who are wolves in sheep's clothing. Jude warns us of them. A remnant of those who did not believe and the angels who abandoned their post, written in the Apocryphal writings in the book of Enoch. This group believes they are the descendants of those angels. There has been no evidence to prove such, but it doesn't take much for humans to think they are greater, or at least equal to God the Father," Mr. Lyemel said.

He reads, Jude 1:10 (NKJV), *"But these speak evil of whatever they do not know, and whatever they know naturally, like brute beasts, in these things they corrupt themselves."*

"If you continue reading, Jude, it tells you what they will become. They believe they can change the outcome of God's plan, and that's how Satan has deceived them. We are in the last days, ladies, and gentlemen. It's time to go to battle for the Lord."

The intention of the moment was to bring the team to praise and worship God in their togetherness, but Tracy's mind went to thinking ahead. It was like when all heads turn when someone bumps into the record player and it makes that scratching sound.

Tracy doesn't experience his moment. "How do you know so much about this group? And how much longer before we reach Cairo?" Tracy's question stops Mr. Lyemel's plans. Tracy gets up, stretches, and waits for an answer.

Mr. Lyemel stands. "I have studied the apocryphal writings and the Holy Scriptures for over 30 years now. I do not have all the answers. There are things that still surprise me. It's no coincidence that things are happening in the world as they are now. You, too, will have to study as much as you can."

"And to answer your second question, we make our pit stop in Morocco in an hour. After refueling, we have another eight and a half hours of ride left." Michael said.

Tracy looks at each member of the team. "After we refuel, we need to focus on the business at hand. Mr. Lyemel, please get as much information as you can on a Joshua Wells who lives in Rabat, Morocco. He may be useful to us if Mr. Banks proves untrustworthy. If you get in contact with him, tell him to pack light, and meet us at the airport. Tell him I said so," Tracy said.

He responds by focusing on the AIM system.

Chapter 6

Picking Up a Stranger of Sorts

Tracy turns to Carsen. "We require as much info on that location as you can find. We prefer no surprises and need a backup strategy for everything. One fact for certain, we've drawn attention. If not with the Apollyon, we have with the locals. Only serious money can buy out two floors of a hotel. It attracts those with equal talents to pursue information. They know we are coming, but they don't know who we are. We have to draw straws. This is so we know who will be your spouse, Michael."

Michael turns his console chair toward Tracy. "My wife? What do you mean, my wife?"

"Egypt is a male-dominated culture. In the early 2000s, there was a shift toward a more balanced culture, but it has digressed. If I arrive there as a lead, it could backfire. They will recognize my wealth, but won't respect me. Michael, you're the dominant figure they'll accept. You must be the one with the power and respect. They'd work to draw you in before me. And as I know they will, I will be along for the ride as your wife, or your bodyguard, which I'd prefer, but I must make this fair and draw straws with Carsen."

He raises his head and squints his eyes. "The question is, can you play second fiddle, Tracy?"

Everyone's eyeing Tracy now.

"Euphrates, fear not. I won't do anything to mess up this mission on purpose, but don't press me. I can break a pinky toe or two."

They laugh, and the ladies draw straws.

"Ah, the bodyguard." Tracy was relieved not to have to play Michael's wife.

"Honey, do you want to know Jesus? He can save your soul," Carsen said.

Michael's head now in his hands, he looks at Mr. Lyemel and Mr. Laemel pleading, "You mean I have to deal with this for three weeks?"

Tracy taps his shoulder and sits in front of him.

"Well, it makes perfect sense. A bodyguard is with you all the time, and a wife isn't. So, while we are gallivanting around with the Apollyon, Carsen can be at the archeological site with Mr. Laemel or Mr. Lyemel. If it gets ugly, they're available to give Carsen an extra hand to kick butt, if needed. I will be there to save yours."

"Oh brother, give me a break. I'm here to back you, not the other way around." Michael said.

"Well, the facts have shifted. Michael, learn to adapt. I assure you you'll see life in a much better way," Tracy said. Sitting back in her seat.

"Who put you in charge?"

She laughs. "You didn't just ask that? Michael, we are here to work together. But I am Team Leader for this mission. I know Egypt like the back of my hand. But once again, to make this all fair, you have until we land in Morocco to come up with a fresh idea. If not, we're going with my plan." Tracy spoke with finality and got up.

Everyone chuckles under their breath and moves to their spot on the plane, allowing Michael to brood in his recliner.

~

The plane lands to refuel in Rabat. Tracy looks out the window and spies on Joshua as they pull into the hangar. A beautiful, sunlit afternoon, the Mousier Redstarts chirp overhead. The brilliant yellow underbellies caught Joshua's eye. His gaze turns toward the jet as it pulls in. His eyes protected from the bright sunlight by mirrored sunglasses. The engines rev down. Michael, unmoving, studies Joshua from his window. The shade in the hangar now conceals the passengers from Joshua's view.

Mr. Laemel and Lyemel open the door and let down the stairs. Rushing down them, they pass Joshua without saying a word on their way to the unoccupied office. Tracy steps out wearing an all-black suit. She approaches him, walks past, and stops. Looking over the top of her shades, "Right this way, Mr. Wells. They will search you, down to your skivvies."

Continuing to walk to the door, she expects him to follow. She moves to the side to let him pass. Joshua was pleased to see Tracy. Although her coldness was unexpected. He stops in his tracks. "Wait! What is all this Mr. Wells stuff? You leave me at the altar and I'm stupid enough to be waiting at this airport for you?"

She turns to him, glaring, biting her bottom lip, wanting to smile but can't show it. She spots Michael and Carsen watching.

"Cairo, Egypt!" she says.

Joshua walks close to her. "I'm in! You realize they have banned me for another year?"

"No problem, we've removed the ban." She winks over her glasses. Tracy waits for him to go into the office. Her hand gestures, leading him to where Mr. Laemel and Lyemel were waiting. He strolls in and she stays outside. Ten minutes later, the office door opens, leaping out, and stumbling, Joshua was no longer grinning. "You know, I feel violated." Sublime tries not to laugh but lets out a snicker. Mr. Laemel and Lyemel come out. "He's clean." They walk back on the airplane. Tracy walks ahead of him. "Follow us, Mr. Wells. We'll leave in thirty minutes. Once in the air, our discussion will include our wedding fiasco and about your invitation to this party of sorts. But before we step foot on this plane..." She turns to him to block his pathway, ensuring, as she looks back, that Mr. Laemel and Mr. Lyemel board the plane without them. "If all progresses as planned, you will be a wealthy man. The alternative is your life. How do you answer?"

Studying her face, a moment. "Well, if it means dying with you, then so be it. I also don't resent the wealthy part. There are things about me that haven't changed." Joshua walks close enough to kiss her.

She spins. "Follow me and let the adventure begin." Sublime says with vigor, as she strides up the four steps into the plane.

Joshua, handsome and tall, manicured beard, and mustache making his light-brown eyes stand out. A potential model in his younger days, he'd only been in the military for a year when they met in Egypt. Joshua was in full satisfaction, walking up the stairs behind Tracy. He bends his body to get through the door. Tracy directs Joshua to a compartment in the back of the plane. There they could talk alone. He greets Michael and Carsen in passing. Noticing the grimace in Euphrates response, "Hey, what's up guy... dude." Awkward was an understatement.

Closing the door behind them, offering him a beverage—he accepts. Sublime waits until they are in the air. She explains the details of their mission. Before she could get a word in, he grabs and kisses her. The intensity of the moment subsides. She sighs, straightening her clothes. "I didn't intend to leave you at the altar or on the island. I did it to save your life if that's any consolation. I know what you are going to say, please let me explain. When I met you, I was in deep and being a Seal Six Trainer was my cover. I taught some classes, but that wasn't my actual job. In my mind, I was free to do and be whoever I wanted. Then I received a message contrary to that fact. The message said if I didn't leave, no one would leave the island alive. Killing everyone to get to me was the plan. If I had stayed, I would have to tell you everything, and I knew you would try to stop me. The risk was too great. If I could stop it from happening, then I would have without hesitation. The threat was genuine, and your life was more important to me than mine. If they wanted to make that little island disappear, they'd have done it. No one else would be the wiser. There would have been no investigation or news coverage. Cover-ups were their specialty. I left without telling you what was going on and I have no regrets about doing so, because here you are, alive. Being accountable for your life and countless others was too much to bear. They had to believe I left you. I needed for you to be in the dark and to hate me for it."

"Don't you think I had a right to know?"

"You are the most stubborn man I know. You crave adventure just as much as you enjoy breathing. I didn't contact you, so you wouldn't become a target. I would never want them to use you as a pawn to get to me. You do not understand what they were capable of. These were people with no mercy and no remorse for anything they did or made me do." Pleading for understanding, she needed him to know her reasoning without hashing out the whole situation.

"Tracy, for goodness' sake. You pretend I am new to this life and what lurks around the corner. I knew the dangers that came with your job. I could have handled myself." He would not let this go.

"Joshua, I was saving you from me!"

"What on earth do you mean? What are you not telling me? Were you a serial killer for the government's use or you couldn't commit to me?"

"You are the only man I've ever loved. You are the only person I could trust. I was not honest regarding who and what I was. My clearance level could take out an entire country if I had to, and they are the ones who gave me that authority. I have trained with monks and masters of every art of war you can think of. You were my best friend, and I was about to marry you and ruin our friendship to the point of no return. I couldn't be upfront about the people I worked for. I was their assassin and for a time, I enjoyed it, until I could no longer be with you. That was the turning point for me. I had to make sure you were safe. I'm the one who told them to put a ban on you from coming to Egypt. And I'm also the one who told the Moroccan Government to hold you in their country and made sure no one knew you were there."

"What?! Why would you do that? Egypt was my home."

"It may have been your home, but your home would have become your grave. With you out of harm's way, I could do what I needed to accomplish to make sure everyone I loved was safe."

"Okay, so what about now?"

"Those who knew about me no longer exist, they're no longer a problem. I wiped every document of my existence as an assassin from their records. Once I was free from the organization, I remained burdened inside. There was no other way to forgive myself for the things I had done. I turned to God for forgiveness, and I must thank you for that. My life now is to serve Him instead of man. My focus is on God's will and being obedient to His Word. As far as your previous home, it's still available to you. It's paid for and I make sure a cleaning service visits once a month. You may return and stay there if you wish."

His body now relaxed. She too could relax a bit. He sat on the couch. Her voice settles, "God has chosen five of us for what's happening, and I believe you were chosen too, for this mission. I know you love God with all your heart and that is why you would be an asset to this team and this mission. The Book of Revelations in the Holy Scriptures is happening as we speak. I know it is hard for you to believe what I'm saying but I am being honest with you. This is way beyond all of us. Give us some time to show you the truth. Once you see all the information, you will know what's at stake here. As of now, three of the team members are on this plane. Mr. Laemel and Mr. Lyemel are our training and support specialists. I want you to join us because you are the best at what you do. We have access to equipment and resources we would not get anywhere else. Wednesday afternoon, we'll meet with a man named Zephaniah Banks who will get us access to the ancient site in Jerusalem." She sits next to Joshua, grabs one hand, and caresses it. "I need you to trust me, to believe without question. We are fighting on the Lord's side." He looks down at her hand.

"Tracy, I believe you. There's been movement in Cairo and Jerusalem, about the place where Jesus met with the Disciples before ascending to the Father."

"Yes, that's a part of our mission and cover. Do you trust me?"

"Yes, I trust you."

"Good."

Her hand raises and injects him with a sleeping liquid. His reflex wasn't quick enough. He was out in ten seconds. She grabs the back of his neck and lays him back in the seat. Tracy opens the door.

"Mr. Lyemel, he is all yours. Joshua will be in a fighting mood. After you inject him with the tracking device, let's sit him in with us so, when he wakes in forty minutes, he won't feel so abused," Sublime said.

"Sure thing," Mr. Lyemel said. She walks out of the door to sit with the others.

"How much do you know about him?" Carsen asks.

"Enough to share for the rest of this plane ride but we'll continue the briefing once Joshua is awake. He can tell you himself." Tracy sits in her seat and directs her attention to Michael. "Would you be so kind as to help Mr. Lyemel bring in Joshua when he's done?"

Michael swivels his chair around and gets up to bring Joshua in, saying nothing.

Within forty minutes, Joshua was waking up. There was grogginess and then the fight. "What's going on here?"

Sublime holds him down by sitting on him and wrapping his arms around her. Everyone's drug reaction depended on their level of tolerance.

His loss of trust in Tracy and the team was possible if she didn't play this right. She releases him and turns toward him and looks him in the eyes. Tracy raises her hand, "I need you to calm down and read, 2 Thessalonians 2:-12." He took five minutes to read the chapter on the AIM system.

"Okay, I've read it. Now what?"

"Our preparation is for this time. We are going to Cairo to gather intel on a group called the Apollyon. Read the Book of Jude," Tracy said.

APOCALYPTIC 7 - SALVATIONS CRY

He then took about fifteen minutes to read. "You are kidding, right?"

"No, I am not." She walks around the table. "This group of men and women believe they are the descendants of fallen Angels. It is their mission to begin the clock for Armageddon but what they don't know will hurt them. First, Armageddon is not a thing, it's a place, Megiddo. They believe this is their opportunity to change what is to come. God doesn't want you to be one of the lost. You can be helpful in the earthly realm of His kingdom. I know you are an expert in ancient artifacts and writings. The plan is to have you work with Carsen at the archeological site. If the contact we meet on Wednesday afternoon proves useless, I need you to take his place and help Carsen decipher the truth."

"Okay, I'm in but I want the truth. Did you put a tracking device in me?"

Tracy knew he would never hurt her, so, she walks over and leans up against the table in front of him. "Yes!" She raises her hands in protest before he could say anything. "It is only until our mission is complete. Once complete, we go back to the Compound and get them removed. If it makes you feel any better, we all have them and it's so *our* people only can track us."

"No, it doesn't make me feel any better but I don't have a choice, do I?" His anger and demeanor were justified. "How do you know they are who they say they are? They could have put the mark of the beast inside of us and you allowed it." Joshua's pacing now, rubbing his hands together.

Tracy took her seat. "I know, Joshua. Because what I've experienced so far could be nothing but God orchestrating what's taking place right now. And yes, you have a choice. When we land, we can send you on a plane back to Morocco or you can go live out the rest of your days in the home I've kept for you and you will never hear from us again."

Thirty seconds goes by. "That won't be necessary. I will go to Egypt."

"Good. We'll continue with our briefing and you can tell everyone who you are. Please welcome X-Ray to the team."

"I'm Joshua Wells—X-Ray when we get off this plane. I was born in (Canno) Nigeria, Africa, and I'm the ripe old age of 36. My background is in Ancient Artifacts. For about six years, I was a Tomb Raider selling to the highest bidder, and I'm a natural-born negotiator. I come from a two-parent home and raised in Nigeria for 15 years. My family moved to Morocco to escape the Apartheid, and I became a Christian at twenty-six. I met Tracy in Egypt and I've traveled the world since the age of eighteen." He finishes, and everyone chimes in with greetings to Joshua.

Michael got up from his seat and touched Tracy's arm. "I need to speak to you now!" Obviously upset, his face contorted with disapproval. He led the way to the compartment area. She closes the door behind them and stands there with her arms crossed.

While they were in the compartment, Carsen wanted to know more about Joshua. "I am an Archeologist. I used to work for the FBI as their top artifacts researcher."

He swivels his chair toward her. "I imagine you never liked my kind?" He was fishing.

Carsen swivels toward him. "Like, would be too soft a word. More like loathe. Since you are a follower of Christ, I can forgive you. You no longer raid the tombs of our ancestors—right?" She lays her elbow on the arm of the chair and places her chin in her hand.

Joshua looks puzzled. He shakes his head. "No...I no longer steal artifacts of significant importance."

In the meantime, Michael and Tracy were not mincing words. Michael started in, "I understand there is a history between you two but what authority do you have bringing in another team member without consulting us?"

Tracy went into defense mode, unfolding her arms. "I have every right to bring someone into this group. I believe Joshua is an asset and brings an understanding to what's needed in Cairo. Why would I bring someone in that may jeopardize our mission? Trust me, I know what I'm doing, and I don't need you questioning everything I do or every move I make. I've been doing this much longer than you have!"

"I understand he will be useful in Cairo but you are talking about bringing him back to base. What's that about?"

Tracy's first thought was to defuse the situation but... "Michael, chill. I know what I am doing. I would never go beyond this group if it weren't necessary and allowed by Mr. Zinkes. He's the one who told me to find Joshua. And if Mr. Zinkes didn't tell you he gave me that authority, then you take it up with him. I am following orders. I suggest you do the same!" The table shudders as she pounds her fist in frustration. "Mr. Zinkes told me to find who I thought was necessary to carry out our mission. Joshua is necessary. Are you happy now?"

"Tracy, this isn't about happiness or lack thereof. This is about being a leader for this team. Sharing every detail there is to know about what is going on and how it affects everyone, and not just you. It frustrates me to no end when you do things on your own and don't give us a heads up. This is not a one man or woman operation."

"No, Michael, this is about your ego. Joshua is here because he is the best at what he does."

"And what is that?"

"He can talk his way in and out of every situation you can think of and he's a master at deception and perception."

"And that's a good thing?"

"Egypt, he knows like the back of his hand and has connections. He loves God, and we had better want him on this team than working for the other side. Are you satisfied now?"

Tracy looks for the finality to this discussion.

"I will have satisfaction once you tell me what your past relationship was with this man?"

"Well, Michael, your satisfaction and gratification stops here. It's none of your business."

Tracy pulls the cabin door open. Carsen, Mr. Lyemel, and Mr. Laemel almost fall in the doorway. Tracy pushes past them, "Oh, brother!"

The three sit in their seats. Tracy sits next to Joshua, while Michael was still in the compartment sulking, "I guess that little tit-for-tat was about me?" Joshua asked.

"Unbelievable! I hope you and the other ego in there live happily ever after," Tracy said. Frustration was clear as day.

With a lengthy plane ride remaining, it was not starting off pleasant. Learning to work together and getting along for this mission was the only way for success. Tracy and Michael would have to restrain their anger and frustration to ensure things didn't get out of hand. Both strong willed and independent, cooperation with the process was necessary. Michael was used to a team and leading it. Communication was at the top of the standard list. He thought Tracy was being stubborn and inconsiderate of her teammates. Maybe she had been but she didn't see it and didn't want to discuss it anymore.

They all took an hour of silence to focus on what was ahead of them. It wouldn't be right away that they all would understand the ramifications of this setback.

Chapter 7

Kelton, Kendrick, and Mr. Zinkes

At the Compound, it was still overcast and no rain clouds were on the horizon. Kendrick and Kelton were the only two having fun. Both were in their element. Mr. Zinkes watches from afar.

Kelton analyzed their computer system and created a new program called G64. His fingers directed his brain to do ingenious coding. Face recognition and previous location monitoring were an understatement. Kelton was giving a lesson while he continued to work creating the G64 program.

The other analysts gather. "I don't mind giving you all a play-by-play of what I'm doing."

"If you don't mind. I'm fascinated by your knowledge," One of the younger analysts responds.

"Good. Gather round. The G64 program will enhance our tracking of a subject from the time they leave their homes to the time they arrive back home at the end of the day. Right now, we are tracking the team going to Cairo. I am adding another team member in real time as they are in the air. Mr. Lyemel sent the information necessary. This program allows for the system to make figurative predictions of a person's moves each day. Of course, we currently don't have tracking devices in us. The satellite system we are using recognizes the movements of employees." He provides an example through another analyst in the room that agreed to be. "For example, Mr. Simpson, you left your home at 7:45 a.m., stopped to get a coffee, headed into work, and went to the bathroom thirty-minutes ago." Mr. Simpson nods his head that Kelton was correct. He felt at home with the state-of-the-art computers and technicians at his disposal. He didn't mind doing most of the work, as they learned from a handsome and stable genius.

~

Later at the airstrip, the day finally clears enough for Kendrick to fly a few of his old favorites. Mr. Zinkes arrives as he was doing inventory.

"Hello, Mr. Roberts." Mr. Zinkes greets him as he walks up.

"Hey, Mr. Zinkes, how is it going? I love this place." Kendrick's face lights up.

"I'm glad. We've gained many worthwhile planes so far. Some need your expertise in retrofitting them with updated equipment. You and Kelton can work together on that. Most are in tip-top shape and waiting for the right person to fly them. Tell me, Mr. Roberts, where did your love for flying come from?"

"My love for flying came when my family and I took a vacation to Houston, Texas, and went to NASA's Visitor Center. At five years old, I got into a flight simulator. It was at that moment, I knew, and there was no changing my mind. I joined the Air Force right out of High School, and I've been flying ever since."

"Isn't it amazing to know early on what you want to do with your life?" Mr. Zinkes asks.

"If you say so," Kendrick then remembered. "Mr. Zinkes, I've been through some hairy missions. Once on a mission over in

Iraq, our chopper got hit by a sniper and had to crash land in enemy territory. We all escaped the chopper except for two, but most of us were injured. Covered in a blanket of dust and scratched from head to toe, we grabbed our weapons. We gathered what we could carry and headed toward a friendly part of town. We had to walk twenty klicks—12.4 miles, over a few hills, when crossfire from Hamas stopped us. Stuck at the halfway mark to our destination, we could not move any further, as they hit one guys on the leg. So, we stayed put for the moment. Dust and sweat in the sweet hot spot of the day, baking in a 107-degree desert, inwardly crying for mercy from God. We had to suck it up, you know." He stops for a moment to catch his breath and gather his thoughts.

"I imagine your adrenaline to survive kicked in?"

"Being caught or captured over there was a terrifying prospect, providing ample incentive. Most of my team suffered injuries that slowed down our progress. There were a few of us who were whole and kept our heads straight. The fire kept coming, and we gave our coordinates to our rescue team. Twenty-three minutes doesn't seem exceedingly long, but when you're pinned down and being shot at, it's an eternity. We could hear the choppers coming. They rescued us, but it was a firefight we had to win before they could land." Kendrick cleans a plane part as he finishes.

"You made it through, that's the important thing, and now you are here flying for God. What are your thoughts on that?"

Kendrick ponders for a second. "I'd rather be here than anywhere else in the world Mr. Zinkes. Thank you for this opportunity. I don't know where or what I'd be doing if you hadn't invited me. If not for this invitation, I was about to give up on life. I'm not saying I would have offed myself, but my path had turned in the wrong direction. The military had no more use for me. Disappointed by my behavior, and learning of my alcohol abuse, my family was fearful that I was going to die if I kept going the way I was. I was feeling useless, but you gave me purpose again. Thank God, I haven't touched none since being here. Not that there's any here, anyway."

"It wasn't a purpose you needed. You needed to get back to what you knew about God. I was the one who put the stamp on you not returning to the military. Your drinking led you astray, and God knew you wouldn't return to Him if you stayed. Being released from the military was your bottom, as they say."

"I guess I could be mad, but right now I am thankful. Before coming here, I repented to my family and gave up the drinking and re-dedicated my life back to Christ. I've sacrificed a lot, Mr. Zinkes. Not having a wife and children. I wasn't a brilliant son in the sense of making them proud of me. So, tell me, Mr. Zinkes, how did you get your abilities?"

Mr. Zinkes was a mystery to everyone. He only spoke when necessary because he was always doing that thing he does. No government agency taught him, and his gift was undeniable. Mister Zinkes sat. "I have known God from my youth. It's interesting. You are the first person I've ever told this story." Mr. Zinkes chuckles. "My mother and father who loved me very much. My grandmother Zelda even more so. She'd take me for walks every Sunday afternoon after church. She was fair looking, lean, and went after everything she wanted in life. Her personality seemed stern to most, and her faith was strong in the Lord. She didn't hesitate to speak her mind and give you a hug in one fell swoop. One day we walked along the red dirt clay roads of Meridian, Mississippi, and she faints and falls to the ground. I was ten then, and I panicked and cried. I didn't know what to do. Looking at my grandmother on the ground, I saw no one around, and she couldn't speak. I will never forget it, hearing a voice behind me. I turn to see a man standing there. He tips off his hat at me. It startled me at first. I needed his aid, and he never said a word. He glances at me. It was as if he was ten feet tall. Looking up at him, I said, *'Mister, you gotta to help me. My grandma has fallen, and I cannot get her off the ground. She's not speaking, so I don't know what's wrong.'*

"The man stooping over my grandmother's side peers at me and says, 'Run to your grandpa.' The thing is, I never saw his lips move once. I turn back to my grandmother. I then look toward the man, and he was gone. Three blocks away, I ran to my house to get my grandfather and parents. When I arrived, I was out of breath, with red clay knees and tears streaking my face. I explain what happened, but I could not hear what I was saying. It sounded to me like a jumbled mess, but they understood me. They race to my grandmother, and when we reach her, she was standing and asking what happened. I said, 'Grandma, you fell on the ground. I tried to help you, but you were incredibly heavy, like a giant boulder and you couldn't talk.' Grandma Zelda was dazed, so they knew something was wrong and took her to the hospital.

"When we arrive, I had to sit in the waiting room back in those days. While there, I saw the same man walking past the reception area. He tips his hat again and smiles. I hear the man's voice again saying, 'She will be all right, and you are too. God is watching over you.' It more so intrigued me now, and the frightened feeling went away. I turn to a woman next to me who was crocheting. I remember it so vividly. She was crocheting a yellow, white, and mint green blanket. So, I asked if she could hear the man speaking? *'No.'* She replied. Then I heard him again. He said, *'Learn to use your gift for me, Giaigo.'* I ran to my grandmother's room and tried to tell them. Realizing I could not say a word."

"Giaigo, what is wrong?" My father asks me.

"Oh! Nothing. I wanted to see how she's doing. It's taking you a long time to come out, and I was getting worried."

At that moment, my dad came over and put his arm around me and told me, "Grandma will be fine. They have drawn blood and took a few x-rays. She may have had a dizzy spell. We will know more information in an hour and then we will go home.

Since it's the summer, grandma and grandpa want you over for a few days to help monitor them." I was so excited.

"Great, and on Sunday after church you can come pick me up and I will give you a full report on their health."

"I am sure. We will talk to your grandparents to see how long they want you to stay."

Smiling, for a moment, I forgot about the strange thing that happened with the man who never moved his lips. A month later, Grandma Zelda and I were walking again, and I got up the nerve to tell her what happened. I reminded her about when she fainted. She remembered fainting, but for the life of her, she couldn't remember what happened after she fainted. I told her she came to on the ground and it was the scariest thing I had ever experienced. I screamed and cried for someone to save her and then I told her about the man and that I heard his voice but never saw him speaking a word, and that he didn't help me get her up either.' Mr. Zinkes chuckles.

"She knew something else was bothering me. She asks me all kinds of questions, like did I know the man, or had I ever seen him before?"

"No, grandma. I've never seen him around here."

"You appear flustered, Giaigo. I will be fine, so you don't have to worry." Trying to calm my worry.

"No, grandma, that ain't it." She stops in her tracks.

"That isn't it. You speak proper English, do you understand?"

I looked up at her with innocent kid eyes. "Yes ma'am, but what happened to you isn't what's bothering me anymore. It's what went on with the man when you fell and at the hospital. Can you promise me you won't repeat anything I tell you now?"

"Scout's honor, I pledge, I won't reveal anything to anyone." She held up her hand with the Scout sign.

"Okay. When you were on the ground, I turned around and saw a man behind me. He tipped off his hat, and I heard a voice say to run and go get grandpa but I did not see his mouth move.

I turned back toward him, and he was gone. Then at the hospital, I saw him again walking by and heard the voice again saying, you would be all right, and I would too. He also said I was to use my gift for God."

I looked up at my grandmother, waiting for her to give me answers.

"Well, between you and me, your parents don't believe... I believe you've had a visitation from an angel and not the bad kind." She grabs me and pulls me close.

"Grandma, there's good and bad angels?"

She let out a giggle. "Yes. I'll tell you about the bad ones when you get older. God works in mysterious ways, Giaigo, and it's up to us to follow God's still, small voice. Whatever the gift is, when God is ready to reveal it to you, I do not want you to be afraid of it. Embrace it with all you've got. We do not know what the future holds for us. The Bible says what will happen and speaks to who God is and the expectations of His people. Whenever you come over, I want us to read the Word of God and see what it reveals from Genesis to Revelations. In the Holy Scriptures, God says many things through man and Jesus—Himself. Love God with your heart, mind, and body, and He will guide you to where you need to go in life."

"Kendrick, I read the Word of God and couldn't stop unless it was dinner, bath time, or bedtime. Astonished at how much I read. My parents never stopped me even though they did not believe as Grandma Zelda. I know now that God gave me this gift to use for His glory and purpose. And Kendrick, he will use you too."

"Thanks Mr. Zinkes. That's an amazing story."

Mr. Zinkes nods, stands, and walks away, leaving Kendrick to continue his work at the air base.

~

Kendrick was up early the next morning, doing inventory in the office inside the hangar. Mr. Zinkes visits the airbase again. Kendrick greets him with a smile. "Hey, how are you?" Kendrick put out his hand. This was a first for Mr. Zinkes. He liked it. Mr. Zinkes finally let go. "I'm doing well this fine day and thank you for asking."

"What brings you to the base again?" Kendrick put his paperwork down on the desk and swivels his chair toward Mr. Zinkes.

"A significant occasion."

"What's the special occasion?"

"Remember, I told you that you had access to every flying machine and could explore for more crafts?"

"Yes, I remember. Has that changed?"

"No! I thought it was time to take you to the Lab. They informed me today that the aircraft they've recently developed is ready to go. You may not have to look any further. Understand, God is equipping us for what is coming. What I am saying is, you haven't seen everything!"

Kendrick rubs his hands together excitedly. "Oh, okay. I must warn you. I've flown just about everything out there, Mr. Zinkes. I'm no stranger to the Black Market. When do I get to see this mysterious flying machine?"

"I suspect now is a splendid time, Mr. Roberts. Take a stroll with me."

They both head toward the double red doors. Reaching the doors, Mr. Zinkes pulls them open and allows Kendrick to go in first. As they head toward a long-slanted corridor, Mr. Zinkes stops at a bright yellow doorway. The sign display stating: 'High Level Clearance Only.'

"Xerxes, you now have high-level clearance." Mr. Zinkes pushes the button and releases the machine to scan his eyes and thumb print. "When we reach our destination, we will scan and computerize your images. What makes this system so different from others is the scanning. The thermal imaging detects the pulse in the thumb and the eye. So, no one can kill you and use your limbs, because it won't find a pulse or detection of a decrease of thermal body temperature. It has cameras to determine the thermal imagery of your body position. If someone was holding a member hostage, the two people standing here must have access. I have the highest security level and can override the feature with a code that's changes every twenty-four hours."

"Wow. I've never seen a system like this."

They step onto the elevator and Mr. Zinkes pushes the only button available.

"You've seen nothing yet. We'll reach our destination in two minutes."

"Two minutes. Where are we going to the moon?"

"Not quite. We're headed in the opposite direction."

The ride was swift and smooth and took two minutes to get there. The doors open, "Welcome to G7 Lab." Scientist and workers moved about. They acknowledged their presence and continued to work. They were using the Black Bell Boeing CV-228 Osprey to transport from the compound to the airbase and had an extra one for use.

"Yes! This is what I am talking about right here!"

"We have the top reverse engineering scientists in the world, and they believe in El-Elohim. This plane has a cloak ability. I am not talking stealth technology but Klingon-type cloaking." Kendrick laughs. "Come and look. We call it the JC-12. It holds twelve passengers, has hydro movement, and does Mach-30 but we haven't gotten to light speed. We have spared no expense getting this plane ready. You will take it in two days, so get cracking on learning how to fly this exceptional machine."

"No more words are necessary. I'm on it." Xerxes was a kid in the candy store. He remembered Star Trek from 60 or more years ago but now that technology was close to reality. Kendrick stops in his tracks.

"Okay, wait a minute. The military claims to not have this technology, but how did you get your hands on this information?"

"Kendrick don't underestimate God. These men and women are scientists from the military, and they are on God's side. I told you God does not keep his people in the dark. There are things top secret to the outside world, and God provides them to us."

"I can't wait to get Kelton over here." Kendrick's excitement was pure joy, but he didn't want to rush into things.

Chapter 8

Getting Their Attention

Arriving in Cairo early afternoon, two smoke-gray SUVs were waiting to transport the team to the Pharaoh Hotel. Euphrates and Leopard were dressed to the *nines*, which meant Sublime's idea won. Michael couldn't come up with anything else since Joshua agreed with the assessment of the current climate in Egypt. The other team members dressed to blend in as the entourage, pilots, and security. Tracy was in a full-length Tiffany Blue leather sham overcoat with an all-white pants suit. As they clear through customs, they head to the cars. Unbeknownst to any of them, Tracy had eyes on her walking through security.

Not arrogant but humble with her talents. It was the opposite for those who crossed her path in times past. Working for the government, she showed no mercy to former targets of interest—except once. She carried herself as the professional she was and didn't give room for doubt about her being head of Euphrates/Mr. Johansen's security.

The Pharaoh Hotel was large, at least twenty stories high. It was where the wealthy stayed, and the poor wished to get a glimpse of the inside. The bellmen waited out front for the cars to arrive. The concierge was waiting inside and took the team straight to the elevator when they arrived.

(Give أعطني حق الوصول إلى كلا المصعدين، ولكن أود أن أتحدث إليك أولا أولا أول"

me access to both elevators but I would like to speak to you first).” Sublime said.

“Sure, I am at your service,” Mr. Sharif said. He was agreeing with everything she requested.

This was unusual for this to happen, especially for a woman. *'I guess money can change things.'* Tracy thought. “Please swipe your card and lead me to your office.”

“Yes, right away.” Mr. Sharif bows several times. His goal was to do everything she said without question. “Follow me this way.”

Sublime didn’t follow him right away but turns to Euphrates and the other team members. “You can go without me. I will meet you in ten minutes.” She walks to Mr. Sharif’s office.

The smell of cleaning supplies penetrates the air as the staff cleans the counter. Reaching his office door, he offers her a seat. He sits, fumbling over paperwork. With a quivering smile, he kept asking if she needed anything to drink or how was their flight. Small talk that was not useful.

“What can I do for you?” Mr. Sharif asked.

“I’m head of security for Mr. and Mrs. Johansen, and Mr. Johansen’s personal bodyguard. I am the only one who will have access to both floors and all rooms. If anyone asks for access other than myself, notify me. I will clear someone else to go into another person’s room. I don’t care if the President or the Prime Minister wants access. No one, and I mean no one, gets in without my clearance.”

“Your request is clear, and I will follow it to the letter.”

“Here is an Imagery Indicator to call me. Even if I am in the shower, I will answer it. It is waterproof, and I expect you to carry it to the shower with you to answer my calls. You will use this to contact me for any reason. Now you can show me to the rooms.”

“Yes, right away.” Bowing, he comes from around the desk, and they walk out the door.

Sublime abruptly turns to him with an indescribable stare, "Let me make myself clear, Mr. Sharif, if I smell corruption leaking from you, I will not hesitate to end any vermin or the hotel itself."

"Yes, you made yourself clear."

"And just so you know I mean what I say, if our stay here is pleasant and uneventful for the next three weeks. When we leave, you can retire and buy your own hotel the next day. If not, you and your family will get a visit at Nineteen-H-Three Street."

His exaggerated exuberance went away rather quickly. "Yes, you made yourself very clear."

Mr. Sharif escorts Sublime to the top floor. Everyone was sitting and waiting on her. She excuses Mr. Sharif and waits for him to get into the elevator. The no nonsense approach seemed to work. "Everyone, here's the deal. Because we have an added guest, here is the plan." One by one, Sublime calls out the team from their rooms. "Mr. and Mrs. Johansen have the master bedroom.

Mr. Lyemel and Mr. Laemel, the two right flank rooms are yours. X-Ray, you have left flank number one, and I will take left flank number two. Let's get moving."

Everyone moves, and Euphrates had to play his part down to the last detail while trying to be funny. His temperament was playful. He still needed discernment, no one else was in a playful mood.

"Honey are you ready to get in the sack!" Euphrates said.

"Not in any lifetime," Leopard said. Peering at the ceiling for God to relieve her of this situation.

Sublime scours the Master Bedroom. She settles the situation for Leopard. "Leopard leave all of your clothing in the master and you can sleep in my room."

Leopard's eyes said, 'God Bless you child.' Like she was a Catholic Priest and just left confession.

"If nothing else, you need to appear to be husband and wife. I will sleep on the surveillance floor right beneath you. That is all for now. Oh, remember, we will meet Mr. Banks tomorrow at fifteen-thirty. X-Ray, you will join us for that meeting."

"Okay but you don't have to give up your room on my account," he said.

"Don't worry about it, I'd rather be close to McBride anyway. Sleep well." Sublime carries her belongings to the elevator.

~

Later that evening, with an empty lobby, Sublime heads to the concierge desk to speak to Mr. Sharif. He rushes out from his office to greet her. "Miss... what shall I call you?"

"You can call me Sublime."

"Ms. Sublime, I hope everything has been pleasant so far? What can I do for you this evening?"

"Sublime will suffice. One more thing about my instructions. The same people will clean our rooms every day. I don't want different staff bringing up our food when we are here. I want to speak to your cleaning and kitchen staff on tomorrow morning. Please set the meeting an hour after breakfast. Please call me on the Imagery Indicator I gave you to tell me where the meeting will take place. Let them know it will be worth their while—and yours."

Afraid for his life, preferring to be rich than dead, he follows the requests Sublime set. There will be more requests putting him to the test to come. His reaction to what she wanted warranted a closer look at Mr. Sharif. He was too agreeable for the cultural times they were living in.

The Pharaoh Hotel was plush and no other like it in the world. It serviced nothing but the high-end wealthy. The walk-in showers, the spa Jacuzzi tubs, and the elegance of warm dark rich colors. Sublime was back in her room on the balcony, feeling the warm breeze, her mind began to drift. Leaning over to view the night lights, she could see there was no shortage of people roaming the streets. She sighs, *'It was enough to just sleep late and relax for one night, it had been a while.'* Sublime thought.

~

The next morning, not so bright but early. Five a.m. to be exact, Sublime was up with the surveillance team. There had been nothing brewing, so she determined they had to make some noise. She heads to the Penthouse rooms at seven o'clock sharp to wake up the sleeping.

Knocking on everyone's door, "Rise and shine. Time to spend money, some dinero." She left them to get ready. Sublime returns to the floor where the surveillance team was monitoring the cameras they tapped into.

"Are there any recent developments on the waterfront to report, McBride?"

"I may have something. While you were speaking to Mr. Sharif, I observed this man taking pictures of you in the lobby. He was subtle but the way he lifts his lapel made me suspicious. I zoomed in on the video and he has a hidden camera. Also, your Mr. Sharif made a phone call right after he spoke to you. I will know who he called in about an hour or so."

"Hopefully, this leads to Apollyon. Let me hear the surveillance on Mr. Banks and turn up the volume."

Unconcerned with the man taking pictures, she expected to have people checking them out. McBride raises the volume. "Yes, I will meet with them today at three-fifteen and provide the information. We will not arrive at the site until tomorrow morning. You make sure everything is prepared for us—understand?" Hearing Mr. Banks hang up, Sublime turns to McBride. "Looks like Mr. Banks oversees the site. I want Joshua to tag along anyway to scope out the site for any mishaps and to know whether this site is real or not."

Returning to the penthouse at seven-forty-five, everyone was in the dining area waiting for breakfast. The spread provided would be a feast. It wasn't often they could indulge in such a breakfast. "I ordered for everyone this morning. It will arrive in fifteen minutes. I instructed Mr. Sharif to use the same people to clean our rooms and prepare our food each day—no deviations." As she was about to speak again, Mr. Sharif calls to let her know the food was coming up and he had scheduled the meeting in the staff lounge at nine a.m. "Mr. Sharif, thank you and I will be there." Closing the imagery device.

The food arrives, it was fresh and hot. The peppers permeated the fragrance of mouthwatering deliciousness. Eggs Florentine, turkey-bacon, and everything you could imagine inside of hash potatoes. They devour it within thirty-minutes. Joyous in their fellowship at the table, laughter consumes the morning. Their guard relaxed to enjoy the meal and each other.

~

Nine o'clock arrives and everyone clambers to find a seat in the staff lounge. Sublime walks in and asks two questions, "Those of you chosen, do you want to retire early? If so, raise your hand?" Everyone raises their hands, one by one. "Does anyone have a problem with not seeing your family for the next three weeks?" Two raises their hands to the question. Sighing heavily, she looks at Mr. Sharif and he dismisses them. "Please give me five minutes to find replacements," he said. She glares with approval. She waits, and he returns with two others who had already agreed before they entered the room.

"Sublime, they have agreed to stay."

"Good, here are my instructions. One, you may not leave this hotel. Mr. Sharif will find open rooms for you. Starting now, make your calls, tell your loved ones you will not be available to see or call them for the next three weeks. Do not tell them what you are doing or who it involves. If an emergency arises, your family will speak directly to Mr. Sharif. He will in turn, relay that information to you. You can explain that it's a particularly important job and you can't leave. If I find any of you talking to anyone outside of this hotel, you will give up your entire earnings. Two, you will speak to no other guest in this hotel. If someone asks questions, direct them to Mr. Sharif. Three, those who will clean the Penthouse rooms will attend to those same rooms every day. You will not deviate from my instructions. You may not clean the rooms when we are not there. If you have nothing to do or are sick, stay in your rooms and direct that information to Mr. Sharif. Four, after your fingerprinting checks out, we take your identification and phones to be kept in a safe. This is for our safety and yours. Mr. Sharif, please make sure there is a cooking crew for your other guests. This crew will not cook for anyone else, but us and for themselves. I expect full cooperation."

"Yes, Sublime."

"All of you, including Mr. Sharif, need to follow me. Mr. Sharif, please make the extra rooms on the south side of the hotel available to the cleaning and kitchen staff on the floor we have paid for. Launder their clothing every evening, so they will not have to leave the hotel. If there are any extenuating circumstances that cause you to need to leave, you run that excuse by me to get it approved. The only reason you can leave is if someone has died. If you must leave, you will not be allowed to come back and work at this hotel until our stay has completed."

Mr. Sharif bows. He rushes them out like cattle.

"Yes, I will make sure I follow your explicit instructions." Mr. Sharif assures her. Everyone waits in the area until they are cleared.

~

Sublime meets up with Euphrates in their living quarters. He was still in his chipper mood and unbothered by her presence.

"Where is everyone?" she asks.

"After eating, they did their own thing. I told them to meet back here at one o'clock." Never looking up.

"Good, that gives me a chance to talk with you alone."

"What's going on?" Now looking at her.

"They've already started surveillance on us. McBride spotted a man taking pictures of me last night. I was speaking to Mr. Sharif about the room and kitchen staff. I guess he caught me lobby. So, we are getting noticed. Also, no matter how you feel about me, I will have your back."

"Sublime, yes, my ego can get in the way sometimes. I can be sarcastic but I am mature. It's not about me, it's about doing the will of our Heavenly Father."

"Thanks, I wish I weren't playing this role. I hate having people under my thumb who don't deserve it. At least for now, Mr. Shariff is an innocent party. The staff, who will clean our rooms and cook our food, cleared the check. They will stay in the extra rooms on the opposite side of the hotel, away from the surveillance team. When we get back this afternoon and after dinner, they are restricted to those rooms."

"It all sounds good but it's better to have them in line than working for the other side."

"We need to go spend money to open the floodgates, after we see Mr. Banks," Sublime said.

"You don't have to say it twice. I'm up for spending serious cash when it's not my money."

"Euphrates don't get too excited. Whatever we buy, we won't keep." She walks away.

"Ah, come on, Tracy! We have money to spend on whatever we want."

She turns to him, "Don't use that name when we're in the field."

"I apologize. You are right but you said nothing to X-Ray. I think it's a double standard here."

"I will rectify that. Make no mistake, it won't happen again. You have two hours to get ready. I need you on your A-game." Sublime turns to leave again.

"Yes, sir, ma'am. Right away, your highness, lady soldier, you." His attempt to be serious turned into goofiness and sarcasm.

Sublime, shaking her head. He was funny, and he made her laugh at his corny demeanor.

~

Down at the surveillance room. Sublime wants to get an update.

"McBride, you caught anything for me?"

"There's further audio on Mr. Banks. He called his wife, and a person called him about thirty minutes ago. They are using an M-80 and we're not able to track that person."

"How do you know they are using an M-80?"

"Because we are using an M-80, and no one can track our calls either. This equipment is on the black market only. Plus, I know how to identify the markings of this system. M-80's gives off a specific signal, and there's no way to pinpoint their location. Plus, your Mr. Sharif called that person last night, I identified a few minutes ago."

So, if we can see their markings..."

McBride stops her. "I know what you will ask. Shadow added a feature to block all our calls coming in or out. I can see their marking but they can't see ours. He did something to it to make us completely invisible."

"Thanks for the info. I think we've got the attention we were hoping for. Unit A-1will accompany us on the spending spree after we meet with Mr. Banks. Instruct them to be ready by seventeen hundred."

"Right away, and we have extra equipment I would like you to try out. Return in about thirty minutes."

Chapter 9

The Apollyon Headquarters

At the Apollyon headquarters, Mr. Frederickson and Mr. Burmese are viewing the flight manifest of the team's arrival and surveillance video. Mr. Burmese was the same as McBride. He monitors the calls out and sent a team to survey A7 at the Pharaoh Hotel. Mr. Frederickson's job is to recruit new members. With the substantial wealth displayed by Mr. Johansen, he will investigate him as a potential member.

"This is the personal bodyguard," Mr. Frederickson said. He points to the image of Sublime.

"She has no identity, and she's off the grid—a ghost," Mr. Burmese said.

"She must be special. I bet she holds lots of information on Mr. Johansen. Mr. Sharif only gave me Sublime as her name. He got nothing else, other than he's afraid of her."

Mr. Frederickson clamps his hands atop of his head while leaning back in his chair.

"If she does have a footprint, it will take a miracle to find it," Mr. Burmese said.

"Mr. Burmese, all we have is time on our side. The thing is, we can't waste it. If anything develops, let me know." Mr. Frederickson gets up to head to his office.

"Yes, sir, and I will ensure our team is working around the clock."

"And why aren't we getting any feed from the Penthouse?"

"Either they have swept the rooms, or they are blocking us. They are using some state-of-the-art machinery. There is no trace of any kind. There are no markings of any kind. They are blocking everything, including our satellite."

He turns towards Mr. Burmese. "Please make sure everything goes as scheduled tomorrow at the site. We want no surprises. I need Mr. Johansen to join us."

~

At 15:15 p.m., the team arrives at Mr. Banks' room. He had a suite with a balcony. The doors to the bedroom were closed. The balcony doors were open, and the sheer, crème curtains blew with the breeze of warm and sultry air. "Pleased, you and your wife's team came to Cairo to explore such a great and historical site. It is an exciting time to have such proof of ancient history coinciding with biblical accountability." Mr. Banks expresses while putting on airs. If Mr. Banks was with the Apollyon, he had no clue who or what they really were, or he was putting on the greatest show on earth.

Sublime thought about the latter but there was no definitive proof at this point of his involvement with the organization. Also, he was not denying the alleged proof at the site, allowing for their defenses to settle for now.

Euphrates takes the lead. "Let me introduce you. This is Mr. Lyemel and Mr. Laemel, Mr. X, and my lovely wife, Mrs. Johansen. This team will accompany you to the archeological site."

"You mean, you will not join us?"

"Mr. Banks, this is my wife's passion. I enjoy her enthusiasm of it as an archeologist," Euphrates said.

"I look forward to taking you all there. It has been extremely exciting news." His attention turns to Sublime. "And who might this lovely young lady be?" Mr. Banks tries to shake her hand. Sublime doesn't oblige.

"She is my personal bodyguard, and she has no name other than Sublime." Sublime stood there seething behind the all-black Ray-bans, unable to say a word. If she could puncture Euphrates lung right now—she would. She imagines it so vividly.

"Surely, she was born with a name," Mr. Banks said.

"Someone abandoned her as a child. The person who took her in was a deaf-mute monk who doesn't remember her name, nor did the monk give her one. Sublime had to play along and couldn't show her dislike for Euphrates. "Trust me, Mr. Banks, her work and expertise speaks for itself."

"Let's hope she never has to use her expertise in Egypt, Mr. Johansen." Mr. Banks smiles. He directs them to their seating to eat.

They dined with Mr. Banks for an hour, feasting on an early dinner spread he prepared for them. Everyone played their part and left.

~

At 16:45 hours, they came back to their respective rooms. Euphrates, Leopard, and Sublime went shopping. Sublime notices two men parked outside the hotel when they took off to go shopping. The initial destination was to the most exclusive jewelry store in Egypt. The Pear-shaped diamond necklace was full of glimmer. For the Mrs., was a class D diamond, which was worth six figures. Sublime stood watch. Curious patrons came to the door but no one gained entrance, as Sublime had the door closed during their purchases. Three bugs were planted throughout the store to see if anyone made calls discussing the acquisitions after leaving. For Euphrates, a platinum Tag Watch, which they ceased making twenty years ago. With the cash spent in fewer than thirty-minutes, they felt someone would reveal or sell knowledge to the highest bidder.

~

When they return to the hotel, the same car and the two men were still there. Getting out of the car as the limo pulls in. Sublime got out just as quick. She bends down into the back of the limo, "Here we go. I suspect they're headed this way. You two do not leave this limo and Mr. Laemel, lock the doors behind me."

Sublime hits the halfway point from the limo and stops the two men, "Can I help you, gentlemen?"

"Yes, we are here to speak with Mr. Johansen."

Sublime motions for them to show any weapons. Only the bodyguard had a weapon on him.

"Please remain here while I speak with my employer," she said. Observing her surrounding, she taps on the limo window. "Put your vest on now! There are two men who would like to speak to you." She waits one minute and then motions them over.

"Sublime, did you search them?" Euphrates asks.

"Of course, I did. There's no need to doubt my abilities. Only one is packing and I will not grant him access. The one who seems to be in charge may sit inside with us. Mrs. Johansen, please exit the vehicle. Mr. Lyemel is waiting at the door for you." Sublime closes the door as she enters behind the unarmed man. Right after she closed it. His bodyguard taps on the window, "Miss."

Sublime ignores him and keeps the door closed. He stays outside the door, waiting. He continues tapping. Sublime puts up her finger up to interrupt the conversation. She opens the door and steps out to address the man. "Forget it! I am his personal bodyguard, and he doesn't go to the restroom without me." Sublime closes the door again, sits back and remains quiet. His bodyguard had no option but to remain outside the limo. Mr. Frederickson motions to speak to his bodyguard. Sublime lowers the glass. "You can stand down. Everything is fine."

Sublime rolls the glass closed. "Mr. Johansen, my name is Mr. Frederickson, and I would like to invite you to an extraordinary gathering of men and women who meet to discuss world issues. I must be upfront, this meeting is by invitation only, and we will ensure it stays that way. Let's be clear, there will be no bodyguards or guns allowed past the main entrance. If those terms are suitable, the invite is available to you."

Sublime lowers her head at Euphrates to say, '*You better not accept.*'

"Oh, one more thing, this is a one-time invitation," Mr. Frederickson said.

Euphrates doesn't look toward Sublime. "I accept the terms."

"The invitation is for tomorrow afternoon. Please be punctual as they will not permit you if you are late."

"Mr. Frederickson, I understand." Euphrates looks at Sublime this time. "Please release Mr. Frederickson to assure his bodyguard of his well-being." Euphrates smiles at Sublime. As soon as she is sure Mr. Frederickson walked away with his bodyguard, she gets back into the limo. Sublime knocks on the glass to signal Mr. Laemel. "Please scan this and scramble us." He grabs the invitation, scans it, and gets out of the limo to open the door for both Euphrates and Sublime.

It upset Sublime that Euphrates accepted the invitation— her dislike was evident through her silence. She let it drop this time. They were to gather intel on the Apollyon only, not meet with them. She said nothing, as she realized this may be their only chance to get a closer glimpse into their organization, transforming irritation to excitement.

~

The team huddles in the living room of their suite. Sublime and Mr. Laemel were standing as the rest of the team rested. "Pale Horizon has shifted into contact with the Apollyon. At seven-hundred-hours, the jet will leave here with Mr. Banks, Leopard, X-Ray, and Mr. Lyemel. They will fly to Bethany, Jerusalem.

That's where the archeological site is, near the Mount of Olives. The rest of us will have time to visit later if everything goes as planned."

Mr. Laemel turns it over to Sublime. "Euphrates and I will head out to this secret hideaway with Mr. Laemel as our Chauffeur. McBride will command the surveillance team downstairs, as they track the Pale Horizon team, and Mr. Faison will command the surveillance for the team going to Jerusalem. X-Ray, McBride has new toys that may interest you. Make sure you have enough gadgets to at least offer a fighting chance as they tolerate no guns at the location—except their own. Being some time away from us, we can't extract your team right away. Mr. Nordic will track your team from the plane and remain in constant contact with Mr. Lyemel and Mr. Faison."

Sublime points to McBride, who joins the meeting.

"They have scrambling capabilities but McBride got a lock on Mr. Frederickson. Sublime planted a tracking device on him when entering the limo."

"Please find out where their headquarters is located. Get as much info as you can on the layout. Once you get a lock on the location, monitor it from the skies. Euphrates and I need to know every inch since they won't allow me in."

"Will do," McBride said.

"Mr. Laemel get comfy with the other drivers. They will seclude the bodyguards and the chauffeurs. I will linger in the limo just in case it's a setup. I can't afford to be with the in-crowd. Mr. Laemel get a tracker on the car tonight."

"It's taken care of," he said. He presents the tracking monitor.

"Perfect, thank you for being ahead of the game." Sublime dismisses them. Everybody left the area except for Euphrates and Sublime. She notices Euphrates deep in thought. She's quiet for a moment. That didn't last long.

"What are your opinions at this point?" she asks.

"I'm thinking, how hot it would be to see you in a ballgown right now and us doing the samba on the dance floor," Euphrates grins her way.

"In your dreams! Are you ever serious about anything? What's taking place right now is scriptural. God's Word is true, and we are right amid the conflict."

Euphrates laughs and takes a minute to stop, huffing the grin away. "Sublime, God is in control. Everything that arises here is because God is orchestrating it all."

"Euphrates don't be foolish. We are here for His plan. Don't you comprehend the awesomeness of it all? We are accomplishing what God has charged us to do and the exciting fact is, we get to experience life in such a way that few people could ever imagine."

"Tracy, what I recognize is that I am here to do my job. No more or no less. I can't concern myself with what you or anybody else expects of me. I stand on what God has given me in brains and brawn and a life to live while I'm down here interfering with Satan's imps. Mr. Zinkes saw something in my ability to get the job done. Look around, this is not a one-man or one-woman show. We are a team of pros, experts at what we do. Take a chill pill, Tracy. Live a little. You're not dead yet." Euphrates walks away and into his room.

Sublime was still standing there at a loss for words, which was rare. She realizes he used her name again. '*I should confront him about it again.*' She thought. Then deciding it wasn't worth expelling anymore breath. They were alone, so no foul this time, shaking her head at his assertion.

Euphrates was right. God was orchestrating and in control. It wasn't until that moment she surrendered it and let God handle it. She shifts toward the terrace doors and marches outside to clear her head. Alone on the balcony with only the night life and her thoughts.

"All right, God. I heard you loud and clear. I am from this point taking the reins off and will follow your lead."

All the stress she felt was of her own making. Rubbing and wrenching her neck back and forth.

'Take a chill pill.' Her only thought was Euphrates words.

Chapter 10

Explosive First Impressions

At five a.m., on the day of the Apollyon meeting, Sublime was up praying. At five-thirty, everyone got ready for the day's events. Sublime taps on Euphrates' open door.

"Everyone is meeting in the foyer for prayer."

Euphrates grabs his coat and Sublime stares as he strolls to his closet and again returns to her. He closes the door and strides past her. "Let's go," he said.

Fortunately for this moment, there was no caddy back-and-forth chatter to contend with. Sublime understood his mood changed from the playful guy of last night to the person she's wanted to see all along. Someone who's serious about what's happening. Would it last?

This day started out promising to be an interesting one.

They gather around as Mr. Lyemel prays, "God, we know everything is in your control. God, we cannot start or accomplish this mission without you guiding and directing us through every situation we will face and endure. We let go of every thought of defeat and conflict of what our purpose is. We are nobody without you, Jesus, in our lives and your Divine Spirit comforting us through guidance and direction. God, all the glory and honor belong to you. In your Son, Christ Jesus' name, we pray. Amen."

They sat to eat breakfast: blueberry flapjacks, eggs, and juice. Once everyone finishes their breakfast, Sublime was ready to move out.

"Let's get to it!" Sublime said.

~

Back at base in Virginia, and a six-hour difference between them and Egypt, Mr. Zinkes calls for Kelton and Kendrick to come to his office. "Gentlemen, I require both of you on watch. The Pale Horizon Team is ready to deploy on their separate missions with the Apollyon and a team will travel to the Jerusalem archeological site. Sublime, Euphrates, and Mr. Laemel will be alone. Shadow will look for anything out of the ordinary around the location. Xerxes get an extraction team together just in case. We may call for you to get them out of there. Prevention is better than reaction." Both Shadow and Xerxes leave for their stations.

Excitement fills their bellies. Xerxes hadn't been in any action for a while-flying commercial airlines. He was ready and willing to take the JC-12 out, but would rather it be for a reason other than extracting his team members from danger. He was up for the challenge and wanted to see what the new toy could do.

Shadow was in the satellite skies, searching for everything at the location range in Jerusalem. He was looking for signs that were out of the ordinary. Were there more soldiers than expected? Were there any new guests invited to visit the site? He determined there was nothing to worry about currently. Shadow identifies other guests arriving at the site, and no one that came up on the G64 system was out of the ordinary. He remained alert and constantly scanned and assigned the G64 team to do the same. His advanced system could observe various territories around the world at one time with live and up-to-date information, even before the authorities knew.

~

In Egypt, Mr. Sharif calls Sublime to let her know a package arrived. Mr. Laemel retrieves the instructions to the Apollyon Mansion and downloads them into the GPS, so Mr. McBride could track them. They knew the Apollyon would tail their every move. It was a standard operating procedure for being vetted into an organization such as this. They took every precaution necessary to ensure Euphrates'—Mr. Johansen's identity was legitimate.

Both teams head out to a beautiful and clear day. Leopard, X-Ray, and Mr. Lyemel go to the jet bound for Jerusalem. Mr. Banks received the hangar information and waits for them to arrive.

Euphrates exits the hotel last, waiting for the other team to be out of sight. Sublime waits at the car for Euphrates. As he arrives at the limo, Sublime opens the door. Down the street, she observes two men waiting for them to leave, making sure no one else follows. The men were not trying to hide.

As team leader, she ensured everyone's head was on straight, especially Euphrates, with this mission. She rolls down the separation glass to speak to him. "Whatever happens today, know I appreciate what you said, and I took it to heart. When we get back, I want to sit down and talk to you and tell you about me and who I am."

"Sublime, I know you are better than me at many things, and sometimes I don't deal with it the way I am supposed to. We are here for each other, and I think that's the most important thing. When it's our time to go, we will be on the right side of things, focusing on the mission God has given us. I look forward to our discussion. Let's see how far we get today."

"Will do, boss." Sublime nods and straightens in the seat. She looks over to Mr. Laemel. He gives her a thumbs up.

~

In Jerusalem, the archeological site team arrives in the jet after an hour and then transfers to a chopper provided by the Israeli Government. They will do an aerial orbit, land back at the base, and get escorted by Israeli soldiers to the site.

"This is so exciting! I can't believe we will get to see truth and history all in one." Leopard said. She and X-Ray are the last two to get off the jet. X-Ray folds his arms and doesn't express Leopards' enthusiasm. He's interested, but cautious.

"Don't get too excited just yet. We don't know what they have found down there or if something else's up Apollyon's sleeve. This is a monumental find if it pans out to be the truth, but we have to keep our eyes and ears open."

"Whatever it is, it must be something, or the secrecy and military presence wouldn't be so great."

"Just remember, secrecy can also hide things, like our deaths."

Leopard turns toward X-Ray before leaving the plane. "Why do you have to be so opposite of positive at a time like this? Remember, to die in Christ is to gain."

"That's good and all, but I'd rather get caught up than chopped up for shark chum," X-Ray said.

X-Ray's sentiment burnt Leopard to the core. She didn't enjoy bantering back and forth with his negativity. She shrugs her shoulders in haste to get the conversation over and moves on with the mission.

Mr. Banks departs the jet first and was talking to the Israeli chopper pilot, as the conversation between Leopard and X-Ray took place. Mr. Lyemel chuckles as he's standing at the jet door, listening. X-Ray knew better than to let his guard down, even on such a joyous occasion. As a Tomb Raider, with his knowledge, he knew they would slice them up and feed them into the ocean waters or the desert sands. "Boy, do I have some stories to tell you when we get back," X-Ray said.

It was obvious to Mr. Lyemel. X-Ray was trying to change the mood Leopard was in. "Well, when we get back, you can tell me all about it," Leopard said.

At the Apollyon Estate, the limo pulled into the driveway. Euphrates was sweating a little. He was not used to being undercover, nor the focal point of an investigation into an organization such as this. Sublime checks on him as they pull into the roundabout.

"You appear nervous. Are you okay?"

"I'm fine. I'll be fine."

"Okay."

She turns around as they are next in line for him to get out. She scopes the top of the mansion and sees armed men guarding all corners. Sublime opens the door for Euphrates, and he's directed to the foyer by the Butler. The butler escorted them to the library after they gathered in silence. They secluded the chauffeurs and bodyguards into a maintenance shop near the parking port. Sublime waits next to the limo.

A half an hour later, the back part of the house explodes. Sublime leaning up against the limo, sees glass and white wood frame particles shoot out from the side of the mansion. She crouched behind the limo until the debris stops falling. She investigates the explosion from the outside and runs back to the limo to retrieve what equipment was available. White and charcoal gray smoke filled the air, and dust was flying everywhere. Everyone except Euphrates ran out, scattering like mice in an unfamiliar maze. The bomb had been placed in the fireplace. The explosion rocked the room, blew the fireplace out on both sides, and the crumbled ceiling fell on some Apollyon members.

One could see the horse stables through a gaping hole in the wall. Euphrates cover his ringing ears to bring them back to normal hearing. As Sublime is searching the limo for equipment, she hears footsteps behind her. A quick glance over her shoulder tells her it's one of the other bodyguards, and the woman pulled out her Sai Swords. Sublime moves to the side as one of the Sai's flies and gets stuck in the limo's side door.

Sublime swiftly kicks the woman, and her body flings into a nearby tree. She falls to the ground unconscious, with the wind knocked out of her. Sublime pulls the unconscious woman into the limo. She closes the door to focus on finding Euphrates and getting him out of the building. Sublime runs into the house to extract him. She's rushed by other members trying to get out. Seeing him walk toward her, carrying an unconscious Mr. Frederickson, she rushes to help him.

"He's hurt, but not unto death. Because of the explosion in the Library, no one could or had time to explain."

"Did everyone get out?"

"I heard the screams of those running out. I saw Mr. Frederickson trapped under a heavy ceiling beam. He was alive but unable to move the beam by himself. I moved it off just in time as the walls flared up with flames. Mr. Frederickson, by that time, passed out from the pain of the crushing beam. I had to cover my nose and mouth to get through the smoke, pulling Mr. Frederickson to safety. Beams from the ceiling pummeled at least two or three men. A poker from the blast flew through the chest of one man standing near it. I couldn't save him."

Euphrates arrived at the limo with Mr. Frederickson, and Sublime explains, "A bodyguard just tried to kill me."

As Euphrates gets ready to put Mr. Frederickson into the limo, he sees the woman. He halts and puts Mr. Frederickson up against the car. In disbelief, "Why did you leave her in here?" Euphrates asked.

"I need answers, and I'm hoping she's a bodyguard of a person killed in there. I'm sure no one will miss her. She seems like a trained assassin, but she wasn't good at it." Sublime grinned. She reaches in the limo to pull the woman out.

Euphrates takes a moment to speak out loud. "You are dangerous, aren't you?"

"I used to kill first. I knocked her out and will ask questions later."

"Did you ever think that's what they want and what if she's a driver of someone not dead?"

"I'm not stupid. My plan was to drop you off and take her somewhere I can get answers, but now we must take him to the hospital. I'll drop you off and then take her to an undisclosed location."

"I don't think you are stupid. Though two heads are better than one."

"Find me another head and I'll think about it." Sublime smiles. In this moment of chaos, she found time to be funny.

Euphrates, still in disbelief, "Give me a break! Put her in the trunk. I have a fish to fry myself. We can find out where their true headquarters is if we get him to a hospital."

"That's fine, but how can we locate their headquarters while he's in the hospital? I need you back at the hotel. Someone needs to follow up with Leopard, X-Ray, and Mr. Lyemel. Once you check on them, you can get back to the hospital."

I'll take another car where I need to go. We've got to know if this was a joint effort to get rid of us or it happened for some other reason.

"I know you have my back, but I can handle this one on my own. I know Cairo well."

"No problem." Euphrates shaking his head and smirking. He was dusty, sweaty, and needed to get out of his clothes. He gets Mr. Frederickson in the car and they head to the hospital. Arriving, Sublime runs into the ER, gets two nurses, and they run out with a gurney. Once they have him, she turns to Mr. Laemel, "Leave Mr. Johansen's number with the reception desk."

~

The team arrives at the location in Bethany. Sunlight beating down as they stroll toward the site. The aroma of a Mediterranean Cypress lay heavy in the air. It was unshakably still, as X-Ray, Leopard, Mr. Lyemel, and Mr. Banks enter the home through a row of Israeli patrol guards. They walk through the stone-faced archway and down the stone steps to notice two windows facing east and west. A lone wooden table stood near the east window. The floor was dusty. It had been untouched. Leopard was in subdued excitement. "I can't believe we are here."

X-Ray bent down to pass through a doorway toward what appeared to be the kitchen area. He yelled to Leopard, "There are bowls in here!" She moves in and Mr. Lyemel and Mr. Banks follow her. X-Ray points to where the bowls are. He wanders past them into the front of the shack. He peers around. "I have been to the sepulcher of Jesus before. This is surreal. The probability that Jesus was here after his resurrection. The visible spot where Jesus showed Thomas his wounds." Leopard realized X-Ray's genuine passion for Jesus.

They trekked outside the home and examined the surrounding habitats. There were only outlines of what remained. Leopard bends down to look at a rust-colored clay pot buried halfway in the soil. "I'm uncertain if this is the exact place, but this experience is astounding. The strands on the back of my neck are at attention. I can't shake the evidence that God's Spirit is here. This is a holy place."

"I am experiencing something I've never felt before!" Mr. Lyemel said.

"I am grateful to have this moment with you all." Mr. Banks says. "We can remain a while longer and then venture to other places if you like before heading back." He stands back and waits for the response.

Mr. Lyemel looks at both X-Ray and Leopard. "I'm okay with viewing other locations."

Both Leopard and X-Ray agree. Mr. Lyemel turns toward Mr. Banks and replies, "We will travel to the new sites."

"Fantastic! Let's head toward the jeep." Mr. Banks leads the way.

The archeological team would not return for another hour. Euphrates reached Mr. Nordic to find out if the team had any signs of trouble. Mr. Lyemel confirmed they were all right and had no concerns about where they were.

~

Dropping off Euphrates, Sublime transfers the unknown assassin to another car and heads to a place she can keep the package safe. The woman regains consciousness and squirms in the back seat.

Sublime knew the place well and backed into the loading dock area. In the clinic office, "Dr. Canno, here's a million. I need you to keep her sedated until tomorrow. Wake her at noon and I will take her in two days."

"I will do as you say and thank you for this."

"When you see him, tell my brother I said hello. Remember, keep it in the safe and do not put what's in the case in the bank."

Sublime returns to the hotel. She finds Euphrates sitting in the common area.

"We will leave in two days."

"Why have you made that decision for all of us? Have you spoken to Mr. Zinkes?" Euphrates asked.

"No, not yet. We need to regroup, and we can't do it here with eyes on us all the time. Tomorrow, I will drive you back to the compound, so the Apollyon can get in contact with you." Euphrates said nothing.

"I'm not happy about leaving without more information on the Apollyon."

They move on and Sublime asks, "How did they say the site visit was going?"

"According to X-Ray, they had no mishaps. I think this was a single effort to disrupt the Apollyon, or they got rid of some of their members on purpose. My gut is telling me someone out there besides us knows who and what these people are," Euphrates said.

"I hope with all the commotion, no one saw me drop my package off. Mr. Laemel, please get to McBride and get a report of anything and everything that was going on around here at the time of the bombing." Sublime asks.

She turns back to Mr. Laemel, "Also, when the archeological team gets back, ask that they prepare a briefing about the site and what they discovered. I will do surveillance at the airport today and tomorrow. Try to rest tonight. We will take shifts on watch. We have a busy day ahead of us tomorrow. Euphrates, I need to speak to you later when I get back."

Euphrates nods and says, "Just keep me updated on your package."

Even though she wanted everyone to rest, she had to stuff her face. Stopping at Al Khal Café for some Egyptian Barbeque. Hunger pains hit, which reminded her she only had a piece of fruit ten hours before. The food vapors steamed through the bag with the aroma of sweet and tangy sauce. She could not wait. It was their favorite from long ago. Sublime arrived at the airport hangar, parked, and turned the car off. She removes the food container from the bag, searching for the fork. Opening the container top, she grabs the rib and takes a huge bite, allowing the meat to follow her pull. Dripping the sweet, smokey sauce on the seat, she wipes it up and finished her lamb-rice and crisp bread meal in fifteen minutes. Sublime waited for the archeological teams' arrival.

The jet lands and she got out to greet them. X-Ray was glad to see Sublime, but he knew the look she gave. She was all business. He stood in front of her.

"We will talk later." He stated.

"You think you know me so well?"

"Am I wrong?" Acknowledging her thought process. He smiled as he wipes the side of her mouth that still had a little sauce on it with his thumb.

"Yum, Khal's." Her lip edges curl up. "And you didn't even think to bring me any?"

The rest of the team walks past them, and X-Ray then heads to the car.

"I'll meet you all back at the hotel. We'll debrief them," Sublime said. She decided not to return with the rest of the group.

She needed time to think about their next move. The jet was a safe, quiet place to think, with no interruption. They left, and Sublime sat in the pilot's seat. Internally, she was questioning how to handle this situation with the female assassin. She wanted answers and if she didn't get them, in times past she would have just killed her, but now, it was different. She prayed, "God, I am looking for you to keep me and to guide me on this mission. I do not take this mission lightly. I know you are guiding and directing everything that's happening for your purpose and your glory." At that moment, the Holy Spirit spoke to Sublime, "Take her and teach her My ways." The voice she heard was clear. She responded, "Yes, Lord." There did not seem to be anything out of the ordinary or out of place as she sat on the plane. Tears roll, and the acceptance of God's plan was undeniable.

Getting back to the Pharaoh Hotel, Sublime checks in with McBride. He would soon receive some shuteye.

Reaching the living room area, everyone was waiting on Sublime. Leopard and X-Ray presented a quick brief of their experience at the site.

"They have established no categorical proof that Jesus was at that location. The region is spot-on corresponding to the scriptural location of individuals seeing him. I must express, I encountered God in that dwelling. We just have to wait to see if they discover any useable DNA samples," Leopard said.

"I agree. Also, Mr. Banks oversees the site, but I have a hard time believing he's a follower of Christ. He seems like it's about the money for him, the recognition if they certify it as authentic. I don't trust him." X-Ray said.

Later that evening, Sublime returns to the penthouse and taps on Euphrates' door.

"Sublime, is that you?" Euphrates asks.

She remained outside, waiting for him. "Yes, can I enter, or do you prefer to come out?" She asks.

"You can come in." Opening the door quicker than Euphrates expected and before he realized it, she was standing behind him. He turned, and it rather surprised him, but he recovered quickly. He inquires, "What's on your mind?"

Sitting on the edge of the burgundy chaise in the room's corner and five feet from the bed, as though she needed to make certain she didn't get too comfortable, Sublime explains her past. "I've been a loner most of my life. Even passing through two branches of the military didn't cure me of that. I worked as a government assassin, and initially, I found my work satisfying. Then, I found out, I was not free and received no gratification in that fact. I'm working at being a team player, and I need you to give me a break."

Euphrates plops on his bed. "I don't get how you work. I function as a team and our missions dictate that we either return together or we die together."

"Euphrates, I've planned a lot of missions and you know well, that isn't regularly the case. Don't try...I'm not like the rest of you. I've experienced tough times, and some people don't make it through, but I'm determined to ensure that doesn't happen now. I'm not suggesting I can stop someone from dying, but I want us...no, I need us to work jointly to prevent whatever we can, and I can't do that without you." She stood as she finished her plea.

"I concur, and for the record, I wasn't trying to pull anything over on you. It's my motto and how I carried out my missions. I never left a man or woman behind—just to make that clear." He stated.

"I get what you are saying, and I commend you for it, and with that stated, I have to take the package back to the compound in Vermont. There are no ifs, and, or buts about it. God declared it, so I must do it."

"Okay, then what?"

"Genuinely, I don't know. She perhaps is to become one of us. I know you question whether I am positive, but I am sure of this because the Spirit of God instructed me to teach her His ways. I am certain God chose her, just as he has chosen us," Sublime said. She sits back on the chaise lounge. Euphrates was unsure of her actions. He could see there was no point arguing with Sublime about this. He was certain he couldn't change her mind about anything. She wasn't taking no for an answer. He walked around his bed.

"Euphrates don't place God in a box. Just because we were the original five doesn't mean God can't use anybody else."

"I know that, but this is the same woman who sought to assassinate you and you don't know why. Now God is instructing you to take her back with us. Okay, whatever you say. Who am I to stand in the way?"

"Understand, my strategy was to interrogate her and leave her in the desert somewhere, but God said otherwise. Can't you consider I question myself whether I heard God say this? But it was so clear Euphrates! There is just no mistaking what God said to me as I was sitting on the jet by myself. If I am confident about anything, it's this." Sublime now stood near his window. "A few years ago, I would be the first one to interrogate her and dispose of her carcass. All that has changed now since we are a team, working for God. I've never played well with others. The military tested what I held dear within me more than anyone can imagine. I know God is in control of what I am saying and doing, and I can't fail God now—not with this." Sublime looks for compromise from Euphrates.

"So, what if she doesn't agree to come with us?"

"There is no option to say yes or no. She will be on that jet of her own free will or I'll drag her on. Either way, doesn't affect me. When we get to the compound, Mr. Zinkes will deal with her. He'll determine if she will have a choice to stay or to go, but I have to take her back."

"Okay." Euphrates yields. "I won't even ask where she's being held. I don't want to know."

Sublime turned and walked toward the door, "Tomorrow morning, I will accompany you and then go speak to the package."

In just that moment, God reminded her in His Word, Isaiah 55:8-9 (NKJV), *"My thoughts are not your thoughts. Nor are your ways my ways, says the Lord. For as the heavens are higher than the earth, so are my ways higher than your ways, and my thoughts than your thoughts."* She walked out, confident of her decision. Mr. Frederickson left the hospital the next morning with a sprained right arm, cracked ribs, and a fractured left tibia. Gone from the emergency room, even though Euphrates offered to take him home. Euphrates, as Mr. Johansen, connected with the Apollyon again, left his information at the mansion with the butler. Sublime did some investigating in the limo that was left by the assassin, and found her identification in the glove compartment. Euphrates received a message they would phone him within two weeks of their new locale. He was in. This was the closest he could be under the circumstances of the blast. The bombing left many questions unanswered.

Sublime had bigger fish to fry for now. After dropping Euphrates, Sublime paid a visit to McBride to get the intelligence she required on the package. McBride contacted Kelton in Vermont to get the information on Ms. Acai.

~

Leaving the hotel, she took her time driving to the clinic. A dusty trail followed as she pulls around the back of the clinic. She  greets Dr. Canno at the double metal doors at the back entrance. She strolls toward where the bodyguard was being held. That proverbial stare down before the gunfight starts, only they weren't in the wild, wild, west, and Sublime had the upper hand.

Kim Acai—Myna Bird, born in Shanghai, China, is thirty years of age, and her specialty is Sai Swords.

When she was two years old, her father killed her mother, and she has been trained to be an assassin since the age of six-years-old. Her father fled into hiding after she finished her training and she declared contempt for him. She had no religious faith.

"Why did you try to kill me yesterday?"

She yanks on her restraints as though there was a satanic presence within. Kim couldn't get loose, and this caused considerable irritation. Sublime grabs an armchair.

"Don't bother, even if you get loose, you will die."

"You're so confident in your skills." Kim spat the words.

In previous years, Sublime would have dealt with an evil person a different way. This was spiritual warfare she had to confront.

"I want to know why you tried to kill me?"

Kim cried out in rage, rattling her shackles. "My master didn't trust your client."

"Why? They approached us and requested to meet. Did your master say this to any of the others?"

"No. He wanted to present it in the meeting. I saw you come from behind the building twenty minutes before the explosion. I knew you had something to do with it, so I tried to take you out myself." Sublime stepped around the gurney to move closer as the woman spoke.

"I am not the one who planted the explosive. Similar to you, I'm a bodyguard. I was searching for blind spots. Otherwise, I remained near the limo. Do you have any idea who I am?"

"I don't care who you are. Let me out of here! I said all I know."

Sublime's expression softens into a smile. "Sorry, Kim Acai—Myna Bird, I can't do that. God has other plans for you."

"What god are you speaking of?" Kim asked. She rattled the restraints again to break out, popping a few blood vessels, but remained chained.

"The Creator of the Universe, the heavens, and the earth, and the God that is over the god your previous boss thought was a god."

"I don't believe in any god," Kim said.

"Yes, we have one of you on our side. Well, he used to be." As the gentle tone didn't ease Ms. Acai's mind. "Oh, yes, Mr. Sokamoto is dead and no, I will not kill you. God has your best interest on this one."

Kim shut her eyes and turned her head in temporary defeat and went silent.

Sublime turns to Dr. Canno. "Can I talk to you outside?"

"Sure." Dr. Canno said. They moved outside of the double steel doors. They walked towards the front of the clinic, but did not go into the lobby of the waiting area. Sublime warned the doctor. "Be careful with her—she's cunning. There is a spirit within."

"I've gone a round or two with it. I am covered by the Blood of Jesus." Dr. Canno smiled.

"That's what I love to hear—keep her docile."

Chapter 11

More to Myron

Silence filled the space for a few seconds. Sublime thought intently.

"On another topic. Is my brother, okay?"

"He is doing fine. Would you like to see him?"

"Yes, if you don't mind."

She turned her focus now to Myron. She put thoughts of Ms. Acai aside. They walked to the elevator, get off on the fifth floor and walked down the hall to Myron's room. Turning slightly as the light by his door flickered, Sublime opens the door to see him sitting in his chair, staring out the window at the view of the city. Motionless, he doesn't acknowledge anyone.

"There has been no change since you brought him here five years ago." Dr. Canno tells her. "The orderlies give him physical therapy twice a day. He loves sitting at this window, but it's the same scenery every day."

"I thought maybe time and persistent care would bring him back to us," she said. Hanging her head in sad realization.

"It is up to God now, and most of all, Myron has to want to come back," Dr. Canno said.

"I don't believe I ever told you the complete story. Myron is ten years older than I am. He fought in the Middle East Wars and, being there, somehow, his mind got lost in the shuffle after our parents died. No one ever knew what happened to him, but whatever it was, he has lost all will to stay in this reality. After the attack on our parent's base, we buried our father within a week. We had to endure an entire month watching our mother suffer and eventually die. Bruised and burned, she fought for as long as she could. Myron and I were by her side every day. One Saturday morning, at nine a.m., while we were resting at her place, the doctor called. Her primary physician stated she had a massive stroke and her heart had stopped. We rushed to the hospital in silence with tears running down our faces in silence."

Tracy was now standing next to Myron, staring out the window with her hand on his shoulder. The view was one of sand and mountains and a few cars rolling by. Upon our arrival at the hospital, the doctors informed us that her revival had taken over fifteen minutes. She was oblivious to the outside world, hooked up to machines to help her breath, and it broke my heart. The doctor said she would not survive another stroke. Both of us stood right beside her bed. I looked at my brother, and he nodded yes. There were no words spoken between us. We knew it was time to let her go. We left the room for the nurses to prepare the medication to ease her suffering and end her life. Within ten minutes, they called us back to the room. Myron and I stood on either side of her bed. We held her lifeless but warm hands as the doctor pulled the breathing tube. For a moment, she breathed on her own, and then her pain was no more. The four colored lines fell flat, showing the state of her existence. She was only the shell that held her soul and her faith. In less than a month, we lost both of our parents.

~

There was a time when Myron would do anything to keep Tracy safe. Now she was returning the favor. He didn't know it, but she saved his life twice.

"Myron guarded my life as his own. We were on holiday once, visiting in Indonesia, and we lost our parents in the crowd on purpose, I'm sure now. Although we were on family vacation,

I realize now Myron was undercover." Sublime reminisced.

"Myron and I rode a rickety old bus one afternoon. Muggy and overcast, the bus hit large-leafed trees as it went by. We were in hiding. There were a lot of Indonesians on the bus with children, smelly chickens in cages, and only one or two men. It seemed like a movie at first. We Americans looking for some killer in a foreign country or seeking safe passage out of the country. But this was real life, and we were running from the police. I didn't know why, but Myron knew. The rain was non-stop, and the bus driver was a short man with terrible, red-splotched, pus-filled acne. I sat next to Myron, scared, still not knowing why we were running. He looked after me in my youth. I felt secure, but I also knew something was troubling him. His sad and angered look was unusual. Myron stared out the window, looking for any signs of the police. The bus patrons were getting loud and my brother for sure liked little noise.

"He got up and walked toward the last row at the back of the bus where all the bickering was taking place. He asked them to quiet down and because they did not understand his American language, they just kept arguing. 'Tenang,' (Quiet!!!) he raged. They kept arguing back and forth. There was no doubt they could hear because they screamed at each other. It was as if Myron didn't exist to them. Myron pulled out his gun and shot all three people in the head. No one screamed in a horrified terror, no one moved from their seats to help these people. No one said to call the police, not even the bus driver. I expected the bus driver to say or do something, but he kept driving like nothing happened. He never once looked in the mirror to see what was going on. I think this was the first time I realized I had no fear - no fear of anyone or anything.

"I guess I was the only one who thought someone should do something. If nothing else, at least pray over their souls. In those times, maybe Myron did them a favor and put them out of their misery. That was my final analysis of the situation. Maybe everyone on that bus wanted to be out of his or her misery. Whatever bad there was in the world for these people to want to die, I knew nothing about their suffering, but I knew how the world was becoming other than peaceful.

"Myron came back to our seats. He hopped over my legs like a gymnast, as though not to disturb me. He slid down in the seat and began looking out the window for any signs of trouble. I leaned over to lie on his lap. He put his arm around me. He was my brother, but did anyone see what my brother did?

"A tear fell, but my love for Myron outweighed the deaths of three unknown people.

"All was quiet, and it was still pouring outside. The bus swerved, he grabbed me and held me tight, and our bus collided with a diesel truck on the wet and muddy road. Screams erupted, chickens scattered, and I suspect a lot of praying occurred because I was praying. Once the collision was over, all the screaming and hollering stopped. It was dead silence again. What was wrong with this picture? No one asked about anyone's well-being. No one asked anything. There was no moaning or groaning from those hurt. No one made a sound. There had been a previous accident ahead that the driver could see as he rounded the curve. The bus driver announced another bus would come to take on his passengers in an hour, maybe five. My brother recognized the road we were on. 'It's time to get off shortcake,' he said. I would follow him to the ends of the earth. He was my big brother. I jumped on his back and we walked into the pitch-black darkness around the corner. I never realized how close we were to the hotel, but I knew Myron would always take care of me." Sublime turned to look at Dr. Canno.

"Myron had gone back to full duty in the military and within a month of our parents' death, I got a phone call. All they told me was that he was in a scrimmage and civilians died. It wasn't until that point they understood he'd snapped. To lose Myron was a lot to bear. To look at him now, you would never think he was a military man."

Sublime turned back to her brother, and asks, "Myron, how are you doing?"

He looks her way and smiles. Myron grabs her hand and holds it for a while and doesn't say a word. He knew her, but he didn't want to come back. She turns to Dr. Canno, carefully pulling away, "Keep Ms. Acai under as little as possible and prepare some drug for the trip home. Take care of my brother. If you need anything, you know how to contact me."

Sublime turned and walked out of the room, leaving without saying goodbye, which she had never done since leaving him there five years ago.

~

At the compound, they were on high alert. Mr. Zinkes called an emergency meeting with Kendrick. He rushes into Mr. Zinkes' office. "What's going on?"

"There is not much information to provide. Nothing is happening right now. Board the plane in the morning and head to Egypt. Take Kelton and Griffith with you to help with flying when needed. Teach them everything about the JC-12."

"You know they need clearance?"

"It's already taken care of." Mr. Zinkes said.

Kendrick leaves Mr. Zinkes and meets Kelton and Griffith in the hall, "You and Griffith are to come with me. We need to head to the airstrip. There's a new toy you need to learn how to work and Kelton. You have until tomorrow morning to decide if it needs any tech upgrades. We're heading to Egypt, gentlemen."

"How exciting!" Kelton said.

"Well, Mr. Zinkes provided little to go on. He just said, we have to leave in the morning. So, we know the team is leaving tomorrow afternoon around four. Kelton get our coordinates and arrival time. That will determine what time we leave in the morning."

As they walk to the truck that will take them to the airstrip, Kelton says, "Gentlemen, what you are about to see amazed me, too."

~

Prior to arriving at the hotel, Sublime prepared the currency promised for those held hostage by her demands. Mr. Sharif's portion was much larger than the others. Sublime debriefed and thanked him for following her orders. "Thank you to all that helped us during our stay. My boss thanks you, as promised." Handing each an envelope, she continues, "After tomorrow, we will be out of your hair." Mr. Sharif was bald. She looked his way. "Sorry." He smiles and says, "No problem. I never want to presume anything, but I hope your stay was pleasant and to your satisfaction?"

"Trust me, if not, you wouldn't get paid. We will leave around four p.m. tomorrow. During that time, we hope to have everything cleared out."

"If you don't mind me asking, if everything was to your satisfaction, why are you leaving so soon? Your stay was for three weeks?"

"My boss has business he must attend to. If that is all, I will see you in the morning."

"One last thing I would like to ask. Since you paid in advance for the three weeks, shall we refund the rest of the days you will not be staying here?"

"A refund is unnecessary. The guests on the floor below the Penthouse will stay and extra few days. Otherwise, please make sure we can leave on time tomorrow.

Mr. Sharif bowed to Sublime and said, "Just let me know if you need anything else."

Reaching the elevators, the Apollyon and the package were never far from her mind. Sublime was certain they would have another chance to meet the members of the organization again. Having infiltrated their system and legitimate proof of their existence, they had to discover who the actual leaders are.

Sublime steps off the elevator and walks to the sitting room where everyone gathered. "I have cleared the bill for the hotel and the staff. We will leave at 4 p.m. tomorrow. In the meantime, we can prepare to leave and relax for the rest of the evening." Sublime continued, but turned the discussion toward the mansion bombing. My gut tells me the explosion, whether intended for us or Apollyon, was a purposeful warning to Apollyon. A warning that someone else out there knows who they are and wants to destroy them. And if that's the case, we need to find them before they find us. It seems to me, why try to kill off their own members if they are recruiting? By the way, I received some intel today that a member was going to express his dissension to Mr. Johansen.

He apparently distrusted you, despite never having seen your mug, knowing you were under scrutiny.

"Did you receive this information from your hostage?" Euphrates asked. His countenance was cool but expressively questioning.

"Yes," she said.

Mr. Lyemel interjects, "What do you think Kim will do once we get her back to the compound?"

"I can only hope we learn more about her and who she worked for. My hope is for her to open her eyes to the truth, Mr. Lyemel. Honestly, I don't know what to expect. She hates my guts right now, so I will be a source of contention for her."

"May I also ask, what are we going to do with X-Ray?" Mr. Lyemel asks.

"Well, we have just become the Apocalyptic 6, Mr. Lyemel."

"I guess we have." He was excited to have an additional person to "torture" during training, and Mr. Laemel grinned.

~

At four p.m., everyone heads to the airstrip. It would take them thirty minutes to get to the tarmac.

Sublime took a side trip to pick up Ms. Acai and found Dr. Canno in his office. Greeting Dr. Canno, she asked, "Are the drug and Ms. Acai ready for the trip?"

"Yes, just as you requested. I gave her some happy juice. She will walk, talk, and eat, but will be docile," he replied, handing the bag to Sublime. They walk out of his office toward Kim. Walking together, he continues, "I am certain they trained her to withstand some drugs on the market. I saw hole markings in between her toes. After testing her blood, I do not believe she's had this drug before. It's not on the market, and I received a sample dosage this month. Give her a quarter cc every ten hours, as needed. If you desire the medicine to be out of her system before then, only give her half the prescription. If I were you, record everything she says. Here is the audio from the last two days."

"Thank you, Dr. Canno."

"You are welcome, Sublime. Understand, I will only reach out to you if something is wrong. Other than that, you will not hear from me."

"I understand."

~

As the rest of the team arrives at the hangar, an explosion blast almost flips one of their cars. The vehicle balances on two screeching wheels until Mr. Laemel corrects the automobile's angle, then it slams onto all fours. AK-47 ammunition pierces the steel frames of the tires and windows. The vehicles come to a screeching halt and the team tumbles out. The rounds are persistent, and Euphrates, X-Ray, Leopard, and Mr. Lyemel return fire, shooting three men on the front line of the fight. Euphrates looks up and spots a Blackhawk in the distance, "We have a bird in the air coming right towards us!"

"I'm hit," Mr. Laemel expressed plainly.

"Are you able to shoot?" Mr. Lyemel asks.

"Yes, it went through, but I have to stop the bleeding soon."

"Stay behind this vehicle and cover me. I need to get to my bag," Mr. Lyemel said. Within two minutes, X-Ray sees Sublime pull up behind the men who were shooting from behind the white brick barriers. Mr. Lyemel stops in his tracks and looks in the opposite direction, "X-Ray, we've got more company." He saw the second helicopter coming in from the opposite direction. "We have to take these down if we plan on getting out of here alive!"

Sublime reached the two men behind the brick barriers. She didn't hesitate. Two head shots. They never knew she was there. Mr. Lyemel took out a rocket launcher from the trunk. X-Ray asked, "How in the world did you get that through customs?" Mr. Lyemel smiles, "I didn't!"

With two shots, one helicopter slides onto the airstrip, bursting into flames. Successfully, the pilot exited the aircraft. The other crashed into the hangar where the jet was sitting. With the plane that would take them home now ablaze, there was no chance of saving it. The jet fuel ignited. Smoke and fire engulfed the hangar. Euphrates comes from around the back of it. "I don't know what that was all about, but I'm sure the hostage in Sublime's car has something to do with it." Euphrates helps Mr. Laemel, as they jumped back in the car to escape the mayhem. The only place Sublime felt safe was at the clinic, but going there would jeopardize her brother and Dr. Canno.

They head back toward the hotel and before they got through the gate, Xerxes arrived. He landed the plane a hundred feet in front of the cars, uncloaks, and steps out as they arrive at the nose of the plane. "It looks like you all could use a lift," Xerxes said. He pulled off his shades.

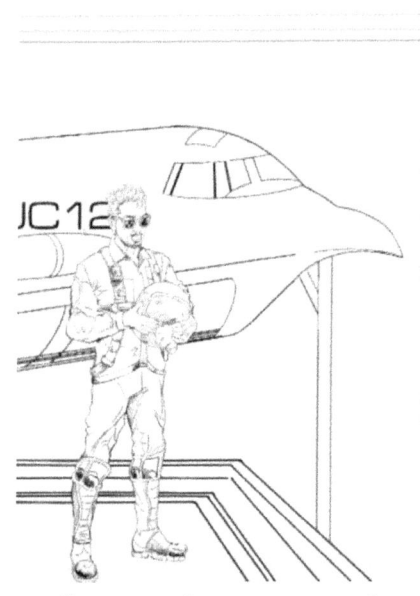

'Mr. Zinkes.' Sublime thought. Euphrates said, "Yes! Let's get out of here before any more arrive to kill us, or the police get here." Everyone jumped on the plane, and Griffith takes flight. Just as the jet was in the air, the police arrive and try to get the tower to stop them. Ignoring their plea, and leaving the other plane behind to burn, Mr. Laemel waved to the authorities.

"Sorry to leave a mess, but we have to go." Just as they took off, Mr. Laemel spots Mr. Banks and Mr. Frederickson running from the airport doors.

At the Cairo Airport, Mr. Banks and Mr. Frederickson stood there glaring at the JC-12's disappearance. Mr. Frederickson said, "You realize we can't track them now. Your idiot pilots destroyed the airplane with the tracking equipment. They were to cripple the plane to provide us with adequate time to keep them here in Cairo and give us more time to discover who they are." Mr. Banks rubbed the back of his neck and wiped the perspiration off his brow. "Mr. Johansen checked out and we need him. His wealth is substantial, and with Mr. Okamoto gone, so is his money. Now, the others with Mr. Johansen, I cannot say. We can lose everything if we don't find out." Mr. Banks walks away in a hurry. Speaking to the authorities, he calls on his people to clean up the mess. Mr. Frederickson ponders and peers at the sky for a second, then turns and leaves.

Desperate times meant desperate measures. The future of the world and Apollyon's exploits, no trivial victory in their view. Approaching their own timetable, Mr. Frederickson and Mr. Banks were in too deep to leave. Fear gripped them as time was running out to get answers. The murky aspects from the bombings to letting the Mr. Johansen go, patience was stretching thin. Blood and war, costly pieces of the puzzle. The picture was falling together. Mr. Johansen is resourceful.

Chapter 12

Why Is She Here?

As everyone settled down and their levels of adrenaline decreased, Euphrates confronts Sublime. "Was the crime scene left behind and the damage to our plane out there for this one here?" He asked, pointing to Kim.

Sublime sitting in a seat across from Ms. Acai, "Startling as it may seem, I don't know if it was for her or you. What difference does it make? They were trying to murder us. That's the point here."

"The fact is, one of your decisions has put us in peril again. Mr. Laemel could be dead right now. Every action you take brings destruction our way. Why can't you just let go of your self-proclaimed righteousness and get on a level playing field with the rest of us?" Euphrates retorts.

Joshua was standing now, hoping this was not a personal attack on Sublime. She looked at him and Joshua knows to back off. Sublime took a moment to settle her nerves before speaking to Euphrates and the group. Silence increased while hearts still pounded from the fight. Sublime had to kill, and she did without reluctance. She couldn't dwell on it now, dealing with it once back at the compound. No one spoke. Silence hung in the air.

A few minutes later, Sublime speaks to the team, and not directly to Euphrates. "Ms. Acai—Myna Bird, is the bodyguard who charged me at the explosion. For the past two days, I have held her at a confidential site. Someone murdered her Master,

Mr. Okamoto, in the blast. They suspect she's dead too, according to the broadcast." Sublime moves from her chair and goes on. "And before anyone takes on the bandwagon of Euphrates here. I got approval to bring her and X-Ray back to base." Sublime sits back in her seat.

Xerxes turned over control of the plane to Griffith. "Since Mr. Nordic is here, please teach him what you've learned."

He could join the others. Xerxes closed the door to the cockpit and explains, "Mr. Zinkes sent us. He felt something was coming. He couldn't explain what it was, but he knew."

"So, what are we to do with the hummingbird here?" Euphrates asks.

"That will be up to Mr. Zinkes and its Myna Bird." Sublime said. She continued, "I'll leave her in his hands. I'm doing what God charged me to do."

Leopard lifts the woman's head from the table, unconscious and unaware of what happened. "Why is she drugged out?" Leopard asked.

She's not doped out." Laying Kim's head back. "The person who kept her for me gave her some happy juice. With all the mayhem that was going on, overseeing her was impossible, so I knocked her out. She'll be out for a time. The man holding her found track marks between her toes. Regular drugs wouldn't suffice. So, if Mr. Zinkes can get to her intellect, God can get to her heart before it's too late. She should come too in about an hour."

"Mr. Zinkes sent me to help with anything needed and to learn about this plane." Kelton said.

"Since I have the floor to speak. As we were taking off, I saw Mr. Banks and Mr. Fredericks together. So, now we know, he was putting on airs about believing what was developing at the archeological site and he is with the Apollyon." Mr. Laemel said.

Everyone remained in silence for the rest of the flight.

Landing at the airbase, everyone peeled off the jet and departed into the G7 Lab they didn't know existed. They rode the elevator up to the chopper pad and headed to the compound in silence.

In the cool night breeze, Mr. Zinkes was awaiting them at the facility entrance. "Welcome back." All greet Mr. Zinkes as they pass him. Michael carried Ms. Acai to the room Mr. Zinkes had fixed for her. Tracy and Mr. Zinkes stayed outside to talk. He stands next to Tracy as she looked out into the field of trees listening to cricket's chirp. "Your obedience pleases the Father. You could have left her there, but you listened to Yahweh's voice and harkened."

Sublime wasn't much for tears, but thanked him.

"Mr. Zinkes, this position you have placed me in sucks. I'm used to being on my own and not answering to anyone. Most of the time I thrive on my instincts and killing without a conscious about it was easy a few years ago. Now, Michael is questioning everything I do and if something goes wrong, I'm blamed for that, too. He assumes I am making things up as I go, and I'm the reason for all the chaos attracted to us. I can't win with him."

"Being a leader always comes with challenges, even those from our own team. I warned you. A few years ago, you would have assassinated her without giving it a second thought, but you didn't. That counts. Now you realize what it means to do God's will and not your own. I know it is tough to let go of what they taught you in the past and personal habits. All you had to count on was you, but now God is in the driver's seat and your team is counting on you to lead. Do not take them for granted. Love and respect them. Michael is not afraid of your leadership., he is afraid of not being as good as you. Understanding someone else's calling is difficult for others to see. We lash out at what we do not understand and wish for ourselves. Give him space to realize his personal growth and mistakes. He won't let you down...but that's not what's bothering you, is it?" He asked.

She looked at Mr. Zinkes and replied, "When I killed those two men, I felt like the old me. I could have knocked them out and left them alive."

"You know that had they realized you were behind them, they would not, for one second, hesitate to kill you?"

"No! I suspect they were there to kill us, but why? I think the reason I'm having a hard time with this is because we don't know why. Why send men and helicopters?"

"We can speculate. Knowing the why may never come. You must forgive yourself. Old habits or thoughts show up, and we must pray to God for emancipation from bondage. Now you know what to pray for but make no mistake, this is wartime in the natural and in the spirit. 'Give unto Caesar what is Caesar's and unto God what is Gods'. Having the discernment to learn the distinction is the key." He spoke with finality and strolled away.

~

Sleeping for a few hours, Kim continued to babble, going in and out of consciousness. After six hours, she came down from the drug. Secure in her room, she came to, confused and angry. Looking at her unfamiliar surroundings. Her room set up like the others with a bed, closet, couch, desk, tv and bathroom. Mr. Zinkes listened outside her door as she yells at the top of her lungs and of her own free will, she collapsed on the bed and fell asleep.

~

Kim realized the following morning that she was in a different location and cried, "Let me out of here!" She could not get out of her room. Mr. Zinkes entered, smacking her nose with the door. Kim attacked him with a round-house kick, and she falls as he grabs her leg and hit her with a palm blow to her forehead. She gets up again and attacks with a double front-snap kick. Mr.

Zinkes gives her a chest blow to make sure she doesn't get up this time. Conscious but reeling on the floor, she moans from the pain and then tries to speak again.

Mr. Zinkes doesn't allow her. He shouts, "Be quiet, and come out of her in the name of Jesus!" The unclean spirit came out and fled through the exhaust vent. Mr. Zinkes could see its essence.

She falls to the floor, unconscious. Bending down to wake her again, she was groggy and free. She feels the pain again and rubs the area of the chest blow.

"Ms. Acai, my name is Mr. Zinkes. I'm the one that hurt you. Although, it's not unto death. It's my intention to help you understand why you are here... you are here because you have a heart God wants to use."

"I don't believe in your God. I told that crazy lady already," she said.

"I understand your reluctance. Since that hindering spirit is no longer a factor, I hope you will give me an opportunity to show and offer information that may change your mind. Afterward, the choice of joining us or leaving is yours." He walks in closer to her. "The reason you are here is that of her compassion. She did not kill you, which you so deserved, when you attacked her. Grateful you should be. She was obedient to the voice of our God."

Kim, expressing her discomfort with her current situation, folded her arms in defiance.

"I will be back in five minutes. If you are willing, we will leave this room." He walks out and heads across the way to Tracy's room—he knocked.

"Hey, Mr. Zinkes."

"Please assemble the team in one hour and yes, include Joshua."

"You still amaze me."

"You have seen nothing yet, my dear. The fun is just beginning. One hour, please."

"Yes, Sir."

He turns but before he leaves, "You have questions, which I can't answer just yet. I need you to trust when you hear from God. It is imperative. I will see you in one hour."

He turned toward Kim's room. Once he reaches her room, she opens the door and is ready to go. He's ready for her and states, "This is not the time to try an escape."

In utter shock, it turns to a scowl within seconds. Mr. Zinkes bends down, "Well, at least I know the demonic spirit isn't the cause of that scowl," he said with a laugh. Mr. Zinkes allowed her to go out of the door first. She huffs as she walks by. "Ms. Acai, once again, we are not here to harm you or keep you hostage, but we have to keep our team safe and our location a secret. All I am asking is to give us a chance before making your decision. Your total lack of trust in us is understandable."

"Okay, Mr. Zinkes, I will give you an opportunity to tell me all about your work here. You only have one week."

"Good, a week is all we will need." He sensed she wanted to belong. She just didn't know it yet.

"But you knew I'd say it, didn't you?" Kim turned to him and asked.

"Yes, and you had to be the one to say it. For you are a woman of your word. You know your first name is a boy's name, meaning 'bold.' Acai is a fruit from Portuguese, Bold Fruit." Mr. Zinkes chuckles even bigger.

For the next hour, Mr. Zinkes gave Kim the tour of the grounds and she still had no clue where she was. He explained what she would have access to and the reason for such a place.

Fascinated at his ability and the facility, she remained reserved in her judgement and acceptance of her current situation for now.

Everyone assembled in the conference room. Mr. Zinkes and Kim enter. He addresses them. "Ms. Acai will stay for a week. After that, she will be free to leave, if she so chooses. If she leaves, she can express where she wants to go, and she leaves unaware of our location. Tomorrow morning, we will begin, but for now, give her history on yourselves. I am sure Ms. Acai will share hers, which is so interesting and colorful."

Everyone stayed quiet until Mr. Zinkes left the room. Sublime spoke first, "Ms. Kim, in earlier times, I would apologize for the way we... I brought you here. I give no apology now as I followed the Holy Spirit and God's direction. For the record, I am not the cause of the explosion. Although unexpected, it gave us insight into this organization your master was a part of. Yes, I was lurking around to see a way in. There were guards everywhere. I could have busted my way through, but I didn't want to compromise Mr. Johansen. As for the drugs Dr. Canno gave you to keep you sedated, they were necessary. I didn't know if or how involved you were in the Apollyon Organization or whether you were an innocent bystander of that explosion like the rest of us. As Tracy said, "My name is Sublime," Kim bowed her head in acceptance. "We will find out what happened. I've trained with many other masters. Don't bother trying to find out who I am if you leave this compound. I don't exist, and no form of government has information on me. That's all I'll give you for now."

One by one, each gave a brief history of themselves, but not too much. Then everyone was quiet. All eyes were on her. Kim speaks. "All right. My father killed my mother and abandoned me on the streets, so they placed me in a Shanghai orphanage. When I was six, they took me from the orphanage and trained me to be an assassin. I worked for those people and completed many missions for them before I escaped. When I was old enough, I made lots of money and changed my face a little. I no longer wanted to be an assassin. I've had this face for ten years, and because of my training, I became a bodyguard to the wealthiest of Japanese. They were skeptical of me as a Chinese immigrant in their country. It was word of mouth that put me in a position to show my worth. I've never lost a client other than from natural causes until now."

Sublime speaks up again, "For what it's worth, the other side of the world believes you are dead. They've kept what happened hush-hush. Your name was among those released as deceased. They claim it was a terrorist attack and did not disclose who or why those people were meeting. We have two ideas. One is an outside group wanted to make a name for themselves, which is the wrong reason. Two, those killings were intentional, an inside job. If the bombings were from an outside group, they've infiltrated Apollyon. How did they gain access to the meeting? Our skeptical connections with the organization didn't give us a foothold in, but we're hoping for another invitation."

X-Ray chimes in, "I'm new to all of this and I need more information. I don't even know where we are."

"For now, X-Ray, the difference between you and Ms. Acai is your faith. See, Ms. Acai doesn't have faith in the true and living God. It's not our job to force her into our belief. Once she hears the Good News, only then will she make a clear and honest choice. To believe or not to believe is the ultimate question. We cannot bring in people who don't share the faith because a house divided will fall. Our differences of opinions are many, but all of us believe Jesus died on the cross for all humanity. We either accept and receive the promise of eternal life or we don't and suffer whatever consequences God has planned for us in this life and thereafter. And as for where we are, disclosing that information right now would be unwise."

"Okay, are we done with the love fest? We need breakfast and can start fresh tomorrow. I'd like freedom for the rest of my day to relax. Ms. Acai, can you get back to your room by yourself? Or do you need one of us to hold your hand?" Euphrates gets up and heads to the door.

"Are you always this sarcastic?" Kim asked. Everyone laughs and chimes in, "Yes!"

Euphrates walks out of the room.

~

"We are across the hall from each other, so you can come with me. Plus, we can get breakfast on the way."

Kim stands up. "That's fine, thank you," she said.

"No problem."

Everyone heads out of the room. Kim and Sublime follow. Kim turned to Sublime and says, "I don't know if I can believe in your God. You've taken me against my will. You've brought me to god knows where and do you people expect me to trust you?"

Sublime turns to Kim. "I expect nothing from you. I know this is a scary situation for you and has shaken your foundation of who you are, but ask yourself this. Do you think our intentions aren't the best for your life? You are alive with only your pride hurt. You won't experience God for yourself unless you open your heart and mind to accept what is happening here and understand it's the truth."

"Who's Truth?"

"Fair enough. We all have experienced God's presence in diverse ways. Yours may differ from mine, but when you do, just keep an open mind."

"How will I know if I do?"

Sublime walks around the table closer to Kim. "The first step is not belief, it's a willingness to listen. God's Word says faith comes by hearing and hearing by the Word of God. It's about wanting to fill that void deep down inside that says, 'there is something or someone out there greater than yourself.' It begs the question, why was I created? I am not talking about joining a religion. The God who created all things, He has given all of us an equal measure of faith to believe God is greater than a statue or an idol we've made with our hands, or any human being who has all the money in the world—but is just as sinful as the rest of humanity. All of us are born into sin. Thankfully, we don't have to live in or practice sin. I did not know Mr. Okamoto, but anyone who joined the Apollyon of their own free will had an evil heart and a weak mind."

Hanging on the wall of the conference room was a picture representing every religion or cult or god ever created by man for reference. Sublime explained to each of those on the wall and what they represented.

"You will know there's a change when the change is in your heart and not by what you can see. It can be instant, or it can take time. It is up to you. The choice is yours to make. Think on this. You tried to kill me and now we are standing here face to face talking with each other. You've listened with your head and not your emotions or what they trained you to do. Trust me, we can use you on our team, but God will not allow it if you don't believe in Him and the one who died for all our sins. Let's go."

Kim, never having a heartfelt conversation with anyone, understood something had to change. Once she had proved herself as an accomplished assassin, Kim maintained the cost of this life was not having any meaningful friendships or relationships. She was where Sublime was years ago. As they walked down the corridor, many of the workers greeted Sublime, and Kim took notice.

"You have profound respect around here."

"I make it a habit to treat everyone with respect." Sublime said.

"How much do you know about Mr. Zinkes?"

Sublime smiled and realized Kim had asked a genuine question. "Come to my room. Let me show you something." They walked to Sublime's room, and she picked up a picture of her mother and father. My parents have been deceased for several years. I gather Mr. Zinkes has been watching us for a while now. I wasn't aware, but he's tested me through the years, even in life-threatening situations. He is a man of God. Someone you can trust. He has special abilities I've never seen. Trust me, I have witnessed many things in my short lifetime. He will never lie to you, nor will he hold his tongue when it comes to improvements in your life."

"Meaning, he can read minds?" Kim asked.

Sublime answered the question as she replaced the picture on the shelf. "Yes."

"He is beyond a Master Martial Artist, too." Kim still feeling the pain in her bruised chest and shoulder.

"I didn't know that about him. None of us has ever seen him fight!" Sublime said, and wondered what she's missed.

"Well, I had the pleasure and even I have to admit, I still have a lot to learn."

"Wow, he's never mentioned it to any of us."

Kim rubbed the area of her chest, still aching. "I learned the hard way."

Sublime laughs. "Don't take it too hard. Stay with us long enough and you will learn things you didn't even know about yourself."

They leave Sublime's room and head to the cafeteria for breakfast and the rest of the day lounging in their quarters.

~

Everyone is asleep. The shadows in the hallway attract no one's attention as they pass the surveillance cameras. One shadow reached for the exit door. A voice came from the dark, "I will not stop you from leaving, but consider this: you have everything to gain and nothing to lose if you stay and learn." Startled, Kim stiffened and stopped.

Mr. Zinkes came out of the shadow and said, "The man you worked for, Mr. Okamoto, was part of a group called the Apollyon. This group is in control of the entire world, meaning the government, the financial system, and the food industry and many others. Your Master was one of a select few who belonged to this group, and his family is the wealthiest in Japan. I am sure you have heard of the Illuminati. Well, the Illuminati have nothing on them. These families not only want to take over their own respective countries, but they want to rule the world by controlling religion, wealth, and government. This is a group that will stop at nothing to have world domination and to bring about Armageddon, the end of the free world as we know it. They believe their evil will bring about Lucifer's rule and bring down God's kingdom. You still have the choice to leave, but I would suggest you at least prepare yourself for what is coming. That is all I am asking of you."

"I will stay for now, but if I stay, you must teach me everything."

"Deal." Mr. Zinkes responded and melted back into the shadows. Kim returned to her room and slept peacefully for the night.

Chapter 13

─ ༄ ♦ ༄ ─

Unexpected Lessons

322 days since it began, everyone was up early and eating breakfast. The steel and olive-greened walls buzzed with conversation. Before Kim came in to eat, Tracy reminded everybody, "Until she is formally one of us, do not use your actual names. If she leaves the compound, it will jeopardize our identities." Everyone agreed and went on eating their breakfast.

Later that morning, Sublime was out on the field training. A mix of Capoeira, Jiu-Jitsu and Tae Kwon Do to make things interesting. Mr. Zinkes found her with her back turned to him. The leaves rustled too swift for the current breeze. She countered his motion, but took a blow to the back-left shoulder blade. Returning with a backside kick, she landed a blow to the back of Mr. Zinkes' buttocks. He countered with a double front snap kick, followed by a jumping roundhouse to Sublime's left jaw. Knocking her to the side, she does a one-handed back flip landing on her feet, which cleared her from another roundhouse blow. There was blood coming from the side of her lip, but it didn't stop them. Playfully, bantering back and forth with twists and turns to counter each other's moves, they sparred for the next fifteen minutes. A crowd gathered to watch. It got up close and personal as Mr. Zinkes landed a palm blow to the right side of her chest. Mr. Zinkes then stepped back for Sublime to recover. It didn't seem to faze her, as it had Ms. Acai. She countered with a back spin to his chest. Mr. Zinkes was more seasoned, but Sublime was both limber and quick. After a half an hour, their session ended. Mr. Zinkes bowed and then Sublime.

"Your heart needs protecting within and without. Leaving it vulnerable can lead to death," he wisely advised.

"Thank you, Mr. Zinkes."

He shrugs his shoulders to stretch. Mr. Zinkes addresses the group, "The reason I told none of you of my fighting skills was because we must learn a lesson in everything we do. Only reveal your strengths when forced to use them. Never let the enemy know the whole of you. They will exploit your weakness and use it against you. Keep them guessing and they will underestimate you. Counter with the truth of your abilities, the strength and power of your being. The deadliest woman alive has learned how to hide in plain sight." Mr. Zinkes looks back at Sublime and continues, "I say to all of you, keep your compassion but take your emotions out of the decisions you make. Listen and focus. Give enough to allow those you want to trust to come in. Use discernment to know when the enemy comes." He finishes with the instructions, "Meeting in the conference room in thirty minutes. Thank you."

As they leave the field, Mr. Zinkes and Sublime rub their respective injured parts—he rubs his buttocks and Sublime her chest. He walked into the building while the rest of them stayed behind in the open field. Sublime leaned on the gray wooden fence that separated the audience from the sparring pair. The team surrounded Sublime as she gasped for oxygen. They realized Mr. Zinkes and Sublimes' abilities were beyond their own. True to form, even Euphrates said so to her, "I must admit, the sparring match between you and Mr. Zinkes was extraordinary. I would have never known had I not seen it with my own eyes," he said. Appreciation clearly showing in his face.

Sublime stayed quiet, humbled by their accolades. Shadow clasps his fingers together. "The possibility of you being an avatar in my computer program would be so exciting. Would you consent to doing some techniques on video and I can create a martial arts simulator?" He asked excitedly.

"Shadow, I am not sure if this applies to our mission, but sometimes, it's necessary to have fun. So, I will consent if you use everyone with martial arts experience." She replied with a smile.

"I will include everyone. This is great. I have a challenge ahead of me. It's so exhilarating, I can hardly contain my enthusiasm." Shadow was smiling from ear to ear, his outward enthusiasm subdued.

Thirty minutes later, they were discussing the Word of God, and Kim had many questions. They could never say there wasn't a heated discussion or arguing over each other's opinions. God's Word and respect won each battle of thought and understanding.

For this week, they trained, and Kim stayed. Kim was a tough sparring opponent for Sublime. Interrogation tactics lasted for two days and then the cell block fast, this time for ten days straight.

Day one, they cart Joshua off first. When he did not return, the others recognized the deal, except for Kim. They took her next and so on. Each had a Bible in their rooms and this time, a desk, and a bucket. Mr. Zinkes, on the observation deck, studied Joshua and Kim. The screaming out of "hello" rang loud, as this was new to them both.

By day three, it became easier to fast. Each one in solitude and meditation.

Day five, Mr. Zinkes observed Kim, now contemplating her decision to stay, she picked up the Word of God and flipped the pages to, Romans 8:38-39 (NIV), 38 For I am convinced that neither death nor life, neither angels nor demons, neither the present nor the future, nor any powers, 39 neither height nor depth, nor anything else in all creation, will separate us from the love of God that is in Christ Jesus our Lord.

She cried out to God. Mr. Zinkes understood the release of burdens she held for so long, telling God she was sorry for all the things she had done. Mr. Zinkes said to Ms. Giles, "They were going for ten days, but I want them out. Send Kim to the conference room after she cleans up."

Workers hose them off one by one and transport them back to the compound.

After showering, Kim met with Mr. Zinkes. He remained in his chair as she steps in. "Ms. Acai, please have a seat." She sits, her body fatigued, and her brain was running a hundred miles per second. The silence was revealing. The teardrops that fell were comforting, her posture unashamed. Mr. Zinkes says, "During this exercise, I observed everyone. I watch for everything, such as illness, evidence of hallucination, hysteria, or extreme fatigue. You did not display any of these factors, but I recognized you were praying. To whom were you praying and crying out to?"

The earnestness of her words was distinct. She answered, "Mr. Zinkes, God has given me a measure of faith. How considerable it has increased and only God can measure. I'd be misleading you if I answered I was not praying to God to leave that cell. I recalled a memory of when I trained as an assassin. They forced us into these brick boxes no bigger than a four by six room and left us three or four days at a time for no reason other than to torture our minds and to break us. Although this seemed comparable, there was something different. It was what I read that made all the difference. Within me, I prayed to God because I want to think God sees me struggling to change. I cried out because I forgave my father for deserting me. I'm unsure if I would have acted similarly in his position, as I'm unaware of his motivations and circumstances. To find out if God would answer, I offered a prayer. Only one minute after I prayed, they came in with the hose and told us to get out of the room. But you can read my mind, so you already know this."

Mr. Zinkes stood and folded his arms. Kim squirms while looking at her hands. "Kim, you can believe me or not. I did not read your mind—it's the truth. I know how to control my gift and when to use it and when not. Observing you praying, I heard you cry out and wanted your honest answer about what you were doing and experiencing. Everyone's experience with God is different. There is always one common theme with everyone's experience. It removes an oppressive weight from your conscious—as though it rises off like air. Serenity and quietness within them—peace. Some cry with emotion, some do not, but they sense something different within them. An intense desire to be and do different from what they had been doing. Because what they were doing before did not complete them—did not make them whole. I wished to discover your point of view without it being tainted." Mr. Zinkes answered.

"While I was praying, peace came over me. Before I prayed, it terrified me inside and then I remembered where I read before when Jesus said, 'I will never leave you nor forsake you.' Those words comforted me, and I knew I could be free. The entire time they were spraying me with the hose, tears fell. I haven't cried since I was five. I want to experience God more." Kim states.

The warmth of his expression made her smile. "Congratulations Ms. Acai, all God wants is a willing heart. God will not make you love Him or worship Him. God wants you to do it of your own free will, as He transforms and renews your mind and heart. We all experienced what you did today. Now it is up to you to continue to seek after God and He will direct the path you must go. That path may bring hard times. Every day will be an unfamiliar experience, and some may not be easy. You will face challenges you can't handle on your own. It is in those times we seek the face of God and His direction and guidance. Even unto death, God says when we die in Him, in His Salvation, it begins our eternal life with Him. When you are ready to accept Jesus Christ as your Lord and Savior, you will express it without guilt or shame, and you will become a child ready for His Kingdom. There is such a thing called the Sinner's Prayer. This is where you confess your sin and accept Jesus Christ and confess Jesus has saved you and forgiven you of your sin. If you believe He died on the cross and rose from the dead for every human. You've begun the faith walk, Ms. Acai. From here, it will be up to God to complete the finished work in you."

"I understand." Kim replies. She stays quiet for a while.

He was now doing that thing he does. "Why don't more people accept what you have received? It is the age-old question, Ms. Acai. Free will governs that someone who does not accept Christ is not willing to let go of their own will. It rules the thoughts of men and women and children from birth. We were all born into sin and God sent his Son as a sacrifice to liberate those who turn to him."

"Thank you, Mr. Zinkes. I have a lot to figure out."

"You are welcome. Please let X-Ray know I would love to see him next." Mr. Zinkes said, dismissing Kim.

~

The next morning, the team gathered in the training area. Sublime asked Kim the smoldering question of the day, "Kim, have you made your choice?"

"Yes, I received Christ as my Lord and Savior. I went down on my knees in my room, confessing to the killings, and prayed the rest of my existence will be different. My mouth said words I've never heard before. It was peaceful and reassuring. When I stopped praying, I felt a terrible burden lift from my mind, and I recognized God's forgiveness. Read Acts chapter 2. It will identify what you encountered. There is a last question I must ask." Mr. Lyemel hugged her like a little daughter.

"What's that? "

"Do you want to stay or get released from the compound? "

She glanced around at all the faces, anxiously waiting for her answer, their expressions accepting. "I would like to stay."

He looked around at all of them. "Now, your name has become the Apocalyptic 7." Everyone hugged Kim.

"One question. Does this mean my moniker changes?" Everyone laughed. Tracy answered, "No. No one has changed their moniker. If you want to change it to embody your new life in Christ, you can, but I believe Myna Bird fits you."

"Apocalyptic 7..." Mr. Laemel speaks up, "You will train through several simulations, advanced martial arts with Kelton's new program, computer training, and any other training we deem necessary. Kim, Kendrick, and Kelton, please plan to instruct your team members in your professions, weapons, piloting, and computer automation. Carsen, you will work with Joshua and get as much updated intel on the Apollyon as possible. Look for any activity. It's been a while since we had an update and use Kelton when needed."

Mr. Zinkes chimed in, "Tracy and Michael, see me at eighteen hundred hours." He nods to Mr. Laemel to continue and exits.

"Thank you, team. It's a free day tomorrow. Please show Kim how to have a good time, Jesus-style, and trust me, this time there will be no staged demonstration." He smiles.

As the instruction progressed, Kim had many queries concerning faith and the sacrifice Jesus made. Reading the entire book of Hebrews was a revelation about why God loved her. Her faith increased in time, and she learned obedience to God's will and His Word was stronger than sacrifice.

Chapter 14

France on the Horizon

After six months, standing as the center of attention, Michael leads the discussion regarding the Apollyon and the next meeting.

"For the last two months, there's been contact with the Apollyon. It was by virtual contact only, which means the Apollyon is still in hiding. They are preparing to meet in Paris, at an undisclosed location. A file will arrive via the web with instructions and I'm sure their Automated Imagery System (AIS) will track us, but don't worry, our equipment is handling the tracking issue. They believe we are in Hong Kong."

Mr. Zinkes now stands. "We will go to France in five days. Once there, this may be our chance to gather as much intel as possible of their plans. Because of the explosion at the previous meeting, extra precautions are necessary. Michael's and Tracy's identities will not change. Kendrick and Mr. Griffith will fly us in the JC-12, and Mr. Nordic will fly with the surveillance team. Kelton, you will be on surveillance and computer systems on the plane and with the command post in France. Carsen, you will continue your role as wife and surveillance.

Joshua and Kim, you are on weapons and extra bodyguard detail for Michael while he is playing Mr. Johansen. Meet with Mr. Lyemel and Mr. Laemel in the morning. There's new equipment available."

Michael rubbed his hands together. "Now, that is what I'm talking about, new toys for the toy-ster."

Joshua motioned to Tracy as they were getting ready to walk out the door. "Tracy, can I speak with you alone?" He touches the back of her arm.

Tracy notices Michael staring. "Sure, what do you want to talk about?" Joshua notices Michael still looking their way. "Not here. Not on the grounds. I need to speak to you, and it can't wait."

"Okay. Give me fifteen minutes to get it cleared with Mr. Zinkes. I will meet you outside," Tracy said.

"Okay." Joshua looks back at Michael and leaves.

~

Driving in silence, they arrive at the virtual shopping plaza. Sitting in the parking complex, Joshua buys two coffees. The android delivers them to the window and the aroma of Columbian espresso permeates the car. The weather was dreary. *'Coffee will hit the spot,'* Tracy thought. Joshua leads the discussion but takes a sip of the black.

"The reason I want to talk to you is I'm still in love with you. You came back into my life for a reason. Holding my sentiments in these months has been a torment. What are we going to do about it?" Tracy was not in shock at his bluntness. This was Joshua, straight to the point. She smiled, remembering their first date, and when Joshua proposed.

Putting his arms around her neck, he said, *'Tracy, I love you and want to spend the rest of my life with you.'*

'Yes!' Jarring back to life, back to reality. "Joshua, events, and times have shifted for us. I love you, too. But my focus is not on marriage right now or any relationship. My focus is on this mission, which you are a part of now. Bringing you back with us was not to pick up where we left off. God wants you here. I am not suggesting it might not happen. It's just, right now our focus

must remain on what God has for us to do. For now, I love you and that's as far as we can take it."

His disappointment vanished as her continued love reassured him. "Okay, so once this mission is over, we can visit this again, can't we?"

"Yes, and maybe then we can seek God's direction for our relationship and where it continues from there."

He nodded and relaxed. He continued, "I need to know something."

"What is it?"

"Do you have feelings for Michael?"

Her stare was priceless. "Are you joking, or are you serious?" Not allowing him time to respond, she clutches his chin and kisses him. "Does that clarify your query?"

"Oh! Yeah." Satisfied.

They finish their coffee and travel back to the compound. Joshua had to let off some steam in the weight room while Tracy went into her room to pray. She heard a quiet tap at her door. She draws up from praying and opens the door. It was Michael. Hesitant, she let him into her room. "You still require discernment, Michael." Closing the door, she waits.

"I need you to know something."

"What is it with you men today?" Tracy asked as she sits on her bed.

Michael stood there, shaking his head, and stuffed his hands into his pockets. "I can't explain it to you right now. I need to pray more." Michael turns and walks out of her room.

Thinking for a second, she rushes to the door. That fast, he was out of sight. She did not pursue the matter. He piqued her curiosity, but she could not worry about it. It was Michael. He was into the theatrical but still. *'What did he wish to tell me?'* She thought.

On a stormy morning, two days before they were to leave for France. The thunder roared, clapping louder than a stadium full of gladiator enthusiasts. The drops of firmament pounded the roof as it rolled over the compound.

Michael sits in a chair in Mr. Zinkes' office. "Right now, my feelings are confused. I don't know whether to act on them or just let them be."

"What is your gut telling you?"

"It's telling me I may rush into something without reflecting, which I repeatedly do. I don't want to make a mistake and there are obstacles in my way, ones I don't know if I can hurdle over."

"What do you want me to say, because I will not give you any answers to that riddle? You must find out for yourself. My only question to you is how are you going to handle it if she does not feel the same way?"

Michael stood and paced. "At this point in my life, I want to meet someone and get married. I know it will happen in God's time, or it may not happen at all. A part of me thinks it's the right time. What better person than someone on our team."

"You still did not answer my question."

Michael adjusts himself back in his seat. "I've never felt this way. She challenges me in everything. She makes me want to be better. I mean, I don't want to be wrong and then get rejected."

"God will not lead you down a pathway not meant to be. You can go against God's voice and do things your own way. It tends not to turn out so good. Sometimes we do not listen when God gives us warning. Seek God first and I know He will lead you to her, or He will confirm you should be alone. Remember, the Word of God says, is it better for you not to marry but if you marry, a man that finds a wife..."

"Yeah, I know Mr. Zinkes."

"The woman you are to join in matrimonial bliss is to be your soulmate, your helpmeet, and the one for you."

"Okay, I will seek God for the next two days and while we are in France."

Michael turn to leave the office and pauses for a moment.

"And you still did not answer my question." Mr. Zinkes said.

~

Leaving the office, Michael runs into Joshua in the hallway. "Hey, you want to work out in an hour?" Joshua asked.

"I can't concentrate on working out. I have a lot on my mind."

"Is there something I can help you with?"

"No! I'll just take care of it myself. I'll see you when I see you." Michael walks off in a hurry.

Michael heads to his room and almost bumps into Tracy. He does not speak and walks by as though she does not exist. Tracy continues to walk, even though Michael said nothing, and encounters Kim coming from the training room.

"Have you noticed Michael is acting funny toward me?" Tracy asks Kim.

"I haven't seen him today. How has he been acting toward you?"

"He came into my room two weeks ago and told me he wanted to tell me something but couldn't, and now he walks right past me and says nothing. Not even anything sarcastic."

Kim's curiosity grew. "What do you think of him, Tracy?" she asked.

Jarring the door open, unaware Joshua was standing behind the door, he overhears their conversation when she stopped to answer Kim's question. "He's brash, stubborn, and unpredictable. Despite all of that, I trust him with my life. Sometimes he is obnoxious. I think deep down, he is a man who loves God. Any woman would be lucky to get him." Tracy finished, and Joshua leaves to the other side of the training facility to workout. She continued, "He's more of a big brother to me. Why do you ask?"

"I don't know." Kim smiled.

"I guess this is lovebird season. Seek God for direction in meeting your mate. You never want to make a mistake and be with the wrong man. If we seek God and His Righteousness, God will give you the desires of your heart. If you wish to marry someone, make sure God sent him."

"Thanks Tracy."

"You are welcome. How are things with you otherwise?"

They link arms. "Walk with me," Kim said.

The storm passed, and only a mist remained. "I can't imagine going back to my old life. I'm part of something good for a change. Not that I do not think about my past. I can see how God has orchestrated my life. I've been alone for so long, and now I have all of you to talk to and you listen to what I have to say, and value me as an individual person."

"Kim, we all have one time or another—felt alone, even though there are many people are around us. Before coming here, I only talked to my superiors about what I was doing. I thought my personal life didn't matter to them. I had never given them any reason to change that course of my life until I met Joshua. They tried to take that away from me. Ultimately, I had to look at my own actions. It is a lonely place to be at the top and you cannot tell anyone. As my eyes are open to how I lived my life before, I see how God has guided and directed my path. God's original plan for me prevailed."

"Why did you accept Christ?" Kim asked.

As she looked out at the rain-soaked field, Tracy recounted, "The military was in my blood. I felt lost after my parents died. Blaming God for their deaths would have been the simple thing to do, but there was something that did not allow me to. Overall, God allowed it, and their deaths were purposeful. In the past, I wish I had died with them. I had lived long enough and no longer wanted to deal with the evils of this world. I think after losing my brother to the war, I was all I had left. Joshua was no longer in my life and I was desperately trying to find my way. I was rummaging through some boxes and came across a bible my mother had given me at sixteen. I had never opened it until that time. In it was a letter from my mother she wrote to me. In it explained her faith. She loved God and wanted that for me, too. It was in that moment I knew. Where the letter was, I read God's Word, and I read we have already won the War. Victory is ours, even if we lose our lives during the battle. God is the victor, and there is nothing Satan can do. Oh! Trust me, he will continue to try to and may win a few battles. The result is a victory for the Kingdom of God. For believers will open their eyes to a place much greater than where we are now. But to answer your question, God filled a hole in my heart. I did some unthinkable things for the government and each time, I lost a part of me."

Kim pondered a moment and asks, "I've been thinking about our trip to France. What if we do not stop them?"

"We can't give up fighting. There will be many battles and some we may lose, but we keep going until God says our mission or time on this earth is complete."

They both look at the forest trees and take in the view before them.

Tracy turns to Kim. "We have two days. Let us make the best of it and prepare ourselves." They both walk back into the building to train.

Tracy saw no one for the rest of the day, except during lunch and dinner. Joshua sat with her both times but kept his affection for her secret, appearing often in deep thought. Michael kept his distance from everybody. Carsen, Kendrick, Kim, and Kelton laughed it up during the whole dinner. No one bothered to wonder why Michael was in such a mood and kept a distance of mind and body from the rest of them. Only Mr. Zinkes knew, and he stayed clear of Michael's drama.

Chapter 15

Who Else is Out There?

It was time to take off for Paris, France. In the JC-12, they were raring to get into some action. With two hours left on the supersonic cruise, no one was speaking. The mood had changed. Mr. Lyemel and Mr. Laemel recognized the suspense and anticipation of what they would find hung heavy in the air, but said nothing. Mr. Zinkes observed it as well and knew the other reason it was tense within the cabin. He likewise said nothing. The perception that this team had become dysfunctional with their desire to be in relationships was apparent. He would discuss it, but now was not the time for it. He knew addressing it now would provoke a detonation amongst a few and it would cause stress in those who didn't know this was brewing underneath.

They arrive at the Orly Airstrip for private jets under the cover of night. They left the airport to drive only fifteen minutes to stay at the Hotel de Crillon, which was still standing after two and a half centuries. The majestic castle motif was as beautiful as a hundred-fifty years ago when they turned it into a hotel.

The surrounding area had many luxurious hotels to choose from and minutes away from the Louvre and the Eiffel Tower.

The streets, damp from the misty rain, were busy with many cafes along the way. Both Sublime and Shadow roll down the windows in the back of the limos. The rich smells from the various cafes permeated the car and their taste buds watered, especially Shadow. Arriving at the hotel, mysterious lights and shadows of the hotel gave it a prestigious character and atmosphere. Buying out the penthouse and the floor below, as they did at the Pharaoh in Egypt, the surveillance team was in place and awaited the team's arrival.

~

Shadow had been born there. If time permitted, he would visit the orphanage again. His heart's desire was to give back to the place that allowed him to be a kid—savior of the bullied. The home was not modern, molded in stone. It saved many children from starving and homelessness. It could not save them from the sting of abandonment. Hoping someone would adopt them from their misery, many would grow and resent society for not caring to love them. Kelton, lucky because someone saw his potential early on and knew how to channel his anger and gift.

They settled into the penthouse and received their room assignments. As they sat in the lounge area, Shadow speaks up, "If possible, we can stroll along the River Seine. As a child, we explored the sixty-one-acre Luxembourg Garden, it was a breathtaking sight to see, c'est magnifique!" Childish excitement evident on his face.

Sublime sitting next to Kelton replied, "I love Paris myself. It's been some time since I've been. The last time here, it was not under the best of circumstances."

Kelton turned. "Were you on the job?"

"Yes. There was a job on a famous tennis player who turned out to be a spy for the Russians. A supposed threat to the national security of France." Sublime said, "Я предлагаю, вы приходите со мной тихо (I suggest you come with me quietly.) Я убью тебя прямо здесь, при необходимости (I will kill you right here, if necessary.)... He was a special case. Afterwards, I determined to stop them. It wasn't enough to threaten people in love, but kill innocent people? It turns out he was never a spy but an activist about to marry a political diplomat. Her parents wanted him dead, and they used their connections to get me to do it. I told them I missed my opportunity and would do it another time. I ended the parents' lives instead and their daughter inherited all their money."

Euphrates opened the floor for everyone to speak of a choice they had to make to do the right thing. Starting the conversation, "My life might not have ever been as exciting as Tracy's here, but when last in Iraq, there was a civilian family hiding out in one of the abandoned buildings we were to evacuate. A mother and two children were hiding on the top floor of the building. She was an American who married a man who turned out to be an Al Qaeda member. She fled with her two children, hiding there for weeks with limited food. With paperwork in hand, she was afraid to go out of the building, because her husband was looking for her. She was about to leave that night. I found her first. I was to expose her to our military personnel. Instead, I got her out and left her at the American Embassy."

Tracy returns the compliment, "Well Michael, I'll take noble over exciting any day." Michael smiles at Tracy.

Leopard reminds X-Ray he was to tell her some stories of his explorations, "X-Ray you promised, so you can't back out now."

"You know, in 2027, while I was in Egypt, an Egyptian archaeologist discovered a 3000-year-old Egyptian tomb in Thebes, the old capital of Egypt. Allowing only five visitors at a time, it was hard to get free from the tour guides, but I did. I was there to steal a scepter of an Egyptian Priest, made of gold and ruby diamonds. Pretending to be ill, I walked out of the tomb, gasping for air, and faking a collapse to my knees. 'I need water.' was all I gave them in a raspy voice. I walked away clean. Six hours later, they discovered the scepter was missing and had no suspects, as I had given them the name of Quinn Lawrence. I sold it underground for eight million. Two years later, I bought it back for 10 million and returned it to where it belonged. I hadn't given my life to Christ, but when I did, I wanted to do what I could to right some of my wrongs."

~

As they sat in discussion, a blast shook the hotel. At nine-forty-three p.m., the jolt was loud, vases splattered, and mirrors fell off the walls. The blast originated on the third floor and took a portion of the hotel down, rumbling for at least a minute. Euphrates and Joshua took charge to make a path of escape. They investigated the elevator to determine if it was yet in operation. It wasn't.

"The elevator is out!" Euphrates said.

Joshua checks the door to the stairs. The explosion shifted the door shut and it wouldn't open. Joshua runs into his room and grabs the ropes from his duffle bags.

He thrusts both down the side of the building. One by one, lowering themselves down the side, they escaped unseen.

Sublime contacts McBride, "Take whatever you can out of the building!"

Sublime turned to the team. "We need to get everything out of here! We all need to grab what we can and help the rest of those in the building that mat be trapped." Around them was chaos and weeping.

"Who's the benefactor of this strike?" Euphrates asked with a grimace.

Mr. Zinkes said, "She is close. I can hear her. I can't see her., it was not for us."

Looking around, Myna Bird runs toward the northwest edge of the Hotel, with Euphrates following. She runs ahead and loses him as she passes through a crowd, following a black trench coat. Myna Bird stops as the trench coat disappears. Euphrates catches up to her.

"Kim, what's going on?" Euphrates asked.

Taking a deep breath, ending in a huff, she answered, "I thought I saw someone I knew."

"Someone from your past?" he demanded.

"Yes, the only person who knows what I might look like now. But why would she run away from me?" She asked.

Euphrates touched her arm. "Let's get back to the others. We have to find out who was staying in the hotel besides us."

"What if it's the same people that took out my old employer? I don't think it's an accident they hit this hotel."

Euphrates turned and walked back toward the hotel. Reaching the others, everyone turned towards Euphrates and Myna Bird.

"Who were you chasing?" Sublime asked.

"A ghost from the past. It's not who I thought it was, because she ran. The woman I was chasing ran because she's hiding. I didn't get a close look at her face. I thought it was someone I knew," Myna Bird replied.

Mr. Zinkes said, "She's connected and ran because she didn't want to get caught."

Sublime turned to Euphrates. "McBride pulled the guest list."

Turning it over to Euphrates, on the mini-AIS, "Do you recognize any of the names from the last gathering?"

He scours through five pages. "There are only two names I recognize, McClendon and my own. McClendon was a family there at the last gathering and the only idiot to use his actual name."

Sublime speaks to McBride on their communication line, "We will find another place to stay. When we do, get your team to that location."

"Will do. I'm here at the elevator doors. Two of my surveillance team didn't make it out alive. They were in the elevator as the blast ignited. It sent the elevator into a free-falling death box ten floors. So, I also have to deal with this."

"What do you need me to do? X-Ray, Myna Bird, and I are staying here at the hotel to investigate. The rest of the team is returning to the plane. We can't leave Mr. Being out in the open."

"Nothing for now. I will keep you posted."

Mr. Zinkes speaks, "We need to know the target, and yes, Mr. Being, I've thought about the connection to the group killing Myna Bird's employer in Cairo. We know Apollyon didn't kill their own members. It is a priority we find this group before they find us."

He turned to Mr. Lyemel and Mr. Laemel. "Find us another place to stay and report back within thirty minutes. For now, we are heading back to the plane. It will be awhile before they let us into the hotel to collect any belongings. Mr. Johansen, Mrs. Johansen, Shadow, and Xerxes return to the plane with me."

Mr. Lyemel responded, "Sure thing, Mr. Zinke's, and Sublime, keep us on your channel." Everyone scatters to their destinations.

~

The Apollyon were watching, and under the current circumstances, they had more to worry about. Mr. Frederickson and Mr. Banks were in a car across the street, watching everything take place. They had previously considered Mr. Johansen might be involved with the mansion bombing. That thought was now eliminated. Mr. Frederickson looked at Mr. Banks. "Whoever is doing this knows our every move."

"Yes. They are taking our members out one by one, and we are powerless at this point to stop them, because we don't know who they are!" Mr. Frederickson exclaimed.

"What if there's a mole amongst us?" Mr. Banks asked.

"It is unlikely this involves one family. We will investigate everyone, and I mean everyone, before we come up missing."

"You don't think they would ever suspect us of doing such a thing, do you, Mr. Frederickson? Our loyalty hasn't been in question for over twenty-five years." Mr. Banks stated emphatically.

"We can't put anything past the Apollyon's fears. Money can turn anyone with the right amount dangled in front of them or the right motivation. If we don't find out who these people are, no one will find us. It's happened before," he said.

"To whom?" Mr. Banks asked.

"The men who we replaced over twenty-five years ago. Thirty minutes ago, I was told no one would know we existed if we don't find out what, who, where, how, and why our members are being targeted and killed." Mr. Frederickson informed him.

Mr. Banks loosened his tie and strained his neck to do so. "I guess we better get on it then."

"I guess so," Mr. Frederickson said.

~

The next day, they found lodging at the Hotel Ritz. They finished breakfast, and the scent of food lingered in the air. They congregated in the sitting room area of the Penthouse. Their contented silence gradually morphed into conversation.

"Getting this group will be a challenge. We don't know who they are for one. We must do it now. The longer we wait, the higher risk it will be," Myna Bird said.

"My concern is the innocent lives being hurt or killed." Sublime admitted.

Mr. Zinkes interjects, "Sublime, always remember, life and death are in God's hands. We will make sure whatever God provides for us to do. We will use wisdom. Our focus is the same. Every life is precious to God. Death is purposeful. It's a tough truth to consider thinking life has no value for those left to pick up the pieces. They are the ones who suffer. Time is ticking. If we don't find this group within the next week, I'm afraid they may go into obscurity, if they haven't already."

Joshua was standing by the window, scanning the street. He turned his attention to Mr. Zinkes, "I think we have some overseers already."

Michael comes to look. "I can't see them. Maybe he's from the group or Apollyon. There's only one way to find out for certain who he is."

Sublime walks toward the elevator. "I'm on it." Sneaking out the back, unseen, she arrived at the car after weaving through traffic. His window was down, so, she catapults through the window and drops into the seat next to a shocked Mr. Frederickson on stakeout duty, "My boss wants to talk to you." Sublime stuck a handgun in his side, "If we wanted you dead, Mr. Frederickson, it would be so. We have fallen onto the same target. They murdered your people and now are trying to murder ours, so I advise you to get out of the car and follow me. I have no intention of hurting you. If we find your organization is behind these assassinations, there will be no place for you to hide."

Mr. Frederickson stared at Sublime. His face concedes. "I assure you. We had nothing to do with it. I will get out and do what you ask. I guess a part of me feels to die now wouldn't be so bad, but providing information to live is more desirable."

Both get out of the car—she halts. "Just to establish we understand each other. If you try anything, a sharpshooter is waiting."

He glances down at the red dot on his lapel. "I get the picture." He straightened his coat.

"Excellent, follow me." She places her gun back in the holster. Once they reach the hotel lobby, Sublime allows him to lead the way into the elevator door. It didn't matter what elevator, Myna Bird and X-Ray were each in one. The doors closed, and Joshua put a black bag over Mr. Fredrickson's head. For a split second, he thought about fighting his way out. He hears Sublime's gun slide from its holster and felt the barrel in his side, changing his mind. Speaking into her wire, Sublime informs Kim, "Myna Bird, the package is in hand."

~

They enter the Penthouse. Joshua guides him to an armchair. He doesn't remove the bag just yet. He squirms like a little kid having to use the potty. Sweat poured out of his glands profusely. It was no guess he was about to have a panic attack—now panting. Mr. Zinkes calmly speaks, "Hello Mr. Frederickson, my name is Giaigo Zinkes. I am the extra security for Mr. Johansen, who is new to your organization. It disturbs us that he has grown into a target of this group attacking the Apollyon members. It is my mission to detect any intelligence you have and, at the least, collaborate with any information we may learn. But make no mistake, if we locate these individuals first, we will exterminate them for the cause."

Mr. Zinkes pulls off the black bag and Mr. Johansen, Sublime, and X-Ray were sitting around him. Everyone else was down on the surveillance floor, listening.

Mr. Johansen speaks, "Ever since your organization approached me, there has been nothing but massacres. Even as we left Egypt, we didn't know whether your team or someone else was trying to kill us. I presume it might have been both."

Mr. Zinkes does his thing. He declared, "Mr. Frederickson, please don't lie to us. We don't like lies when we're only trying to help."

"Yes, we were there but we were only there to do surveillance." Mr. Frederickson replies.

"No, no, no you weren't. You lie again. Your men were to impair the plane to detain us from leaving. You reprimanded Mr. Banks for the screwup, but you covered for him to the Apollyon."

"How do you know that? There was no one around us. Have you kidnapped Mr. Banks to torture him for information like you are getting ready to do to me now?"

Mr. Zinkes chuckled, "I know what you ate for breakfast this morning, Mr. Frederickson. I assure you we are not torturing Mr. Banks."

"Sure, why don't you tell me? You could have read that from my hotel room ticket."

"We aren't playing games here. On your serving tray was the one element that reminds you of your wife—your dearly departed wife. Strawberries and Crème. It was the day after your twelfth-year wedding anniversary. That morning, at the same time she delivered your favorite strawberries and crème, a bullet came through your hotel window and pierced her brain. She dropped right on the bed as you were laying there. You didn't move from your spot. Not terrified that your wife was just murdered, nor did you get down on the ground to protect yourself. You lay there on top of the covers with your black terry robe and black plush slippers dangling from your toes and did not move a muscle. See, this came as no surprise, as you suspected she was a spy. A spy for the Italian government against your precious Apollyon. In fact, when Apollyon brought you the news of her desertion, you urged them to allow you to kill her yourself, to show your allegiance. You got up from the bed, took a shower, gathered your belongings, and left just as calmly as you entered, because Mrs. Frederickson got the room under an alias. Guilt has plagued you all these years, since finding out the horrifying news during the autopsy she was bearing your offspring!" Mr. Frederickson broke down and couldn't contain his emotions. "Big mistake!" Mr. Zinkes did not let up, "Not only did you learn she was carrying your child, but you also found that the Apollyon was mistaken about her and it was another man's wife who had turned on them and defected to the United States." There was no benefit in tormenting his conscious anymore. He was now sobbing, his face dripping with tears and mucus.

Joshua was at the window, peering. "We've got company." He spotted two men running across the street.

"Mr. Frederickson, tell your people to stand down. We need answers only you can give." Mr. Zinkes warned him.

Mr. Frederickson hesitated, and then shouted, "Stand down! Do not engage."

Mr. Johansen came and sat in front of him. "Your organization approached me. I want in. I want this other group just as much as you do. It is not in our best interest to leave this place without knowing who they are and why they are trying to kill us. My life is at stake because they have linked me with your organization in Cairo. We need your help and if you don't trust me by now, then you never will. I need an answer before you leave. Am I in, or do we walk away and leave Apollyon holding the bag?"

His face was red and fully soaked with tears and sweat. "For now, it would not be in our best interest to see you leave, but the final decision is not mine to make. Fifteen powerful families will protect what is theirs, to the ends of the earth. I will take the information back and contact you tomorrow morning by eight a.m. That information will detail where they will be meeting. Believe me, I am on a time frame to find these people. My life is on the line. The Apollyon make people disappear." Mr. Frederickson finished with desperation in his voice.

Sublime spoke calmly and gratifying, "So, do we, Mr. Frederickson—so do we."

Recognition dawns on his face. "I will get back to you either way by tomorrow morning."

Chapter 16

Assassins Credo

Sublime escorted Mr. Frederickson to the elevator, through the lobby and out the front door. Two men met him at the door, and he instructed them to stand down. Sublime recognized one of them from when they were in Egypt. As she was about to turn to go inside, she sensed someone staring. It was a woman from across the roadway. A crowd walked by, impeding her view. She disappears. Sublime goes up to the surveillance floor. McBride's busy monitoring the M-80. "I need you to roll the video back fifteen minutes from the front of the building, specifically, across the street." Scrolling back, two minutes later, she says, "Stop the tape." Sublime called out to Myna Bird, "I need you to look at something."

Myna Bird recognized the woman, covering her mouth. "I need to speak to you."

"Sure, follow me." Behind closed doors, Sublime asked, "Is that the woman you were chasing yesterday?"

"That's her." Myna Bird asserted.

Sublime said, "She scowled at me as though sending a message. It was a little weird, because it reminded me of the time we were in Cairo and you attacked me."

Myna Bird silently pondered this. She places her fist under her chin. "She is here to kill me because of our past."

"Who is this woman and what does she want with you?" Sublime asked.

"Her name is Ty Chin. She was more of a sister when we were training to be assassins. I befriended her, and we fled together. When she revealed her plan to kill our master's son, who was only five months old, I refused to allow her to do it. I opposed her to save his life. He lives today in an undisclosed adoptive family, and she's never forgiven me for my betrayal. Early on, she was better at everything. I soon surpassed her. I didn't want to kill her, but to save the child—I tried. She survived because the police came, and she ran. I ran with the child, pretending he was my own." Myna Bird turned to Sublime, "I must face her and one of our souls will leave their body."

"Your soul will stand before God in peace. Your life is different now, and God has forgiven you. Isn't there another way to deal with this situation?" Sublime asked.

"Ty Chin has not forgiven me, and she will wait for her chance. Now that she knows I'm alive, she will never give up."

"She will have her chance with all of us," Sublime said.

"Promise me." Kim put her hand on Sublime's arm.

"What is it?" Sublime asked.

"If we meet Ty Chin face to face, I want no intervention. If we must die, then I prefer she goes by my hand and mine alone."

"Remember, life and death are in God's hands. You will only take her life if God allows it." Sublime tells her.

"I understand, but she belongs to me, so promise me!" Sublime agreed and left the discussion on Ty Chin for later.

~

The day was long, and the night even longer. She sees the shadowy figure through the sheer curtains in the night lights from below. Myna Bird wondered whether Ty Chin was head of the group or just a pawn, as they always had been to the Credo. Sublime finds Myna Bird outside on the terrace practicing Tai Chi. There was only silence as Sublime leans on the railing and waits for Myna Bird to finish. Myna Bird stands with her hands in the prayer position and opens her eyes to see Sublime standing at the rail. Myna Bird moves next to her and the silence continues for a few seconds.

"You're worried about having to face Ty Chin?"

"Not worried. I'm aware of her hatred for me. Back then, as teenagers, she and I sparred secretly, where no one could hear us. She said one or both of us would die if we don't follow, as they say. Ty Chin thought out our plan of escape. I told her my goal was to do as they said. Endure everything they've got and when it's time, I'd kill them. She would always tell me to keep my voice down. I would always tell her it didn't matter if they killed me. Either they kill me now or they'd die later. We both grew as experts. I became their top assassin, and Ty Chin followed. They never allowed us to leave, except for jobs. Our master's security force escorted us to each location. They kept us chained and beat us until they knew we were loyal to them. Used and abused for their pleasure, we would do anything to comply and not get tortured to death. White cement shakes with a metal cot and half-moon brick tile roofing. One week earlier, unnoticed, I hid in a delivery truck. Travelling back and forth from the main house and Assassin's Edge. Once I knew how to get to the home, I traveled back to Assassin's Edge on foot. Ty Chin covered for me, and I made it back without being noticed. We planned to carry out our escape during the graduation ceremony of other recruits the following week, and they were unsuspecting of our egregious disloyalty. The night we escaped. We lurked outside of where our master lived. Ty Chin seethed with revenge. The home was a mile away from the training facility at Assassin's Edge. That night, we took the lives of the master and his wife. Ty Chin found their child lying in its crib. As she was about to cut the child's throat, I pushed her away from the crib. I told her, 'We can't take this child's life. A curse will come upon us.' She was so sure the child would grow up to seek vengeance, and she wasn't willing to take that chance. I was now pleading with her. Letting her know he'll never know what we did tonight—no one would. She was adamant and tried to go after the child again. I grabbed him from his crib and told her I would kill her where she stood. She looked at me with instant hatred and she said, 'If you keep the child alive, we part right here.' Still holding the child, I told her, 'Do what you will. This child will not die by our hand, and he will never know what his father did to us.' I could see my words hurt her. The fact that I would side with this child over her. She called me a stubborn fool. She then tried to go after the child again and I blocked the knife with a Shuriken. I lay the child into its crib and pursued Ty Chin. We fought for ten minutes, breaking everything in our path. We heard the police coming. Ty Chin turned and disappeared through an open window and into the dark. I gathered what I could find for the boy. As I was searching, I found ten thousand dollars in a desk drawer. We disappeared into the darkness. I later found out that a servant we missed, found the parents dead and called the police. I saw her on the news. Before sunrise, exhausted and weary, I snuck into a military cargo van headed north and stayed on the road for three hours. I boarded a flight out of Hong Kong with the child and landed in Australia. I left the child on the steps of an orphanage without being seen."

~

Myna Bird only dozed for a few hours before getting up from her dream of Ty Chin. Groggy, she asked Euphrates, "How long have I been out?"

"Just a few hours. I didn't want to wake you. Sublime and I traded places on surveillance watch. Can I ask you a question?"

"No problem. I have to make a run to the lavatory first."

"Sure." When she came back, Euphrates was pacing the floor.

"Are you okay?" Kim asked.

Fumbling, he said, "Yes, no, yes! Um, I wanted to ask you if you are interested in me!" Euphrates didn't move, holding his breath.

Her quirky response eased his nervousness. "Uh, huh?" She sat. "Uh, I can't answer yes or no to that question right now. I have a lot on my mind. I will say I like you and if we make it out alive, I'd consider going out with you. To be honest, I can't think about it right now."

"Okay, I can live with that. I wanted to clear the air and my head of any uncertainties or misconstrued banter between us," he told her.

"I'm glad I got that cleared up for you." It wasn't sarcasm, but bewilderment. *Why did he pick now to express his feelings?* She thought. Euphrates walked out of the room and headed to the penthouse.

~

Waiting to hear from Mr. Frederickson, A7 acknowledged their top priority was to stop whoever was doing the killing. With speculation of Ty Chin's involvement in the bombings, Myna Bird was the enticement to draw her in.

"I know she will watch us," Sublime stated with confidence. As she was about to continue, McBride called, "There was a note left for Kim."

"It's Ty Chin." Myna Bird said.

"Pick up the note and bring it." Sublime instructs McBride. They still had two hours to go before receiving their answer from Mr. Frederickson.

McBride brought the note, "Package delivery."

"Thanks McBride."

"You are welcome." Sublime turned and closed the door. "Here you are." Sublime handed the note to Myna Bird.

"Thanks." She opens the note and reads it out loud. "I need to speak to you. Meet me at the River Seine, Pier 33 at three p.m. Don't be late, because you will not have this opportunity again, Ty Chin." She folded the note. "I assure you she is not looking to talk. She's out for blood."

Mr. Zinkes spoke up, "I realize your passion and investment in this matter. We will honor what you have requested and not interfere in this matter with you and Ty Chin, but it is not up for deliberation whether you will go alone. It will compromise Euphrates to be in the open, so he will not go. Sublime and X-Ray will go with you and they will not interfere. If you can reason with her without battle, then do so. If you are not, then you must do what you must."

"Thank you, Mr. Zinkes," Myna Bird said.

Sublime turned to X-Ray and Myna Bird. "Let's get ready. We don't want to walk into a trap." They head to McBride, giving him the pier coordinates to get intel. "If we're to meet at the pier walkway, these positions here and here are our weak points." On the imagery scope, it showed both spots with red dots. "I will take the left flank. I guess you get the right." She looked at X-Ray. "You can have whatever side you want. The choice is always yours to make. I would never stand in the way of you making your own choice," he responded sarcastically. Sublime looked at X-Ray as though he had lost it. Maybe he had.

He never confronted Sublime about the exchange between her and Myna Bird in the training room he overheard. She ignored him and the commentary.

At one o'clock, they headed toward the wharf, taking thirty-five minutes to arrive. Sitting in the silver van, with two windows in the front doors, McBride raised the scope camera to scan the area. Myna Bird searched to determine whether Ty Chin would show up early and looked for any unexpected movement. At two-thirty, they made a last review of their weapons. The rear doors to the van opened and the three get out and head toward their destinations on the wharf.

Myna Bird stood at the pier's edge as Ty Chin walked up without making a sound. Although her back was turned, she sensed Ty Chin's presence and said, "I see you are early."

"I see you haven't squandered your discipline, and I see you have brought company." Ty Chin said.

Myna Bird now shifts toward Ty Chin. "Yes, they are my colleagues. They will not interfere."

Ty Chin grinned, "Are your people trained assassins as well?"

"No, their training is beyond what we received at the Assassin's Edge."

"Oh! I can see that since both of my people are out cold," Ty Chin observed.

"Ty, we are not here to kill your people. They're unconscious. I am here to reason with you, if possible. To ask you to stop what you are doing with the Apollyon." Myna Bird considered her words, trying to get info on the group doing the bombings. "There are members of my team you have put in jeopardy and you killed two in that last bombing. We have the situation under control. Your group can stop and let us take care of Apollyon. that way, we will reach our two goals."

Ty Chin postures with smugness, folding her arms in stout opposition. "You don't seem to get the point of why I called you here. I'm not here regarding Apollyon. I'm here to finish what we started ten years ago. Plus, Black Rain won't be going anywhere because we are all over the world. We will stop at nothing to wipe out the Apollyon members, and that includes you if you've joined them."

"First, you have murdered innocent people." Myna Bird stated.

"Collateral Damage and if you don't get that by now, then I feel sorry for you." Ty Chin smiled.

"Ty, I have changed since we left Hong Kong ten years ago. I accepted Jesus Christ of Nazareth as my Lord and Savior. God loves you and He doesn't want you to perish in this life without knowing who He is. Please listen, I'm not your enemy. I wasn't ten years ago and I'm not now. If you continue down this road, our two groups will be at war. Our goal for the Apollyon is the same, but Black Rain is going about it the wrong way. Within the

Apollyon organization, we can only break it down from the inside and you don't have the resources to do it. We have someone on the inside. Black Rain will continue to kill their members and innocent people, but will never destroy Apollyon. One person dies, they recruit someone else for their plot for world supremacy. If you keep killing these families off, they are just going to go into hiding. We'll never find out who their true leader is until God says so, but killing them off will not bring that any faster."

Ty Chin never shifted from her position. She stared at Myna Bird for a few moments. She explains, "Black Rain's mission is to exterminate Apollyon and take back the free world."

"Let me ask you a question. Are you the leader of Black Rain or are you a pawn for the mad person who can't control their people?" Myna Bird is now tired of talking.

"If you must know, I am the leader in Paris." Ty Chin replied.

"I am asking you to back off. If you continue to pursue this, we will come after you with everything in our power. You don't understand what we are capable of. I've learned things you can't even fathom. My life and my perspective have changed. To die in Christ is to gain eternal life, so I will die for what I believe. Are you willing to die for Black Rain?" Myna Bird asked.

"Kim, I don't know who you're with, and I don't care. Rest assure, we will die for our cause." Ty Chin.

"One last question I must ask. Were you involved in the Cairo bombing?"

"No, I have been in France for five years. Before that, I lived in Australia, making sure there were no stones left unturned." As Ty Chin finishes her statement, Myna Bird moved in to destroy Ty Chin, going straight for the jugular. Ty Chin countered with a left elbow to the back of Myna Bird' spine. She stumbles and regains her footing. Ty Chin smiles, "I am not your shadow anymore, Kim. I have trained and waited for this day to come."

"So, have I, Ty." Kim attacks with a spinning back kick and as she lands on her other foot, the knife pulled from her leg holster strikes Ty Chin's left cheek. Ty Chin postures again and touches her cheek, wiping the blood off and onto her clothes.

"Ty, I am giving you one more opportunity to leave alive. Our purpose does not have to be our deaths. If we continue this, one of us will die."

"Death was the purpose of my asking you here today. I'm confident the person leaving alive will not be you." Ty Chin counters. Myna Bird returns to her stance. Both glaring at each other as they know this will be to the death. Kim flashes back to the fight with Mr. Zinkes. She smiled. The ferocity of their fight increased with each blow and cut. Matched, Myna Bird runs to attack Ty Chin, ramming her head into her abdomen. She grabs hold of Ty Chin's legs and did a back-hammer kick to Ty Chin's cranium, crushing the bones in her face. Ty Chin falls backwards on the concrete. The dust surrounds her as the force of the fall crushes the back of her skull. With her eyes wide open, her face falls to the side, blood runs from the side of her mouth. From the blows Kim received from Ty Chin, she limped over to Sublime. Myna Bird grabs a hold of her and cries. Sublime grabs her, and they walk to the van.

"I can't wait to get back to Vermont." Sublime states. She lays Myna Bird across the back seat in exhaustion, crying for a soul lost.

At the hotel, in the lobby, were several patrons wondering whether Myna Bird was the victor. There was no enjoyment, only grief for the young woman lost long ago. Now, with their leader gone, it would take time before Black Rain could regroup, because there were other players to consider and now one of theirs was dead. They had to move on the Apollyon while they had the chance with no obstruction.

~

Arriving at the penthouse, X-Ray helped Sublime put Myna Bird in her room to rest. She turns to X-Ray. "Can you get me a clean towel and bandages to clean her wounds?"

"Sure. She's going to be fine. A few bruises and minor cuts." X-Ray says.

"Her body is not what I'm concerned about. Another person is dead, and we don't know how deep that wound will go."

"We'll be there for her, but that's something she's going to have to forgive herself for." X-Ray expresses.

Myna Bird moans as Sublime pats her cuts.

"I'm thankful she made it out alive."

X-Ray leaves to get more badges. Euphrates sees X-Ray leave Myna Bird's room and knocks at the door. "Is Myna Bird all right?" he asked.

Sublime comes to the door and closes it behind her, and they both sit in the living room. She sits in front of Euphrates on the coffee table. "She will be fine. This was a tough battle. She prevailed by killing Ty Chin."

"You know I have feelings for her." Euphrates states. He was waiting for a sarcastic remark.

"I never want to presume, but I could tell. She likes you too. We long for human connection and relationships, and sometimes we must make tough decisions. I am in love with Joshua and although he knows, I can't think of being with him during this mission. My goal and priority are to do the will of God and complete my purpose and God's Holy plan. You need to decide what's most important, then act on it or let go. Tomorrow's not promised to any of us, and the fight today could have gone the other way. With the love growing inside of you for Myna Bird, can you let her go if the time comes? I love Joshua and if God says the same after this mission is complete, we may continue our journey. It seems harsh to say this now, but I can let him go with love," she states.

Sublime gets up and walks toward the window and stares over the skyline of the green mountains standing at attention. The horizon cast its glares off the sun and sky's illustrations of warmth. Glows of amber and orange. Another day would set on sadness and wondering. The overcast day retreated to let the sunlight's ray's breakthrough as it went down to the west.

X-Ray returns with the bandages and he sees Sublime by the window and Euphrates on the couch. She asks, "Can you bandage her wounds? I'll check on her in a bit."

Sublime, speaking to Euphrates, "What did Mr. Frederickson say?"

Euphrates sits back. "They have agreed to meet. We will get our directions soon."

"Well, we should have at least a month before Black Rain is back in operation again here. We can't waste any more time. We must complete this mission within a month, or our ties can be severed, and we lose our contact with them forever." Sublime turns away from the window and heads toward the room where Kim was recovering.

Euphrates stops her. "I'll check on her. You get rest. We have a busy day tomorrow." Sublime nods her head and walks past Euphrates to her room. She turns back as she reaches for the door handle. "Good night, Mr. Johansen."

"Good night, Sublime."

X-Ray leaves before Euphrates gets to Myna Birds room. He enters his room and they all rest for the night.

Chapter 17

30 Day Countdown

Euphrates was on the phone. "Mr. Frederickson, there's some good news. The positive is we've determined the identity of the group harming our families. Black Rain involves many cell groups across the world. The bad is their present whereabouts are unknown. The head of the Paris group is dead. So, we have twenty-nine days before they regroup and come after us again. Their leader was a woman named Ty Chin. She was an experienced assassin from Hong Kong. I'm offering you this knowledge because there's limited time to act."

Mr. Frederickson swiped his brow and realized time was of the essence. "Thank goodness, they've pushed the meeting up to two days from now. They will contact each family two hours before the meeting. So, make sure someone is available to receive the call."

"Mr. Frederickson, I need you to call the heads. Meeting without having my bodyguard present is not wise. If it isn't doable, then I will not make this or any other meeting. I need that to be clear to the families. I am not prepared to risk what occurred in Cairo."

"Mr. Johansen, I will communicate the information and will get back to you within the hour."

"I will wait for your call." Euphrates ends the call.

~

A7 gathers in the dining area at five o'clock, and Mr. Frederickson had not called back concerning the bodyguards attending the meeting. Remaining around the dinner table eating and standing by, "I pray Mr. Frederickson convinces them to let in the bodyguards. I don't want to go in there alone with no backup. I think they are letting me in because of Black Rain. There's something very sinister developing."

Mr. Zinkes said, "It will depend on how lengthy the meeting goes. Euphrates construct the talk your way. You both will have recording mechanisms, so we will lose nothing. Our mission is the same. Find out who the antichrist is and take out Apollyon."

Sublime wants to make sure Mr. Zinkes just stated a change in their mission. "So, according to your statement, our mission has changed?"

"Yes, Sublime. That change will happen down the line. We will not engage to destroy but will continue to gather information—for now." Sublime continues to eat.

As Euphrates picks up his cranberry juice, his mini-AIS buzzes. "You are late, Mr. Frederickson," Euphrates states.

"Unfortunately, necessary. Calling the families takes time. Concurred with your position and they will bring their guards along. The struggle to keep clarity of purpose and keep everyone intact is troublesome at this stage, and they selected not to take any chances, since the threat is undeniable. Reminder, they will contact everyone in two days."

"Okay, Mr. Frederickson." Euphrates drops the signal and calls McBride, "Are we veiled?"

"Yes." McBride replied.

"Frederickson will call in two days. With bodyguards approved. I will require a few tracking mechanisms. Tracking these individuals is a priority once we leave France. There's much work to do."

They concluded their meal and met in the penthouse's boardroom. "Tonight, we will head to the JC-12 to work out our plan. I don't wish to do it in this hotel. For the next forty-eight hours, establish your posts at the airplane, the vans and everything else belonging to us." Mr. Zinkes directs, "What are you waiting for? Let's get a move on, time delays for no one!"

Everyone jumped out of their seats. Xerxes and Shadow were on airplane duty. Sublime and X-Ray took the vans. Euphrates and Myna Bird checked surveillance and weapons with McBride, and Leopard watches the perimeter of the hotel for any signs of trouble with Mr. Laemel and Mr. Lyemel.

~

X-Ray and Sublime were alone at the vans. "How do you see this ending? And what is the probability of us getting out of this alive?" X-Ray asked.

"My apprehension is the distractions surfacing. Myna Bird with Ty Chin, Euphrates with Myna Bird, among others like Black Rain. I'm wondering if everybody recognizes the consequence of our actions. If we don't get our brains out of the clouds, the likelihood of us getting out of this alive has significantly declined."

X-Ray grabs Sublime's arm and realizes her rationalization of relationships was faltering and was not looking at this as a life experience. Rubbing her forearm, "Expand your knowledge and consider the significance of how love works. Your previous employers forced you to set your emotions aside. The events are different now, Sublime. Consider, we are in a life-threatening situation. We can't lay our finger on it. But if nothing else, Christ was the greatest illustration of love. He accepted His mission and aim. I'm certain He saw someone being whipped and crucified, and the image came back to His remembrance in the Garden of Gethsemane. Jesus knew what to expect in the visual but He could never imagine the anguish, suffering, torture, and pain he had to endure on the cross. I can think of how much He endured, but I'll never know unless I go through it myself. We can't have the mentality that what we do here will shift, prevent, or alter what God's plan and purpose are. God chose us, knowing what was to arise between us. The obstacles are purposeful, Sublime. God understands what we are facing and knows who the antichrist is. God knows how each of us reacts to love, war, pressure and just dealing with our own existence. I've studied and according to the scriptures, he will be a Jew, because he will sit on the throne in the temple. If he's not a Jew, they will accept him. He will deceive many because he will claim to be a god and he will do wonders. With or without us, they will reveal him. This group can't be a part of that revelation. We are not here to stop the plan of God., we are here to fulfill it. I love you and that will never change, just like you can't alter the distractions that are cropping up. My love for you is part of God's fulfillment, and the same goes for Euphrates and Myna Bird. You will not stop love, because God blessed it. Quit fretting about everyone screwing up this mission. Each one of us realizes what we must do and what our failure may mean. Each of us knows when the Father calls us to stand before Him, then there will be no avoiding it. Trust God, He knows what He's doing, or is it you don't trust yourself?"

"It's not that I don't trust myself, it's everybody else I don't trust, when their minds are on other than this mission."

"Again, you are not depending on God, because God is who formed this team."

"How can you believe that?" Sublime asked.

"Because depending on God is to depend on His plan. He will lead and guide you if you are living for Him and seeking Him to establish your steps and lead you by the Holy Spirit. Your faith can not be in us. Sublime, your faith must be in God. We are his earthly vessels, nothing more, nothing less." X-Ray Said.

Sublime didn't want him to see her upset, but he saw it. "I will rest in the van."

Hours pass, and Sublime emerges from the vehicle, sliding the door open. "Did you take a nice nap?" X-Ray gets his coat out of the passenger side as she still stands at the open sliding door.

"No rest. My mind was in a wrestling match with God. He won. I repented to God and I owe an apology to you and the others. I make no excuse for how God has created me and I can't get so bound up in this flesh that I can't see I am struggling. It's just tough not knowing. It's hard not to be the one in authority, in control."

X-Ray walks around to the open slide door and hugs Sublime, "Actions illustrate surrender. Self-control and turning your will over to God is the hardest thing any of us can achieve. That means we are trusting without seeing. Remember, faith is things hoped for, and waiting on the manifestation of a miracle, needs, desires, and not we wished it to happen. Hope delights me most. God can do all. It's the promise of what He does that is most cherished by me. You are not walking in faith if someone lays everything out before you and you know what will take place. Where's the adventure of living like that? What astonishes me is the scriptures expose so much to us but most of humanity yet don't believe. Now that's foolish."

"I love you Joshua, and I pray whatever God's will is, we do it together, you, me and the team." Sublime says with a smile.

Still embracing, car tires grab the concrete, speeding up the garage ramps, when Sublime spots the two men in a classic model of Citroën e-Mehari. Sublime pushes X-Ray to the side. "Get down now!" Bullet's fly, and they crouch behind the van, the car passes. Sublime comes from behind on the other side to put a round behind the driver's brain. The car plunges into the wall next to the elevator, and the passenger staggers out. The would-be hitman lifts his hands while walking toward X-Ray. He then reaches for a gun and X-Ray puts a slug in his heart, and one between the eyes. He falls backward to the car door, sliding down the door to the ground. They left the wrecked car smoldering and the other dead body on the side of it. Two dead, and there was no logical reason. X-Ray walks up beside Sublime, "This isn't Apollyon, it's Black Rain. We must leave now. They know where we are." Joshua runs up the stairs to let them know what happened in the parking structure. Joshua speaks to Mr. Zinkes, "We believe it's Black Rain. We need to leave now before others arrive. Knowing our location can compromise this mission."

Mr. Zinkes got up from his chair. "The surveillance team can stay for now. Pack and move to the jet." Sublime told McBride to delete the footage. Recorded in the cloud, the manipulation was easy. No Law Enforcement came, and no one saw what transpired. X-Ray packed his and Sublime's belongings and helped her transport the vans to loading. Myna Bird, still sore, Euphrates, Mr. Zinkes, and Leopard throw their gear and sacks into the rear, and Euphrates and X-Ray closed the doors.

"Let's move! Xerxes, Shadow, we are on our way." Sublime spoke over the transmission frequency. Arriving on the tarmac, everyone didn't bother taking their baggage out. One by one, they ran onto the JC-12, as Xerxes and Shadow were expecting their arrival. They drew the window shades as they sat around the conference table. Mr. Zinkes knew their thoughts. He says, "As we have left McBride and his unit, I am sure within a few minutes, the police will scour the area. Someone should have discovered the bodies by now. It does us no good to face Black Rain unprepared. We will wait for the opportune time to deal with them. Shadow, I need you in constant contact with McBride to give us any intelligence filtered through the hotel. After this meeting, Euphrates and X-Ray, please secure the vehicles out of sight. This move should have Black Rain at bay for now. Everyone needs to rest. An interminable day awaits us tomorrow."

Within 36 hours, Mr. Frederickson called, right on schedule, "We will meet at 2:00 p.m. Please make sure you will be ready to leave by noon. We will provide the directions as you drive. The information I can report to you right now is that you will reach the Canal Saint-Martin Area. Be ready for driving instructions by twelve noon. If you do not answer the first time, they will not attempt again." Euphrates hangs up.

"We have to be ready to go by twelve. The meeting is at two o'clock. We will need to return to the Ritz to pick up the tracking GPS, which will be there by 11:00 am. It will give us directions as we drive. They will track our movements but won't be able to track the van following us. McBride needs to clone the device to track me." Euphrates states.

Sublime, now giving out orders, "X-Ray, Myna Bird, and Leopard, you will trail us from the van. We need you to block any interference as we drive. Black Rain will continue to search for us and may follow as we leave the hotel. Euphrates, you cannot retrieve it from the hotel. It will have to be Mr. Laemel or Mr. Lyemel. McBride needs to do his magic within fifteen minutes. Once we are in, we will not move on the Apollyon. We'll get as much information as we can for now."

It was eleven-thirty and McBride finished duplicating the tracking device. Everything was progressing as designed. Shadow and Xerxes drop the contact GPS off to Sublime, two blocks away. Everyone was alert, and the adrenaline was pumping. Sublime handed it to Mr. Laemel, "We're on." The rules dictated it had to be on five minutes before noon. At noon, the GPS beeped, transmitting instructions to their destination. Two hours and many turns later, they reach the Polmier Mansion. Everyone arrived simultaneously and a silent greeting followed. Locked in the lower level of the compound, the butler says, "Good afternoon." Bodyguards stand directly behind each of the representatives The Butler directs them to their respective places at an oblong, cherry wood table, with chairs covered with blue velvet material. Natural light seeps through the windowpanes with crushed blue velvet drapes hanging from the ceiling. As if on cue, they all sit at the same time. Recognizing none of them, it was an essential thing for Sublime that none of them knew her either. The other bodyguards stood there and had no inkling of what their employers planned for the world.

Silence crept in, and this was the moment for Mr. Johansen to take over the dialogue. He stands. "As the newest member of this most distinguished group, I must inform you of a terrorist organization called 'Black Rain.' We have disposed of the leader of the Paris unit, but there are more units in other countries. While in Cairo, you approached me to join the Apollyon. There was never an opportunity to learn why this group exists and how I could be of use."

A man they had never seen before got up from a side chair and spoke. "My name is Redford Morgan. I am the Ambassador for Apollyon. Our purpose now is to learn who you are and for you to know who we are in return. Today, we stand unafraid of this group called Black Rain. Until you identified them, we could not turn up any information on these individuals."

Mr. Johansen, confident in his ability, "Well, that's odd, having the women and men in this room who represent many of the world leaders of today. How is it my family could find them? No disrespect meant, but your man Frederickson was sweating bullets. I'm not seeking for any credit here. I want what's best for the entire world order, and not one of us can take this group for granted. They will die for their beliefs and I am not sure what this group's position is yet. Black Rain threatens our way of life. At this stage, I wish to learn who you are and what's the intensions of Apollyon?"

Mr. Morgan walked to the head seat but remained standing. "Mr. Johansen, is it? The time has arrived for the nations to learn of our existence. Since creation, when the Watchers, the Angels from the universal cosmos, slept with the Women of Men, ancient writings state the figure most claim as the god of Noah wiped our glorious race out. What the ancient writings didn't state in simple expression or revelation was that someone would and has discovered a seed from our ancestors and is alive as we speak here today. The Prince of the power of the air will rule the universe. He is just waiting for the appointed time. He will rule and govern with a just hand, and he is seeking for us to establish his throne. Our place is at his feet during his advancement to power. He expects us to succeed, where there will be a Universal Government. He is looking to us to fulfill our destiny and be by his side in the new kingdom on earth. For now, your pledge to take your place in history and give your lives, resources, and allegiance to reign with him to achieve the goal of peace for this world. We are talking no more wars or people going hungry for food or knowledge. There will be no more homelessness and disease. This achievement will not be without your cooperation and dedication to be a part of this history-making event and bring in a Universal Order."

They all clap like trained seals. Euphrates claps as a seal, too. He made it look real. The other bodyguards and Sublime stood still as good little soldiers, motionless. Euphrates knew inside she wanted to destroy them—it wasn't time. Knowing the whereabouts of as many of the families was more important in keeping track of them. They'd leave for their home destination until summoned to meet again. We were one step closer to the leader of the Apollyon. Euphrates stood as Mr. Morgan was going to dismiss them.

"One more thing Mr. Morgan, I understand you are representing the man-watcher but I'm not the only one who wants to meet him in the flesh as I have given my allegiance to such a one who will bring our day of triumph."

"Mr. Johansen, in due time. He is eager to meet all of you. It will be in the next several months. Timing is crucial. With Black

Rain running rampant, we must be careful to make sure our leader has the utmost security, and we are sure they are no longer a threat. As Mr. Frederickson informed me, you'll handle them for us. I wish you speed and luck. If this satisfies your answer, I adjourn us."

Just as they came, everyone left in silence. '*If Mr. Zinkes was here, then we could know what they were thinking.*' Sublime thought.

The guessing game continued. Euphrates got in the car and they did not speak, because they didn't know whether they attempted to bug the limo or us, just as we had done to them. Having ample opportunity to do so, they didn't want to take any chances. Sublime wanted to take them out but understood the timing was not right—yet.

~

In the airplane and heading home, they debriefed. It was now a waiting game. Although they met Mr. Morgan, they were yet extremely far from the end. They would wait longer to meet this man of perdition that was to save the universe from extinction. Such a dismal reflection, Satan had deluded them without dispute. Could any of the members shift to the right side? To receive the truth and renounce the lies before them? Entrenched in their own belief and deception, Apollyon could not perceive truth. They were blind to it.

Silence was the mainstay of the trip back home. They felt relief from the past tension. Michael expressed his intentions to Kim, and Kim gave him hope for the future.

Mr. Zinkes wanted to express himself and his sentiment. "McBride and his team will stay for one week and meet us back at headquarters. I thank you, Sublime, for restraining yourself and not destroying the Apollyon."

Michael jumps in, flying his arms around, "I knew it. I could feel your emotional outrage at what was being said!"

"Yet, you knew I wouldn't. I have more self-control than that, don't I, Mr. Zinkes?" Tracy wanted him to vouch for what she was saying.

He overlooked her childish petition for affirmation and went on, "I trust you all realize we are close and must remember our mission. We are to destroy this group in time, but are not to destroy the leader of the Apollyon. His purpose and destiny haven't changed, but it cannot be with this group of men and women. There are others who will lead him into his false glory." Mr. Zinkes said.

Carsen states, "In my study of the scriptures and other writing material, I came across a book by Thomas Horn, who discussed the return of Apollo/Nimrod in 2012. In his book, he says how it was possible this could happen through a biotech resurrection. They found a sacred coffin or casket of Osiris at the Giza Plateau in 1998 by a man name Zahi Hawass. They found someone used DNA to resurrect the Apollonian tissue. This was forty years ago. Which if this is true, then he is now a full-fledged adult?"

Kelton opened the Holy Scriptures saying, Revelation 17:8 (NKJV) says, 'the beast that you saw was, and is not, and will ascend out of the bottomless pit and go to perdition. And those who dwell on the earth will marvel, whose names are not written in the Book of Life from the foundation of the world, when they see the beast that was, and is not, and yet is.'

"Do you mean they found DNA from one of the Fallen Angels and created the son of perdition incarnate?" Michael asked.

Mr. Zinkes gets up from his chair and said, "Yes, this could be conceivable. They have been engineering animals and plants for over sixty years. It was just a matter of time for them to crack the code with humans. We have to do more research on this phenomenon." Mr. Zinkes seemed disconcerted at this news Carsen and Kelton provided, and it also surprised Tracy at his reaction to the news. What was bothering him? Was this an unexpected revelation? It looked like Mr. Zinkes was unaware of the situation, or he was deliberately keeping the team in the dark. He was unaware of Tracy's questions because of his focus on what they learned.

Chapter 18

Black Rain

Experts predicted Y2K to be a doomsday event that would turn the world's economic system upside down. Computers running the world's banking systems would not recognize the double zero for the calendar year and crash. However, nothing happened, and no one died. The actions of terrorists in 2001 made the United States vulnerable by using our own planes as weapons of mass destruction. The USA, its own worst enemy. Not only had enemy terrorists abroad, but domestic terrorists but our chickens returning home to roost. God's wake-up call for His people to return to Him. The housing market crashed in 2008, and so did Wall Street. People lost homes, their life savings, pensions, and the economy was slow to recover. By 2010, they predicted gas prices at ten dollars a gallon. It didn't happen. Ancient Mayan calendars were reported to have predicted more dire predictions of the world ending, or some other life-threatening event in 2012. No one knew what the end of the calendar meant if anything. The Mayan Civilization had long vanished, and only ancient writings and ruins remained. Speculation could only prevail, as those with historical knowledge suggested they may not have had time to complete the calendar because of a catastrophe, natural or otherwise. They disappeared from the face of the earth. Was it a natural disaster or as some thought, *'Aliens?'* In 2020 was the most tumultuous time our generation had ever experienced. A worldwide, Corona Virus Pandemic. A Pandemic that cost hundreds of thousands of lives, just in the United States alone. Not only were they dealing with death, but a presidential election for the ages. Both sides of the aisle blamed each other for stolen elections and voter fraud. 2021 saw the beginning of people's rights being taken away by vaccine mandates. It was hypocrisy. We could get an abortion, but we had no say in the matter whether we took a vaccine or not. By 2030, they turned to extreme measures and called themselves States of America. Un-united in saving itself from destruction. White nationalists, atheists, Black Lives Matter supporters, Blue Lives Matter supporters, and people of all faiths all desired their rights.

People felt as though it was Sodom and Gomorrah all over again. It threatened every move made in politics, health care, the schools, and our livelihood. We had taken God out of everything and even churches. It was now a production of feel-good services. In 2044, we were closer to knowing this man of perdition. The world was going through a major shift in thinking in realistic terms. They speculated the anti-Christ would come out of Spain or the European nations. Good, or indifferent, the True and Living God was in control and most of humanity ignored His Word.

Heading back from Paris, the Dark Web clearly knew of Black Rain. The creeping place where Black Rain communicated with each other and for A7 to gather information on them to dissect their intelligence. Shadow had no issues in hacking into their network. They would soon learn the reason this information would be so vital to their mission and operation. Mr. Laemel spoke on the matter, "This is what Shadow found, countless figures who they've called antichrist, including Holy Roman Emperor Frederick II, Russian emperor Peter the Great, Pope John XXII, Benito Mussolini, American President Barack Obama, both George W. Bush's, Saladin, Napoleon Bonaparte, American

President Donald Trump, and German Dictator Adolf Hitler, just to name a few were of the Apocalyptic Prophecy era. Mysteries and parables that Christ left to the world were for our learning. Some took it to the extremes on both ends. Black Rain and the Apollyon are the same, having jobs to do before the end is to come. Interpreting the mysteries and parables according to their own knowledge and understanding. Both will end in the same place: eternal damnation."

Mr. Laemel finds the information needed on Black Rain's beginning on the dark web. "Beginning in the early 1900s, Benjamin T. McCloud discovered the prophecies of Michel De Nostradamus, born in 1503, a physician and seer. 1 Samuel 9:9, "Formerly in Israel, when a man went to inquire of God, he spoke thus: *'Come, let us go to the seer,'* for he, who is called a prophet, was called a seer." He continued, "Nostradamus wrote an Almanac containing information on future events. He did not foresee his theories being used to stop and ultimately kill people. The premonitions that had already taken place and those Benjamin could research, such as The Rise of Napoleon, The Death of King Henry II, and the French Revolution. He also followed many other prophecies, which sparked his path of destruction on God's behalf. When in 1917, as the First World War ended, three sisters from the Portuguese city of Fatima declared they saw an apparition of Mary, the mother of Jesus of Nazareth. Mary told them that a cosmic sign in the night would arrive before a second world war.

On January 25, 1938, an immense aurora appeared in the sky in Europe. The glow was so great, they could see it from Africa and America. Six weeks later, the annexation of Austria into Germany took place: (Annexation is the administrative action and concept in international law relating to the forcible acquisition of one state's territory by another state and held to be an illegal act. It is distinct from conquest, which refers to the acquisition of control over a territory involving a change of sovereignty, and differs from Cession, in which territory given or sold through treaty, since annexation is a unilateral act where territory seized and held by one state. It usually follows military occupation of a territory.) Thus, the Second World War became inevitable. In 1925, Benjamin began Black Rain officially, and turned it into an organization to monitor future prophecies to ensure other organizations didn't disrupt what was to take place. Considered a local conspiracy group, radicalizing perpetrators to an 'Eco Chamber' of thought, norms, and ideology. Benjamin lived another forty-years, and lived to see that the Atomic Bomb, and the 1966 London Fire, which happened. Benjamin held on tightly to his belief of what was to come through the Almanac book for future prophecies he determined would surely come. The Black Rain organization grew under Benjamin McCloud's leadership. At his death, Black Rain continued under the authority of Stephen Maringer, who took it further by studying, not only secular world prophecies but also biblical prophecies and spawned its mission to include the Apollyon and organizations like it, by attempting to dismantle their functions to take over the world. Succeeding many times, they too didn't realize their purpose for being would one day get extinguished.

"What conspiracy and how has it been effective in bringing about the destruction of so many lives?" Sublime asked.

Mr. Laemel answered, "It came about when powerful and secretive groups (the Illuminati, the Bilderberg Group, and other shadowy cabals) plotted to rule humanity with a single world government. We now know that groups have used political finance, social engineering, mind control, and fear-based propaganda to achieve their aims. They say signs of such underground thinking to be the pyramid on the reverse of the

Great Seal of the United States, strange and disturbing murals at Denver International Airport, and pentagrams in city plans. International organizations such as the World Bank, the IMF, the European Union, the United Nations, and NATO listed as founding organizations of such groups like the Apollyon."

Organizing with cell groups in other countries, since the 2028 elections, conspiracy theorists at heart, their aim was to hunt and kill every Apollyon member they could find. The theory of Black Rain was the Apollyon made up of International Elites' controlled industry, media, and their organizations. Most of all, they believed the Apollyon held high guard in government agencies with the goal of global domination. Black Rain had implicated their involvement in most of the major wars, famine in certain countries, and secretly staged events to bring in martial law to manipulate the economy, food, and drug industries, and handled the Covid-19 outbreak. Their Apocalyptic Prophecies, under the guise of self-preservation claims about the End-Times, have fueled their conspiracy theories. As there may be truth to some of it, when you don't do it God's way, you lose. Their motto: the Apollyon will bring about the antichrist, a leader who will supposedly create an oppressive world empire. Proven at this point to be true according to God's Word, but they're looking at the truth with blinders on.

"We must stop the Apollyon and Black Rain." Mr. Laemel states.

Chapter 19

Deserted Compound

Under the cover of darkness, and with added information about Black Rain at hand, they arrive at the Compound Headquarters to discover it empty.

"What in the heck is going on here? Everyone's fled!" Xerxes shouted.

Mr. Zinkes walked ahead, "Everybody, follow me. Ask no questions, Euphrates."

He flipped his hands up in protest. "Why do I bother to think around you humans?"

Mr. Zinkes put his palm on the pad and allowed the scanner to read the image of his eyes. The doors open, they get on the elevator and the floor drops a little as they descend to the Lab. They reach the bottom level and walk off the elevator. A computerized voice greets them. "Hello, Mr. Zinkes. Welcome back." The lab is clear, nothing but white walls, tables and an eerie silence of florescent lights flickering. They stand in front of the computer panel, "Hello R.U.T.H. (Remote Utilization Technology Hub), can you show the footage from the last thirty days and play any messages?" Mr. Zinkes asks.

"Yes, Mr. Zinkes, you have two unopened messages from Captain Collier. I will play the messages for you now."

The Compound surveillance intercepted a conversation onboard an airplane that indicated they knew the location of the airbase. That evening, we received an anonymous tip someone would raid the base. They had to act and remove all indications of staff and machinery, with or without positive verification. They couldn't take the chance. It was not a genuine threat. Within a few days' time, they moved everything and left it spotless. To protect their location, they took everyone to a deserted military base, and left R.U.T.H. to provide the information for Shadow. Everyone was on high alert. A second message followed, "Hello Mr. Zinkes, please write these coordinates as the messages will self-encrypt, erase, and RUTH will self-destruct in thirty minutes as Shadow created her to do." Everyone headed to the elevator.

"Goodbye, Mr. Zinkes."

"Goodbye R.U.T.H. We will communicate again."

"No, from now on you will talk to my clone."

"I will not forget you, R.U.T.H."

"And thank you, Shadow, for creating me."

Shadow stopped, "I will see you at our new location R.U.T.H. and will make certain you remember everything. A backdoor motherboard holds the self-destruct mechanism." Shadow ran and extracted the original processing unit. R.U.T.H. would stay as the original. They head back to the JC-12. Sublime walks to the cabin, "Cloak, and inserts the coordinates. We want no one to track our system or whereabouts."

"I'm on it." Xerxes responded.

Watching the surveillance footage, they recognized none. Mr. Zinkes expresses, "It was Black Rain who stumbled onto our compound to catch us off guard. They think we are a part of Apollyon."

Euphrates sat back in his chair and states, "We're in too deep to stop now. Immobilizing Black Rain before they do anymore damage is a priority. The question is, how did they find us?"

Sublime points to the guy on the screen, "We take him. We strike the head of the serpent. He's sloppy, but they're organized. Tomorrow, we go to war with Black Rain. If Apollyon suspects this group is no longer a threat, they may push their plans up."

Mr. Zinkes walks around the plane. "Tomorrow, I have to take a trip. I cannot tell you where I am traveling. I will return in two days."

~

Leaving everything else behind, their new home was over 2,040 miles away. At the base, they unloaded, and Captain Collier, Ms. Giles, and others gave them a cheerful welcome. It operated as a thriving airport, which opened to the public in 1995. Back in 2011, construction continued underneath the airport, which led into the mountainside. There were so many speculations and conspiracy theories about why and what they were building there. Below, the Denver International Airport (DIA) was a Deep Underground Military Base (D.U.M.B.) Constructed for presidents and the elite. This was being done because of the imminent doom that was predicted for 2012.

When 2012 came and went, something disastrous happened. The economy could never recover, as the government claimed. Inflation was too much for people to handle. Tired of big government, the movement became Operation Occupy, and they trampled big government and the money system as we knew it crashed. They bartered gold, silver, and other precious metals to the highest bidder, and money that existed was less than twenty-five cents on the dollar. When the Elite could no longer afford to hide in their million, billion, and trillion-dollar bunkers, they abandoned them. People had to help each other survive. A meteor or a pending disaster didn't force them in the place they were in. It was their arrogance that led them to believe they were in control. It had been fifteen years. There was no need for powerful military forces with resources limited. Many of the military bases were abandoned and supplies left behind. Leaving smaller forces to contain unsolvable problems, and create bigger ones to mass murder the unwanted.

Tracy gets off last. She had been here before with her father, at age nine. She remembered hiding in the men's barracks and not wanting to leave. *'Daddy, I don't wish to move from here.'*

'I know sweetheart, but daddy has to transfer to a different state. They are closing this base down and If you don't leave with us, mom will be very unhappy. She will miss you and Buster won't be able to stay with you either.' Thinking of the irony, if they hadn't closed the base, they may never have left, and her parents would be alive today - maybe. Joshua found her in the barracks hallway.

"Are you all right?" he asked.

"Yeah, my parents, and I and my dog, Buster, lived on this base. My dad knew where to locate me when I'd go missing. I always drifted to the guys, who were about eighteen or nineteen, because they looked so scared. I loved being around them. They reminded me of Myron."

"So, you have memories of this place?"

"I have wonderful memories." Joshua hugs her.

"Rest, because bright and early in the morning, we track Black Rain."

"Yes, I need to rest. I guess everyone does at this point. How's the bunker?" she asked.

"A little stuffy, but it will do for now." Joshua grabs her hand and starts down the corridor. Joshua kisses her on both of her cheeks and leaves her at her door. "Have pleasant dreams."

"Good night, Joshua." It had been many years since she lived, hid, or played in such a place. It was familiar, which brought back fond memories.

Chapter 20

Mr. Levi

Back to Paris, and Mr. Alerion Levi was the aim. Kelton used his R.U.T.H. Face Recognition Program to find Mr. Levi. Sublime was certain this man had the knowledge to dismantle Black Rain for a while, or for good. McBride was still in Paris when A7 returned to bring back Mr. Levi. McBride tailed him for two days prior and tracked him to his home. Sublime and X-Ray enter his apartment. Mr. Levi walked through his front door at midnight. Sublime used the *"special sauce"* Dr. Canno gave her and shot him in the neck to take him out without being heard or seen. X-Ray caught the bag in his arm, and Mr. Levi sank to the floor like a rag doll. Both carry him out the door, leaving down the fire escape from the apartment complex hallway. Mr. Lyemel was waiting below with the car, and they head to the plane.

Within three hours, Mr. Butler was on the JC-12, in route to Colorado. He awoke after an hour. "What am I doing here? Who are you people?" Sublime sits in front of him and smiles. Contemplating whether to confront him with his deeds or give him the silent treatment until they arrived at DUMB. His frantic and uncontained emotions led her to believe the latter would cause a heart attack.

"Mr. Levi right now is not the time to ask a lot of questions. We are on our way to another country, where the questions and answers will begin. For now, is there anything we can give you? Perhaps a building you can blow up or a group you can stalk and murder for your sick and wicked purpose." Sublime looks at him and relaxes back in her armchair. With the silence came increased anger. But he couldn't do anything but blow a blood vessel. She needed him to talk and to spill any information.

"Just to make sure we are clear about your purpose here, Mr. Levi, you have placed yourself in a dangerous situation. You have put your family in danger. We are monitoring them to ensure no one hurts them because of your involvement with Black Rain. Our hope with the knowledge I provided you just now, you will see fit to offer us the knowledge we seek on Black Rain." Mr. Levi's anger escaped him, and his posture slouched as he considered his family.

"Please, don't hurt my family." There were no tears. The quiver of his words was revealing.

"Mr. Levi, we never threaten innocent people. You have no reason to trust me in this area. You have my word nothing will happen to your family. We are not in the business of killing innocent people like Black Rain and the Apollyon. Is it casualties of war you call them? Well, we are specific to the targets we remove. We need to make sure you understand what our position is and what we will do to get the information we need. Levi, can I call you Levi?" Sublime asked.

"Oh, so this is about Apollyon?" he asks. "Whatever," he said, peeved.

"Mr. Levi, we are not bad people. We are trying to do the same thing you are to Apollyon, but we prefer to do it in a way that's pleasing to God. What we first want to know is how you found us?"

"It was Ty Chin's idea. She was sure she'd win. She planted the device on Myna Bird to track you. We gathered intel on you as you headed into the Ritz. One of you said, 'I can't wait to get back to Vermont.' Once you got to a certain area, we could no longer listen to anything you said." Sublime knew it was her-own screwup. "The two men killed at the hotel were our attempt to scare you off our trail. When that failed, our only course of action was to see if hitting you in Vermont would send you packing. We sent intel to our cell group there to track the whereabouts of your headquarters. Because of their lack of capability to advance in the facility, they sent me with a team. When we arrived, the facility was empty. It was unclear to us whether this was the facility, we heard the voice speak about. We had to try."

A7 didn't consider anyone else would have the tracking ability that they did. A7 underestimated Black Rain, 'It won't happen again.' Sublime thought. She continues, "In eight hours, we will offer a deal you won't be able to refuse." Sublime gets up and walks out of the cabin.

"Euphrates, please un-cuff Mr. Levi and let him know we can see his every move."

"Sure, thing Sublime, anything else you demand me to do, your highness?" His sarcasm didn't bother her anymore. Euphrates delivers the message and releases him.

As Euphrates walks out the door, Mr. Levi screams out, "Hey, I believe in God, too! You said you were doing this for God!" Sublime's tactic was working, and his lips ran on and on. They left him in the cabin room with the thought of never being released again.

~

Eight hours later, they land at the D.U.M.B. Euphrates looks at the scan of the room and discovers Mr. Levi was resting on the lounge. He opens the door and handcuffs Mr. Levi to walk him into the base. Shaken by the thought of torture, Euphrates led Mr. Levi to an empty bunker and left him there. The team meets back in the conference room. Tracy speaks, "We'll work on Mr. Levi at five a.m. and see if we can catch his brain off guard." They rested except for Euphrates and Mr. Levi. He stayed up with the night shift crew monitoring the airwaves, and Mr. Levi was having nightmares regarding the possibilities of what would happen to him soon. They woke Mr. Levi at five and put a black material bag over his head and led him to the Interrogation Room (IR), sitting him in a cold, metal seat.

"Mr. Alerion Levi, I assume you've had enough time to grasp the seriousness of this situation and what part you can play here? You've had enough time to decide whether your life is more important than Black Rain." Sublime states.

"I am ready to give you with what you need. The only request I have is, you promise to take my family out of there and get them to a safe place." Sublime takes the bag off his head and looks up at the security camera.

"Alright, Mr. Levi, I need the locations and the leader of each cell group for Black Rain." Placing the paper and pen in front of him on top of the gray steel desk. The room had a double mirror you'd see in an Interrogation Room at the police station in times past. It was concrete gray, depressing the suspects to death or making them beg to confess.

"Alerion, I assure you, if you cooperate and the locations and the leaders check out, no harm will come to your people or you. We will transport you and your family to a secure place where you will not have to worry." Sublime promised.

"I will accept your offer," he said.

Mr. Levi started writing as Sublime left the room. Sublime reaches the Communication Room and sits next to Leopard. Sublime was hesitant. Something was bothering her.

"Something isn't right," she said.

"What do you mean?" Leopard asked.

"This was too easy. Mr. Levi is a Black Rain member in high command and trained for capture. He had to know the Apollyon, or the authorities could capture him. Mr. Zinkes isn't here to read his mind, and we have no way of getting in contact with him. Does anyone else feel what I'm feeling, or am I making a big deal out of nothing?" Sublime asked.

Euphrates speaks up. "I am not sure what to think at this point. There are many variables. Do we trust our gut, or do we trust Butler? We have accurate information on his household and their whereabouts. He signed up for Black Rain and understood the consequences of getting caught. Could it be we have him right where we want him and he's willing to give up Black Rain to save his family? Maybe he's become disillusioned with them."

Just as Euphrates finished his sentence, Sublime turns to the monitor to check on Mr. Butler and saw blood spraying out the side of his neck. "My God, we have to get to him quick!" Yelling, Sublime was the first out of the room and everyone else runs behind her. She grabs the first-aid kit. She screams at Leopard to find Mr. Laemel and Mr. Lyemel. Within thirty seconds, Sublime and Euphrates reached the IR. He was unconscious, face down on the desktop where he was writing, and blood was everywhere. They laid him on the floor to see if they could stop the bleeding by pressurizing his carotid artery. Euphrates grabs whatever he could find to press it against his neck. The impact punctured a major artery on the side of his neck. Sublime did CPR, and after ten minutes, there was no response. She checked his pulse once more and got up off her knees. She walked over to the table to see what information he wrote. There was a list of names and locations and a note next to the writing pad. It was a note he left to Sublime.

'Ms. Sublime, I understand the ramifications of my actions and the information I have provided is correct. I hope you will carry out your side of the bargain and get my family to a safe place. Once recruited into Black Rain, I couldn't get out. They threatened to massacre my family if I tried to quit. Please inform them I love them with all my heart and never meant to put them in danger. I was true to them and felt it best that I was not part of the equation to protect them. Black Rain won't look for them if they believe I took one for the team. I need you to deliver me to the doorstep of the address below when you are ready to move in on Black Rain with the knowledge I have provided on the list. If you deliver me before you are ready, they will go underground and look for ways to attack. They will continue to plot the doom of Apollyon, and now that they believe it involves your organization, they are coming after you full force. They will work their way back to the surface to kill them and any collateral in their way. I hope you have better luck in steering their efforts in the right direction and if there is a God, and the Bible is true, I guess I won't be seeing you on the other side.'

Mr. Lyemel and Mr. Laemel were standing there listening and observing the whole time. "We will take care of Mr. Levi, Sublime. The morgue is still functional." Mr. Laemel touched Tracy's arm, "Get cleaned up, the both of you, and we will take care of him." Tracy walks out the room and says nothing to anyone.

~

For a day and a half, everyone tried to get Tracy out of her room with no luck. At the end of the second day of her self-sabbatical, Mr. Zinkes arrived. There was no need to hear what was going on from the others. He went to her room and knocked on the door.

"Please go away. I'll come out and eat when I'm ready. Please, just go away and leave me alone."

"I know you need to talk."

Recognizing his voice, Tracy ran to the door and opened it quickly. Hugging his neck, she almost crushed him, but her guilt, hurt, and anger released. Sobbing, she fell to her knees and asked God to help her. Mr. Zinkes picked her up and closed the door behind him.

"Mr. Zinkes, when I came to my room and looked at myself in the mirror and saw the blood I had on my hands and face, I undressed, got into the shower, and cried for hours. It wasn't so much that I had never seen death. I cried for his soul. I've taken lives many times before and if they repented to God, then they too would be in heaven. But with Mr. Levi, I'm not sure of anything. He took his life to save his family's. Although, he didn't have to."

"Tracy, your grief is considerable. It was not your fault. You did what you had to do to get the information, and you followed God's plan. You can't take on yourself the burden of Mr. Levi's.

The choice to take his own life was his and his alone. He was not a believer in the God you and I serve. He chose his path, just as everyone else has to make that choice to live eternally with Him or damnation in the lake of fire."

~

Trying to make sense of the tragic circumstance with Mr. Butler, Tracy emerges from her room the next morning. She steps into the command area and McBride addresses her, "Glad to see you back, Tracy. I've just finished up the Intelligence on Black Rain. I will present it to the team in an hour."

"Thanks, McBride. I...."

"You don't have to explain. All of us have been there a time or two," he said.

"Thanks." She left the control room and headed to Joshua's room. She knocked on the door.

He spoke loudly from behind the closed door, "I thought we didn't have to be there for another hour!"

"It's me, Joshua."

He opened the door and grabs her and hugs her tight. "Come in. How are you feeling?"

"I guess I won't get annoyed at the question, since I've only seen you and McBride so far. At least, can you tell the others not to bother with asking. I'm alright? I'm out of my room. That should be sufficient." Tracy sat at his desk.

"There's the Tracy I know. You can't blame us for worrying and Euphrates appeared to take your absence the worst. I saw him twice go by your room and almost knock but stopped himself. I think none of us wanted to get our heads chopped off for caring. Mr. Zinkes came back just in time."

"Yes, and speaking of Mr. Zinkes. I can't put my finger on it. Wherever he was, he came back different."

"Well, when he got back, he didn't speak to anyone of us. I saw him walk past, and he went straight to your room, like he knew what you were going through, and he was the only one you could talk to. I wish I could have been that person."

"It wasn't so much I couldn't talk to anyone else. I felt he was the only one who could give me the answers I needed, when I needed them. I guess he does that for everyone."

"It was urgency I saw on his face when he arrived. What was going on with you?"

"Walking away from this team, mission and everyone was an option. He reminded me that God elected me to lead, and He doesn't make mistakes. Joshua, I thought God was through testing my faith and love for Him. I guess you never get past learning from life experiences until you finish your race. I blamed myself for Mr. Butler's death and turned this tragic event into a pity party for Tracy. My self-consumption impeded me from knowing and doing God's will. I thought about how the other disciples felt when Judas betrayed Jesus. Could they have stopped what Judas did? There was nothing they could have done. That's how it was supposed to be. Now I know Mr. Butler chose his own path. I have to make good on my promise and get his family out and into safety."

"Look at it from the other perspective. Not caring about his soul is just as detrimental."

"You are right. A few years back, that's exactly where I was. No compassion."

"I'm glad you didn't walk away from us. I need you."

She kisses him. This time with passion. "Thank you, Joshua."

~

Heading to Paris, they retrieved Mr. Butler's family and took them to an abandoned bunker in Utah, abandoned about ten years prior. His ailing father would not survive the trip, so they took him to a Hospice Hospital, paid for his care to wait on his death in peace. A7 provided the rest of the family with money, transportation, and other necessities to live out the rest of their days in moderate peace of mind. Of course, the family was saddened but not shocked by their son, husband, and father's actions. Shadow provided them with new identities to be safe and free from the authorities and Black Rain. They chose not to accept the offer of salvation in Christ. They were not willing to convert to believe in the truth. Completing this task allowed them to focus on Black Rain. The A7 team returned to the D.U.M.B. base after relocating Mr. Butler's family. Time was of the essence, to develop a substantial plan to stop Black Rain.

Chapter 21

Global Breakdown

Now, identifying the primary cities where Black Rain operates could take several months. A7 knew Black Rain had suffered a setback and it would take time for the cell groups to reorganize. Even though there were hundreds of cells in most of the larger countries, they established seven main headquarter hubs that had the economic support to continue to kill Apollyon members in Australia, Canada, Egypt, America, Brazil, China, and Rome. Each one was far enough from each other to take months before the news to travel to any other headquarters in their estimation. They would have to take each location out one at a time and put the high-ranking members on ice. Taking a week to complete the critical planning stages of the attacks, they would carry out the execution at once in each region, first hitting their weapons' depots, then communications and equipment, and finally food supply. America was a distance from the other bases, and A7 was already there, so they struck them first. The trucks transporting the A7 teams hit in three locations, taking out communication, equipment, and their weapons stockpile.

Sublime, Euphrates, and X-Ray would lead the three attacks and the others were backup with Capt. Collier's men.

"Is everyone in position?" McBride asked.

Sublime, Euphrates, and X-Ray acknowledge. As trucks ram through the gates, missiles strategically hit the communication tower first. Guards fired on them as they busted through the gates. Each site had two regiments of soldiers but could not match A7's firepower. There was a helicopter to the left of the building. Euphrates didn't hesitate to blow it up. They storm the north side of the communications building and the men left inside gave up without incident. The MK-31, focused grenade launcher, devastated the warehouse, and those on the balcony rails around the buildings fell, screaming to their deaths. Using M-77 Carl Gustaf Recoilless Shotgun Rifles, they rounded up the remaining soldiers, dazed and confused by the smoke, dust, and debris, in the untouched parts of the building. Destroying all communication panels at the facility and leaving the remaining captured tied up in a locked storage area on the grounds. We would provide the authorities with enough information to charge and implicate them. The combined effort was a victory with a minimum loss of life. Some casualties were unavoidable.

The team then hit bunkers in Canada, Brazil, Egypt, Rome, and China next, leaving Australia for last.

They arrived in Australia, just as winter was ending and the weather was turning toward warmer temperatures.

They landed in the Northern Territory of Alice Springs and located an abandoned warehouse ten miles away from the Black Rain site. Black Rain Australia, better armed and forewarned of their approach, more than doubled the facility's security compared to other earlier destroyed facilities. The team surveyed the facility for two days.

"They are on high alert. We need a different approach." Sublime admitted.

"What do you suggest?" Captain Collier asks.

"Let's fall back and plan the attack on the jet. Euphrates, are you in agreement?" Sublime asks.

"Yeah, let's. I'd rather die knowing we had the best plan possible."

"Everyone fallback and regroup at the jet," Sublime instructs.

Everyone arrived at the warehouse, unloads, and Captain Collier joins the team to discuss the plan.

"Shadow, can you get the aerial view of the facility on the AIS?"

"No problem. It'll take a few seconds. Okay, here it is." Shadow finishes.

"My recommendation here is to plan a decoy attack at the front gate, while the actual insurgent drops from the JC-12 inside the back exit. The JC-12 tech can handle a minimal amount of artillery. If we drop at the back gate, Xerxes can get the plane out and wait for us here, two blocks away in that open field. With the gate already blown from the decoy attack at the gate, we escape in that truck out the front gate once we destroy their communications tower and network. Everything else is immaterial since they are the last on our list." Sublime finishes and looks around for agreement.

Euphrates nods his head. "I like that idea, but we need another armory truck. The first is the decoy, the second is for our escape. We'll position the escape vehicle outside the front gate. That first truck can destroy this part of the building, where their communication hub is located. We wire it to explode within that facility."

"What are your thoughts, Captain Collier?" Sublime asked.

"I like both of your ideas. If we are only going after their communications, we only need one decoy detonation truck to go through the gate and hit the communication building. We know this back building holds the leader. Sublime's suggest, we drop in the back, Xerxes flies the JC-12, and Shadow sends the truck. We drop out of the JC-12 and the second truck is at the back gate. With most of their manpower focused on the first truck, we can have a quicker escape out the back with the leader. It's up to you what you want to do with him afterwards. What are your thoughts?"

"I like your plan, Collier." She said. Sublime and Capt. Collier looks toward Euphrates to see if he agrees.

"I like it too. I prefer your plan over Sublime's." Euphrates said with a laugh.

"OMG, you are never serious. We will go with your plan, Cap." Sublime said, shaking her head.

Sublime looks at X-Ray and asked, "Can you find us another truck?"

"I'm on it," he said.

Euphrates, Sublime, and Capt. Collier discuss the plan. Taking a few hours to locate another truck, X-Ray had the second truck back at their location within six hours.

Inside the warehouse, Sublime asked, "Euphrates, how long do you and Shadow need to get the explosives and the remote ready?"

"The explosives are ready." He looks over at Shadow.

"I require two hours to trigger the truck, and another to attach. We can strike by tomorrow or whenever it's best to hit them. I'm thinking more about the cover of darkness. The JC-12 can cloak."

"So, tomorrow night it is." Euphrates said with finality.

She gestures to Euphrates and Capt. Collier, "We need to decide who drives, and who drops."

X-Ray chimed in, "Mr. Laemel and Mr. Lyemel drive the getaway truck. You, Euphrates, Capt. Collier, and I should hit the leader. Capt. Collier's team covers us. That's my two cents, for what it's worth."

Everyone looks X-Ray's way and smiles. "There we have it." Sublime said. "Let's get to it."

The next evening, they execute the plan. As the truck drives through the gate entrance, crashing into the communication building, Shadow detonates the explosive, and the building goes up in flames. Soldiers run toward the communication building as the team drops inside the back gate. Ten minutes later, the drop team reaches the back exit, carrying the leader out the back gate, dodging gunfire. Two of Captain's team members are carrying the leader out the back gate, dodging gunfire. Gunfire struck Black Rain's leader twice in the back, causing him to fall. They pick him up and carry him in the van. The rest of Capt. Collier's team reaches the van and speed away to rendezvous with the plane.

When they arrive at the plane, they carry the leader onto the JC-12 and move toward the back of the plane to tend his wounds. "He's still alive and breathing." Mr. Lyemel prepares the scanning bed on the opposite side of the room. Euphrates and X-Ray carry his body onto the body scanner. After the scanning is complete, Mr. Lyemel looks over at Sublime, shaking his head, and covers the body with a sheet. Sublime lets out a sigh and sags down onto the seat. Her goal was to grill him and leave him on the other side of the world. Mr. Laemel worked on the two soldiers who had through and through gunshot wounds. They would live.

~

The team had been involved in the attacks to bring about the disruption to suppress Black Rain for four months. The team took a week off for a much-needed rest. They couldn't put off any longer tackling Apollyon and their members. Euphrates got in contact with Mr. Frederickson to set a meeting to share the report of Black Rain's collapse. Mr. Zinkes then called a special meeting to discuss the next steps on Apollyon. Tracy and Mr. Zinkes were the last ones to leave the discussion area.

"Are you withholding something from us? When you left the last time, where did you go?" she asked.

"I can't divulge that information to anyone. When the moment is relevant, I will approach you first and afterward, the others. For now, I need you to continue to serve this team like you have been." His demeanor was firm but caring. "Trust me, in and of yourself, you will not fail God. Keep your mind stayed on Him and He will direct your path. We know what the end will be. All of us have to perform a part for that appointed conclusion."

Tracy left Mr. Zinkes and had dinner with the rest of the team. The evening's menu was Latin inspired. After scarfing down her meal of chicken enchiladas and Spanish rice, she headed to her room to pray. A while later, she sees a vision of men standing before a great owl, with fire crackling out of its belly. An angel swooped down and everyone around falls into a heavy slumber. The angel studies her and stands before her. She's trembling and doesn't know what to do. She continued to stand there, paralyzed, staring at a faceless entity. The glow illuminating so brightly. She turned to avoid going blind. The voice says, 'Don't fear, you will be triumphant.' The angel flies toward the sky like a rocket, leaving a bright trail that she could still see as she looked up to follow its ascent. Still on her knees, coming out of the trance, she steadied herself by grabbing hold of her bed, sweating and panting. Tracy quickly looked around and realized she was still in her room. The strangeness of the moment grips her, and she could not determine if it had been a daydream, a vision, or a genuine encounter. She decided not to tell anyone what had transpired, as she was unsure of herself.

Returning to the Mess Hall, she sits with Michael. "Has Mr. Frederickson followed up yet?"

"Yes, and no. I received a message from Mr. Frederickson, but I haven't spoken to him personally."

"Let me know when you hear from him tomorrow."

"Tomorrow! How do you know he won't call now?"

"He won't. Trust me." Tracy gets up and walks away.

~

The next morning, at nine a.m., Mr. Frederickson called to affirm he set a meeting with Mr. Morgan in two days. Michael is in the conference room alone.

"He is in Cairo and can meet you there." Mr. Frederickson says.

"Inform Mr. Morgan. I am eager to give him the splendid news."

"Mr. Johansen, I will deliver the message and set the meeting for Friday at ten a.m. Please be on time. He doesn't appreciate being kept waiting." Michael hangs up with Mr. Frederickson and calls the team in. He had forgotten what Tracy said the night before. Mr. Zinkes and Tracy arrive first. Michael tells them, "I just spoke with Mr. Frederickson. We fly back to Cairo. I have a meeting with Mr. Morgan in two days." He glances over at Tracy, she smiles. He then remembered and wants to ask how she knew but let it go.

~

Mobilizing the teams, McBride, and his unit of five left that evening for Cairo. After McBride was on his way to Egypt, A7, Mr. Zinkes, Mr. Lyemel, and Mr. Laemel prepare the JC-12 for their trip to Cairo. As they assemble around the imaging table, Mr. Zinkes broke the silence, "This mission will soon end. Mr. Morgan will offer us key information to allow us to conclude this part of God's plan." Everyone remained silent. Tracy recalled her vision. She wondered, 'Does my vision have anything to do with the ending of our mission?' Mr. Zinkes turned to her and said, "Tracy, all you have to do is accept God's plan and He will direct your footsteps." She looked toward him, and their eyes met. She knew he was aware of her vision.

Arriving in Cairo, Mr. Laemel, Euphrates, and Sublime disembark from the JC-12. McBride had a limousine waiting for them at the airstrip and Mr. Laemel would escort them to the meeting place, which was at the Apollyon Estate again. Mr. Frederickson greeted them and guided them into the mansion's library this time, as construction was still underway in the previous meeting room. Sublime carries an AIS imaging screen to explain the process of what transpired with Black Rain. As Mr. Morgan entered the library, Sublime and Euphrates stand to greet him.

"Welcome back, Mr. Johansen and Ms. Sublime, is it?" Mr. Morgan asks.

"That is correct. She is head representative of our security team, my personal bodyguard, and the deadliest woman in the world. I'm more than thrilled to have her in my service. Her skills are impeccable." Euphrates was getting quite good at putting on airs.

"You mean she is a precision killer?" Mr. Morgan retorts.

"No matter how you describe her, she is that and more."

"I am so glad you have such trust in her capabilities. Please sit, both of you," he said, gesturing as he takes his seat. Sublime remained standing and opened the case.

"Mr. Morgan," Sublime begins. "The problem of Black Rain is no more. If you view our imaging screen, my team took out all seven Black Rain bases, without mercy. We destroyed their communications and weapons supplies. Those major seven areas of interest were the central hubs for communication." Euphrates directs Mr. Morgan's attention to the screen.

"You have proven your value to us in manpower and wealth. This is impressive, and since you have satisfied us with this extraordinary help, I would like to return the favor. We wish to welcome you to Apollyon. In two weeks, we are convening for an annual celebration of festivities in San Francisco, California. We welcome your organization to show up, but our practices would prohibit them from experiencing certain sections of the club, those of the female persuasion. There are sufficient spaces in the lodge to support their activities and pleasure." He stands and moves from his chair. "Although Black Rain is no longer a threat, we will proceed with our security protocols and provide the location a day prior to the gathering. If this is enough time for you, then I will let Mr. Frederickson know to contact you."

"We accept and look forward to seeing you in two weeks." Euphrates smiles. Shaking hands, Mr. Morgan departs from the library. Euphrates looks at Sublime as she was closing the case. He grins at her. She doesn't smile back.

Leaving the estate, everybody is back on the JC-12 heading to Colorado. Tracy opens the Word of God and reads Isaiah 66. Tracy looked out the window and thinks to herself, *'This is where it may end.'*

~

Hours from the Colorado Base, Tracy trots out of the cabin. She goes straight to Kelton. "I need you to search any material on any secret associations in San Francisco, California."

"Allow me a few moments." Kelton takes a few minutes to research., then said, "According to our records, there is only one existing club in San Francisco left." He puts the material on the imaging screen for everyone to see. "Here is what I have found. Since 1873, a Global Society has held secret sessions in the Ancient Redwood Forest of Northern California. Members of the so-called Bohemian Club included former American Presidents and the wealthiest men of every country. Each year, members put on crimson, black and silver robes and conduct Occult Rituals, wherein they worship a Giant Stone Owl, sacrificing an individual being in effigy to the Great Owl of Bohemia. They have held the society's famed annual function for over 100 years at the 2,700-acre Bohemian Grove in Monte Rio, about 70 miles north of San Francisco in Sonoma County. The annual gathering near the Russian River opens with the 'Cremation of Care' ritual, in which it burns the club's mascot in statue, symbolizing freedom from care." Kelton spoke after everyone viewed the material, "From other material I've read, in the 1980s, Gascon Kratky exposed the correlations between the Bohemian Club, Skull and Bones, and other occult secret societies and examined the roots of the Grove and its link to occult networks dating back to ancient Egypt and Babylon. In scripture, they used the

Egyptian god Tophet for this same custom."

"We will take them down at this gathering. We won't have another chance at this," Tracy states. Michael looks at Tracy as she zones out.

"Tracy are you, okay? You look a little out of it," he observed.

"I'm fine. It's just I need to work through some things and make sense of it all. What I recognize is, we have to conduct surveillance before we're called by Apollyon." Tracy looked at Mr. Zinkes and says, "When we return, I desire to speak to you."

"I realize the answers you seek are within you. Accept the move of God." Mr. Zinkes scans the room. "And that's for all of you. We will take a few days and prepare ourselves. We must follow the leading of God."

Joyous to return to the base. They were happy to receive the message that their mission goal was near. Tracy focused on what awaited them. Would they do the right thing and if so, what would happen to them after it was all over? Sublime retreated to her room to pray, "God, is this how it will finish? Did I see the future, because everything I have just learned points to the vision I had? I saw only myself. God, please tell me." Sublime cried out and Mr. Zinkes knocks on the door. She attempts to clean her face and eyes of the tears.

As Mr. Zinkes enters, she tells him, "I need answers and you are the only one who can give them to me."

"Tracy, my presence here is to help all of you. I am here to guide you in the truths of God and how to live for Him and instruct you regarding your work on this earth for God. EL ELYON is the ruler of all humanity. Abba Father is EL OLAM, the eternal God, and no matter what, His Word will not return void. It declares in His Word that His word will come to pass. God will not leave you alone in life or death. We can't fear it." Mr. Zinkes tells her.

"Mr. Zinkes, I had a dream or a vision. God was giving me a glimpse of the future or my fate. Far back from the woods, I saw the owl and a fire flaming out of its belly. Figures stood around this fire. I couldn't figure out what they were saying, and couldn't recognize any of the men standing there surrounding it. An angel swooped down, and a gust rushes from its wings and either made them unconscious or killed them. After they were down, the angel looked at me, and instant terror came over me. I couldn't talk or run or do anything. The angel said not to fear that I would be victorious. I am not afraid to die Mr. Zinkes, it's the unknown that's making me crazy. Does it mean I will be victorious, or all of us will be victorious?"

"According to the scripture in Isaiah, God will allow some to remain to proclaim His Glory to the utter parts of the earth. Was this a message from God?" Tracy asked.

"Trust that God will never leave you nor forsake you. I don't have the answer. Thoughts are something I read. I'm not one to predict the future. The eerie cringe of the moment and trace of anger did not leave Tracy for a while. Mr. Zinkes was not giving her the answers she was longing for. She shook it off to move forward in what A7 needed to do. They would rest and then prepare for the trip to San Francisco, California. Researching nearby places to purchase, they knew they needed to buy out the entire place this time, so that there would be no one around to recognize them."

Chapter 22

Life is Lost

In preparing to survey the location, Sublime and McBride's unit went ahead of the others to gather intelligence. McBride rented a small, private hotel called the Cavallo Point, which was 6.6 miles away from the Bohemian Coppice in Monte Rey, California. Hunter green Lone Cypress trees scattered across the mountainsides. Trust was not the issue Sublime had to fret over anymore. A7 knew their mission and when it would end. From Colorado to California, the vision ran through her mind repeatedly, and it remained a disturbing account of possibilities. Arriving, the team settled in and sets up surveillance around the area, taking an aerial trip the next day around the Bohemian Club. McBride pulled up the map on the AIS to show Sublime the area of view of the Coppice.

"According to the floor designs and the aerial view, we can't fly over, but we can circle around it. I've already chartered a chopper." McBride informed them.

"Excellent, you are one-step ahead of me." Sublime smiles as she crosses her arms—thinking, considering the steps ahead.

"You seemed a little pre-occupied on the ride here. What's going on with you?" he asked.

"Nothing I can reveal right now. All I can say is I will have it together by morning. You don't have to worry about me. I'll be fine."

"All right, we have to be there by seven."

"I'll meet you out front. The less anyone sees us, the better. I'm sure Apollyon is here on the Bohemian grounds, making sure security is top-notch." They both return to the hotel.

At seven-forty-five a.m., observing most of the area on their route back to the airfield, Sublime spots the enormous owl through the forest brush. This settled her vision and misgiving that Mr. Zinkes was withholding information from her. Secluded, you couldn't see any buildings for miles around from the grounds or the air. The helipad was visible behind the camp hotel. Although the location was beautiful—trees greener than luminescent algae in murky brown lake water, there was no doubt dreadful things went on in this place. By the time they gathered all the intelligence, it would be four days before Euphrates would get the call for the meeting place and time and wouldn't get the directions to the Coppice until the day of. They already had the place. He needed the directions to show up. The festivities would start on a Sunday morning.

Friday morning, Sublime wanted to go up one last time to survey the campgrounds, and this time, they would go up in a one engine Cessna. The forest is green, beautiful, and tall. McBride turns the plane towards the campground. Artillery shots fired, hitting the rear-side and tail of the plane. Black smoke flew from the tail with sparks of gasoline dripping towards the ground. As they turn the plane, sporadic gunfire hits the front, and it hits McBride. Sublime's mind spaces out for a quick second. Had she been wrong about her dream or vision? He slumped over the side of the seat and she unbuckles him to take the controls. As she grabs the wheel, pulling McBride toward her to check his pulse, she confirmed he was dead. Her arm and the top of her body are now covered in his blood. Spitting out more black smoke and losing gas fast, the old plane was now heading downward—nose first. Falling fast, spinning out of control, leveling the plane was her first thought. She had to find a place where she could somehow crash land. She hadn't flown a small aircraft such as this for fifteen years. Not knowing how bad it would be when she crashed the disabled plane, she wondered if it could get any worse than this. Three hundred feet in the air, the landing gear wouldn't budge. "The landing gear is not engaging." Grunting, the words out, hoping—pulling on the lever would jar them loose. It didn't. She looks up at the top of the plane. "Hey God, can I get a little help here?" Sublime asked. She skids across the tops of the trees, and the plane spiraled. Sublime, screaming at the top of her lungs all the way down, plunging to her death, the plane comes to a complete stop without blowing up. Two large tree branches stop the momentum of the fall. She slammed her head on the control panel, and this knocked her dizzy. Groaning, conscious but confused, she realized she was alive, dangling from the seat straps, and staring directly at the ground. Sore, with a bloody mouth and a bruised forehead. She unbuckles herself and crawls and pulls her way to the door. She couldn't help but notice McBride's body on top of the flight panel and partially in the other seat. Sublime climbs out the door and grabs onto the tree branch and jumps down. Getting out of the plane in one piece with a minor headache, bruising, and groaning with every move, "Thank You for the help, and ouch," she said to God. She knew they would come looking for the plane since there was no explosion. The radio was busted and although her imagery visual was intact, she could get no signal. She didn't know how far she was from the campgrounds, hotel, or civilization. At least she had plenty of daylight to figure out which way to go. She had to get moving and hated to leave McBride's body behind. 'This was no accident,' she thought.

Checking her surroundings, she climbed back into the wreck to remove any identification from McBride and grab all the supplies she could carry. She knew how to survive anywhere, but the clock was ticking. Her priority was to get away from the plane quickly, before whoever shot them down found the wreckage, and then rendezvous back with the team to finish Apollyon. Sublime doubled back through the woodland and continued moving. Three hours later, she reached a dirt road, and no vehicles were in sight. She didn't want the wrong people to discover her or leave footprints they could follow. She had to get close to a water source. On the other side of the road, a ridge of trees blocked her access to get the watery stream, giving her access to drinking water. This was also better, as they would look for the plane on the other side.

With no flashlight, she didn't want to risk setting up a fire and get discovered. She would have to risk it after midnight to keep predatory animals away.

~

Twelve hours in Euphrates found Mr. Zinkes. He starts right in. "They should have been back by now." Euphrates was clearly anxious and worried.

"Yes, something has happened. Sublime is alive, but something worries her. I do not feel McBride at all, he's gone." Mr. Zinkes said.

"We have to search for her. It's already getting dark." Euphrates said, pacing.

"Euphrates, Sublime knows what to do and how to do it. There are a little over thirty-six hours before you show up at the Bohemian Club. It's too much of a risk for anyone to see you right now."

"We just can't sit here and wait to see if she's alive!" Euphrates said emphatically.

"By morning, if we do not hear from her, I will send out a search party, but you will not be part of that search. More than likely, I will send out McBride's team, Mr. Lyemel and Mr. Laemel. A7 has a job to do, and that is the only mission you will do the day after tomorrow." Mr. Zinkes said with finality.

Frustrated and angry, Euphrates makes his way through the kitchen and out toward the lake on the back side of the hotel. Myna Bird followed him. The dock creaks as he walks to its end. He hears Myna Bird behind him. There was silence for only a few moments as she stands next to him. Euphrates bends over the railing.

"I recognize your frustration and there is no one in there who doesn't feel the same." She said, motioning back to the hotel. "I've observed and learned a lot from Sublime, and she knows what to do in a crisis. Mr. Zinkes believes she is alive, so think positive. She may be on her way back here right now. Euphrates, we all want to look for her, but we cannot risk the mission for one individual. You know Sublime would do the same if it was her standing here, and you were out there."

"I know what she had to do. She had to leave McBride so she could get her way back here. She could be anywhere in that vast forest. We have to wait and see if we hear from her by dawn."

They stand looking out over the lake, crickets chirping as loud as the planes going by. They walk back in and go to their rooms for the night.

~

Morning came. Mr. Zinkes sent out McBride's team, Mr. Lyemel, and Mr. Laemel for an all-out search party. The roads provided no clues, nor did their fifteen stops in the woods to see if they could find any of her tracks back to the hotel. By four o'clock, they were back and had not found Sublime or the wreckage.

Euphrates was the first to interrogate them, "You couldn't find anything?"

"We didn't even find any wild animals around that place." Mr. Laemel said. "We couldn't find any wreckage of any kind, so we assume the plane went down in the mountains. She had no tracking device on her and her imaging visual has no connection for us to trace. She is out of range. If she is walking her way back, it could take her days or weeks for all we know."

X-Ray, frustrated with the entire process asked, "Can't we take the plane? It can cloak, so no one would see it."

Xerxes tries to explain his point. "X-Ray, we can't risk taking the JC-12 or any other aircraft in the air. We don't know what caused their plane to go down and if it wasn't because of pilot error, whoever attacked them wouldn't hesitate to do it again. My guess is, someone did something to that plane, because McBride was an expert, but anything is possible. Plus, we wouldn't see smoke from the crash anymore by now. She has left the plane and we don't know where they went down. We can't risk it right now. If they Apollyon gets spooked, they could cancel this meeting and we don't know how long it will be before they all meet again. We just can't risk it, and Sublime wouldn't want us to."

"Xerxes, how can you even say what Sublime would want? I know her better than all of you, and she would want us to look at every option. I know the JC-12 is special to you, but if it's between it and Sublime, I'm taking Sublime." X-Ray said.

Mr. Zinkes stepped into the conversation. "I need everyone to calm down and listen. Sublime is and will be fine. I need all of you to focus on what we need to do tomorrow, with or without Sublime. Sublime is in God's hands, and we can't fall apart now when we are this close to the goal. I need everyone to rest until dinner time and after dinner, we will walk through the plan one last time. Do I make myself clear?" Surprised at his tone, they followed orders and felt some sense of relief he recognized she would be fine.

Sublime, miles away from the campgrounds, made it through the night without being discovered. She continued through the forest terrain, which allowed her to move quickly in some areas and fighting through some minor impediments in others. Occasionally, she winced from the bruising from the crash. She pulled out her imagery phone. Still no reception. She continued to scan for any sign of reception, trying not to be discouraged at the thought of not getting back in time to take part in the mission. She stopped to drink water before moving on.

At six a.m., Euphrates spoke to Mr. Zinkes, "We know she is alive. Right now, we have no clue where she is or whether she will get there in time."

"Euphrates, no matter the outcome, Sublime is fine. You never know, she just might surprise you. Your job hasn't changed, this team's mission hasn't changed, and you can't go in there worried about her. God is watching over her, as He is watching over all of you. Yahweh chose you all for this day, for this very reason and purpose. All of us have our destinies in God's hands. Make Abba Father proud to call you son."

The festivities would start at nine a.m. and the ceremony wouldn't take place until nine o'clock that evening. Once the evening ceremony begins, Euphrates would give a signal to the others and they would put the Apollyon down. Sublime had no clue what the completed plan was. Would she reach them in time?

Reality hit Euphrates, as he was in the Bohemian Coppice Hotel preparing himself to meet with all the members of Apollyon. He wasn't alone, but he didn't have Sublime. Not that he couldn't complete the mission without her but playing this part put him at a disadvantage when he knew she was nowhere to be found. With Sublime by his side, that disadvantage was never a concern. At nine-thirty a.m., they met in the Presidential Conference room to hear the day's events. Euphrates wore a specialized camera phone on his jacket. The surveillance team was in place about a half a block from the campgrounds. They could hear and see everything going on, but Euphrates could not hear them speak. Everyone gathered like sheep.

"Good morning, my fellow Apollyonians. Our master's rise to power begins today. Only the Apollyon knows the true meaning of world peace. Today marks the day we no longer hide from Black Rain. Thanks to Mr. Johansen and his team, we can freely roam the world that belongs to us." They all shouted and cheered in adoration. "Today we press towards the mark of the highest calling of our god, Apollyon. For the next two weeks, we will eat, sing, and be merry to the point of death. Tonight, we begin our journey to a world where our god is king and lord, where we rule this universe and everyone in it. Are you with me, Apollyonians?" Again, screaming out like trained seals, Euphrates couldn't help but wonder how they could be so blind to what they're about to experience. He looked around and recognized current and past presidents, politicians, and many wealthy elites. Afterwards, everyone was free to roam and enjoy the campgrounds until the ceremony that evening. Euphrates saw Mr. Frederickson and requested to meet with Mr. Morgan. Mr. Frederickson whispered into Mr. Morgan's ear. He walked back to Euphrates. "He will meet you back in the conference room in thirty minutes." Mr. Frederickson said.

"Let him know I will be there." Euphrates headed to his lodging to freshen up and make sure everything was working properly.

~

In the forest thicket, Sublime makes her way south. The humid weather made her drink more water than usual. She questions whether she will make it. She believes this was where it would conclude, with or without her there, though several miles away, it could have been a hundred for all she knew. None of the area looked familiar. She had only observed the area from the air. Halting for thirty minutes to rest her body from the pack she was bearing, she heard the voice of the Lord speaking, *'All will be fine.'* Encouraged and her heart joyous, she gathered energy to maintain the course journey toward the Coppice.

~

Euphrates and Mr. Morgan met. Euphrates shakes his hand, and Mr. Morgan leads the discussion. "Mr. Johansen, I hope your lodging is satisfying?"

"Yes, handsome it is. I have been in many parts of the world but I never learned of this place." Euphrates was confident of what was to happen, and he sought to put Mr. Morgan at ease. "Yesterday morning, my team performed a security check around the periphery of the hotel where we are staying. The location is well-hidden. We never knew this was here. My team reported that traffic control provided news that another plane crashed on Friday. I hope it wasn't anybody you know."

Mr. Morgan studied Euphrates for a minute before answering. "I learned the same from Mr. Frederickson yesterday. He claimed that when they arrived at the airplane, they found just one body inside the plane, deceased. Is there any concern you have?"

"No, I was just wondering if it was a representative of the Apollyon. I wish to make certain everyone arrived safely."

"Our society has a vast history, and this place has been one of our best-kept secrets. I do not believe we have anything to worry about from any outside source. You have taken care of Black Rain for us, so there is no one else we need to be concerned about. Anyway, tonight's ceremony will bring to light all we have worked for, generation after generation. They have corrupted this world since time began. The one we serve. The one veritable god of this universe wants to restore order. Tonight is the great revelation." Mr. Morgan explains.

"Do you mind giving me a glimpse of what will happen tonight, since I am new to all of this?" Euphrates laughed and expected Mr. Morgan to join in. But that didn't happen. Mr. Morgan obliges, "Tonight begins with a pledge to the only veritable god of the universe. We then feast on wine and there will be a special surprise, I do not want to disclose. I guarantee after tonight, you will not only feel powerful but be powerful. Tonight's festivities are all about letting go of any inhibitions you might have about us, Mr. Johansen. Our forefathers knew what it would take for this wonderful world to survive all the damage we allowed to happen to it. It was because of our ignorance that caused us to be sleep, for so long. How can a man believe in a god they have never seen? Tonight, we take the blinders off Mr. Johansen, and reveal the true and living god to everyone here. The truth, Mr. Johansen, will set us free." With a menacing smile, he finishes the conversation.

"Thank you, Mr. Morgan. I look forward to tonight's festivities. I will take my leave and bid you a pleasant afternoon. I want to enjoy the campgrounds."

Euphrates left Mr. Morgan in the Presidential room to meditate on God's Word and what he had to do tonight. There was no question Mr. Morgan was out of his mind. By five-thirty, there was a knock on the door. Euphrates answers, "Yes, can I help you?"

"This is your robe for tonight's observance. Please remember, we serve supper at six. They do not tolerate tardiness." Euphrates allows the man to come in and place the garment in the closet, and he closes the door behind the man. "God, where is Sublime?" He asks out loud.

Chapter 23

- ❡ ◠◠◠ ◆ ◠◠ ◠ -

Is This How It Ends?

Miles from the Coppice, it was now dusk. She rested for a moment, not allowing the exhaustion to overwhelm. Her imaging visual, now active, picked up an incoming call signal. She continues to move forward, a gleam of hope that she will connect to life outside of the forest trees and its nature. Sublime called X-Ray. The visual beeps. "Oh my God! Sublime. What happened? Where are you?" Turning aside from the others so they couldn't see, he almost breaks down from the relief.

"Someone shot our plane down and McBride is dead. Leaving him behind in the airplane, I hiked my way back to civilization. I prayed I was traveling in the right direction. Lacking a compass, the imagery phone just picked up a signal. I am uncertain how far I am away from the Coppice. What's going on and what is the plan?" she asked.

"He's on the grounds. We are a mile away in the surveillance truck, viewing and listening. Once it gets dark, we will move in. We can see and hear everything, but we can't communicate with him, so he doesn't know you are close."

"We will have to keep it that way."

"I'm tracking you now. You're approximately three miles away, and you're headed in the right direction." X-Ray informs her. With no time for small talk. X-Ray continues, "Tonight, at nine o'clock, they're having the blood sacrifice. We plan to take them during that ritual, so everyone is in attendance." Sublime thought back to her vision.

"That only gives me about two hours to get there," she said.

"Sublime, once this business is over, the JC-12 will be there hovering over the helipad near the owl. We're going to the hotel area to be nearby, and we'll attack when the time is right. There will only be a few members remaining. Euphrates will ensure those members never show up at the sacrifice. I need to know if you are all right," he said, still concerned for Sublime's well-being. Stating the facts, "Yes, I crash landed. I walked away with a few scratches and bruises. They shot McBride, and I can't say for sure who shot our plane down. I am sure it had to be the Apollyon protecting the Coppice. Tell the team I am okay, and I'll see them on the other side of the owl." X-Ray and Shadow look at each other with great relief and conclude their conversation. X-Ray then contacts Mr. Zinkes and Xerxes, "Yes, X-Ray, I know she contacted you. We will continue with our plan."

~

At eight-thirty that evening, after supper, Euphrates tracks the targets, Mr. Ford, Mr. Beaumont, and Mr. Frederickson. Euphrates tranquilized each of them and hid them in his room. The intelligence they gathered on each one proved they all had a fascination with art. Euphrates intrigues them into his room with a promise of seeing an original Rembrandt that hadn't been in the public for over fifty years. Most everyone was halfway drunk during and after dinner. He swore them to secrecy, or they would not see the painting. As each one sat for the show, Euphrates came out and shot each one with a tranquilizer gun. Yes, it seemed primitive, but it worked to keep them alive and quiet. A7 given strict instructions: execute all others! Why was it necessary? Because it was the instructions given them by Mr. Zinkes, a message from Yahweh Himself. When He gives instruction, you follow it. A7 had been and wanted to remain obedient to what God had instructed. There would be no deviation from what God said. They didn't want the failure of destruction to befall them.

Mr. Morgan was closest to the man of perdition. He would not be the one to help reveal Apollyon to the world. Because of financial standing and backing, the others would be the ones to make the revelation at the ceremony. Delayed maybe. Nothing would stop this group. But all things are in God's time.

Euphrates put on his robe and walked out of his room. The halls were empty and the only personnel standing in his way to the ceremony were Myna Bird, Leopard, X-Ray, Mr. Lyemel, and Mr. Laemel. They took care of the inside security and locked all the staff into the kitchen with a bomb strapped to the door that would go off if anyone tried to open it. At least they didn't have to be casualties of this battle. It was 9:14, and the ritual had already begun. Euphrates stayed on the ground, while the others went up top to take out the remaining guards, hovering over the ceremony like ravenous wolves. The guards could see everything going on down at the owl. No one down at the statue could see the guards because of the cover of darkness. Leopard came upon a guard that was already dead. She stopped in her tracks. "I have several guards already down. Do you copy? They are dead."

"This is X-Ray. I just found the same thing."

Myna Bird from behind strangles and breaks a guard's neck. "This is Myna. The last guard on the west wing is down."

Everything was going as planned. Then a commotion started down at the owl. Guards down on the ground grab Euphrates. He resisted to no avail. They stood him in front of Mr. Morgan. With a glass of wine in his hand, the flickering ambers flowing from the belly of the owl behind him, Euphrates asks, "What is going on, Mr. Morgan?" With his back to Euphrates, he turns toward him and answers, "Mr. Johansen, we need some blood and since you seem to be a great mystery to all of us, we had to wonder, how could you be so gifted in taking out Black Rain and being so efficient in staying from under our radar? Mr. Johansen, we have no clue who you are and that does not sit well with our master, and it doesn't sit well with me." Mr. Morgan came close to Euphrates, and the guards hold on to Euphrates tight. Handing his glass to one man, giving Euphrates a blow to the gut. He drops to one knee, and they stand him up again. Mr. Morgan continues to ask questions, "Before we proceed, can you tell me where your bodyguard is right at this moment?" After being punched, Euphrates was praying Sublime was somewhere close.

"Mr. Morgan, I have no clue where she is. I wish she were here because if she were, I know you would have never gotten this close. If I had to guess, she was at the hotel where the other female guests were. Why don't we just get on with this, shall we? I have better places to be," he spat. Further agitating the situation, intentionally. Mr. Morgan says, "You are mistaken. We didn't bring you all the way out here for to have a glorious time. Our intentions are unrecognizable to such weaklings as yourself. You have money, but you have no actual power. You lack insight into the true reality of what we are doing here. We are sacrificing to the only veritable god and tonight, you are that sacrifice, Mr. Johansen." He moves in closer. "Not some of your blood, but all of your blood shall spill tonight." Feeling satisfied no outside forces would rain down on his parade, Mr. Morgan snaps his finger, and the guards drag Euphrates to the altar.

Euphrates struggles and gets loose. With the men holding him, in a swift movement, he cracks the head of the guards. He pulled guns from his hidden holsters and from the guards and throws off the robe. The fireworks begin. From above, the firepower rains down on those scattering to run. In the chaos of gunfire, Mr. Morgan runs towards the woods.

As he came to the edge of the owl altar, looking back, he turns to find Sublime standing in front of him and runs into her knife. She whispers into his ear, "There is a way that seems right to man, but that way leads to death. You and your god will burn in hell for eternity. Your allegiance to your master has led you to eternal damnation." He drops to his knees. Sublime pulls out another weapon and continues to complete the mission along with the rest of A7. Close to Euphrates, she looks down and sees a guard on the ground, his gun pointing to shoot. She jumps and pushes Euphrates out of the way. The gun fires. Her body lays still. Euphrates runs over to Sublime, falls to his knees, and checks her. "Sublime, Sublime!" Euphrates calls out. He leans over to see if she was breathing. There was no sign of life. "No, no, no.... this can't be happening!" He screams her name one last time. Her heart was no longer pumping.

As the JC-12 hovers over the trees with Xerxes at the helm, the deafening sound of gunfire was no more. Euphrates and the rest of the team stood, except for Sublime. All they could hear was the wind from the JC-12 blowing the tops of the trees surrounding the camp. Everyone froze. Hovering over Sublime with a wingspan immeasurable was Xariel the Archangel. Her body rises. "Father, I am at your command. What am I to do?" The sky rumbles with a thunderous sound. A7 is awakened. Xariel looks down on her, "You have done well, thou good and faithful servant." They look up to see a glimpse of what was, and then they look down and Sublime's body was no more. Xerxes lands the plane on the helipad, and everyone got in.

X-Ray was the last one to get on, as he had to run back to the kitchen to take the explosive device off the door. The plane was leaving, and the silence of death rang true over the camp. X-Ray asked the ultimate question, "Where is Tracy?" No one could answer.

A sea of bodies lay over the court in front of the stone owl. The service people did not move until they saw the kitchen doors flapping back and forth by the wind. The kitchen staff searched all the rooms and found Mr. Frederickson and the two other men awaken from the tranquilizers and released from their bonds. Conscious and frantic, they all rush out to the wooded area towards the burning owl statue. Mr. Frederickson was in the lead. As the light became brighter, he stumbles over a body, "What in god's name happened here?" They all looked at each other in horror at the sight of the sea of bodies before them. One by one, they checked to see if anyone was alive and there was none. Death came for them all.

~

The flight back to Colorado was in silence. Their only thought was, what happens now that she's gone? Mr. Zinkes disappeared and provided no answers. An hour and a half later, they were landing, and Ms. Giles greets each one as they enter the base. "Welcome back. Please adjourn to the meeting room in one hour. There is a message from Mr. Zinkes."

"Ms. Giles, if it's all the same to you, I don't think we can wait an hour. We need to know some information now." Euphrates states.

"Euphrates, as you wish. I will prepare everything and meet you in the imaging room in fifteen minutes." She said.

"Thank you, Ms. Giles." He hugs her.

Each one walks past her. She sensed the loss. Sitting for thirteen minutes, Ms. Giles came in and closed the door behind her. She sat down in the head chair. "When you all started this mission, you had a common purpose and a not so common plan for your individual lives. I have watched you grow in all areas of your salvation, your faith in God, and with that faith there are sometimes questions only God can answer. Mr. Zinkes has left you a message. Rest assure, God will leave none of you nor forsake you." Ms. Giles turns on the imaging viewer.

"Hello everyone, as you can gather, I am not with you and neither is Tracy. The mission all of you so selflessly accomplished this evening has brought not only a glorious victory to the Kingdom of God but sorrow to your hearts as well, I'm sure. God understands your sorrow, your feeling of loss, and your heaviness of heart. And because Tracy is not with you, understand tomorrow starts a brand-new day. Each of you must face your journey, as Tracy has faced hers triumphantly. I know she felt this burden as she was traveling through the woods to be with all of you and to complete what God called you to do. I know she is looking down on all of us and smiling because she loved us. Trust, she is in Christ's presence and one day you all will see her again. Each of you has a letter from Tracy Ms. Giles will pass out once we have concluded this session. I will see you all a few days from now."

Chapter 24

─ ❦ ◆ ❦ ─

Seeing to Live On

Each one resting in their perspective rooms read the notes from Tracy. By the time they completed reading the messages, everybody was in tears, including Euphrates. The consensus was that she knew this would take place and didn't tell anyone.

'To Joshua, I love you and I didn't tell you because I knew you wouldn't support me in completing my mission. Trust me, I wanted to express my feelings, you were the only one I wanted to tell. Just like our wedding day, I couldn't bring myself to put that burden on you. I won't see you for a while. I didn't know how my death will come, but God knows me best, and His plan will manifest before my own. You were the one man I could grow old with. I loved you so much, and only God's plan could have separated us again. I leave this message with you because I know you love God, and you wish to please Him. Listen to Mr. Zinkes and receive his instructions plainly and adhere to them. Your salvation depends on it. Trust God and the team you are with. God didn't make you one of us for nothing. He has a purpose and a plan for your life, and A7 will need you to fight with them. I love you, Joshua. Tracy.'

"She's not gone. She's with Mr. Zinkes somewhere. Wherever he goes, I know she's there with him." Convinced of this, he heads to speak to Michael. He knocks on his door.

"What's going on, Joshua?"

"I need to know what happened out there. Can you explain what happened?"

Michael could sense he was angry. He asks Joshua to come into his room. They sit, "When I broke loose from the men who were holding me, I looked around to see Sublime rushing toward the edge of the Coppice. I see Mr. Morgan running in her direction and I was going to run that way, but he ran into her. I saw him drop to his knees and knew she took care of him. Man, I was excited when I saw her. I knew my backup was here. As much as I complain, I knew she had my back. I continued with our mission and I had my back toward her, facing the men on the ground. She came from behind me and pushed me to the side. I lost my footing and fell over a body. When I looked back, she was lying on the ground. I scooted over to her. She was unconscious. I looked for any wounds. There was blood coming from her chest, near her heart area. I felt for a pulse. It was like in an instant, everything went black. I had no perception of anything. When I came to, she was no longer in front of me. All I saw was a speck of light when I looked up and around."

"I don't think she's gone. She's with Mr. Zinkes wherever he is. She may have thought something was going to happen, that's why she left the letters. I won't believe it until Mr. Zinkes gets back. That makes more sense to me. The rest of this is not making any sense."

Joshua left Michael's room without saying goodbye. Michael looks around the door to see Joshua walking down the hall. Michael walks over to Mr. Laemel's room. He knocks, and Mr. Laemel answers, "What can I help you with?"

"You might need to monitor Joshua. He's in denial that Tracy is gone. He thinks she's with Mr. Zinkes wherever he is."

~

Euphrates' love for God increased in fervency and determination. He advanced in his learning of the Holy

Scriptures, and it all became clear. Amazingly, it did for all of them. The authenticity of life and certainty of death, what they were warring for was surreal. Remaining at the D.U.M.B. in Colorado, Mr. Zinkes finally arrives. He had answers they would never accept until it was time they had to serve without a doubt. "We're instructed to travel to India. There we will locate our next member, Maharashtra, in Mumbai. Griffith's team has paid for the top two floors of the Taj Lands' End. We will head there in two days. Most of you will remain in the hotel to continue your rest. Euphrates and Myna Bird will leave with me. Mr. Laemel and Mr. Lyemel will maintain your training and your required study is Revelations."

~

Mr. Zinkes instructs them, "As you are studying Revelations, please adhere to the warning. Lean not to your own view. If there is something you do not understand, ask the Living God to reveal it to you. Have discussions, receive instruction from each other spiritually. Remember, our warfare is not carnal. We must train ourselves to fight sometimes in the physical."

Joshua still dealing with the loss of Tracy, loved her with every part of his being. She wasn't coming back and was at rest. The difficulty of carrying on was overwhelming. Joshua walks over to Mr. Zinkes. "Mr. Zinkes, can I talk to you for a moment?" Joshua waits for his response.

"Yes, Joshua. Come with me and we will talk for as long as you need."

~

They walk to Mr. Zinkes' room, and he offers Joshua a chair. Mr. Zinkes sighed, "Before you ask your questions, I need you to understand Tracy loved you, but she loved God more. You will get to that place of loving God more than anything else. Her not being here won't matter because one day nothing from this life will matter to you in the big scheme of things."

Joshua falls to his seat. Tear's stream, "Where is Tracy, Mr. Zinkes? Why didn't she come back with you? Where is she and when is coming back?"

"Joshua, your anger is justifiable. God knows exactly where you are. Tracy is not coming back. Her life has ended in the most courageous way."

"Mr. Zinkes, I get what you are saying, but you are the one who knows where she is right now and if she cares I exist. Does she care I love her?"

Mr. Zinkes asked, "Are you expecting an answer to that question?"

"Mr. Zinkes, I need answers. Tracy told me in her letter to listen to you. To listen and learn how to discern what you say to us. What we are doing is so secretive, why should people care about whether we succeed? Why should we genuinely care about a society that's hell bent on destroying itself, even though they see what's happening to them daily? God is absolute and with everything we have been through, I want to know if we will ever know each other again. There is so much speculation as to if the Bible is complete or not. What they left out or whether our loved ones will remember us once in our transformed bodies, whatever that means. I depend on God to never lie. He will carry out all He declared in His Word. Am I missing the mark? Am I doing what is necessary for me to make it in?"

"Joshua, self-preservation is the quickest way to losing your path to everlasting life. Some do not see and will not care what we are doing here for the Kingdom. We have an enemy out there who is betting on our failure. We do not work for the kingdom of God to seek validation from people. It is purposeful to bring clarity and salvation to those called. For now, I will not further discuss this, as it is not time for its revelation. Trust the answers will come and you will see its fruit manifested. As far as your other questions, Christ will be the Judge in whether you are in the Lamb's Book of Life. If you are not, then you will stand before

God and be accountable for what you have done with the life God has given you. God's Word is simple and true. People have had their own interpretations of the Bible for thousands of generations. God says, do not add or omit from His Word. This was the problem with Black Rain and Apollyon. God's revelation is just that. It will not alter unless God changes it. And we know God will not change it, because then it would make His word a lie, which could never be, because God is not a man that He could lie. God's Word tells and explains its meaning all by itself. Seek first the Kingdom of God and His Righteousness, and all understanding will come to you in time. God will reveal everything you need for your course. Even though you all are a team, each one of you has a plan, a purpose from God as an individual. To show you an illustration of what I am saying, Revelation and Daniel interweave with each other. If you study both, God will show all you desire to learn in His Word and for what is coming. The reason I am informing you of this is that God has elected you to be one of His representatives to this unit. Be the one to sustain the others with the Word of God. Joshua, your purpose is of extreme value to this team, because of Yahweh's design for you. You will become the Teacher. When you asked yourself a while back, why people do not see the truth? That is how Satan works. He starts with a lie with that has a bit of truth in it and perpetuates it until it becomes so vast that no one ever thinks it is false. Question God and ask Him to show you. As much as I hear from God, I do not have all the answers. There are some mysteries kept from me until it is time. Get in the Word and study and seek His face and He will give you the answers necessary for your calling. God will use you if you plant His Word in your heart. Trust, when you hear His voice and the world around you will grow strangely dim. For the ultimate question, Tracy is with the Lord. She ran her race and finished well, and you will achieve the same when He calls for you. All of you will. Until time arrives for a new Heaven and Earth, the work must continue. What you will experience and who you may remember is not a question I can answer, because God will declare it in the vortex of your thinking as time. In the theme of being simple, you will just have to wait." He finished with a laugh.

"Thank you, Mr. Zinkes, for taking care of Tracy for me. I mean, for watching over her all these years. She told me about the tests and although I don't understand it, I thank you for bringing us back together again. I know you can read minds, but you can't plant thoughts and feelings for someone else and make them do things, so I am grateful you gave her the authority to seek me out."

"You are welcome, but I take no credit. It was all Father's plan from the beginning. I'm just obedient to God's will. Just so you know, I tested you as well. The scepter you stole and returned. You were at the precipice of you downward spiral. It took you a while, but you came around to do the right thing. So, you see, all of you."

Joshua turns to go out and suddenly paused in his tracks. He senses there was something different. Joshua did not open his mouth but thought, *'I know what you are, because God revealed it to me.'*

Mr. Zinkes stood, and his wings filled the room. In a whirlwind, he grabs Joshua and transports him to the Holy Mountain. They were now standing on a mountain peak. His wings kept Joshua warm as the mountain top air was close to zero. "I have brought you here for you to know the truth. To know who I really am. To know that Tracy is in the resting place of our Savior."

Joshua turns to look out at the stars that seemed so close in proximity that he could touch them. Mr. Zinkes lowers his wings for Joshua to see the earth down below. He instantly shivered. He grabs him close and transports him back to the room.

Joshua dropped to his knees. "Therefore, Abba Father chose you to teach the Revelations of God to this group and to others. To see Joshua, not just with your eyes but see the plan of God for your life and others with your heart." Joshua walked out of the room and down the hall to his room, falling to his knees again.

~

That hour, Joshua received a vision. He could not describe his experience. He went down on his knees and worshipped God. The light drew him in, and Joshua declared, "Your Word I have hidden in my heart that I might not sin against thee." As the voice uttered to him, Joshua fell prostrate.

'You have found favor, Joshua. Teach My word. Search, study, read, and protect the good news in your heart. Teach others as I have appointed thee, and you will surely live.'

"Yes, Lord. I will serve as you say." When Joshua came to, he was back in his room. The tears fell uncontrollably. He steps into the steel, brushed bathroom and washes his face. "OMG, that has never happened to me before and I can't tell anyone." He stared in the mirror. "God, I will undertake what you have asked me to do."

~

Later that evening at supper, everybody was laughing and enjoying a wonderful moment. Joshua could not get his mind off what transpired in his room and what he learned. Euphrates notices and sits next to him as he comes in to enjoy dinner. Michael sits down with his steak and veggies and a big cup of water.

"Joshua, you miss Tracy. We all do. You are still alive, man. Stop moping and live." Michael tries to cheer Joshua up.

A part of Joshua felt sad for Michael because he didn't realize what had happened. How could he know? The heaviness was on Joshua to not utter a word about what transpired, nor tell them who Mr. Zinkes was.

"Michael, I thank you wholeheartedly for your concern, but we know Tracy is in a better place. I miss her, but I'm working to get where she is and no matter how long it takes, I will serve God's will. Don't worry about me, brother, I'll be fine. We all will be fine. God has given me a task for our team. I am to become your Spiritual Teacher, so when we reach Mumbai, I will be in solitude for a time. Once Mr. Zinkes has located our next member, I will come back to the group."

"Okay. All I wanted you to do was cheer up." Joshua chuckles and got more food. "I will Michael, I promise." They shook hands.

Chapter 25

In Search Again

Heading to Mumbai in the JC-12. While they had been at the Colorado base, Griffith dispatched a unit to Cairo, monitoring Mr. Frederickson. They assembled around the table as Mr. Zinkes explained the culture of India, "In 2020, Mumbai, hit with a great heatwave, the temperature reached 130 degrees and people fled to Brihan, Mumbai, because the National Forest had enough cover for people to survive. It took two years for the climate to drop to a level where the cities were habitable again. They have observed a change in the weather there again. It used to be a bustling town and now only those that have wealth can remain there. Families from various parts of India used to come to this city for trade, commerce, education, and employment. It was a dream place for many families and the hotel where we will live depicts what it used to be. The cost of living is expensive in Mumbai and powerful industrialists found Mumbai to be their fit place for business. It's next to Pune, so back then college students would visit the city. It was a city of hope for their society. Unfortunately, it developed into a den of thieves. They would have an enormous spectacle called Ganesh Chaturthi. It was a Hindu Festival that lit up the metropolis every August and September. The city is not what it formerly was, but God is sending us none the less. We seek an individual, accomplished in the arts of Cheibi Gad-Ga, Kalari Payattu, Silambam, Thang-ta and Thoda. We will go to the only Martial Arts School left in the region, Sport City Martial Arts Academy. When we go there, we will talk to Master Bakinaka. He is not the person we are searching for, but one of his pupils is. I recommend you read up on their culture and prepare yourselves for whatever comes. I will go lie down now and Joshua, we may speak after I have had my rest. Thank you. Mr. Lyemel, please take over." Mr. Lyemel brought up another image on the AIS for them to examine.

"If we look at the viewer, Mumbai and Delhi were terrorist targets, because Delhi was the political capital and Mumbai was the economic metropolis of India. The fundamental reasons for them being targets was because of the religious conflicts played out between India and Pakistan. It doesn't matter what theology, country, or era there is, history seems to repeat itself and religion is the catalyst for it all. Thank God we don't live for religion. It's important to have a relationship with our Heavenly Father, through His Son, Jesus Christ." Michael wanted to ask a question of Mr. Zinkes before he headed to get his nap.

"Go ahead, Michael, ask the question. And mind you, it is not just for your benefit. It helps the team."

"I wanted to ask why you sought this individual when you sent for us."

"The Lord instructed me to go myself. If I did not go, the next member would not come. God found that person faithful, like Abraham, and that person was in God's presence. My presence will reassure him or her they can accompany us. One day you will be in His presence Michael, and will realize that it's correct when Jesus declared, my sheep hear my voice and a stranger they will not follow."

~

Two hours later, Mr. Zinkes asked Joshua to join him in the compartment area. He closes the door behind him. Michael wondered what that was all about. He had learned with Mr. Zinkes. It was best not to interrogate him too often.

"I inquired of the Lord for the answers you require. You are to travel to Kalsubai. It is the highest mountain crest in Mumbai. There is a secluded cabin there. Take this Calibrion with you to that holy place and let me warn you, it is sacred. It bears the Word of God within it. This is what the Lord has revealed. You must fast for three days and nights and pray at noon, three, six, nine, and so on. You will rest from prayer from seven a.m. to noon and remain in that state of prayer and fasting. On the fourth day, you will eat nothing but broth. You will then fast another two days and on the third day, you will consume nothing but broth. Thereafter, until we come for you, you will eat nothing but fresh food. God will make certain someone will take care of your meals. Read, study, and show thyself approved. God is with you." Mr. Zinkes finished the conversation. Joshua stepped out of the cabin and prayed in his seat.

Mr. Zinkes comes out of the compartment. He sits, and they focus all eyes on him. He relaxed back into his chair. "I want to assure everyone that I am with you for the long haul. In previous times, I would not go on a mission. I want you to know that I love and respect all of you for the choices you have made, and I don't take it for granted that you could be elsewhere. I just want you to know I appreciate you." Mr. Zinkes folded his hand and closed his eyes and rested.

Michael couldn't help himself. "Man, what is going on? Why are you talking to Mr. Zinkes? I just want to know?" Joshua opened his eyes and recognized why God would have him flee into solitude.

Joshua smiled. "Michael, I am not at liberty to discuss what God has planned for me. All I can tell you is that when we get to Mumbai, I will go into seclusion until the next member of this team is on board. I want to do the will of the Lord, and it's not helping that you disturbed me during my prayer. Ask God for discernment, please!"

Leopard laughed when she heard Joshua's answer. "I told you, Michael, and you didn't listen to me before. My prayer is you'll listen this time. Anyway, just as an update, we will arrive at our destination within an hour. There is no civil unrest right now and looks to be calm in Mumbai. However, they are preparing for the weather to change in two months."

Michael got up and went into the pilots' compartment and waited in solitude for the rest of the flight with Mr. Griffith. They were eager to be on the ground and gear up for the next mission.

They had received little intelligence, as they were still unsure of what their next mission would be after collecting their new member.

~

Jeeps waited for them at the airstrip, overcast, hot, sticky, and it didn't take long to feel miserable. Stepping off the plane, wet with perspiration and praising God, there was a warm breeze blowing, but wasn't enough to provide a reprieve from the intensity of the heat and humidity.

Mr. Zinkes spoke to Joshua before he left the rest of the party. "Mr. Wells, you will leave us here and go to your destination. Make certain you following the directives given you." Joshua took his pack and left with the two guides. He glanced back and waved goodbye.

"Everyone else", Mr. Zinkes said, "Let's move out. Tomorrow, we head over to the Martial Arts Studio." They took their belongings and headed to the hotel, which took a half an hour to reach. The once bustling metropolis was no more. The skyline, beautiful with one of Mumbai's accomplishments, the cable-stayed bridge linking Bandra to Worli. Part of the Western Freeway which linked their suburbs to South Mumbai's largest business district, Nariman Point. The citizens relied on local trains for the daily commute. If it weren't for the people left in the towns, you could consider it a wasteland of architecture and nothingness. The wealthy ran the government, ignoring the poor.

At the hotel, you could see they struggled to maintain it at a standard of luxury that would attract customers. The recession and politics didn't support it. They were grateful for A7's business. To avoid being tracked by Apollyon from a credit card payment, they paid cash, but this drew the attention of the hotel employees. They trusted no one and others trusted only hard cash and the meager value it held.

Once in the penthouse suite, so used to Sublime giving out the orders, they were at a loss of what to do about assigning rooms. There were six rooms to go around. Euphrates spoke up first. "I suppose I'll pick this room. Sublime was better at this leadership thing." They followed his lead and Mr. Zinkes decided he would remain on the lower floor with Griffith. Since X-Ray was not there, Mr. Laemel and Mr. Lyemel took the room that would have been his.

An hour later, everybody gathered in the common space. At that same moment, Joshua was arriving at Kalsubai. As Joshua entered, the men carried in his bag and the pre-prepared packages silently. Trees and a beautiful river's edge surrounded the secluded log cabin. Much of the water was still until the waterfall dropped within a quarter of a mile of the riverbed. He could see it from the cabin window as the moon gleamed across the skyline. It was seven p.m., and he would start his fast at midnight. Although Mumbai was hot, at this high of altitude, it was cold at night. He lit a fire in the fireplace and laid down on the couch and relaxed. When he woke from the snooze, it was nine-thirty. He consumed his last meal and as much water as his body could handle to keep hydrated. When midnight arrived, he prayed, "God, what do you have in store for me?"

At daylight, up bright and early and searching for breakfast, Mr. Zinkes, Euphrates, and Myna Bird head to the martial arts studio after inhaling a bland breakfast of oatmeal and berries.

Walking into the studio, Master Bakinaka greets them, "Welcome to our martial arts studio." Mr. Zinkes bowed and thanked him. They observe the students for a while, Mr. Zinkes keeps his eyes on the one he is there for. Mr. Bakinaka stood next to them, smiling.

"You realize why we are here?" Mr. Zinkes asked.

"Yes, but she doesn't. I knew someone would come someday. I didn't know when or who. God has been preparing her since a toddler of two years of age. She is my only daughter and God instructed me long ago she was exceptional. Her course is to leave this place and accomplish something remarkable. I must caution you still, she will not go without confirmation from God." Mr. Bakinaka Said.

"That is why I'm here. We must present ourselves trustworthy." Mr. Bakinaka called out to Surya.

Surya Bakinaka, Vashti, was born in Mumbai, India. Now, at 20, her specialty was Martial Arts. Born to an Indian mother and Japanese father, she studied martial arts since she could walk. A disciple of Yahweh since birth, she teaches the arts in her father's school.

She directed her students to proceed without her. She acknowledged her father with humbleness and suspicious of the others. Her curiosity was unsettling to Euphrates and Mina Bird and Surya did not hide it.

Mr. Bakinaka asked for everyone to move to the other side of the studio to talk. Surya bowed to her father, the others, and allowed them to walk ahead of her. Mr. Zinkes read her as she inquired why they were here. Reaching the other section of the studio, Myna Bird attacked Surya with honorable intentions. Mr. Bakinaka screamed to Mr. Zinkes, "What is she doing?"

He wanted to rescue his daughter. Instead, Mr. Zinkes grabbed his shoulder. "Myna Bird will not hurt Surya. I will have to stop it. Surya is stronger."

Her fighting style was formidable. Surya was fast, punching blows to Myna Bird's chest and backside kick to her mid-back. Myna Bird attacked again, not taking her current defeat personally. Surya counters front-sidekick to the side of Myna Bird's face. Surya returns the attack and aims for Myna Bird's leg. "STOP!" Mr. Zinkes yelled. If he had not stopped the sparring, Surya would have snapped Myna Bird's leg. He then requested to meet Surya alone.

He asked Mr. Bakinaka, Euphrates, and Myna Bird to return to the other side of the school. Once gone, Mr. Zinkes bowed to Surya. It was the same as the test with Tracy, but as Surya slid backwards from a punch to the chest, she at once stood.

"I know what you are."

"I am what God designed me to be. He sent me, so you would join our team?"

"I will join you because I know it is what I'm expected to do. The others do not recognize who you are, do they?"

"No, and we must keep it that way. There is one who knows. God has commissioned him to become the Spiritual Teacher for this group. Joshua is on Mount Kalsubai in study. God revealed my identity to him, as He has to you. As for the others, when it's time, God will let them know. We will leave Mumbai in eight days. That will allow you enough time to say goodbye to your father and pupils. You may bring only what you need. You have access to your own accounts, but it's not required. And to be clear, I am human in various facets of the concept. I have the deteriorating condition of the mortal reality. I can suffer and get hurt."

Surya bowed to Mr. Zinkes. He allows her to walk out before him. She walks to her father and hugs him. Tears fall, and Surya continues working with her pupils. Mr. Zinkes walks up to him and they bow to each other.

~

At the hotel, they were sitting in the communal living area, waiting for Mr. Zinkes to speak to them. At eleven-fifty-one, Mr. Zinkes appeared from his suite. "We will leave in eight days with Joshua and Surya. We will head back to the compound and there, you will receive your instructions for your next mission. For now, enjoy the rest of your stay here. Leopard, I require you along with Mr. Laemel and Mr. Lyemel to catalogue as much material as you can of India. This part of Mumbai will no longer be standing after a year. Try to go on most of your exploration in the evening. Everyone else take this occasion to unwind. That is all for now."

~

While on the Mountain, Joshua was heavy in prayer and fasting, building himself up in his most holy faith to serve God as He called him to do. It was an ordained sabbatical that he didn't request but necessary for seeking God, and to learn and accept the design God had for him. Fasting was not a painless task. He was in the best situation imaginable in seclusion. No interruptions from the outside world, and solitude.

The full day one, he wrestled within himself. Hunger pains and a slight headache interrupted his sleep. He prayed, drank water, and fell asleep until day two. Waking every three hours did not help the headache. It diminished after drinking some vegetable broth and sleeping from seven to noon. By the third day, he could focus on prayer and studying the Word of God. It was on this day his heavenly language remained consistent during his prayer hours. No longer having his flesh war against him to get into God's presence. Crying out to God, being broken to get filled anew with the Holy Spirit. He sprawled on the plush marbled rug, prostrate, and surrenders all at the feet of Jesus. Crying out from the sting of losing Tracy, "God, why did you take her from me?" Hearing His still small voice, *'She is where she belongs.'* He cried out even the more and begins the healing process of letting her go but never forgetting her. He had never experienced this closeness to God before adhering to the directions without compromise. On the seventh day, he understood the will of God for his life and for the team. He prepared to leave the Mountain that evening, so as not to arrive in the violent heat of the day. When he reported to the hotel, they saw the renewal in him. Mr. Zinkes smiled.

Unfortunately, the wise cracking Euphrates was himself. "The way you look, I should have gone up there with you. It was a Moses on the Mount experience, but not the same glowing presence."

Joshua laughs so hard, his belly started cramping. He says, "Euphrates, everybody has their own pathway to walk. I can confirm for you, you will go on yours as God intended. Trust me, God has excellent works in store for you. He has wonderful things in store for us all." Joshua turned his attention to Surya.

"You must be our new member."

"Yes, I have consented to come with you," Surya said.

"Good. Welcome, and I look forward to working with you."

They gathered on the JC-12 that evening with the greatest purpose ahead of them. To see their next mission accomplished to its conclusion.

Chapter 26

- ⟨ ⟩ ◆ ⟨ ⟩ -

Getting to Know You

On the JC-12, in route to the D.U.M.B., relaxing around the table thinking, Michael was now leader of A7. Tracy was on his mind. Reminiscing back to a conversation they had. '*What we do now will establish our own destiny. Obeying God and being in His perfect will is all we desire to aim for. Everything else is a means to an end. Michael, this is not our home.*'

Kim interrupts his thoughts. "I've been meaning to talk to you. You've been a little distant."

"I had to work out some things. It wasn't until this moment I realized Tracy knew she'd die, and if she didn't, there was something she wasn't telling us."

"Why are you so certain?" Joshua asked.

"Because of a discussion we had. She said all we are working on is to prepare for our end. This is not our home."

"So, do you think we are all going to pass away like she did?" Kim asked.

"No, it's not as straightforward as that. Kim, we only have bits and pieces of the puzzle. God and Lucifer will have a last battle. Everything in between now and then is what we are a part of. Will we know like Tracy did? I don't know."

In the many conversations they had, his tone sounded like Tracy. She rubbed off on him without him even recognizing it. Kim continued their discussion. "Tracy is with our Holy Father and as much as I'd like to be there with her, I have a purpose down here on earth. Gods not finished with me yet. Michael, look around us. Even in the state our world is in, there is still the beauty in God designed. Trust me, we will all experience our conclusion." The tables had turned. Michael was now acting and speaking like a leader focused on God. Now, thinking deeper and more purposefully. He was observing more, but Kim had to bring Michael back to the present. God still had things for them to experience, see, and accomplish.

Mr. Zinkes asked Surya to give a brief history of her life while she was snacking on some dried, seasoned celery sticks. She placed the bag down and gulps down what remained. "I am twenty years old. I was born in Mumbai and I am not full Indian. My father is of Asian descent from the Mughal Empire. When my mom fell in love with my dad, her family renounced her birthright and declared her non-existent to the family she loved. Being disowned leaves you without a name in the Indian society, you are less than a hound. My mother knew the repercussions, but her love for my father was deeper than her tradition. My parents left Mahim and migrated to Bombay, so no one would recognize who she was. She died when I was three years old, because of an aneurism. My father was the strength I needed when my mother passed and then my father turned to God. I began my martial arts training at age two. Although I have sought no glory, I am a Grand-Master. My code name will be Vashti from the Book of Esther." No one made any remarks or asked Surya questions. They nodded their heads in acceptance.

Two hours remained on the flight back to Colorado, when Mr. Zinkes comes to address the team, "When we get back to the base, I will need to go to the Holy Mountain. Everyone will have the next week to do nothing other than read and study the Book of Revelations. Once I get back, you will train." Mr. Zinkes gets Surya's attention. "During this week that everyone is studying, you will spend no less than six hours with each of your team members getting to know them." Everyone's expression told the tale of discomfort, except for Joshua. "When I return, Mr. Laemel and Mr. Lyemel will give me a detailed summary of your progress. If you have questions about what you are studying, please talk to Joshua." Joshua smiled. There was no time to question anything. He understood his assignment.

"What happened to doing nothing?" Michael said.

Carsen raised her hand. "You can start with me tomorrow." Surya nodded in approval, as she thought it was their custom since everyone did the same thing earlier.

Michael was in his curiosity mode again, "Hey! Mr. Zinkes, where's this Holy Mountain you keep speaking of? Why haven't we gone there? And why is it such a secret?"

"Michael, I am not at liberty to speak of the Holy Mountain just yet. For now, it is the place where I get my instructions and have solitude." Surya and Joshua looked at each other.

~

Arriving at the D.U.M.B., it was clear skies and a full moon over the base. They were glad to be back. It also reminded them Tracy was no longer with them. Michal directs Surya to Tracy's quarters, which had already been prepared for someone to stay in.

He turned to her. "This was Tracy's living quarters. We had planned to clean out her belongings but we agreed to keep it as it was. Maybe you can learn a little about her from the things she left behind."

"I appreciate all of you accepting me as a team member."

"Oh! We haven't accepted you yet. You are required to work your way into acceptance on this team. Just because Mr. Zinkes wants you, doesn't mean you belong," adamant in his posture.

"I understand Michael. I'm not here to take Tracy's place. My aim is to be a part of God's plan and missions we need to complete. I have no wish to lead this unit."

"Let's be clear, and please don't take this the wrong way or think I'm being mean. No one and I mean no one can ever take Tracy's place."

"I take no offense. I know all of you are hurting from her loss. She must have been someone special." Michael relaxed his clinched jaw.

"Yes, she was. Are you anything like Mr. Zinkes?"

"No, I don't read minds. He is quite beyond my years. I can receive a lot from him. I can learn from all of you, if given the chance." Surya walked through the door and glances back at Michael.

"Thank you again," she said and closes the door.

Michael heads to speak to Mr. Zinkes but finds he's already left to the Holy Mountain. Michael heads to his quarters and retired to sleep, as they all do.

The moon, bright and unassuming to man, it was there like it had always been. Life turned, day by day with natural disasters increasing in foreign lands and in diverse places. It was just the unknown of all factors that kept them on their toes and constantly wondering what it would truly be like. Life had forever changed for the A7. Tracy was no longer with them. They had assured resolve they too must move on. The flickering flame of passion between Michael and Kim in Paris had mutually blown out. As they too recognized, it was an earnest but fleeting fantasy. This mission and the vitality of their involvement were never so prevalent. Nothing could impede what they needed to do. Feelings would have to take a back seat, and that would not change soon.

~

The following morning, the twins gathered the team for a pre-meeting. Mr. Lyemel begins, "Now begins our study and getting to know our new member. Carsen has come forward to start out with Surya. Before that happens, Mr. Zinkes has instructed he wants each of you present a question you want him to answer when he returns and before your training starts. Please take as long as you need to come up with your question and turn them in before leaving this room today." Mr. Laemel gives out the pen and paper. He says, "Also, you need to identify who will be two through six on speaking with Surya."

"I will go tomorrow with Surya," Kim states. They all one by one spoke up.

"Kelton is next."

"I will continue after him." Joshua said.

"Kendrick will go next, and then Michael will be last to speak to Surya." Mr. Lyemel Said.

"All of you know what to do this week. Please take the rest of this hour to complete your questions for Mr. Zinkes." said Mr. Laemel.

With their questions turned in, they head to their quarters, or whatever they wanted to do until mealtime. Mr. Lyemel read the questions to Mr. Laemel.

Kendrick laughed at his own question before leaving it with Mr. Lyemel. He knew Mr. Zinkes wouldn't have the answer— Will we all die this time?

"Michael asked, did Tracy know she'd receive a bullet for me? Ms. Surya, why are there only seven of us? Ms. Kim, is there something we are missing in the Bible? Mr. Wells, what is our next mission? Ms. Carsen, where is our next mission happening? Mr. Johns, how long before the rapture takes place?"

"They have some valid questions." Mr. Lyemel states.

"They do. I would like to know some of these answers myself. We have been with Mr. Zinkes the longest, and he's still a mystery to us. I'd like to know where the Holy Mountain is. Why don't we question him more often?"

"I don't know. It's not like we followed him without knowing what we were getting ourselves into. We both agreed as we sought the Lord for what to do with the rest of our lives. He sought us out. So, what is our end?"

"That goes without saying. I'm sure that's on all our minds. It's just more important to Mr. Roberts at this point."

Mr. Laemel and Mr. Lyemel, identical twins, were born in Boston, Massachusetts. Premature, they fought for their lives at 4.5 pounds when born. Following each other's footsteps, they became CIA Support Integration Officers at twenty-six. Considered at the top of their profession, when Mr. Zinkes approached them, disillusioned with the CIA, it took little for them to leave, and at thirty-five left to work for God.

As they walk out, Mr. Lyemel says, "I guess it's unimportant."

"Yeah, let's do what we came here for to the end. No need to stop now."

~

The 'getting to know you day,' started with Carsen and Surya. Carsen started, "I am an archeologist by trade, with military training. Being an FBI Agent afforded me to travel the world. Even that doesn't compare to what I've experienced here. Not knowing I was to be a part of something larger than what my mundane experience had led me to believe, my career was all there was in life. I just didn't realize with all my studying and learning about archeological artifacts and life from thousands of years ago, I was letting my life pass me by. Perplexed, when my parents didn't fight me after I told them I may never see them again, a part of me felt ashamed. Was I missing something? Why didn't my parents fight for me? Why did I feel so excited about doing something other than what I had always done? Mr. Zinkes gave those answers and more, and I am grateful I'm no longer lost in that way."

"Have you seen your parents at all?"

"No. I am sure they are fine. The one obstacle I had to overcome when I joined in was to let them go. My parents are believers, and I didn't appreciate how much faith they had in that moment standing in their living room. It wasn't until Mr. Zinkes explained my bond of weakness, that I realized they probably understood better than I did." Carsen walked over to her bunker chair and continued, "Today, you begin the course of figuring out what you have to conquer before our mission is complete. All of us, including Sublime, had too as well."

"Who's Sublime?" Surya asked. Carsen smiled and answered, "Tracy."

"Please forgive me, I keep forgetting her moniker."

"To be honest, Sublime was as much part of her as Tracy." she answered with a big, kind grin.

Their conversation finished, and Carsen showed Surya the location where Tracy finished her journey and the archeological site they found in Jerusalem. Ending up at dinner in that space, there was freedom of expression and laughter. They would share war stories and reminisce about the good they had experienced together. Their constants had remained in Ms. Giles, Griffith, Mr. Laemel, Mr. Lyemel, Mr. Zinkes, and a squadron with Captain Collier. Egypt had been a distant memory. What was next?

Tuesday, Kelton met with Surya. She tapped on his door. "Ah! Yes, Surya, you are to gain knowledge about us and our skills. Come and go with me." They walk a few feet to the computer area. They stopped outside the door, peering through the plate-glass window. "My name is Kelton Johns. I was born in Paris, France. The only man who accepted me for who I was taking me from an orphanage. They had no background information on me or any part of my ancestry. My dad saw the gift in me I had with computers. I've written protocol codes for NASA and every military branch there is, or isn't, known to the outside world. Planting viruses on any computer in 4.3 seconds is my weapon of choice, which is my claim to fame around here, hence the name Shadow. My job on this team is to research and to access any system necessary to gather knowledge for our advancement. As you can see, I am part of the team, but they don't need me for the muscle. I'd just get in the way. Anyway, when Tracy was with us, she was unaware I accessed her information. That is how deep I can reach. She was top secret—classified, you know. She lived up to the hype of how deadly she was. I use my ability for God now. I have no desire for our adversary to win on any front. He must feel like he will prevail. Do you have questions for me?" Surya put her hand on Kelton's arm.

"I like you. There's a presence around you I've never felt before. You are open, you don't see how much God loves you and how great He will use you. There is an innocence about you."

"Thank you and I receive what you have spoken over my life, Surya. For clarity, I am not innocent. I've had to overcome some areas of my life. I wrote programs for some bad people, albeit I didn't know they were bad. Once I found out, that didn't stop me from continuing my work with them. I've repented, as we all have, but I hear what you have said. I am not as well versed in the ways of life and relationship as the others. As it stands today, I have never been in a relationship period. I guess that would be odd for someone so young as you. Now let's move into the computer area and I will show you some features I've developed."

Surya absorbed everything possible. There was no question unanswered that she asked. Both Surya and Kelton walk into the mess hall, smiling and laughing. Michael continues to chew his chicken as he looks their way and says nothing.

Chapter 27

Getting to Know Israel

The warning bells rang, "This is not a drill", repeating over and over. "A7, report to the computer lab."

"Griffith, what's going on?" Michael asked.

"We have movement at the airfield. Someone just touched down, and it's not one of ours. It reads Israeli. Whoever landed may not know about this base, but knows there's an airport."

"What type of plane?"

"Appears to be a one-man fighter."

"Captain Collier, a small group with me. Everyone else stay here for now."

"You got it," Captain Collier responded.

This was right up Michael's alley—his element of expertise. He would never pass up the chance to get into some action. Michael, Capt. Collier and three security personnel put on their tactical gear and headed out. As they move out the exits, the base was on lockdown. They arrive at the jet in pitch black darkness and discover the pilot was nowhere to be seen.

On the coms, Michael said, "The only place the pilot could be is in the airport. Lights are still out, and coms are on. We have to search the airport."

Twenty minutes pass by and Michael sees lights near the tram that passengers used to take to and from the terminals. "It looks like a male. He's in the tram terminal." They corner him, and Michael points a red dot on his head, and Captain Collier puts another red dot on his heart.

"I don't know where you came from. If you have any weapons on you, I suggest you drop them. Kick them to the side before you are no longer a factor on this earth." Michael commands.

The pilot drops the weapon and his flashlight. "I'm no threat."

"I'll be the judge of that." Michael said.

"My name is Jacob Zuriac. I am from Jerusalem. They invaded our base, and my plane's controls went haywire from the impact of the plane next to mine received. It didn't show any damage until I got into the air. They no longer read accurately, and so I had to land. I couldn't land at any base, so I escaped the area and landed at the nearest airport friendly to Israel. And because my controls stopped working, I got lost. Fifteen minutes passed before I realized I was flying alone, not knowing my destination. I could no longer find them, as I searched for another fifteen minutes. I had to land several times for fuel at different AirForce bases. From Jerusalem, I traveled to Africa. From Africa, I took off to South America, from Brazil, I flew to Mexico and from Mexico, I came here. Each time, I landed at a base where I thought someone could help me fix my navigation system. I found each base deserted, except for when I landed here... If I told you the entire story, you wouldn't believe me, anyway."

With guns still pointing at him, "Try me, I've seen more than you can imagine. I will cuff you now and put you in a holding cell until we can verify who you are and whether you're a threat."

Droplets of sweat ran down his brow—fear.

"Sir, I am no threat. I will do as you ask."

"Turn around, Mr. Zuriac, and if you try anything, my men will drop you where you stand."

"Okay, okay."

Michael Euphrates went to Mr. Zuriac and handcuffed him without incident. "We will not hurt you unless you give us a reason."

"No problem. You will have no troubles from me."

Captain Collier covered his head with a material bag. "Mr. Crosley, you, and Mr. Jones get fuel in that jet and get it out of sight. Mr. Nordic and I will take Mr. Zuriac here and get him into a room. Capt. Collier, head to Shadow, tell him we need knowledge of who this gentleman is."

~

They all leave out. Michael gives a green light to the D.U.M.B. base and takes Mr. Zuriac to the interrogation room. He leaves the man handcuffed and blindfolded for the moment. "Mr. Nordic, please monitor Mr. Zuriac here. We don't want another episode like we had with Mr. Butler." The rest of A7 was waiting when Euphrates walked into the computer lab.

"Kelton, do we have any identifiers for Mr. Zuriac? Is he a resource, or we need to neutralize this threat?"

"Capt. Collier gave me his personal info and I'm still working on gathering intel on him."

Surya paced back and forth. "What's on your mind, Surya?" Michael asked.

Still pacing, Kelton broke her thought, "Give me twenty minutes. I may have to work through some channels to get inside Jerusalem." They all waited. It only took him twelve minutes.

"It shows Mr. Zuriac is deceased. They think his plane went down over Iran."

"Something doesn't seem right." Kelton and Kendrick say.

"What do you mean?" Carsen asked.

"He claims his navigation system went haywire, and he got lost from his squad. You fly from Iraq to Colorado. Why didn't he contact his base prior to now? From Jerusalem to Colorado is close to seven thousand miles. There's no way he didn't stop and call someone," Xerxes said.

"Yeah, what he said." Kelton says.

"Something does not smell Kosher. Get it?" Everyone looks at Michael.

"What? It was a joke. Don't you guys make jokes anymore? You guys have to lighten up."

"Michael, the potential of a threat is great. Those fighter jets come standard with a tracking device. What if they sent him out to scout for any military presence?" Carsen asked.

"You guys for the past two years have been telling me to ask God for discernment. Well, I've asked God. My gut says he's hiding AWOL. Jerusalem is as unstable as the rest of the world. We need to learn why he's here. I don't trust being a scout is his purpose. This far from Israel, and they think he's deceased."

"Michael, do you mind if I interrogate him while everyone watches?" Surya asked.

"Be my guest. My interrogation tactics may be a little harsher than yours."

~

Everyone walks to the IR waiting room behind Surya, and she walks into the IR by herself. Mr. Nordic leaves her in the room with Mr. Zuriac. A quiet ninja, she speaks to him in Hebrew. "(מר Yacob, שמי ושתי) Mr. Yacob, my name is Vashti."

"כמו המלכה ממושמע, לאחר?" (Like the disobedient Queen?)

"Mr. Zuriac, interpreting Queen Vashti, is up for debate. Paraded in front of men to dance, who only gawked at her for her beauty and not for her self-worth. I understand disobeying God would have been one thing but a man who loves his wife for her self-worth, wouldn't parade her in front of men to lust after her?"

"I guess not."

"Hence, being in that time, I can't know why she disobeyed the King. I'd want my husband to love me enough to ask why I didn't dance instead of banishing me. And that leads me to you, Mr. Zuriac. Why would a man who's travelled seven thousand miles to Colorado not contact his government to tell them his navigation failed, and you lost your bearings?"

Silent. He stared across the table at Surya. "You will not believe me if I tell you. You'll think I am crazy when I am not."

"Yacob or Israel, if I may, you do not understand what I've seen. Why don't you try me? After all, your life depends on it?"

The others look at Michael with concern. "What could she do to him?" Michael does not respond and continues to watch.

Mr. Zuriac understands the seriousness of the threat. He still hesitates — a big mistake. Engaging him in conversation was not working. She stands, and hands hit him in the neck and puts two of her fingers down under his clavicle bone near his heart and it paralyzed him.

"Yacob." She bends to his ear and speaks loud enough for everyone to hear. "You cannot move any extremities of your upper body. Every second that goes by the pain will travel both ways until you pass out. If you'd like this pain to stop, I suggest you tell me the truth and the whole truth. I will know if you are lying."

The pain was now traveling. "Okay, okay. Please stop this. The pain is too much." Surya returned to his side and gives him a blow to the chest and snaps his neck to the side.

On the other side of the glass. "She's good. I need to learn that." Euphrates said.

Mr. Zuriac was relaxing his face as the pain was subsiding.

"Are you ready to tell me why you are here, Israel?"

"Yes. Can I have water first, please?" Surya looked at the empty glass. A minute later, Mr. Nordic brings in water. Shaking, he gobbles the water, like it was his last. He sighed.

"The reason I am here is that a voice told me to come."

"A voice in your head told you to come here?"

"I was in Africa and I was going to contact someone. As I was standing there getting fuel from a deserted base, I heard a voice telling me to go to Colorado. At first, I ignored it. I thought maybe my brain was exhausted. Then the voice said I'd die if I went back. A tingling came over me so strong, I could no longer ignore it. It said, I'm needed here, and the plane too." He searched her face to see if she believed him. "I am telling you the truth."

"Mr. Zuriac, do you believe in God?"

"Yes, yes, I do."

"Do you know what's going on in Israel right now?"

"All I know is we've been fighting factions for years, and God has given us grace and mercy to win those battles. Jerusalem has increased their military presence tenfold. I've followed the traditions since my childhood, but I was never a religious man. As an adult, I have followed Messianic doctrine. I believe Jesus was the Messiah and He will return."

Surya smiled. "Mr. Jacob, I am not sure what your purpose is. But God knows your purpose and will get the glory. I will be back soon." She walked out of the IR and conferred with the others. "I know he's telling the truth. He was sincere."

Euphrates wants a second opinion, and he would not back down. "Surya, I trust what you say but we have been through too much to be trusting of anyone. We keep him on lockdown until Mr. Zinkes gets back." They discussed how to handle the 'visitor,' and decided Surya would oversee Mr. Zuriac until Mr. Zinkes returned from the Holy Mountain—whenever that might be— as part of her initiation. Mr. Laemel wanted to make sure Surya stayed on task. He touched her arm and took her aside.

"Although you have the task to care for Jacob, your responsibilities this week go unchanged. You must work out a schedule and continue what you started. Mr. Zinkes will not allow this as an excuse."

"I understand, Mr. Laemel. I will ensure I complete my tasks."

Later that night, Surya walked to Joshua's door. He didn't answer right away. When he opened the door, he didn't have on a shirt. Joshua was six-three and well built. He had never been without the attention of the ladies in the past. Surya turns her head to the left and stared down the hall.

"Oh, sorry Surya, let me get my shirt." He walked away and returned in a few seconds with a shirt on.

"What can I do for you?"

"I was wondering if we could visit with each other tomorrow. I've already met with Carsen and Kelton."

"Sure, no problem, I can meet with you after eleven a.m. or one p.m. or before three p.m. or after four." Surya was amused.

"Your prayer hours?"

Laughing. "Yes. After taking care of Mr. Zuriac, come and get me. I am okay to break the routine occasionally. I understand you have to spend a significant amount of time with each of us."

"Mr. Wells, you will prove to be an interesting discussion on tomorrow. I will see you at eleven a.m. tomorrow and thank you."

For the rest of the evening, everything was quiet. They remained on edge and the base stayed on high alert. The unexpected could happen again.

~

Surya dreamed of her dad. Waking, she recalled him stating, "There will be seven." Pondering the dream, she readies herself for the day's tasks. She took Mr. Zuriac's breakfast.

"Thank you, the coffee is heaven sent. A decent meal is scarce these days."

"I'd take you to the mess hall, but I didn't wish to wake you early or take you there in handcuffs."

"Sleep is not a part of my DNA right now and thank you for not parading me as a prisoner."

"You realize we must take every safeguard. This is God's work and must contain any troubles."

"Don't fret. Understanding why I'm here is what's heaviest on my mind, not the fact I must stay in here. God sent me, to what end remains a riddle."

"Well, Jacob, I'm sure He knows your presence. I'm speaking of Mr. Zinkes. When he gets here, he will give the answers we all desire, or he may not. Tell me your history, details, please."

Mr. Jacob explains Jerusalem's history and how he was now in the military. "Since Israel's rebirth on May 14, 1948, its military served as a critical necessity to keep this tiny nation safe from its Arab neighbors and terrorist organizations who threatened to annihilate it. To meet this security challenge, they instated conscription, or 'the draft,' to enforce mandatory enlistment. All Israeli citizens over the age of 18, male and female, except for non-Druze Arab citizens, must enlist. They require men to serve three years and women two years. Although military service is compulsory, there are exceptions, exemptions based upon religious, physical, psychological, or other legal grounds. Half of those men and women are yeshiva (Jewish seminary) students (Haaretz). For 88 years, yeshiva students were exempt from military service based on an arrangement made with Israel's first prime minister, David Ben Gurion, in 1948. For two years, I was a part of that exempt group. I removed myself from the sacred study and lived in military service full-time. They base this Netzah Yehuda Battalion off the leaders, telling the soldiers they were fulfilling the opening words of Deuteronomy 20: 1-4 (NIV), that say, *1 'When you go to war against your enemies and see horses and chariots and an army greater than yours, do not be afraid of them, because the Lord your God, who brought you up out of Egypt, will be with you. 2 When you are about to go into battle, the priest shall come forward and address the army. 3 He shall say: Hear, Israel: Today you are going into battle against your enemies. Do not be fainthearted or afraid, do not panic or be terrified by them. 4 For the Lord, your God is the one who goes with you to fight for you against your enemies to give you victory.'*

In 2018, battles raged with in-fighting of different Prime Minister regarding whether yeshiva students must fight within the confines of military responsibility and continued religious opposition from the ultra-orthodox Jewish Leaders wanting to keep the battalion as is. Their argument remains that we can see in the Tanakh that participation in physical warfare has spiritual implications. In the Book of Numbers, God orders a census of the Israelites to prepare for military service. He sets apart the Levites to serve the Lord in the Tent of Meeting. Numbers 8:14 &16, (NKJV), *14 'Thus, you shall separate the Levites from among the people of Israel, and the Levites shall be mine... 16 For they are wholly given to Me from among the people of Israel.'*

"Moses emphasized that all the other Israelite men of age, except the Levites, were morally and ethically required to serve in the military. He made this clear when he rebuked the tribes of Reuben and Gad for requesting to settle on the east side of the Jordan, thinking their intention was to avoid fighting alongside their brethren." Numbers 32:6 (NKJV), *'And Moses said to the people of Gad and to the people of Reuben, 'Shall your brothers go to the war while you sit here?'*

"This remains a rhetorical question echoing in the hearts of so many Israelis until five years ago. Upset, because religious Jews sought to use Yeshiva study to avoid enlisting in the Israel Defense Forces (IDF). I did not want to subject my children to such short-sightedness. I continued to study the Torah, and I also wanted to know more about Jesus and read Daniel and Ezekiel. Ms. Surya. I know God sent me but I don't know why. I cannot say what my purpose is here. I joined the IDG out of obligation to my city, my people and God but I continued to stay because I wanted a better life for my children."

"Thank you for that lesson. I will leave you now." Surya left him to eat his breakfast and then returned thirty minutes later to find Jacob sleeping. Taking the metal tray, he never moves to acknowledge her presence.

Chapter 28

Getting to Know All About You

Surya gathered with the others to eat, waved at Joshua, and sat next to Michael.

"Good morning, Surya, or do you prefer Vashti?" He asked cheerfully. Skeptical, she's slow to sit.

"I only want Vashti when on a mission or around Mr. Zuriac until he's cleared. How are you this morning?"

"Good and I am stupendous."

"That's great. I wanted to ask if it's still okay to speak with you. Joshua and I are meeting today, then I'm speaking with Kendrick, Kim and then yourself."

"I don't have a problem with that. Can I ask you a question?"

"Sure."

"When we were in India and we first met, meaning when we walked in, did you know why we were there?"

"Someday, I knew someone would come. I didn't understand it would be for me. I assumed they would come for my father because of my mother's death. My mother's family would come to their senses and look for her, but never did. That's why I trained hard to avenge my mother's honor. I soon found my vengeance misplaced and wanted to make sure I could protect my family."

"You and I will have an enjoyable conversation when it's my turn."

After eating breakfast and checking on Jacob, Surya found herself at Joshua's door again.

"Nice to see you have on a shirt this time."

"You're welcome to sit anywhere."

"I think at your desk chair will do the trick."

"Suit yourself."

"So, let's start from the beginning." Surya said.

"I guess I'll leave out the boring stuff. Let's see, I joined the military when I was eighteen, then got out at twenty-two and went to school for archeology for six years. The fascination and passion were intense. I became a Tomb Raider."

"Wow! You're young. Well, I travelled around the world looking for ancient treasures. I had a team, and we followed clues, looking in well-known places that might hold significant finds or monetary caches. Sometimes I was lucky. I'd sell the artifacts to museums or very wealthy people looking for certain memorabilia."

"So, you are like Carsen?"

"To a certain extent. Carsen learned the languages of ancient archeological texts. She studies artifacts recovered or discovered by men or women like me, Raiders. If someone finds an artifact, she travels to the locations and studies them."

"Ah, I see. So, do you have any family you have left to fend for themselves?"

"I had a mother and father. They are both deceased. No siblings, it's just me now."

"So, how did you come to be with A7?"

"Wow, okay, we have five hours left." Joshua gets comfortable on his bunk.

"I was living in Egypt for a while, raiding tombs for the military. There were wars, and it just so happens. I had an office in a special clinic. As I was coming out of the elevator, she walked in, looking bewildered and confident. She was too beautiful and coherent to be in that place for herself, so I ask if she needed help. She politely and sternly says, 'Yes. I am looking for Dr. Canno.' I show her where the doors to the clinic were. She said, 'Thank You', and walked through the doors and never once looked back at me. A week later, I saw her again. This time she walked past me and then turns around, smiles, and then walks out of the clinic. By the time I came to my senses and ran after her, I couldn't find her. She had disappeared that fast, so I went to ask Dr. Canno about her. He wouldn't give me any information and seemed terrified that I even asked. I back off and didn't see her again until one day she knocks on my office door. She was even more beautiful up close and personal. I let her in my office, and she got straight to the point. 'You've been enquiring details from Dr. Canno.' I didn't deny it, and I ask if she would like to sit down. She obliged me, and we sat for hours talking. She knew my life's history, and all I knew was the fake name she gave me. I was in love and we dated for a year and were engaged another year after that. I knew she worked for the government. It was top secret, and I trusted her. We were to marry our third year together. The night before the wedding, she stayed in her room, so I thought nothing of it. The next day, she never showed up. No explanation, no thought of sending me something down the line to explain. I went back to Egypt to find her, but she was a ghost. Vanished, no trace of her anywhere. I still to this day don't know why she was at that clinic. Five years later, I'm living in Morocco and I get a phone call from God knows who. I believe it was Michael telling me to meet the woman who left me at the altar, at the airport. Dumbfounded, scared, angry, and happy, I experienced all these emotions simultaneously. She's the only woman I ever loved and when she walked off that plane, I was in love with her all over again. When I consented to get on the jet and go with them to Egypt, it was the first time I ever knew who she was and the skills she gained. She was deadly, a killer, and she was good at it."

"You were in love with Tracy, even though you knew nothing about her until she sought you out again. You gave up everything to be with her?"

"Yes, and I still miss her. She's gone and I'm still here." Surya took a few minutes to gather her thoughts and allowed Joshua to do the same.

"So, why the nickname, X-Ray?"

"Superman. I'd love to say it was just because he had x-ray vision."

"Who's Superman?"

"You are young! Superman was a mythical superhero that did good things for the people of Metropolis, a fictional city. He fought crime and was from a planet called Krypton. Kryptonite, the color of emerald-green, was the only thing that could sap his strength and kill him. He had x-ray vision with laser beams coming out of his eyes and he was in love with this ordinary girl Lois Lane, a news reporter for the Daily Planet Newspaper. Every time you turned around. He was saving her from disaster. She'd get into trouble snooping in places she shouldn't be. On the practical side of this, I picked X-Ray because I used x-ray machines to view artifacts. Also, I can read people and can talk my way out of things, that's what Tracy used to say."

"How did you find out about Mr. Zinkes?"

Joshua stopped. "Are you referring to his abilities or the other thing?"

"The other thing."

"So, you know about him?"

Joshua hesitated for a moment, thinking about how to express his experience at that moment. "After Tracy died, I was distraught, and I had plenty of questions. Like now, he disappeared for two days back then." Joshua realized Mr. Zinkes had been going to the Holy Mountain on his trips. "Only now, he's told the others the truth about where he was going. When he returned, we talked alone in his room. God spoke and revealed who he was. Mr. Zinkes confirmed it, and I lost my mind for a moment. I can only tell you my experience was beyond imaginable. I broke down and he said I would become the spiritual teacher of A7. That's why you didn't see me at the hotel in Mumbai. During the time we were there, I was on the mountain in prayer and fasting. I experienced God in that holy place like I had never experienced Him before. You and I are the only ones, so why reveal himself to you?"

"God required him to do so. He's the only reason I would leave my father and come here, leaving everything behind."

"So, why were you chosen?" Joshua asked.

"My true purpose here is unknown. Leading up to this point, my mother had been barren until she accepted Christ. She got pregnant with me. She prayed for me as Samuel's mother prayed for him, and she dedicated me to the work of the Lord. I have known nothing else since my birth. My father continued after my mother died, teaching me, and guiding me down this path. When I was eleven, I saw a vision and God told me I would leave one day, and a special man would show me the way. A part of me knew when they walked through the door. God also knew I needed confirmation. I will be part of what is coming, no matter how long it takes."

"You are in a position other people may never experience firsthand. I take it as an honor God considered me. My past, to put it mildly, is not spotless. I'm forgiven. That part of my life is long gone. I guess we better head down so you can feed Mr. Zuriac for his lunch." Joshua stood to leave the room with Surya.

"He prefers you to call him Jacob."

"How many languages do you speak?"

"I speak my native language. I also speak Hebrew, Arabic, and Farsi. I may never get to use the Farsi. I think the Hebrew and Arabic will come in handy."

"Tracy spoke many languages."

"You truly loved her, didn't you?" She said as they walked out the door.

"I do. Her contributions to A7 and our brief, meaningful relationship are what I remember most. I know she is in a better place. She was the only one for me and I will miss the fact we won't be able to grow old together or have children. We will see each other again in our heavenly places." His body straightened. "Let's get some chow." Their connection sealed with affirmation of what they knew and what the others didn't.

~

'How many days of life shall I fumble around in the universe not knowing where I belong? My heart pounds to know the real me, and I see the molten lava of my existence. Existing to be that shooting star, the first curl on a new baby's head, the rusty nail that enters the stride parts of flesh. I delight in knowing you, who am I, the ink that writes the exceptional story, the owl that saves its babies, the healing tendon, and the water that saves. Who am I?'

Surya awakens, sweat dripping. Tears flow with the sweat, her head now in her hands. "I have to let go. This is not good for me." She pulled the covers off and the dampness of the cool breeze of the blanket reminds her to take a shower. Another day and it was only five in the morning. She showers, prays, and got herself ready to tend to Jacob's needs. Her silence was not uncommon. The others noticed her somber demeanor.

Two tables away, Michael asked Joshua, "You think she's homesick?"

"No, something is bothering her and being homesick is not it. She was told she was to come with us way before we ever showed up on her doorstep. It looks more like she is in search of something."

"So, how do you know so much?"

"I spoke with her on yesterday. She's looking for answers we can't provide."

"Well, I speak to her in two days. I hope she's not trying to get all deep in the business."

"I don't think so. It's like pulling a camel through the eye of a needle to get you to open up to me. You don't share yourself with anyone. You had that one thing in common with Tracy."

"Hey, what's that supposed to mean?"

"Why have you and Kim backed off from each other? The attraction was obvious."

Michael got up from his seat and took his tray. "That's none of your business. Stick to the spiritual stuff."

Joshua didn't challenge the issue. Looking around to see the rest of the team staring at them both.

~

Surya met up with Kendrick after finishing with Joshua. It was on the JC-12. Weather normal outside, with broken clouds to shade her way. She learned the ins and outs of flying, and there would be a lesson soon. For now, he showers her with his passion for flying. Their day ended in the mess hall and for a moment, Surya had forgotten her dream that woke her up in a cold sweat. Kendrick was grateful for her company and conversation even though he knew it wouldn't be for long. She left to see Jacob.

"Jacob, can you tell me more of your experience since fighting in the war?"

"Ms. Vashti, I've told you all there is to tell. The only other things are when God spoke, I felt peace doing what I was told to do. I couldn't explain the feeling if I tried. It was almost as if nothing else mattered or existed in that moment other than getting here. There was urgency and there was peace. When I arrived, it was as if someone lifted a significant burden. I cannot explain it any more than that."

"I understand Jacob, and call me Surya. That is my God given name."

"Do you really understand, Surya?"

"I believe I do Jacob. I have waited a long time to be in this place and yet, my questions are still unanswered. It's patience I am learning and there's nothing I can do about it."

"Can you tell me how much longer they'll lock me in this room?"

Surya sighed for them both. "Jacob, your fate, I'm afraid is in the one being that can clear up everything for you and for me. Mr. Zinkes won't be back for a few days. Then you can get your answers and so can I. Have a good night." Surya retreats to her quarters. Stepping through the door, she looks at her bed and remembers the dream. That night, no dreams came to her.

~

The next couple of days of routine were the same. She met with Kim. It was the last day, and she was to meet with Michael for their one on one. They could only express relief because Mr. Zinkes would turn up soon to ease them of their apprehensions and questions. Finding Michael busy in the weapons room, it was befitting to recognize Michael's fondness for action.

"Surya reporting for our conversation, sir."

"No need for formalities here, Surya. I'm certain most of my teammates gabbed your ear off. I'm one who prefers to listen as much as I talk, so this will be a two-way exchange."

"I see. So, would you like to open?"

Michael postures and leans on a crate, tumbling, almost landing on his derriere. Surya caught his jersey in time. He perched on the crate and straightened his shirt.

"I was born in Northern Iraq."

"Ah! Hence the Euphrates River."

"Yes. I entered the military at an early age. It was all I learned until I became suppressed with the world's ruling systems and the senselessness of the wars we continued. The higher the position I got, the higher intelligence information I collected on what we were doing, which made no sense anymore. I retired and then I found myself with A7 years later."

"What is your relationship now with A7? Do they recognize you as their leader? The reason I ask is that your demeanor is angry and apprehensive about change."

He snickered. "Be it far from me to criticize. I will take the time to do what Mr. Zinkes asks. Who knows, I might be next to take a slug for one of you." Huffing, he continued. "I received Christ, and I didn't know what it meant to live for Him until I joined this team. A part of me still doesn't get all the mysteries there are to discover. When I came to A7, I was pompous and confident of my qualifications, as you seem to be Surya. Never in my wildest dreams did I think there was someone better than me. I succeeded in all my endeavors, but joining this team shattered my self-imposed bubble, a change I'm grateful for. I recognized my existence was not on the right track, and God brought me here to restore me, because He was the only one who could, and that part of the story seemed to be across the board for all of us. Something about us needed adjusting, and you're no different. We have the concept down, but we weren't moving about our lives down the right path. When I got here, I met Tracy Pimbridge, Sublime. I disliked her and tumbled hard on her at the same time. Now, that's something I've never told to anybody before, except Mr. Zinkes. Well, I never said it, just read me and knew." He points to Surya. "You seem to have that effect on people. They just want to spill their guts around you. Anyway, because of our mission, I could never tell her how I felt and if I had, it would have been for nothing, anyway. I'd appreciate you protecting that bit of information. Only you, Mr. Zinkes, and Kim know. I had to learn hard lessons, and the one thing I'll never forget is that I can do nothing without God."

"So, you loved Tracy too, and you never told her. Why?"

"It was because she was in love with someone else and she reached out to him and their love for each other was still there."

"Ah! Joshua."

"Yeah, and their love was true, and I didn't have a shot. She's the only woman who's ever challenged me in every way. Having a comeback for every shrewd, sarcastic thing I used to say to her, she kicked my butt, and I liked it. She loved me, not the same way I adored her, and because I knew she wasn't for me, I directed my affection elsewhere, which wasn't true either. I am not sure if anyone told you. On our last mission, Tracy took a bullet for me. She died, so I could live. So, you see, Surya, I'm not bitter about what she did. I am thankful and angry at her for making that decision without telling me. I desired her to stay alive and keep me grounded, to keep me on my toes. No one else challenges me as she did, but I must concede you might challenge me in the physical department. I look forward to our training together."

"So, are you upset I am on the team?"

Michael set aside the rags and the gun he was cleaning. "No, I'm not upset. I give everyone a hard time, and I meant what I said. Prove your worth to this team because we depend on each other. We don't have to be perfect and training will teach you that. Don't be reluctant to challenge any of us or respond to a challenge. What we do cannot change because it's God's plan. What that plan is from here on and with you remains unknown. And don't get it twisted. You are not here to replace Tracy. No one can ever replace her."

Surya sits down on the crate next to Michael. Grabbing the rag to help him clean. "Can you at least be the big brother I never had?"

Michael was right. She had a way with words to rival Joshua. She knew just what buttons to push. "I can do that, as long as you don't annoy me as a little sister would. Surya, you have skills. You showed that to Jacob, but you haven't been in the field with us. So, it will take time for us to trust you with our lives out there."

"Thank you for recognizing the gift of God in me, and I can help this team, and I promise I won't annoy you."

"Are there any other questions you have for me?"

"No, but I want to be a part of this team and if it means proving my loyalty, then so be it."

"Surya, your loyalty belongs to God. Know this. It could be to our end this time. We don't know what's ahead of us, and a part of that is the beauty of God's plan. We must trust ourselves and each other. Not to change the subject, but Mr. Zinkes should return soon. How is Jacob?"

"He's doing well and he's as anxious as we are for Mr. Zinkes to get here."

"Mr. Zinkes, now there's a riddle."

The rest of her day was learning about all the weapons available for their use and training. Michael was the tour guide for the day, and they talked until there was nothing left to say. Michael dropped Surya off at Mr. Jacob's room and went about the rest of his day.

Chapter 29

The Holy Mountain

On the Holy Mountain (שמיים הצעיר-Youngest Sky), where time doesn't exist, the mountain peaks have beginnings of snowfall. In an internal cavern, an Archangel was there with Xariel on the last day before he was to return to the base. Gabriel the Archangel speaks:

"Our Father has sent me this day to prepare you. Find the one who has the ancient Reed. He must go before the Witnesses. You must not fail, or Archangel Michael will come. Once the end comes, you will hear my horn. You'll stand before YHVH." Gabriel says.

"I will do as Our Father says."

"Know the day is near, for the end is at hand."

"How long before the trumpets sound?"

"That is not for us to know."

"As YHVH commands His Spirit."

Mr. Zinkes arrives at the base, unbeknownst to everyone. They all gather for breakfast. Michael ate berries and pancakes. "Man, these pancakes are delicious this morning," he said to Joshua.

"I prefer waffles, and I like an occasional blueberry pancake."

Over the loudspeaker, "A7, report to the conference area in one hour."

Michael looks around the table. "Mr. Zinkes must be back. Good, now we can get some answers."

Joshua finished eating his oatmeal. "Did everyone finish reading Revelations?"

One by one, they acknowledge they had. "Are there questions you have before we meet with Mr. Zinkes?"

Michael gets up from the table. "I can't speak for everyone else and I always have questions. I think it's too much to talk about right now."

Joshua gets up from the table. "All right, you all know where to find me."

~

Mr. Zinkes is in the room with Mr. Zuriac. "I apologize for my absence when you arrived. My name is Mr. Zinkes."

"Ahh! You are the one we've all been waiting for. Shall I tell you the story I told the others?"

"No need. I know why you are here. God sent you and the plane for His purpose."

"So, they told you?"

"No, I have seen no one since I arrived. I came straight to your room."

"So, how could you know the reason I am here?"

"Mr. Yacob, you heard a still small voice three times tell you to come here to Colorado. You are here because we need you when we arrive in Jerusalem. Your expertise in Israel and how to get to a certain Chief Priest, Anai Bethlem, is crucial. He holds an ancient artifact, the qeneh hamiddah, that will measure the temple. Created out of pure gold, it collapses from six cubits to one cubit. The others do not know this information yet. So, I would appreciate you keeping this information between us for now. I need you to come with me. You are no longer confined to this room."

"You are amazing, as Surya told me." They leave the room and head to the conference room.

~

Finishing their breakfast, most were in the conference room thirty minutes early. Joshua, the only uncurious one, strolls in five minutes before it was time to meet. Surya bounced in her seat with excitement, looking around at everyone. They all were eager to receive the answers they were looking for and to discover why Mr. Zuriac was here. They sat around the table in silence, as breathing was their only choice. Ms. Giles, Mr. Laemel and Mr. Lyemel walk in together and then Mr. Zinkes walks in last with Mr. Zuriac. It surprised them to see Mr. Zuriac out of his room and walking into the conference room. "Looks like you all are eager to receive news and answers, which I have plenty but first you must read, Ezekiel 14. The Lord God is declaring war on this world. In the next six months, we must train and complete the second part of our mission. God wants us to prepare leaders for the Remnant. As for Mr. Zuriac, he is no threat. God sent him to us for a purpose, specifically his jet plane and his knowledge of Israel. We will need it in Jerusalem."

~

Mr. Zinkes sat in his chair. "But before I get to that, I will answer your questions. Michael, Tracy saw our last mission in a vision, and although she felt her death could occur that night, she didn't know in what manner it would happen. She didn't know she would save you. What she did revealed the love of Christ, to die for a friend. Tracy considered you a brother, a friend, and she laid down her life so you could complete the work God had for you, for all of you. Her selfless act allowed all of you to get out alive to finish what you started for God, to be here right now. I hope that forever clears up your question as to if she knew. Surya, seven, is the number of completeness. God sends His word to complete His work. If nothing else, Revelations should have revealed that to you. I know you want to speak alone and that will take place soon. As for the rest of you, the number seven is significant many times in the bible. Just as an example,

Jude 1:14 reveals that Enoch was the seventh son of Adam. There are seven beatitudes, seven churches, seven spirits, seven golden lamp stands, seven stars, seven seals, seven horns, and the list goes on and on." Next, he turns to Kim. "There is nothing missing. Everything is there for our learning. Are there other books we can learn from, yes? God doesn't leave His children ignorant. Seek Him and you will find Him. Ask for knowledge and the Lord God will reveal to you all what He desires you to know. Your insight and level of understanding are all up to you. Joshua, our next mission is to travel to seven continents and establish cells for the Lord. Those left behind will need help when they come to Christ. It will be our responsibility to convince them through God's Word. Carsen, part of your answer was in the answer for Joshua. We will end up in Jerusalem. Once we leave on our mission, this base is going dark. Kelton, all I can tell you is soon, as I stated to Joshua. No man knows the hour or the day when the Son of man will return, and that includes me. Kendrick, life, and death belong to God and the Lord God alone. When it happens, I'm sure you will be pleased. The Lord God reveals so much to us during this time. All of you should trust your own instincts and know God's plan is infallible." Mr. Zinkes headed toward the door. "Your training will begin tomorrow." He instructed as he walks out of the room.

Mr. Lyemel stands, "I trust all of you read Revelations?" Everyone had. "Kendrick, you will not train with the others. You will need to lead the upgrade on Mr. Zuriac's jet to the JC-12 technology, and he will aid you. We require his craft ready before we take off for the seven."

~

Prior to dinner, Mr. Zinkes requested Surya and Joshua to meet him in the conference room. He was already present when they arrived. Both Joshua and Surya sit with anxious inquiry now.

"The reason I am meeting you both alone now is because YHVH wants me to reveal some things only to the both of you. In the twentieth century, man came upon knowledge, as it once was in the garden. Back in ancient times, man gathered with the fallen and they too received knowledge not meant for them to know. This has been Lucifer's plan all along. To create something that would not honor YHVH or acknowledge the Lord God's existence in forming humans in the likeness of YHVH's image. To bring us where we are now, in a time such as this, it has happened again. This time the Apollyon completed the transfer of knowledge with the Fallen and there is no delaying the results. In our last mission, we were to delay the coming of the world destruction. Now things must take place as foretold in the Revelation." As Mr. Zinkes was about to continue, the Spirit of the Lord came upon Joshua. He falls to his knees. He speaks in his heavenly language, Mr. Zinkes interprets: "Rest in Me, trust in what you hear. Seek after Me. Love Me with all your heart. Trust Me past your tears. Love Me beyond your fears. Happiness and joy are within Me. Trust Me with your heart and trust the Holy Spirit within you. Seek me, seek me, seek me. For my glory shall reign in the heavens and in the earth. Trust Me and I shall not leave you nor forsake you. Trust me past the hurt you feel. Love Me beyond what you can see. I will use you for my glory and I will lift you up and enlarge your heart. Listen to My word and hear, thus says the Lord. This is for you to see and to understand your place in Me. Fear not, for I AM is with you. Lean not to your own understanding. For I come quickly, I come quickly. I shall use you for My will, for My purpose, says the Lord, trust Me. Amen." Mr. Zinkes continues to speak, "Because God has chosen all of you at such a time as this, you cannot faint and lose heart. Only God knows our expected end. YHVH has given us hope through the Lamb, and our future is in him. This is upon us."

Chapter 30

Faithful Cells

Memories of lives past, children racing up and down the fields of daydreams. Colorful, hunter green pasture, palm trees and glass filled sands. The innocence of them long passed, their faces swollen with desperation and yearning to see if they would endure. They could recognize the grace now and the faithfulness of God. Hope fades with every occasion of wondering—what if? Is it too late for me now? My gut told me redemption is nigh but my inner man warred against me and won.

~

The end of this age was near. The Apollyon wanted the people without hope.

Meeting after breakfast, as Mr. Zinkes reiterated, "Our mission is to create faithful cell groups that will remain when the time arrives for testing of those who will survive. After we carry out our mission, the testing will take place and then the Two Witnesses will appear. They delivered the son of perdition, but it is God's design we do not end his efforts. God's plan will continue according to His word. You all are part of His Kingdom that encompasses you, Mr. Zuriac. YHVH will write His name on you all and those to come. We will travel to Africa, Mongol, Australia, Greenland, Canada, Brazil, and Jerusalem will be the last place to establish cell groups in those countries. Joshua, you will advise those God has qualified. Michael, you, and the rest of the group will create a uniformed tactic to train them how to combat, stockpile weapons, food, water, and the Word of God.

Once the day has arrived for us to train no further, we will settle in Jerusalem. I perceive you are thinking, why weapons? They must be able to defend themselves against chaos in the land. If they must take a life, it's because the depravity has increased."

The task before them will not be pleasant, and they will encounter significant resistance. Fasting and praying on their own to prepare themselves, Joshua helped Kelton search for the seven individuals who would help bring those to Christ. Kendrick retrofitted Mr. Zuriac's jet fighter with the JC-12 tech. Taking three months to get everything into place, their time would begin in Greenland with Hans Egede.

~

A7 reached a descendent of Hans Egede in the early afternoon. The JC-12 landed near the Egede home, tucked away in the woodlands, while it was still light out. No one could see them from the central road, and Kendrick and Mr. Nordic landed in his backyard. There was no disguising the disruption in the trees from the plane's landing. Mr. Egede came out with his rifle drawn. He was shouting and squawking at the trees stirring. "Come out from behind those trees. Who's out there?"

Mr. Zinkes walked off the airplane first and orders everybody to stay put until he signaled them forward.

"Preacher, Eli Egede, we are here in the name of our God."

"And what God is that?" his tone questioning in high pitch.

It was a humorous moment and if Mr. Egede weren't holding a weapon, he would have laughed till his belly ached. Mr. Zinkes giggled. He hoisted his palms and declared the moment a serious one. "Jesus Christ, you received twenty years ago when you thought you were dying of cancer. You promised God, you would serve Him if He healed you."

"Everybody knows my history. You must do better than that."

"God healed you and you've kept your word all this time. God is pleased you are fearless and unwavering in your faith. Not that you haven't stumbled or made mistakes. He now seeks the hardest task of your life in maintaining that faith, even during the tribulation period. You have questions. I require you and your wife to listen to what we have to say."

"How did you learn about my wife? Are you part of some government organization?"

"No, we are not part of any government." Mr. Zinkes answered cautiously.

"It's the same way I recognize that your kids are dying in their bedrooms at this moment." He drops the weapon. "My team is on a plane you can't see right now. May we enter your home? There is no reason for alarm. We are not here to hurt you. If you provide us some time, I will explain everything."

Cautiously, he waves them forward. "Yeah, what do I have to lose at this point?"

"Your hope, Mr. Egede, which we are here to build." Mr. Zinkes yells to everybody they can come out. As each entered the home, Rachel, his wife, comes from the children's bedroom. She suppressed her torment as though it had been there for years and she could turn it off like a water faucet to display to others she was okay. Mr. Zinkes asks them to sit.

"My wife can sit. I'd rather stand."

"May I offer you some water?" Rachel asked.

"No, thank you Mrs. Egede." Mr. Zinkes wasted no time in disclosing what's taking place. "Our normal way of life is ending soon. God has instructed us to prepare those left behind to help others come to Christ. You, Mr., and Mrs. Egede, must hear us. Even though you will not leave in the Rapture, those who come to Christ will require your spirit during the three and half years of tribulation. We are here to teach you what you must achieve to bring others to Christ during those years. Again, God is not disputing your belief in Him. He requires using it. He will strengthen you through the battle, but you must not waiver. You will need to teach others as we are advising you. If you give us a week, we will supply you with all you need. A tumultuous and perilous time is coming, and it is our job to prepare you. And before you ask, I understand your agony and grief for your children and there is nothing you can do to make them better. They are in the bosom of Christ now." Rachel wanted to jump up and run to their room. She couldn't move. Paralyzed with grief. Surya went over to her and grasps her hands and prays with her. She glances at Eli. "Prepare the children." He returns sobbing and they comfort each other in accepting their children were no longer with them.

"We will help you bury them if you agree?"

"Thank you, we appreciate it."

"We will provide you time. Come and retrieve us when you are ready."

"I will." He soothed his wife.

The next dawn, they buried and eulogized the children, and it was another day before Mr. Egede was ready to work with A7. Joshua talked with Mr. Zinkes earlier that morning and gathered information useful for storage of needed items. With clear skies and sunny afternoons, Joshua began each day by expounding on the word of God and what was to happen for the day.

"Mr. Zinkes says you have a storm shelter, is that right?"

"Yes, how did he....?!"

"Eli, the only thing you won't receive an answer to is how he does what he does." The confirming glance Joshua gave was satisfaction enough.

"Yes, there's a storm shelter. We haven't used for fifteen years."

"Well, that's where we'll start, and it will be your base of operation, for now, your food and weapons shelter."

The shelter was large enough to hold a church meeting and pack it with food and weapons. It was a dusty old place needing major fixing. They replaced the broken wooden slats, which let in light, with steel slats to keep out sun and moisture. Transporting shelving more easily was the reason for widening the cellar doors. They had to reinforce the doors to ensure no one could just break it open, hammering and sawing the days away. Money was still available to spend, to buy them whatever they needed. Supplying the shelter, they stayed there for three weeks. The Egede's missed their children. They no longer mourned as others with no hope would have. They knew they would see their children again. Within the fourth week, it was time for them to leave. Euphrates shakes Mr. Egede's hand. "Our time here has ended. I can only tell you to stand strong and continue to increase your faith. It doesn't get easier from here. Trust only those that are into God's word, and you will know them by their fruit. Be watchful and never let your guard down," he said.

Mr. Zinkes stepped up, "No, you will not see us again in this life. We have to continue our work down here until we finish it."

"I still don't know how you do it. I consider all of you God's angels and my wife and I thank you for your help and your presence during this season of sorrow and trouble. Do you mind if we pray before you all leave?" No one denied prayer. Eli prayed, and no stone was unturned.

~

Flying under the dark and harmony of night, they now headed to Canada, to a descendent of David Livingstone. When they arrive, they rest for a day before seeking Christine Livingstone, which was no longer her last name. Married for twenty-three years to Charles Wreckbaum. Although they lived in a rural sector, the JC-12 could not land there without being seen. They would find shelter for the jets and seek for alternative transport to take them to the location. The large cottage home, painted charcoal grey with white trim, played well with the overcast clouds of the day that let through enough sunlight to make it bright outside. Mr. Zinkes steps out the van and heads to the porch. To the left was a bay window and a porch swing. Mrs. Wreckbaum was in the rural area of Kerrobert in West Central Saskatchewan. Both she and her husband were in their late fifties, and their son, in his mid-twenties, was home when Mr. Zinkes knocked on the door. Mrs. Wreckbaum comes to the door all spry and happy. Mr. Zinkes could hear her through the door until she opened it. The instant smell of fresh baked goods wafted out the door.

"My word! You are a tall fellow, aren't ya? Hey Charles, are you expecting anyone?" Mr. Zinkes could hear Charles coming to the door.

"No, Christine. I'm not expecting anybody." He walked out the door and greeted them, "Yes, sir. Can I help you?"

"My name is Mr. Zinkes. I'm here because God sent me. Mrs. Wreckbaum, you are the heir of one David Livingstone?"

"Oh, my word! Yes, he was my great-grandfather. He's passed for a while now. What's going on?"

"God sent me to you to prepare you for what's about to happen around the world. I know it sounds peculiar. Give me time to explain, and you'll understand everything."

Just like the Egedes, Mr. Zinkes and his abilities mystified them. Shocking and humbled, they received their call to serve as God instructed. Each place was distinct from the rest, and each descendant continued to be in wonder at Mr. Zinkes and his prophetic awareness of their history and present. Mr. Zinkes never talked of their futures, but warned the days ahead would be in chaos and hardship. Six months to wrap up their tasks in the places God had instructed them to prepare souls, they would head to Jerusalem in two weeks.

Chapter 31

Salvations Cry

Before heading to Jerusalem, they stay in Mongolia for the moment, being near the Khovsgol Lake (Dark Blue Pearl), a hundred-mile-long pristine alpine lake in North Mongolia (Dalai EJ, the Mother Sea). This was the last place to establish a faithful cell. Secluded from the public, to pray, fast, and enjoy the serenity of what God had created the weather cool and brisk, the water majestic, laying as flat as the iced over lake. With the sounds of a moving lake, Mr. Zinkes was standing at the edge of the blue array of water. Mr. Zuriac was standing there next to him. "I am glad God allowed me to observe this place and to experience everything, never thinking my story would turn out this way. I'm grateful. It is still a blur how I got here. I wouldn't want it any other way."

"Because YHVH has called for a time as this, know that what's ahead is for Judah and Jerusalem. All the nations rise against the All Mighty, shall utterly fall. It shall be in the days of the prophet Zechariah. Christ will return to do as stated in His word. There has always been an outcry for repentance and more so now. There are blinded eyes and deaf ears to what Yahweh is saying to those that were formed in His image. You have seen the difference between the righteous and the wicked, between those who serve God and those who don't. Soon, you will only see the righteousness of God. Fire will consume the wicked like straw. For those who fear His name, the Sun of Righteousness will rise with healing in his wings. We all will be free. It is our time to tread upon the wicked, says the Lord of Heaven's armies. God has provided enough warning. The time has arrived to complete our mission and it will not be easy for any of us from this point on. Enjoy the view, Mr. Zuriac." He turns and walks away to leave Mr. Zuriac at the pristine view.

~

Later that morning, everyone gathered around the table, eager to get the information for the next move. "We will go to Jerusalem in four days. Apollyon has begun the destruction of humankind and God in their own infinite wisdom. We are not about to stop them. It is to get into Jerusalem and extract Anai Bethlem, as he is now the Chief Priest. We must get him into protective custody, as his life is in danger. He will be the one who will rise for the righteous. His warning to them about the false man they shall call a Savior. The man who signed the United Nations Peace Treaty ten months ago. Anai Bethlem is a descendant of Mary and Joseph. He is unaware of this. He is the last descendant we must prepare. The two witnesses are near, and it is our job to get him to them. They will seal him and then our mission will be complete. Mr. Zuriac will be our lead on the ground when we land in Israel. Kelton, we need you to find the Chief Priest and we need him found like yesterday. Once we find Mr. Bethlem, we need an extraction strategy. Leopard, you will need to find us a safe place until we can get him to the Witnesses. Time is of the essence." Mr. Zinkes informed them.

~

Mr. Zinkes requested Surya and Joshua to join him for a walk. "The three of us will walk one day's journey to Mt. Otgontenger. I have something to show you there. Prepare to leave in one hour. Do not bring bread, you won't require it. Water alone is vital." The hour arrives, heading toward the mountain. They would travel to the other side of it. The mountain top was nippy and crisp. There was no snow, which was unusual for that time of year. Twenty-four hours into their adventure, they reach their destination, daylight was still available. He ordered them to wait before they proceeded. There was a lone rock entry way Mr. Zinkes entered. Coming out five minutes later instructing them, "Remove your shoes, as this is holy ground." He went back in and Joshua and Surya followed behind. It was dark, and the temperature was not as it was outside. "You will be in prayer for three hours. I cannot tell you what transpires here, but know the Spirit of God is in this place. After prayer, we will move further into the mountain."

The presence of God was so strong there, it was overwhelming to anything other than worship. Caverns deep provided glowing lights of amber and sky-blue rock. Winds whistling melodies of praise as they uttered in prayer and cried out to ABBA Father. As they wrapped up the three hours, Mr. Zinkes says, "It is time."

They walked through another entry way, Mr. Zinkes transformed into his angelic form, and they kneeled. His wingspan glowed as the sky-blue rock intensified its light. His body appearing to the light transformed into a translucent rainbow-colored presence. They could still see his mortal shaped body. He rose in full array and then landed in front of Surya and Joshua again. A bright light filled the space, Gabriel entered, and both Joshua and Surya fell into a deep sleep. "They will know nothing of their former lives. I will write on them the word of I AM. They shall not know time has lapsed until thus says the Lord God Almighty."

Mr. Zinkes returned to the JC-12. Everyone looked up but did not ask the question. "Joshua and Surya will not be coming back. YHVH has taken them. I am not at liberty to explain their whereabouts." He relaxes in his chair and prays.

~

Two days before they would take off for Jerusalem. Euphrates gathers the rest of the team to prepare Mr. Zinkes on the plan. "Kelton has located Chief Priest, Anai Bethlem. He's being held prisoner in the temple. They have done nothing to him yet but he cannot leave the synagogue on his own accord. We will extricate him and deposit him in Egypt until it's required for us to come back to Jerusalem."

"Since he is not here now, Joshua told me where to take Anai before you all left. Dr. Canno, if yet alive, will help us. He said to give his and Sublime's name, if he questions us further, to let Mr. Zinkes speak to him and give him one million in cash. He will allow us refuge for as long as we need it." Leopard says.

"What is the extraction procedure?" Mr. Zinkes asked.

"Well, since we've identified where he is, Mr. Zuriac will fly the Israeli jet just in case the towers are active. Once we enter the base, will have access to generals and soldier uniforms. He will get them and return them to the JC-12. He will put on the generals regalia, along with me, and Kelton. Mr. Lyemel, and Mr. Nordic will have on regular uniforms. Kendrick and Mr. Laemel will wait with the airplane along with Leopard and Myna Bird."

"I will come with you." Mr. Zinkes said.

Euphrates looked at him. "Are you certain about that?"

"I'm positive."

"Well, we can use all the help we can get. We don't want a large group that will draw too much attention. Once in Egypt, we will stand by for your directions on how and when to get him to the Two Witnesses. I'm confident there will be a crowd and military presence, which I'm sure won't be friendlies to our cause."

Mr. Zinkes heads toward the jet's exit door. "We'll worry about that when we get to it. Let's take one mission at a time. The alternative is to die without completing our mission and Jerusalem's complete annihilation from there." He leaves the jet and looks at the horizon. Euphrates remains convinced that Mr. Zinkes is not telling them everything.

~

Leaving at the break of dawn, two days later, both planes rise and descend towards Jerusalem. They land at a military base known to Mr. Zuriac—no one was there. The flight tower had no one in it. The planes on the ground were unmoved. They could hear a bustling city but, it differed from car horns and people chattering. The eerie existence of the day. It wasn't clear to make out what it was.

"Something is strange. It looks abandoned months ago. There was a full-fledged base here when I left. Now there is nothing."

"It looks like they left the base. The planes are here, equipment, and tanks." Euphrates observes.

"I don't understand this?" Mr. Zuriac expressed. "Is this a sign of the peace treaty signed months ago? To disband our whole military. None of this is making any sense."

"Jacob, God never ceases to amaze me." Euphrates laughs. Euphrates walks into the General's quarters. "General Zuriac, your suit awaits."

Everyone gets what they need and head back to the JC-12. On board Euphrates tells them, "As easy as it was getting here, and those suits were, I don't think the rest of this mission will be so easy."

Mr. Zinkes stops everyone in their tracks, "I must confess something to you. On this morning, Abba has called out from the heavens. There is no need to worry. Your souls will have peace. We are exempt from the Salvations Cry." Mr. Zinkes speaks the Holy Scriptures word for word.

"Well, isn't this great? All we have left to deal with is the wicked. What are we going to find next, the anti-Christ sitting in front of the door waiting for us to at the temple?" Euphrates said. Everyone glanced his way and shrugged their shoulder. Mr. Zinkes read them, *'They all think under the circumstances, it's possible.'*

~

Their mission remained the same, extract Anai Bethlem and take him to Egypt. The extraction plan would begin at midnight. To see turmoil in the streets, confusion and hearing the wails of the suffering, they could not allow their empathy to outweigh the mission. Having to push past what they saw, screaming mothers weeping for their babies. Men in violent delirium. Women in instant madness. Those left, now recognizing the truth. They made the wrong choice to listen to the world and not the Word of God.

"Ease your spirits. Eternity is ours to hold." Mr. Zinkes assured them.

The city, 1500 miles around, they arrive at the Temple Mount to find there were few guards around it. As they enter, they could hear the sporadic shouts of people longing for the loved ones now gone. Visibly shaken guards met the team as they entered the temple in pandemonium. They were in the dark about everything that was going on outside the temple walls and didn't defy orders or move from their stations. Jacob approached them and demanded to see the Chief Priest.

"Yes, sir, can you report to us what's going on out there? We have orders not to leave. They won't allow us to go check on our families," the soldier pleads with Jacob.

"Sir, the Word of God is true as He spoke in the Holy Bible. We have suffered many lives lost today, and some will not get the chance to repent for their sin. You have that moment now. If you confess Jesus Christ as your Lord and Savior and continue to believe in your heart until death, you too can have salvation. God's last Salvation's Cry has gone out to the world. Follow Christ and believe. Do not let this government deceive you. The devil's schemes are at work here. To have eternal life, you must believe Jesus is the Son of God and He has come back to redeem His Bride, the people of God, and establish his Kingdom that will reign for eternity."

The soldier dropped to his knees. "I want to follow Jesus!" Just as the phrase fell out of his mouth, a group of guards came rushing through the corridor of the Temple. The guards opened fire, striking the man through the heart, causing him to fall over. Euphrates, Jacob, and Mr. Nordic return fire while Mr. Zinkes looked for Anai Bethlem. There were steps on both sides of the corridor, and they all reached the top of the stairs and returned fire to give Mr. Zinkes more time.

All the while, bullets were flying. "I knew this being easy wouldn't last," Euphrates said. Laughing at a time like this was unexpected. It made him freakishly calm under the circumstances of being fired upon. As they ran toward the end of the hall, Mr. Zinkes came running toward them with the Chief Priest in tow. "I have him. We need to get out of here now!" They all ran towards the stairs again, only to meet more gunfire. Ducking and dodging, Euphrates drew extra ammo and showered the area from top to bottom to get out and survive. There would be no jumping out of windows. Euphrates ran out in front of Jacob and covered him as the bullets kept coming and missing. He shot each one going down the steps. Wounded but not dead, the team escapes the Temple with Anai Bethlem, and because of the chaos that continued among the people outside, they concealed his identity and got him to the JC-12 in one piece.

Both Leopard and Myna Bird saw the jeep rolling toward them from the side window of the plane. Myna Bird jumped up and ran to the cockpit. "There's a jeep heading our way, and it's moving quick. Get this jet humming. We need to get out of here fast." Xerxes fired up the JC-12 and looking through his binoculars, spotted Euphrates heading fast toward the jet. The jeep turned the corner around the plane and stopped. Euphrates grabs the Chief Priest and takes him to the plane steps. Mr. Zinkes kept an eye out as everyone got on the plane. "No one is tracking us, so we are in the clear." Speaking to Euphrates. Hearts still pounding, the plane lifts and they are in the air within thirty seconds. They departed with everyone intact.

~

At the temple, the smoke was clearing. Mr. Frederickson came in fuming. Yelling, "I want him back here now!" The Captain found his men dead and the Chief Priest missing. "I have no clue what happened here. We have no cameras in the Temple. It's forbidden, so we have no clue who did this." Mr. Frederickson shot him in the head. "Lieutenants search the surrounding areas for any signs of Chief Bethlem. He couldn't have gone far. Do not disappoint the Master. This will not please him at all. You find him, and you find him quickly or you'll be next." The Lieutenant scurried off with the remaining regiment of men.

Heading to Cairo, Egypt, A7 could relax only briefly. The Chief Priest was praying the whole time on the plane. They arrived in thirty-five minutes. At the abandoned airport they had previously escaped from. A mild sprinkle of rain covered the plane. There would be no fire fight this time. This tower had no one inside. Cars, vans, and trucks with keys still in the ignition, plenty to choose from. There was one to fit everyone. Xerxes and Shadow went on the hunt. Everyone else stayed on the plane. They returned to the plane with a van.

As usual, Euphrates wanted answers, and he wasn't taking no, or it's not time yet, for an answer. "Chief Priest, why have we risked our lives for you and why were you being held in the Temple?"

"As the High Priest, I've been in that position for the last five years. I am not self-appointed. God put me in the position for His purpose and use. I am the only priest who has defied those in government." He cleared his throat.

"I am the only one God warned about the peace treaty and who was behind it. Once I voiced that knowledge and my concern, God put a hedge of protection around me. Then I was no longer accepted in the meetings. I spoke to all that would listen—it fell on deaf ears. My own brothers turned on me, blinded by greed and position. It was so sad to see their souls lost. Because of the Rapture this morning and not being taken, I questioned my faith and whether I genuinely believed. Questioning everything I had done in my life and asked God why? Continuing to pray, He didn't answer. It wasn't until Mr. Zinkes busted through the door and said, 'follow me.' that I realized there was a reason. Because I am not dead right now or locked up waiting for execution, which was their plan for me, there must be a purpose why I'm here. God still has something for me to do."

Mr. Zinkes answered his question with certainty, "High Priest of the Most-High, you have something that must go to the Two Witnesses in Jerusalem. In seven days, we will take you to them. The Witnesses present God's Word and His Holy Spirit. You will give them the relic entrusted to you five years ago. You must not show it to anyone of us, we are not to look upon it. It is for the Witnesses' eyes only." Mr. Zinkes said.

"Thank you for explaining. I understand now, your life was in danger. Let's head to the clinic at daybreak."

They gathered on the plane, ate some granola and nuts, and slept for a few hours.

Chapter 32

The Last of Their Stand

Clinic Egypt was in their sights and to discover it still untouched and functioning as before was not short of a miracle, God's holy arrangement, they were sure. Leopard, Euphrates, Myna Bird, and Mr. Zinkes got out of the van and walked into the clinic. No one was there to receive them, the hallways deserted, and only the flickering fluorescent lights guided their way. They continued through the double doors to locate Dr. Canno sitting in his office. He stared up at Euphrates and was further terrified to see Myna Bird. He recognized her from before.

"What are you doing here? I have no money, I have nothing of importance, please, we just have mentally sick people here. Please don't murder me!"

"Dr. Canno, please calm down." Euphrates said, bringing his hand up. Dr. Canno instantly perspiring, wiped his brow. "We are not here to kill or take anything from you. Sublime and Joshua told us where to find you and hopefully you can help us. We require your cooperation and need shelter for seven days." Myna Bird gave him the briefcase with the payment. He patted the case in thanks. His look was more to say it was a waste on him at this point. "I will help you. Keep your money. It is no longer useful here." Myna Bird opened the case and turned it toward Dr. Canno. "I think you are mistaken." The case was full of gold. "God bless you," Dr. Canno expressed. He dropped to his knees, sat on the floor, and wept. Sobbing harder each second.

Mr. Zinkes steps forward. "You are wondering why you are still among the living? It was not because you lack faith. Yahweh has kept you here to support us with our mission. We require to be out of sight for seven days and again we will leave for Jerusalem. Do not fear, your soul belongs to God. Please let us know if there is room here or not?" He got up off his knees and studied Mr. Zinkes briefly. Resolved not to ask the question. "Accompany me, I will show you to the vacant rooms." Dr. Canno continued to have a perplexed expression. Mr. Zinkes could see his posture relaxing. After he settled everyone, Mr. Zinkes asks, "Take me to her brother's room." In a questioning posture, he complied, "Right away."

~

The building's interior was tranquil. On the outside, the turmoil continued in the distance, miles away. Mr. Zinkes could see it from the hall window. The desert sand dunes visible in the distance. The sand blowing mild in a funnel cloud landing near a valley low.

"He has been catatonic for years. I told Sublime long ago it appeared he never wanted to come back to the real world. His brain received no damaged, he just didn't want to return."

"I know." Once he clears the door to Myron's room, they step in, Mr. Zinkes turns his torso back to Dr. Canno. "You can go, he will be fine. Please prepare enough food for everyone. Do as you would ordinarily do, act as if nothing has changed. If your staff asks who we are, you can tell we are here to help with the clinic and the patients for this week. Let them know we are not your enemy and will not harm any of you. God has assigned us here for the time being." He grins and then left the room. It was just the two of them now. Mr. Zinkes sat on Myron's bed and spoke to him his way. His brain had suffered no damage. Something clicked where he remained stuck with images of the war. Daily replaying the same battle, and him taking a noncombatant's life by accident. It was psychological trauma—guilt. His unit was in

Yemen, helping to fight against Iran, as they were in the crosshairs between the Saudi-backed government and Iran's rebel militant Houthis. Myron shot a young boy and his grandmother, not realizing they were fleeing the apartment building that was just blown up on the other side. The child came out first, coated with ash from the debris. Myron reacted to the movement instantly, shooting him in the chest and arms. His trigger didn't stop shooting until the grandmother who ran after the boy to protect him, was also lying beside him. Running up on the bodies, there was too much blood to save them. The grandmother was now gasping for air, but no air was going on now. He stood over the bodies, unable to move. A fellow soldier ran past him and brushed him in the shoulder, saying, let's go but he didn't move. Myron dropped his gun on the street and sat in front of the bodies, wailing. From that time until now, he never returned the normal man he once was. The military discharged him, and Tracy was told of his mental state. His care remained with Dr. Canno the whole time.

Myron turned to Mr. Zinkes, "I am ready to go now."

"Where would you like to go?"

"I want to go with you to see Tracy. You know where she is. I want you to take me there with you." For the first time, Mr. Zinkes had no answer to his request, knowing what he meant. He experienced the anguish of Myron's human existence. Mr. Zinkes would have to seek God about this. It was the only time he spoke. Mr. Zinkes guided him to his bed, and there he remained until the next day.

Later that afternoon, supper was ready, and Mr. Zinkes returned to the lunchroom. No one questioned his whereabouts. Mr. Zinkes sat at the dinner table to eat his soup and a torly casserole. "At the cover of darkness, Euphrates, and Mr. Nordic, you will need to secure us more hardware and ammunition. In six days, we will head to Jerusalem to deliver Anai Bethlem to the Witnesses. Our path toward that destination is uncertain.

We will need to prepare for all situations."

"Mr. Zinkes, we know where to locate them." Euphrates said.

Day two, they were antsy and continued to prepare themselves and the weaponry they confiscated from the abandoned military base not too far from there last night. They all took turns doing security for the clinic and watching for any signs of disturbances within a mile.

~

Day three, they trained their bodies for battle. Mr. Zinkes and Myna Bird sparred. Euphrates came behind everyone, watching the sparring match.

"This should amuse. The last occasion this took place, it didn't end so well for Kim." As soon as he finished the words, it happened again. "I've learned from their mistakes not to mess with Mr. Zinkes. Why do they continue to get beat in public?" he said, speaking to Shadow and Xerxes.

Mr. Zinkes overhears, "It's better to be in the conflict and lose, then not fight at all."

"I hear you, Mr. Zinkes, but when the fix is in, it's best to live to fight another day."

~

Day four, Mr. Zinkes told everybody to prepare through prayer. Rest, eat, and have fun. There was a game room in the clinic they could lounge in and play pool and listen to what false news was being reported to the world.

~

Day five, Mr. Zinkes decides he would twist on his teacher's hat once more with Leopard and show her martial arts skills, if ever attacked.

"Mr. Zinkes, why is it you never instructed me before?" Leopard asked.

"Your skills were effective where needed. We never considered your hand-to-hand combat skills. Plus, you never asked me. You have military training and I never inquired if it interested you to learn more advanced techniques. You are an excellent shot."

Mr. Zinkes paused, because he could discern the shift in Leopard's body language.

"Carsen, I didn't mean how that came out. I am not always precise with words. There is only One who is perfect in every respect. I apologize if I insulted you by my remark. Our focus has been to use your skills for archeology and scripture. There are things I learn as they take place."

"No explanation needed Mr. Zinkes. Some comments should roll off my shoulders. In the past, I constantly had to prove myself. I should realize by now it's unnecessary here."

"Every one of you is unique to God and me. My love for you all is unshakable. You have become my children just as much as you are His."

"Mr. Zinkes, no worries. There are factors you must keep from us. I trust you and I always have, and that's no different from the truth. You've done nothing to damage us physically, spiritually, or emotionally. Even though you've disappeared often, you've always been here to encourage us in every area of our lives and struggles when we needed you most." Carsen stopped and hugged his neck tight, pecking him on the cheek as she let go. Mr. Zinkes returned the hug and then strolled away. He stopped and turned back toward her. "Prepare your heart and your soul Carsen, prepare your mind." He turned again and walked away toward the other side of the clinic.

~

Day six, everyone was up right away for prayer, for the run through to get Chief Priest, Anai Bethlem, to the Witnesses. They check their weapons to make certain the JC-12 was secure and ready to fly. That evening, everyone ate together and discussed general situations in their lives up to this point. No one was concerned about the future. They were simply living for the moment. As they experienced, plans could change in times of existence. While everyone slept, unaware and unafraid of what they were to do on tomorrow, Mr. Zinkes paid a visit to Myron. "I have asked the Abba Father, and he has released you. I do not know where you are to go. It is Abba's decision. Sleep well." Mr. Zinkes placed his hand on Myron's chest, and he took his last breath.

~

Day seven would be substantial for all. Everyone was up early and ready to take off. They fly at daybreak to head back to Jerusalem. Mr. Zinkes speaks to everybody, as the jet is in the air, "Now, we must bring the ancient item to the Witnesses. Today, we will be the victors, as they don't know we are coming. What you will encounter today, you may never experience again."

At the abandoned base, the JC-12 lands, and they were one mile from the Wailing Wall and the Temple. Euphrates gives his last orders, "I will run point with Mr. Nordic. Mr. Zinkes will bring up the rear with Xerxes. Shadow, you, and Myna Bird will run right and left flank. Leopard, you will be with the Chief Priest. Do not leave his side."

Mr. Zinkes spoke, "Once we drive to the wall, we will be on foot. Even though it's only been a week, the people of this time are yet at a loss and we can't concentrate on them right now. Our mission is to get him to the Witnesses. Are we clear?"

Everyone said, "Yes."

All getting into the two jeeps, they drive right outside the Wailing Wall. They took their positions and received no trouble until they approached the street where Christ traveled to Golgotha before His crucifixion. They were now a hundred yards from the Temple, and they fired on militants loyal to the enemy of Jerusalem and the Witnesses. Bullets flying in all directions, they didn't realize right away. Leopard fell to her knees. Mr. Zinkes pulled Leopard into a doorway, and the rest followed behind them, to ensure no one else got hit. He laid her on the stairs. The bullet critically wounded her. She couldn't walk on her own. Xerxes was now carrying Leopard, as they ran down the corridor of the building and behind the building where soldiers followed far behind them. The decision was to continue running and come around the other side of the Witnesses. They could lose the soldiers running after them. They were now running and blasting their way through anything that gave them opposition. As they reached the Witnesses, barricaded by police and rifles, one by one, they drop to the lawlessness and the madness before them. It was now Mr. Zinkes and Anai Bethlem. Euphrates tried to get up but drops backward as they hit him under the arm of the bulletproof vest. Anai takes out the ancient relic. Just as they drew close to the militia, Mr. Zinkes grabbed him and transforms into Xariel. He flies him over the barricade and the Reed measuring stick drops in one of the Witnesses' hands. Euphrates sees the true nature of Mr. Zinkes and gives up the ghost. The Witnesses open the Reed and time stops for those lost souls that would not transform to meet Jesus face-to-face. Xariel lays Anai Bethlem on the ground, he would not see death but live. Xariel stands in front of the Two Witnesses. "It is the hour for you to go before the Father, Xariel. They are to leave with you and join the others. Completion of our times and half-times is beginning. Then it will be time to judge the dead and reward His servants, the Prophets, and His holy people, and those who fear His name. From the least to the greatest and it will be time to destroy those who have created iniquity and destruction on the earth. Xariel collects A7. As they rise, the three meet them, familiar. The sky breaks open and Xariel lifts them within his power. Joshua, Surya, and Tracy smiles.

"Until the established hour, we will stand before the Great and Mighty Lord of Hosts."

*To be continued in the established hour,
as the Apocalyptic 12,
become the Angels of Heavens' Armies.*

ABOUT THE AUTHOR

The passion to write for A. R. Leonard, started in High School, where an English Teacher, Mr. Katzman, encouraged folly, fun learning, and the joys of literature. In her early twenties, having vivid dreams, *Amethyst Love* (Amazon, 2019, Rev. 2025) and *Mercy Undercover* (Lulu,2025) were born. There were many dreams that followed, which spawned other books, such as *Unconditional Counsel* (CFP, 2020/Lulu.com, Rev. 2025). *Apocalyptic 7-Salvations Cry* (Lulu.com, 2021, Rev. 2025), birthed from a dream during her writing *Unconditional Counsel*. Current projects for *Embrace the Dawn to Live Again* (Amazon, 2024) and future Works in Progress are, *Unconditional Counsel 2: Fate Unbroken, Apocalyptic 12-Angels of Heaven's Armies, The Container, Opposing Fruit, and The Heart of an Untold Legacy: A Father's Story.* In 2016, she created Nita Nae's Books to fuel the imagination of readers. In 2014, encouraged to start publishing her books, she is now paying it forward by helping others realize their dream of writing and completing books.

AVAILABLE & COMPLETE

Amethyst in Love, (KDP, 2019, eBook only, Rev. 2025)

Unconditional Counsel (CFP, 2020, Rev. Lulu, 2025)

Embrace the Dawn to Live Again (KDP, 2024)

The Ghosts of Slavery's Dance: No More Chains (Lulu, 2025)

Mercy Undercover: A Det. Brenda Sayers Story (Lulu, 2025)

FUTURE BOOKS (WIP's)

Unconditional Counsel 2 – Fate Unbroken!

Apocalyptic 12—Angels of Heaven's Armies

The Container

Opposing Fruit

The Heart of An Untold Legacy: A Father's Story

www.ingramcontent.com/pod-product-compliance
Lightning Source LLC
Chambersburg PA
CBHW050158030726
47505CB00005B/1426